PRELUDE
for a LORD

PRELUDE
for a LORD

CAMILLE ELLIOT

ZONDERVAN

Prelude to a Lord
Copyright © 2014 by Camy Tang

This title is also available as a Zondervan ebook. Visit www.zondervan.com
This title is also available in a Zondervan audio edition. Visit www.zondervan.com

Requests for information should be addressed to:

Zondervan, *Grand Rapids, Michigan 49530*

Library of Congress Cataloging-in-Publication Data

Elliot, Camille.
  Prelude for a Lord / Camille Elliot.
    pages cm
  ISBN 978-0-310-32035-7
1. Christian fiction. I. Title.
  PS3605.L4425P74 2014
  813'.6—dc23   2014018868

All Scripture quotations are taken from the King James Bible.

Any Internet addresses (websites, blogs, etc.) and telephone numbers in this book
are offered as a resource. They are not intended in any way to be or imply an
endorsement by Zondervan, nor does Zondervan vouch for the content of these
sites and numbers for the life of this book.

Publisher's Note: This novel is a work of fiction. Names, characters, places, and
incidents are either products of the author's imagination or used fictitiously.
All characters are fictional, and any similarity to people living or dead is purely
coincidental.

Cover design: Laura Klynstra
Cover photography: Richard Jenkins
Interior design: Lori Lynch

Printed in the United States of America

14 15 16 17 18 19 20 / RRD / 20 19 18 17 16 15 14 13 12 11 10 9 8 7 6 5 4 3 2 1

To Sue Brower, for your vision in suggesting this book and our shared love of all things Regency.

CAST OF PRIMARY CHARACTERS

Lady Alethea (al-EE-thea) Sutherton, daughter of the seventh Earl of Trittonstone. Alethea's brother inherited upon her father's death, becoming the eighth Earl of Trittonstone, but he died only a few years later, and Alethea's cousin, **Wilfred Sutherton,** inherited the title and became the ninth Earl of Trittonstone. Alethea's mother died when she was very young, but her neighbor, Lady Arkright, loved Alethea like a daughter. Her closest friend is her half sister, Lucy. Contrary to the strictures of proper English society, Alethea has learned to play the violin, although she also plays the harp and pianoforte.

Miss Lucy Purcell, illegitimate daughter of Alethea's father. Before Lucy was born, her mother married a sailor who gave Lucy his name. He died in the war. However, everyone in Alethea's village knew Lucy was the by-blow of the seventh Earl of Trittonstone. After the death of her mother, Lucy went to Bath to work as a maid, and she rose to become a lady's maid. Her employer is Mrs. Ramsland.

Mrs. Ebena Garen, Alethea's aunt. Ebena was the younger sister to Alethea's paternal grandmother, Darla. Ebena and Darla's father was Baron Winterscomb. Darla married the sixth Earl of Trittonstone, while Ebena married Mr. Tar Garen, a younger son of the Earl of Danners.

Margaret Garen, twelve-year-old niece of Aunt Ebena's late husband.

Lady Arkright, (deceased) Calandra was an Italian woman trained in music in the Ospedale della Pietà under the composer Vivaldi. It was in Italy that she met and married her husband, Sir William Arkright, and they lived nearby in Trittonstone Park, Alethea's home. They had no children. When Calandra died, she bequeathed her violin to Alethea.

Bayard Terralton, Baron Dommick, known as "Bay" to his close friends and family. Lord Dommick only recently inherited the title when his father passed away, about seventeen months before the story opens. (When his father was alive, Lord Dommick was known as Mr. Terralton.) He plays the violin and flute.

Miss Clare Terralton, Bay's younger sister. Clare is about to make her debut in London in the coming spring.

Lady Morrish, Bay's mother. She had been Lady Dommick until a few months before the story opens, when she married Sir Hermes Morrish.

Sir Hermes Morrish, knighted several years ago and married Bay's mother after the death of Bay's father. His nephew is Mr. Morrish.

The Quartet, (Lord Dommick, Lord Ravenhurst, Lord Ian Wynnman, and Captain David Enlow) four noblemen extraordinarily accomplished in music performance and composition who have been friends since they were in school together. After they graduated university, they performed for private concerts in London and became quite popular due to their wealth, handsome faces, and musical talent (in that order). Then Bay and David bought their commissions and became officers under Wellesley on the Iberian Peninsula, battling Napoleon Bonaparte.

Captain David Enlow, third son of the Viscount Enlow. He has one sister and two older brothers. He saved Bay's life at the Battle of Corunna and helped him back to England. After a few months, he returned to the Peninsula to continue fighting against the French. He plays the pianoforte and the flute.

Arion Mercaren, Marquess of Ravenhurst, known as "Raven" to his close friends, inherited his father's title when he was very young. He has two sisters, one of whom married the Earl of Windmarch. During the summer after Bay returned from Corunna, Raven took his friend to Ravenhurst Castle to recover. He plays the violoncello and pianoforte.

Lord Ian Wynnman, second son of the Marquess of Crallworth. His older brother is the Viscount Dinswell, and he has a younger sister. He plays the pianoforte and violin.

PROLOGUE

October, 1809

Trittonstone Park, Somerset, England

*L*ady Alethea Sutherton sank onto a thin-cushioned chair in the dark, dreary drawing room opposite her cousin and his wife. "Would you care for tea?" Alethea asked, which struck her as odd since her cousin now owned this house, and the master arriving at his new home could hardly be considered a visitor.

Wilfred, the new Earl of Trittonstone, frowned at the threadbare carpet. Alethea was about to mention how her father and brother had never spared the funds to refurbish the home when Wilfred slapped his hands on his knees and said, "No sense putting it off. Alethea, you have a week to pack up your things."

It was the same sensation as when she was twelve, riding her horse through the woods. She'd arrogantly thought that as she knew every tree and twig, she'd be perfectly safe if she sped up to something faster than a walk. A low-hanging branch had thwacked her in the throat, dislodging her from her horse. She'd landed hard on her back, so in addition to her throat constricting, she hadn't been able to make her lungs draw in air. She felt that way now.

"Good gracious, Wilfred, she's going to faint." But rather than assisting her, Mona leaned away from Alethea as if unconsciousness were contagious. "I told you to introduce the topic with more circumspection."

"She should have expected it," Wilfred groused. "It's my house now, after all."

Alethea managed to gasp in a breath. Yes, she had half expected Wilfred to arrange for her to leave, but she hadn't thought she'd only have a week to pack and say good-bye to her childhood home. "Where . . . where will I go?"

Wilfred's wrinkled brow cleared. "Is that all that's worrying you? You'll stay with Aunt Ebena in Bath. You remember Aunt Ebena, don't you?"

For Alethea, her brother's funeral had been a blur of faces, but she did remember Aunt Ebena—tall and thin, with a pinched mouth, a gigantic beak nose, and chestnut hair streaked with ash. "She wants me to stay with her?"

"I didn't ask," Wilfred said. "But she'll do what I say, now that I'm the head of the family. Especially if I sweeten the deal with some money for your upkeep. Ebena's always looking a little shabby."

Alethea realized her cousin was against her like an icy north wind. A gust blew her down, and once she got her feet under her again, another gust knocked her over once more. She wanted to leave the drawing room, but she didn't think her legs would support her. "I've lived here in the country all my life," she said faintly.

Mona gave a lusty sigh. "Now, don't be melodramatic, Alethea. You had your season in London, after all." Mona's nasally voice had an edge to it since her family hadn't been wealthy enough to sponsor a season for her.

Alethea swallowed the metallic taste in her mouth. The majority of her time in London had been abject pain and humiliation, on account of her height and lack of social skills. And Trittonstone Park had been her haven from her father and brother.

But her father and brother were gone. She didn't need a haven anymore.

And the last few years, with neighbors who avoided her because they thought she was odd, and with the two people closest to her heart gone, she had been fighting the bleakness of her life alone, the suspicion that there was something fundamentally wrong with her, the fear that the way her family had treated her was the way she would always be treated. Perhaps now was the time to find a new community. And hadn't Wilfred said . . .

"Aunt Ebena lives in Bath?" Alethea asked.

"Of course. Isn't that what I said?" Wilfred frowned.

Mona looked at her shrewdly. "Do you have an acquaintance in Bath?"

"Yes, my sister."

Mona's nostrils flared almost as large as her watery blue eyes, and Wilfred's narrow face turned purple. "How dare you mention—" he sputtered. "You are never to mention such persons in this house."

Considering they had ejected her from her home less than twenty minutes after arriving, Alethea had lost all pretense of politeness. In addition, she had an unfortunate tendency to rebel when someone told her what she could not do.

"Are you referring to my half sister, Lucy Purcell?" she said in a loud voice.

Mona's narrow shoulders flinched. Wilfred's grey eyes bulged and grew bloodshot.

Alethea's anger sent strength to her wobbling knees and she rose, shaking out her brown woolen skirts. She had forgotten about the broken fingers on her left hand, and the motion sent a stab of pain up her arm, but it only stoked the fire in her chest. "Yes, Lucy lives in Bath. It will be nice to be close to her again. We have only exchanged letters since she moved two years ago to take a post as a housemaid. Your cousin is a lady's maid now, Wilfred," Alethea said sweetly.

"She is not my cousin!" Wilfred choked out.

"Half cousin," Alethea corrected herself. "Pray, excuse me." She swept toward the door, half amused when the butler opened the door from the outside of the drawing room before she reached it. She gave him an impudent smile, which the very proper servant did not return with so much as a crack in his stately facade, although Alethea could have sworn his chin twitched.

As she climbed the stairs, her smile faded, and her anger burned to ashes. This was no longer her home. Gone were the long hours walking the hills and running down them when no one was around to see her. Gone also were the long hours playing her violin . . .

She checked herself. She hadn't played since the day her brother broke her fingers.

But perhaps in Bath she would find a better doctor, one who would enable her to play again. And Bath had more concerts she could attend, more access to published music. And Bath had Lucy.

What did it matter where she lived? She only had three more years to wait. She had thought she would spend them here, but instead she could spend them close to Lucy, where they could make plans and ready themselves.

Three more years before she would be free.

CHAPTER ONE

12 Months Later

A prickling sensation spread across the back of Alethea's neck, which had nothing to do with the brisk air of Bath in the winter.

She looked up from the cabbage she was considering and glanced around the busy marketplace. People shifted in and out of her vision, none looking at her. She twisted to look in the other direction, but again no one paid her any attention.

So why had she felt as if she were being watched?

The farmer, John, looked at her with brow wrinkled. "Something worrying you, miss?"

Alethea had never corrected him. By now, she was used to being called "miss" as opposed to "my lady." After all, who would believe an earl's daughter was out in the market buying potatoes and parsnips? But today it took her a moment to realize he was speaking to her. "What? Oh, I beg your pardon, John. Yes, I'll take the cabbage."

The prickling feeling returned. Alethea casually turned to the side as if considering some leeks and quickly glanced up.

She caught a man staring at her.

He looked away as if her gaze burned him. Alethea continued to watch him, studying his grey thinning hair, dirty leathery skin, cadaverous build. She wasn't sure what she was searching for, perhaps something silly like an indication he'd been watching her, but then he entered into a conversation with a man selling knives, apparently bargaining for something.

Had he been watching her or did he just happen to look in her direction? She would have been a terrible spy.

She slipped the cabbage into her market basket, then paid and thanked John before leaving. She was being ridiculous. Who in the world would care enough to want to follow her? She had no money of her own that she controlled, and no social connections since her one season in London had been so uneventful. Besides which, she was a tall, plain, eight and twenty-year-old and not some pretty, dewy-eyed young miss just out of the schoolroom.

She turned up Milsom Street, which bustled mostly with maids, manservants, and merchants this early in the morning. The more fashionable set would emerge in several hours, but for now she was relieved that, as usual, no one would recognize her. It was the reason she'd flown against convention and volunteered to do the cook's marketing—the opportunity to stroll the streets of Bath, breathe in the crisp air, and walk for an hour or two with no young ladies to titter at her strong stride, no old biddies to disparage her rosy cheeks from the exercise.

A year ago she had arrived in Bath with the hopes it would have a more diverse, broad-minded set of people. Instead, Bath contained a fashionable set who professed to be liberal and intelligent, but who all seemed to disdain Alethea's passions as ungenteel. Their wit could cut as sharp as the people in London, and for some of them, politeness was merely a veneer.

She could not avoid them at the evening parties, but she could shake their influence loose from her mind during early mornings like these, when she could disappear into the servants of Bath. She strolled through a cluster of shopkeepers, completely unnoticed.

Almost.

A coach-and-four barreled down the street, much too fast for the narrow way. Several people leapt out of the way of the horses with cries of alarm, but the crowds forced the coachman to finally slow his headlong dash, right where Alethea stood pressed against a shop wall.

"Why are we slowing?" a deep male voice demanded from the depths of the coach.

Alethea had been breathless on account of being forced to the side, but now the air stopped in her throat.

It couldn't be him. Not here, in Bath.

She glanced up just as a man from within the coach looked out—and met her eyes.

Dark eyes, shadowed, solitary. He had always reminded her of a hawk, its power and beauty, its lonely existence. But she now noticed that there was a dark pain, something that had aged him beyond the eleven years since she'd seen him last.

His eyes flickered, and she tensed. Surely he wouldn't recognize her. She had been one woman in a crowd of hundreds at his concert in London who had danced at the same balls, attended the same operas. Fallen half in love with dashing Mr. Terralton, son and heir to Baron Dommick.

No, he was Lord Dommick now—she had read that his father died last year, three months after Mr. Terralton returned to England, injured from fighting Napoleon on the continent.

But his gaze didn't leave hers for a few heartbeats, as if trying to place her.

Then he turned away as the man sitting next to him said, "Bay, I'm sure it would hamper your rescue attempts if you were arrested for killing a bystander with your coach."

Alethea recognized him as Lord Ian Wynnman, and sitting across from them was the Marquess of Ravenhurst.

Her heartbeat galloped. Three of the Quartet, here? She would have expected them to be wintering at their country estates, not mouldering in Bath with invalids taking the waters.

"Bay, your stepfather is a fool. A delay of a few minutes will not mean your sister's ruin," Lord Ravenhurst said.

Alethea recalled an announcement in the papers about Lord Dommick's mother remarrying, although she couldn't remember to whom.

"He may be a fool, but I know nothing of his nephew," Lord Dommick replied as the coach pulled away from Alethea. "I intend to allow him no time for any malicious scheming . . ."

Alethea stared at the back of the coach as it continued down the street, her heartbeat returning to normal. For a moment, she'd thought the Quartet was in Bath to give one of their famous concerts, but that was a silly notion. After Lord Dommick and Mr. David Enlow had gone off to join the fighting on the continent, the Quartet had not played together in seven years. She had not heard anything about Mr. Enlow but supposed he must still be in the army.

The Quartet's concerts had been glorious, but the pain of the memory of her first meeting Lord Dommick made her insides twist like a kitchen rag being wrung of water.

She straightened her shoulders. She was a fool to allow old memories to hurt her. She continued up Milsom Street, although her steps resembled a march more than a stroll.

If those three bachelors were to remain in Bath, she would more than likely see them at the social entertainments of the winter months. One or all of them would be trapped by some well-meaning older woman into being introduced to Alethea, and she would need to admit they had already been introduced years ago in London.

But perhaps they were simply here for a day or two before

travelling on to London or their estates. She might be worrying for nothing.

Alethea walked toward her aunt's home in Queen Square. It had been a new, expensive development during the time Aunt Ebena's husband had bought it, but in more recent years it had begun to fall out of favour, inhabited by a more dowdy set than the fashionable residents of the Crescent and Laura Place, and now the homes in Queen Square reminded Alethea of aging baronesses attempting to hide the ravages of time and neglect.

She was near her aunt's home when she heard from behind her, "Pardon me, milady. Might I have a word?"

She froze, partly because of "milady," and partly because the male voice was unfamiliar to her, uncultured, with a slick overtone that reminded her of cold congealed beef.

She should have simply walked on. After all, it could be nothing but trouble for a lady to be so rudely accosted on the street by a stranger. But because he'd startled her by knowing she was no ordinary miss, it gave him the opportunity to hurry around her stiff figure to stand before her.

She had anticipated the sticklike grey man from the marketplace, but she was almost relieved to find this man was different. He had a round belly that strained his bright yellow-and-green striped waistcoat and spindly legs encased in puce breeches. The puce at least matched the amethyst stickpin in his starched cravat, and the yellow stripes almost matched his blond hair.

Something tight coiled in Alethea's stomach at his audacity and the fact they were alone on this remote street. The general stamp of her neighbors were unlikely to bestir themselves to chivalry and rescue her.

"Mr. Golding at your service, milady. I wish only a moment of your time." The man's mouth curved in a strange V shape that tilted his eyes up at the corners and made his face seem to leer at her.

How did he know her rank? Was it a guess? Nothing in her plain straw bonnet, dark blue dress, and wool cloak indicated she was anything more than an upper servant. "Pray excuse me." She attempted to sidestep him, but he blocked her way.

"I have a lucrative proposition for you."

"Let me pass," she said.

"Perhaps you have in your possession a violin?"

Of all things he could have said, that was the last she expected.

"My employer is willing to pay a substantial sum, if you were in the mind to sell it," Mr. Golding said.

"Who is your employer?" she demanded.

"My employer wishes to remain anonymous."

"Of course he would," she said dryly, then realized the man hadn't identified his employer as a man or woman.

"You may name your price," he said. "Enough to buy another violin. Enough to afford better lodgings for yourself and your aunt."

The cold of the season suddenly made itself known to Alethea through her woolen cloak. How did he know about her aunt? Perhaps the same way he knew about her violin and her rank. The words had been amiable, but the man delivered them like a faint threat.

No, she was being silly. This was exactly like the time the new butcher in the village had tried to insist that the rotting meat he had delivered was the same quality as always. As lady of the manor at Trittonstone Park, she had put him in his place when she had the cook prepare a piece and demanded the butcher take the first bite.

She drew herself up. "I refuse to have any interactions with someone of whom I know nothing."

Mr. Golding's brown eyes narrowed, and his V smile flattened.

"However, should your employer wish to call with a note of introduction, I would be pleased to receive him. Good day."

She stepped around him and continued down the street as quickly as she dared. She half expected him to follow her, but instead she heard the heavy stamp of his footsteps moving away. She peeked around and saw his broad back, encased in purple superfine, as he headed away from her. He had turned the corner and was out of sight by the time she reached Aunt Ebena's door.

She was surprised by a post chaise stopped in front of her aunt's home. The coachman who stood holding the horses' heads gave her an insolent grin, which she froze with a cold glance. Raised voices sounded from behind the front door, causing Alethea to quickly enter the house.

The narrow front foyer was chaos. A trunk took up most of the space, while the rest was filled with a woman twice as broad as Alethea, shouting at Aunt Ebena, who stood firmly at the foot of the staircase.

"'Tis your responsibility now. I wash my hands of her!" The woman shook her meaty paws at Aunt Ebena.

Alethea's aunt was a good stone lighter but taller than the woman, and her gimlet stare could have set a small fire. "I was present at the funeral. The solicitor clearly stated that the girl was the responsibility of her blood relatives. Of which I am not."

A light voice piped up at Alethea's elbow. "You might as well sit down. They've been at it for at least fifteen minutes."

Alethea started. A small girl sat in one of the hallway chairs shoved against the wall. She had been partially screened by the door when Alethea entered the house, and she hadn't noticed her.

The girl calmly sat as though awaiting an audience with the queen. She could be no more than eleven or twelve years old, with light brown hair in rather wild curls. Her dress was too short for her, exposing tanned forearms and dirty shoes and stockings. She also had a dark smudge of something across her nose, and another streak across her chin.

Alethea had rarely interacted with children. She had not been close friends with the women in the neighborhood of Trittonstone Park since they did not understand her love of music and considered her something of an oddity, so exposing their children to Alethea's unconventional notions had been the last wish of their hearts. At a loss, Alethea blurted out, "You have something on your face."

"Oh?" The girl scrubbed at her cheeks with a sleeve, which caused a grey mark to appear.

"I think it's from your dress."

The girl peered at her sleeve. "That must have been from the dog at the inn. He was quite dirty."

The woman in the hallway bellowed, "You are expected to undertake your husband's responsibilities."

"Expected by whom? The *blood relatives* who should be taking a more active interest in this matter?" Aunt Ebena shot back.

"What is happening?" Alethea asked the girl, feeling foolish doing so.

"They're arguing." The girl's tone implied Alethea was a bit of a simpleton not to have deduced that already.

Alethea's gaze narrowed. "That much is obvious. What are they arguing about?"

"Me, of course."

"What about you?"

"Why, if I shall come here to live."

❧

Alethea had a coughing spell for a few moments. "Here? With Aunt Ebena?"

The girl's eyes brightened. "She's my aunt as well. That means we are cousins."

"Who are you?" Alethea asked belatedly.

"Margaret Garen."

Garen. The name of Aunt Ebena's husband. Alethea realized Margaret was looking at her expectantly. "I am Alethea Sutherton."

"Pleased to meet you," Margaret said as if they had been introduced over tea.

"Why would you stay here? Wouldn't you rather be with your mother?" Alethea glanced at the strange woman, still arguing. The sounds echoed off the walls of the foyer.

"She's not my mother. She's my Aunt Nancy. My parents are dead." Margaret said the words with unconcern, but Alethea noticed the tightening of the small mouth, the clenching of her hands in her lap.

"When did they die?" Alethea asked gently.

"Eight months ago. I have lived with Aunt Nancy since then, but she is terribly stuffy."

Something about the way Margaret said the word made Alethea remember her own childhood, ruled over by nursemaids and governesses. Alethea had grown old enough to rather pity those poor women. "Does your definition of stuffy mean intolerant of frogs in the drawing room seat cushions or something of that sort?"

Margaret grinned. Her blue eyes lit up, and twin dimples peeked out from her round cheeks. "I knew there was something about you I liked."

Alethea realized with a powerful sense of dread that perhaps she was being punished for all the mice in shoes and charcoal drawings on bed sheets that she had inflicted upon her childhood servants.

"Try and stop me!" roared Margaret's Aunt Nancy. She whirled around.

Alethea jumped aside before the large woman crashed into her and then was nearly clocked in the forehead by the front door being yanked open. She stumbled backward and ended up sitting in Margaret's lap. The girl gave a great, *"Umph!"*

A swirl of chill wind, then the deafening slam of the door. Alethea was left staring at the suddenly quiet hallway, broken only by the sound of Aunt Ebena's angry gasps. "How—! How dare she—!"

Alethea felt squirming beneath her.

"Could you get off me? You're terribly heavy." Margaret pushed at Alethea's back.

Alethea regained her feet and stood. She caught sight of the butler, the housekeeper, and the cook peeking from around the corner of the stairwell, round-eyed and pale. The other servants were probably peeking from the top of the stairs.

Aunt Ebena pressed a bony hand against her chest, which showed up white against the black silk and lace of her gown. Her wide grey eyes took in Alethea, standing awkwardly next to the trunk, then Margaret's small form in the hallway chair. Aunt Ebena took a breath as she straightened to her full height, pressing her thin lips closed and looking down her beaky nose at Margaret. "Hill, send for Mr. Garen's solicitor," she ordered the housekeeper. "We shall get to the bottom of this."

Aunt Ebena turned and made her way back up the stairwell. A scuffling from the floor above indicated the other servants were scattering before being caught by their mistress. "I don't know what she was thinking. I have no use for a child," Aunt Ebena muttered.

Earlier, Margaret had borne the argument with an almost quirky sense of humor. Even now, she kept her chin raised and her back straight, but Aunt Ebena's words made her eyes flicker downward. It was not there on her face, but Alethea could see the bruise formed on her soul. How often had Alethea heard her own father say, "What use is a girl to me?"

The sight of Margaret's face caused a burning in Alethea's chest. It had been the same as when the village women told her she should not play with Lucy. It was the sense of an injustice she had the ability to right, or to ease. Others had disregarded her existence, but she would ensure she did not do the same to anyone else.

"Did you ever try spitting crickets?" Alethea asked conversationally.

Margaret blinked at her. "Crickets?"

"They feel quite odd moving about on your tongue, and their flavor is distinctly earthy, but spitting is highly accurate for proper placement of said cricket into, for example, a governess's teacup." Alethea couldn't quite believe she managed to speak with a straight face. "Or at least the vicinity of the tea tray."

In addition to her dimples, Margaret's wide smile showed a slight overbite that made her look like a darling fairy child. "That is quite a good idea."

Alethea wondered if she was welcoming chaos upon her aunt's home, but Margaret reminded her of how she had felt, abandoned to Trittonstone Park year after year by a father who despised her and a brother who only sought to use her. Alethea had been unwanted and unappreciated by any except her half sister, Lucy, and her widowed neighbor, Lady Arkright. She would not let this child feel as she had.

"Let's get your trunk upstairs."

Margaret looked distastefully at the battered trunk. "Don't you have servants to do that for you?"

"Our aunts have chased the servants away, so I would need to send someone to collect them, and there is only the butler, who's got sore knees, and the cook, who's making breakfast. So, would you rather haul your own things or not eat?"

Margaret hopped to her feet. "Where is my room?"

Responds well to threats of starvation. She recalled being the same at that age. If Margaret was here to stay, it may not be too bad. Really, how difficult would it be to care for a young girl?

∽✤∾

Bayard Terralton, Baron Dommick, leaned against the squabs of his coach as it continued down Milsom Street. That young woman had looked at him as if horrified.

"You've lost no time, Bay," Ian remarked with a sly smile. "She seemed taken by you."

"Who?" Ravenhurst demanded.

"That pretty young maid on the street."

"She looked at me as if I were a corpse come back to life," muttered Bayard.

"Did she recognize you as the Mad Baron?" Ian asked flippantly.

Bayard's mouth tightened at the nickname his former betrothed had given to him during the season in London when she was spreading rumours about his sanity.

Raven's foot shot out and kicked Ian's boot where it rested atop his knee, knocking it down. Ian straightened more in surprise than anger.

Raven said nothing, simply gave Ian an ice-cold stare.

Ian grimaced, shrugged, and looked away.

Ravenhurst turned to Bayard. "We are here in Bath to rectify that situation."

Bayard was not so certain, after the damage done by Miss Church-Pratton, the woman he had almost married. But he had to succeed for the sake of his sister and his mother. He would not cause them pain again. "Can't this coach go any faster?" Bayard pounded his head against the leather squabs.

Raven wisely ignored his whining and addressed the root of his concern. "You're certain Mr. Morrish is here in Bath?"

"My sister's letter said he arrived the morning she wrote to me."

"Your mother's chaperonage in the house isn't enough to guarantee your sister's safety against Mr. Morrish?" Ian waggled his dark gold eyebrows.

Raven snorted. "Please. You know Bay's mother as well as I."

Bayard wasn't offended. He knew that Raven, Ian, and David—his close friends since Eton—loved his mother as if she were their own. But Bayard's mother, while kind and generous, preferred to be pampered rather than responsible for others.

"I didn't tell you about this summer." Bayard's sister, Clare, would kill Bayard for revealing this, but he depended upon his friends to help protect her.

"Do tell." Ian grinned, his dimples peeking out from cheeks showing a golden-brown shadow.

"The squire's younger son—a nasty piece of work, the kind to pull legs off of frogs for a spot of fun—tried to force himself upon Clare in an empty stable."

Ravenhurst's icy-blue eyes glittered. "Did he, now?"

"The idiot also confessed he wanted to ruin her so she'd be forced to marry him." Bayard's knuckles ached and he looked down, realizing he'd clenched his hands into fists.

"Please tell me your resourceful sister did not stand for such treatment," Ian said.

"She remembered what David taught her and hit the boy in the throat with her closed fist. She then ran out."

"That's my girl." Ian grinned.

Raven sighed. "I will never again complain about David teaching your sister those fighting tricks."

"It was so she could hold her own against the village bullies. I was surprised she remembered after all these years."

"Bullies, suitors. Same class of chaps, don't you think?" A lock of straight blond-streaked brown hair had fallen over Ian's eyes, and he swiped it away impatiently. He happened to catch the eye of a shopgirl as they rode past her on the street, and he flashed her a smile.

Bayard was used to his friend's easy way with the opposite sex, but after the disastrous end to his betrothal last year, the gesture now caused a pang in his chest. He did not have Ian's charm, Raven's title, or David Enlow's powerful presence. He was simply . . . Bay.

"I will never understand how women flock to you even while you need a haircut and a shave." Raven tugged at his immaculate cravat. "You look positively uncouth."

"Artful disarray," Ian corrected him. "And women prefer it to starchy."

"Enough," Bayard said before the insults escalated.

Ian's grin widened. Raven's white-blond eyebrow angled upward, but a smile hovered around his stern mouth.

"We need David around to keep us in line," Ian said. "It's boring for Bay to have to do it."

But the fourth of their group, Captain David Enlow, was fighting with Wellesley somewhere on the Iberian Peninsula. Last year David had returned to the war three months after saving Bayard's life in Corunna.

The squeal of horses, the acrid smell of gunpowder, the screams of men dying . . .

Bayard drew breath and forced his mind from the memories before they overwhelmed him. Again. He needed to have more command over himself. *Lord God, help me learn to control myself.*

"Bay?" Raven's voice was cautious.

"I'm fine," Bayard said.

"We're here." Ian opened the carriage door.

The front door to the house opened, and Bayard's sister hurried down the steps to throw herself at him. He staggered backward even as he wrapped his arms around her. His injured shoulder twinged, but he did not loosen his embrace.

"Bay, thank goodness you're here." Clare was usually as correct as Ravenhurst, and the fact she embraced him so exuberantly showed her relief at seeing her brother.

"My welcome is distinctly lacking." Ian gave Clare his most

devastating smile, but it only provoked a frown from her that could have come from the strictest of governesses.

Raven interrupted her glare at his friend with his courteous bow. "Miss Terralton."

She released Bayard to curtsey to Raven and then, grudgingly, to Ian. "Ravenhurst. Ian." Clare turned to Bayard and shook his coat lapels, creasing them. "It took you long enough to get here."

He frowned down at her. "I left within an hour of receiving your letter."

"Mr. Morrish has been here every afternoon, and Mama has given him permission to escort me to Lady Woolton's ball next week." Panic flared around the edges of her dark eyes.

He tucked aside a lock of fine dark hair where it had fallen across her nose. "I will be escorting you to the ball. And for good measure, one of the three of us will be within sight of you always."

She was so relieved that she kissed his cheek, even with the servants watching from the house's open doorway. "I knew I could depend on you, Bay."

"Come inside, come inside," called a jovial voice. Sir Hermes Morrish, Bayard's stepfather, waved to them from the front step as he leaned upon a cane. "It's too cold to stand about, and your mother is anxious to see you."

"Has Sir Hermes pressured you in any way?" Bayard whispered to Clare as they headed inside.

"No. But he doesn't prevent his nephew from pressing his suit. He seems to think it a lark." Clare sniffed in indignation, then sobered. "Bay, I don't like how Mr. Morrish looks at me." She shuddered. "The way we used to look at the Christmas pudding."

Bayard's hand tightened over hers. "You will have no need to fear. I have a plan." He nodded to his stepfather as they approached the front door. "Sir Hermes."

"Good to see you, m'boy." Sir Hermes gave a boyish grin that made him look decades younger. His curly brown-grey hair had been disheveled by the breeze, but he did not seem to notice. He ushered them into the house he had procured for the winter.

It was a fine house, not too far from the Roman Baths where Sir Hermes's doctor had ordered him every day for his gout. The golden Cotswold stone looked warm even in the fitful sunlight, and the inside was richly furnished with classically inspired furniture boasting more gilt than the ancient Greeks had ever seen. In the drawing room, Bayard's mother reclined on a chaise lounge, but she sat up as he entered the room with Clare on his arm.

She held round, white arms out to him. "Bayard, how good of you to come."

He stepped forward to take her hands, entering into the thick cloud of her perfume. He kissed her cheek. "Mama, how are you?"

"Bath is lovely." Her soft, high voice, usually languid, was alight with excitement. "I have become reacquainted with several old school friends whom I have not seen in ever so long."

"Your mother is well able to entertain herself while I take the waters." Sir Hermes beamed at his wife as he sank into a nearby chair. He grimaced only slightly from his gouty foot and rested his cane against the chair arm.

Lady Morrish greeted Raven and Ian like additional sons, and they both kissed her cheek in turn before seating themselves.

"Will you be staying in Bath?" Lady Morrish asked Bayard. "Clare said she has asked you."

"Yes, and I have even better news." He nodded to his stepfather. "Sir, this house you have let is very fine, but Ravenhurst has offered us the use of his house and servants here in Bath."

Lady Morrish's mouth opened in an O of surprise and delight. She turned to Raven with a rapturous smile. "But what of your mother?"

"Right now she is with my sister at their estate in Devonshire," Ravenhurst said.

"Ah yes, she wrote to me of your sister's new baby boy."

He nodded. "Mother has extended an invitation to you, madam, to stay with her at our home on the Crescent, provided you and your family do not mind rattling around her house alone until she returns to Bath in a few weeks."

"We should be delighted." Lady Morrish clapped her hands. "It will be wonderful to see your mother again, and her home is so much larger than this one."

"But, my dear," Sir Hermes said, "what of my nephew?"

Clare stiffened.

"What of Mr. Morrish?" Bayard's tone was harsh.

"Just this morning Sir Hermes suggested we invite him to stay with us," Lady Morrish said. "His rented rooms are small. But I am afraid we cannot invite him if we will be accepting Lady Ravenhurst's generous offer."

"Yes, Mr. Morrish is a stranger to her," Bayard replied.

Sir Hermes frowned at this change of plans, but then his amiable nature reasserted itself. "Whatever makes you happiest, dear."

Bayard had to admit that in the three months of his mother's marriage to Sir Hermes, the fine lines of stress that used to radiate from her doe-brown eyes had disappeared in the light of his stepfather's more easygoing nature. Bayard's father's stern nature had heightened his mother's nervous temperament, but that nervousness had faded, and he owed his thanks to Sir Hermes's influence.

At that moment, there was a rap at the front door, and moments later the butler entered the drawing room and announced, "Mr. Morrish."

Clare shot to her feet, her hands clenched together. Bayard rose also and reached out to fold her hands in his. She gave him a grateful look and relaxed slightly.

Bayard studied Mr. Morrish as Sir Hermes performed introductions. The ginger-haired man looked only slightly like his uncle in his rosy cheeks and curly hair, but where Sir Hermes had an open artifice and bright, dark eyes, Mr. Morrish's half-lidded gaze shifted slyly from side to side. His smile toward them all, and especially Clare, was wide and ingratiating, but never reached his eyes. The man was not handsome—he had protruding front teeth and a weak chin that made him slightly horselike in appearance—but he carried himself with an easy confidence that made one feel he ought to be handsome.

"Lord Dommick," Mr. Morrish simpered when they had all reseated themselves. "I had no idea you were coming to Bath. Were you not at Lord Ravenhurst's estate for the past year?"

Bayard stiffened. While it was no secret he had been at Ravenhurst Castle since last winter, the sneering way Mr. Morrish mentioned it seemed to indicate he knew the truth about why Bayard had been buried in the country for the past twelvemonth. The specter of the ugly rumours threatened to overshadow Bayard, and he tightened his jaw.

"I had always intended to support my sister for her come out," Bayard replied coldly. "When I heard she would be spending the winter in Bath, I naturally came to escort her about in society."

"We all came," Ravenhurst added. His icy demeanor seemed to make Mr. Morrish's civility falter.

A flash of something ugly passed across Mr. Morrish's pale face, then it was gone.

"Miss Terralton is like a sister to us," Ian drawled, although Bayard caught the edge to his words. "It's as if she has three older brothers."

A twinkle shone in Clare's eyes as she glanced at Ian.

To his credit, Mr. Morrish recovered quickly. "Why, that is how I feel about Miss Terralton myself. It is a relief to know she has other such friends as I."

A wordless sound escaped Clare's lips as she had difficulty containing her outrage.

"She has a great many friends," Ravenhurst said. "My mother has offered to Miss Terralton and her family the use of our house here in Bath."

Mr. Morrish started in surprise, then turned to Lady Morrish. "My dear lady, how fortuitous for you. Surely the Marchioness of Ravenhurst's home is one of the most elegant in Bath."

"We shall be very comfortable," Lady Morrish said.

Mr. Morrish's smile seemed to indicate he thought nothing more delightful than her removal to the Ravenhursts' home, but Bayard noticed the man's hand clenched in his lap.

The rest of Mr. Morrish's visit passed with gentle gossip that delighted Bayard's mother. Mr. Morrish had a rapier wit that sometimes bordered on cruel, and his manner of conveying a story seemed to indicate how he despised the characters he spoke of. He appeared to be watching Raven and Ian to see how long they would stay, but Ian brought up at least five or six times how they considered themselves family to Clare and her mother and seemed entrenched in the chair he lounged in. At last, despite the fact Sir Hermes was his uncle, propriety forced Mr. Morrish to depart.

Bayard made a point of walking Mr. Morrish to the door, accompanied by Raven and Ian.

Mr. Morrish had an assurance that was faintly like a challenge as he donned his beaver hat. "I bid you good day, gentlemen. I expect we shall see much of each other this winter."

Raven stiffened, but Ian said, "Good day," and all but ushered Mr. Morrish out the front door.

"I should like to darken his lights," Raven said in a chilly voice.

"What did you think of him?" Bayard asked Ian. Of the four of them, Ian's ability to assess a person's character surpassed them all. Perhaps it had to do with his successful interactions with the fairer sex.

"Completely mercenary," Ian said. "Although there is something refreshing about a man so transparent about it."

"*Refreshing* is not the word I would use to describe him." Raven frowned at Ian.

"He should never be allowed an opportunity to speak privately to Clare, for he seems the sort of man who might press his advantage to force a marriage out of the situation."

"That much is obvious," Raven said.

"Pity you can't forbid him to dance with her," Ian said. "Although, Bay, if you allow him to guide her outside a ballroom for a moonlit stroll in the garden, I should have to shoot you myself."

"If Bay did that, I would suspect someone had slipped some tonic into his tea to make him stupid," Raven said.

"I had forgotten how jovial and complimentary your company was," Bayard replied.

Before they reentered the drawing room, however, Ian said in a low voice, "Be very careful, not only of your sister, but of your reputation as well. He is the sort of man to exploit any weakness he can ferret out."

"I shall be careful." Bayard could make no mistakes for the next year. His sister's season, and his mother's sensitive heart, depended upon him.

CHAPTER TWO

lethea's half sister, Lucy Purcell, stumbled as she stepped outside St. Mary's chapel after church on Sunday morning. "Surely you're jesting."

"I have had five exhausting days of attending to my aunt as she spoke to her solicitor and preventing Margaret from sliding down the bannister and terrorizing the shopkeepers as we acquired fabric for some new clothes for her. I assure you, I am not jesting." Alethea breathed in the cool air after the musty atmosphere of the chapel. She appreciated that the church in the square was small and not as crowded as other more public churches, but the sermons and prayers wove around her ribcage like a corset pulled too tightly. None of those lofty rectors preaching obedience had been abandoned by God to a neglectful father and cruel brother. She had no use for a God like that.

"You, caring for a child?" Lucy peeked around the edge of her bonnet to study Alethea. "You, who have always been unfashionably direct with gentlemen where other women were demure, because you have no interest in marrying? If you did not look so unwell I should find this quite diverting."

Alethea glared. Lucy laughed.

Alethea looked for Aunt Ebena, who as usual had not sat with Alethea and her sister during the service. Her aunt's lined face made her seem to be forever frowning whenever directed at Alethea or Lucy, which made Alethea relieved she didn't impose her company upon them, but she felt the pain of the slight for Lucy's sake.

Aunt Ebena was speaking to one of her numerous friends, and would likely remain with them until Lucy left Alethea's company to return to her employer.

"I take it Margaret is staying?" Lucy asked. As the day was fine, they made their way toward the formal gardens laid out in the centre of the square.

"Aunt Ebena's solicitor found nothing in Margaret's father's will to allow her to refuse this responsibility." At least Aunt Ebena had kept her disappointment to herself and Alethea, and had not expressed her reluctance to Margaret directly.

"But Margaret is niece to Aunt Ebena's late husband. She is no relation of yours."

"She's a closer relation to that Aunt Nancy woman, who was third cousin to Margaret's mother." Alethea ran her hand through a shrub of rosemary along the path, breathing in the pungent scent. "However, I gather that Margaret's . . . liveliness had been trying."

Lucy crowed, "What did Miss Jenkins say to you before she quit her post? That she hoped you would one day have a child exactly like—"

"Miss Jenkins was the worst governess of the lot," Alethea protested. "She wanted me to curl my hair. Every morning."

"The curling iron *did* work for two entire minutes before it all straightened again."

"Miss Jenkins's curse has not come to pass," Alethea said. "I have quite enjoyed having Margaret about."

"Have you now?" Lucy regarded her sister with narrowed eyes. "And what of her education?"

The elms rattled in the wind like a thousand fingers shaking at her. "Education?"

"Is she adequately prepared to be enrolled in a ladies' seminary?"

"Er . . . no," Alethea said.

"I assume Aunt Ebena has not funds to hire a governess, so her schooling must fall to you."

Alethea coughed. "Me? But . . . I haven't the faintest idea where to begin."

"Surely Margaret brought some school books with her?"

"None except an atlas that had belonged to her father and several books of published journals from personages who have travelled to various parts of the world."

"So . . . no French or history?"

"No. I must teach her French?" Alethea felt panic begin to set in.

"And not only book learning, but she must learn to sew, paint, and play music." Lucy ticked off the items on her fingers. "And above all, genteel deportment."

Alethea steered them away from the obelisk at the centre of the gardens. "Are you hungry? I am hungry. Let's go have tea." Anxiety always made her want to eat.

"Where is Margaret this morning?" Lucy looked vastly entertained by Alethea's discomposure.

"She had nothing fit to wear to church. Her clothes are too small for her, and apparently she spent a great deal of time roaming the woods near her Aunt Nancy's home."

A choked sound came from Lucy that sounded suspiciously like a snort.

Alethea ignored her and continued, "Aunt Ebena wouldn't

allow her to attend church in a muddy petticoat. So, this morning Mrs. Dodd is teaching her to bake a cake."

"Good. If she is like you, she will eat vast amounts of food."

Alethea halted in the middle of the path. "I do not eat vast amounts of food." She might need a bit of extra nourishment because of her active nature, but surely not *vast* amounts.

"To be fair, as a child, you spent a prodigious time out of doors, escaping your governesses." Lucy gave her a toothy smile.

"As I recall, I often visited you and your mother."

"Unlike you, I would have welcomed a governess with open arms. And now you will need to become one." Lucy sounded positively gleeful.

Alethea continued walking out of the gardens and across the street. Her eye sought out her aunt's door, a gold colour slightly darker than the Bath stones of the building. However, that uncomfortable prickling sensation at the base of her neck had her rubbing it roughly, and then a furtive shadow just at the edge of her bonnet made her turn toward the corner of the square.

Church-goers had filled the streets, walking and conversing, and Alethea did not recognize all of them. How to know if she was imagining things or if someone had been watching her?

"What is it?" Lucy asked.

Alethea didn't answer, but hurried to the low, arched doorway to her home. The butler opened the door to her, and Alethea didn't breathe easier until it closed behind them. "Tea in the sitting room, please," she said to the butler.

"What has upset you?" Lucy persisted as they entered the sitting room. The old-fashioned furniture, its shabbiness enhanced by the faded burgundy and blue colours, today appeared soothing and safe.

Alethea sank into a rickety chair. "I think someone was watching me at the marketplace a few days ago."

"Watching you?" Lucy dropped onto the settee.

"I'm not certain. I had a peculiar feeling." She explained what had happened, pausing only when the butler entered with a tea tray.

After he'd left, Lucy said, "I've told you that you shouldn't be doing the marketing for the cook. The marketplace is not safe for you."

"It is safe for *you*—"

"You and I, no matter how you pretend differently, are not the same." Lucy stared hard at her sister, her face and dark eyes making Alethea almost feel she were staring at a mirror. Except she was certain she never looked at herself like a recalcitrant child as Lucy did to her now.

Alethea gave a cup of tea to Lucy. "Mrs. Dodd is grateful for the help when her rheumatism is acting up. And she makes sure I get extra seed cakes with my tea."

"What were you saying earlier about not eating much?" Lucy took a sip of tea, which didn't completely hide her smile.

"And if I did not help Mrs. Dodd, I should go mad within these walls. I enjoyed twenty-seven years of galloping across the fields and walking up the downs every day. Bath is a prison. It is not considered genteel to walk for the sake of walking—that sort of thing is much more acceptable in the country." Alethea had not wanted a lack of her normal vigorous exercise to force her to adjust the fit of her gowns, so she had kept active as best she could.

Lucy understood her sister's energetic nature and sighed as she nodded.

"I am not certain if it is related, but a man spoke to me on the street when I was returning from the market." Alethea explained about Mr. Golding. "Did Calandra mention anything unusual about her violin?"

"Not at all. She would be more likely to speak to you about it than to me."

"I know her husband bought it for her as a wedding gift," Alethea said. "They returned to Italy for their wedding journey so she could visit her relatives. He bought it for her from a peddler. It was in terrible condition and not very expensive."

"Is it very old?"

"I am not sure. I don't know how to find out."

"Do you or your aunt know anyone who might help?"

Alethea's thoughts immediately flashed upon Lord Dommick's lean, dark face in the window of the coach. He, along with the others in the Quartet, played their favoured instruments as well as any professional musician, which was unusual among noblemen. Lord Dommick was considered an expert in the violin, in addition to the violin compositions for which he was also famous.

He had told her women ought not to play the violin. She would not ask him for help if he were the last man on earth. "Aunt Ebena's friend Lady Whittlesby is a well-respected patron of music. She will perhaps know a violin maker or instrument repair tradesman."

"Perhaps I should go in your stead. Those may not be places appropriate for an earl's daughter."

"You will not waste your half day running errands for me," Alethea said.

Lucy glanced at the clock on the mantel. "That reminds me, I must be going."

"So soon? It has been barely an hour."

"Mrs. Ramsland requires me to return early today to help her prepare for a dinner party tonight."

Alethea frowned. "She is an unreasonable employer."

"She pays me every quarter," Lucy said calmly. "And an abigail's life is preferable to being an upper housemaid."

Alethea grasped her sister's hands. "Two more years. Then we shall be able to go to Italy and keep house for each other and you will never need to serve another woman again."

Lucy smiled warmly before leaning over to kiss her sister's cheek. "Two more years."

Lucy had left barely a minute before the front door opened and Aunt Ebena entered the sitting room. Her thin eyebrows rose at the half full tea tray. "Had no appetite today?" Her deep voice was stiff.

"Lucy had to return early."

"Ring for more tea."

"I'll get it myself." Alethea took the cold teapot to the kitchen, where Margaret was washing dishes sulkily.

"This is most unpleasant," the girl said to Mrs. Dodd. "Don't you have maids for this sort of thing?"

"There are no fine ladies in this kitchen, so if you dirty the dishes, you wash them," Mrs. Dodd told her. She turned to Alethea with a tray already prepared with a fresh pot and extra cup. "I heard Mrs. Garen come home. Your sister didn't stay long."

"Her employer requested her to return early."

Mrs. Dodd sniffed. "And Mrs. Ramsland wonders why she can never retain her servants."

"Who's your sister?" Margaret said. "Is she my cousin too?"

"Yes. She's my half sister."

"Why doesn't she live here?" Margaret scratched her nose with a wet hand.

Alethea, used to the scandal of her friendship with her sister, was suddenly acutely aware of the impropriety of explaining that relationship to a twelve-year-old girl.

She was rescued by Mrs. Dodd. "Never you mind," the cook told the girl, and Alethea escaped the kitchen.

"It took you a long time." Aunt Ebena frowned.

Used to her aunt's complaints by now, Alethea ignored her and poured tea. After all, she had lived with her father's and brother's criticisms for too long for her aunt's abrasive personality to affect her much.

Aunt Ebena had already appropriated a piece of seed cake for herself. "It's cold," she said with a touch of petulance.

"You could have joined Lucy and me when they were still warm," Alethea couldn't resist saying.

Aunt Ebena sniffed. She took a sip of tea, then set the cup down. "Contrary to what you believe, I do not impose during your sister's visits, not because it is unseemly for me to take tea with a lady's maid, even though that is still true."

Alethea blinked at her aunt.

"I do not impose upon you and Miss Purcell because I cannot abide the giggling that inevitably erupts when you gather over tea and cakes."

"We don't giggle."

Aunt Ebena gave her a speaking look that made Alethea's cheeks grow warm, but she smiled at her aunt. The older woman did not return her smile, but it was not an unfriendly omission. It was simply Aunt Ebena.

Her aunt sipped her tea, marking the end of the topic. Alethea hesitated, wanting to say something but uncertain what to say, yearning for . . . she knew not what.

She'd had difficulty getting accustomed to her aunt, especially since Wilfred had forced them together. But did this comment about Lucy indicate Aunt Ebena was starting to unbend, perhaps even appreciate Alethea more? Would they achieve more than this polite veneer?

The problem was that Alethea did not know how to relate to respectable women. The women in the area around Trittonstone Park had been polite, but they had also avoided her because they disapproved of the "low company" she kept. Alethea would never have changed her behaviour to gain their approval, but their neglect made her feel lonely.

Did she want to develop a closer relationship with her aunt? Or would it be better to be alone and unhurt by disappointments? She did not expect her aunt to treat her as her father and brother had, but Alethea's experience with family members had been less than ideal. She realized she was idly massaging the two last fingers of her left hand and stopped.

She was simply missing Lady Arkright, she decided.

"Where is Margaret?" Aunt Ebena asked.

"Still in the kitchen. Cleaning up."

"Allowing her time in the kitchen is acceptable until her clothes arrive and she is more decently attired." Aunt Ebena didn't quite sigh, but she breathed heavily as if the remembrance of Margaret's wardrobe had been a particular trial. "However, since it is apparent the girl is staying, you must take her education in hand."

Alethea looked at her aunt incredulously. "Not you too."

"What?"

"Lucy said I should teach Margaret French." Alethea shoved a bite of cake into her mouth.

"Among other things." Aunt Ebena sipped her tea. "Lady Whittlesby's youngest granddaughter has just left the schoolroom, so she may still have the girl's schoolbooks. I shall ask her when next I see her."

Lady Whittlesby's name reminded Alethea of Mr. Golding's interest in her violin, and it occurred to her that perhaps the man knew of her violin because of her aunt. "Aunt, did you speak to anyone about my violin?"

"Whyever would I do anything of the sort?" she said irritably.

"Many of your friends are fond of music . . ."

"They are also exceedingly proper. Why would I confess that my niece is so unladylike as to play a violin? And against my advice." Aunt Ebena gave her a pointed look.

Alethea's warmer feelings toward her aunt dissipated. Why must people insist on telling her what she could not do? She realized with a surge of annoyance that it had been Lord Dommick telling her that exact piece of advice during Alethea's season that had spurred her to master her violin over her pianoforte and harp.

And why was she remembering that unpleasant experience with Lord Dommick? She must take herself in hand.

"Why would you think I have spoken to someone about this?" Aunt Ebena asked.

Alethea hadn't decided if she ought to tell her aunt about Mr. Golding, but now she must. She explained briefly.

Aunt Ebena grew grave. "Why would anyone want your violin?"

"I must speak to someone about it. I thought perhaps Lady Whittlesby might know to whom to direct me?"

Aunt Ebena nodded. "That is a very good thought. She had an expert repair a violin that belonged to a great-uncle and could give you the tradesman's direction. We shall visit her tomorrow. Is your violin safely hidden?"

"Yes." Thanks to Lady Arkright's husband and his woodworking abilities.

"Anyone passing by on the street would have heard you practicing," Aunt Ebena said with a touch of asperity, for she considered Alethea's hours of practice excessive. "But how would they know what particular instrument you owned?"

"Only Lucy knows." And there was no one in Bath who would understand Alethea's passion for an instrument unusual for ladies to play. Most of the ladies she knew would be shocked.

"I am curious to see it. Bring it down."

Alethea headed upstairs to her bedroom. She doubted Aunt Ebena could shed any light on the affair, but this was the first time she'd shown any interest in her music. They attended every concert faithfully, which her aunt enjoyed although she did not play herself, but at such events, Aunt Ebena equally enjoyed the company of her cronies, who were more avid musicians.

It took Alethea a moment after opening her bedroom door to understand what she saw. Then she gasped, the air scraping against her throat. Her chest tightened until the ache blossomed down to her stomach.

Bedclothes were strewn across the rug. Dresses had been pulled from the wardrobe. Stockings and petticoats tumbled from drawers. Furniture had been shoved askew, leaving deep scores in the wood floor.

Someone had torn through her bedroom.

Possibly while she'd been inside the house.

Alethea found herself at the bottom of the staircase, her breath coming in heaving gulps and her body trembling. Her knees wobbled and she dropped to the bottom step.

She had to tell Aunt Ebena. Was the intruder still in the house? She grasped the bannister and hauled herself to her feet. She staggered to the sitting room and flung open the door.

"What is it?" Aunt Ebena's voice was more irritated than alarmed.

"My room . . ." Alethea stopped, took a breath. She had to be rational or her aunt would never understand what had happened. "We have had an intruder in the house. May still be here."

"Impossible." Aunt Ebena rose to her feet.

"My room . . ." The vision of her things tossed about by unknown hands made her shudder.

Aunt Ebena exited the sitting room. Alethea followed her to her bedroom, and so was directly behind to catch her aunt when she cried out and stumbled backward at the sight of such disarray.

After a moment, Aunt Ebena shook Alethea's hands off her and straightened. "Dodd!" She hurried back downstairs.

"Madam?" The butler appeared at the base of the stairs.

"Someone has been in Lady Alethea's room. Make sure the intruder is no longer in my house."

The butler broke his professional facade and stiffened for a heartbeat, but then quickly snapped his fingers at a footman who had found his way into the foyer at the commotion. "Come with me."

Alethea wanted to go with them, as if facing the intruder would somehow help her face the violation of her room and give her a sense of control. She did not like feeling helpless and weak—she did not like feeling like a victim, as her brother had made her feel.

And was her violin still in its hiding place? Had the intruder searched beyond the more obvious places? Her panic grew from a simmering to a boiling. She could not lose Calandra's violin. Its value, both emotional and professional, was undeniable.

"Alethea!"

Her aunt's voice brought her attention back. Alethea followed her into the kitchen.

Soon all the servants except the butler and the footman had gathered in the kitchen, and Alethea stood against the back wall with Margaret by her side. Aunt Ebena spoke with precision. "An intruder has been through Lady Alethea's room. Dodd is checking the house to ensure they are gone." Aunt Ebena had to raise her voice as several people gasped. "Who was last in Lady Alethea's room?"

The upper housemaid, Sally, began to tremble violently. "I was, to straighten up. Just before church, ma'am."

"Did no one hear anything?" Aunt Ebena said.

"Most of the servants went to church," Mrs. Hill said. "Mrs. Dodd and I were here in the kitchen with Miss Margaret."

"I made a poultice for Mrs. Hill's knees." Mrs. Dodd swiftly inhaled. "I went to the herb garden and noticed some broken branches on the bushes against the back wall, but didn't think much of it."

"I cannot believe it," Mrs. Hill said, her hand at her chest. "In broad daylight, with us in the house."

Aunt Ebena questioned each servant in turn, noticing if any-one hesitated or seemed to recall something.

"Will we be safe?" Margaret whispered to Alethea.

Alethea feigned a confidence she was far from feeling. "We shall be quite safe."

"Do you have a secret treasure?"

"What?"

"You must or someone would not break into the house to search for it." Margaret's eyes gleamed. "Is it gold? Jewels? Maybe a cursed pirate's treasure?"

"If I had a pirate's treasure, cursed or not, I would be on my ship, sailing the high seas, rather than taking you for dress fittings at the seamstress."

"I would too. And I wouldn't need dresses because I'd be in man's breeches and wielding my deadly sword."

Dodd and the footman returned now, confirming the intruder was no longer in the house. The room exhaled as one, and Alethea squeezed Margaret's shoulders.

Aunt Ebena went to Alethea. "Go and see what has been taken," she said.

"May I come?" Margaret asked.

"I am going to clean my room, not go to Astley's Circus," Alethea said dryly.

At the word *clean*, Margaret's enthusiasm dimmed a trifle, but she quickly said, "I still want to come."

Since it would keep her out of Aunt Ebena's way, Alethea nod-ded and headed upstairs.

The sight of the room caused nausea to rise up in Alethea's stomach, but she stood in the doorway and took quick, shallow breaths.

"A biscuit helps," Margaret said.

"What?"

"I would steal a biscuit from the kitchen before I had to clean my room."

"I have no need for you to steal a biscuit for me," Alethea said. "And for your information, asking Mrs. Dodd politely will usually accomplish the trick as opposed to raiding her larder."

"Oh," Margaret said. "Our cook was not so nice."

Alethea took a deeper breath and plunged into the fray. She first went to her trunk to ascertain her violin was still in its hiding place and breathed a sigh of relief.

It was not so terrible a mess once Alethea picked up her clothes from the floor. She shared Aunt Ebena's lady's maid, so she set aside the clothing she would give to the maid to be washed, pressed, or mended. Gradually she realized Margaret was depositing various items into the wardrobe willy-nilly.

"What are you doing?" Alethea said.

Margaret froze. "Helping?"

"Why did you put my hairbrush into the wardrobe?"

Margaret looked into the wardrobe at the pile of random items, then back at Alethea. "It was on the floor."

"So why not place it on the dressing table?"

Margaret looked at the dressing table. "I'll put all that in the wardrobe too."

"What? No. Why?" Alethea was beginning to feel as if she were in a farcical play.

"Aren't we cleaning?" Margaret asked.

Understanding dawned. "Is this what you did when you cleaned your room? Throw things into the wardrobe?"

Margaret nodded. "It's fastest."

So she could go out to play as quickly as possible, Alethea would guess. "I have a thought. What if we put things back in their proper places?"

"That'll take *forever*."

"Things will be much easier to find than rooting through the wardrobe."

Margaret looked at the wardrobe again. "I suppose so." She picked up the hairbrush from the pile and placed it on the dressing table.

Alethea folded a petticoat. "Surely your mother did not allow you to fling all your things into the wardrobe that way?"

Margaret's movements stilled for a long moment. Her back was to Alethea, so she couldn't see her face. "No, she didn't like it." Margaret's voice was softer than normal.

Alethea bit her lip. Margaret was so cheerful a child that she often forgot the girl was still in half-mourning for her parents.

Although Alethea still missed Calandra, she remembered that in the months after Lady Arkright's death, it made her feel better to speak of her to others. There hadn't been many in the neighborhood who were close to the widow because she was Italian, but when Sir William Arkright's heir dismissed all of Lady Arkright's servants, Alethea had visited them and helped them find new positions. Speaking to them of their mistress had given Alethea great comfort.

But how to get Margaret to speak to her? Alethea again felt that pang of awkwardness because of her lack of experience with children.

"So, um . . . tell me nice stories about your mother." Alethea winced as soon as the words came out of her mouth. She half expected Margaret to burst into tears or run from the room.

There was a long silence. Then the girl half turned toward her. "Mama never let the maids clean for me. She wanted me to learn to be neat. She didn't like it when I threw my things into the wardrobe." Her voice was soft, but grew in strength as she continued. "So, one day she sent the maid to tell me to clean my room. When I went to the wardrobe and opened the door, she burst out at me." Margaret giggled.

Alethea laughed. "That is a good trick. I think I would have liked your mother."

"I think so too." Margaret picked up a shoe, then put it back in the wardrobe. "Papa was like Aunt Ebena, but Mama could always make him smile."

And now she was here with Alethea and Aunt Ebena, with no mama to make any of them smile and an intruder alarming the household. What if Alethea or a maid had interrupted the intruder? Would he have hurt her before escaping?

Alethea needed to uncover the truth about her violin quickly. She prayed that Aunt Ebena's friend Lady Whittlesby would be able to help her.

Pray? No, she had given up praying a year ago, the night she had been locked in her bedroom, still shaking from the pain of her broken fingers and from the fear that she may never be able to play again. God had not helped her then and would not help her now against this trouble. She could only depend upon herself.

She could not lose her violin. It was the key to all her hopes and dreams.

CHAPTER THREE

❧

*B*ayard danced with his mother in the Upper Assembly Rooms while keeping watch over his sister, dancing with Mr. Morrish.

"Bayard, I don't understand your prejudice against Mr. Morrish," his mother said as they danced.

He pulled his gaze back to his mother, looking particularly fine tonight in a cheerful gold dress he hadn't seen before. His mother seemed to dress in brighter colours since his father had died over a year ago. They suited her.

"I don't know Mr. Morrish well," Bayard said. "I am simply exercising the rights of an overprotective brother."

"Take care you do not stray into *overbearing.*"

"Clare would scold me if I did." Clare did not look particularly happy with her partner, although Mr. Morrish danced well. He was light on his feet with far more graceful movements than Bayard could ever produce.

"Bayard, do stop staring at them." There was a note of hurt

in his mother's voice. "You will offend your stepfather with your suspicions."

"You know I would never deliberately do anything to upset you." Especially now, after the pain he had caused her this past spring in London. The *ton's* barbs and slurs had produced tears she had tried to hide, but he had seen how they had wounded her.

"Then do try to be friends with Sir Hermes's nephew. If you accept him, then perhaps Clare will warm to him."

The movements of the dance separated them, which rescued Bayard from trying to hide his surprise. When they came together again, he said, "Do you wish Clare to become more intimately acquainted with him?"

"I should like them to be friends, and if they discover a deeper connection, I shall not object. His disposition is so cheerful, much like Sir Hermes's. He would bring light and laughter to Clare, who has a tendency toward too much seriousness."

"But what of his fortune?" Bayard disliked being so blunt with her, but her fancies sometimes overlooked practical matters.

"Sir Hermes believes Clare would be very good for Mr. Morrish. He is not a wastrel, and with Clare's good sense, he could become even more respectably established. Maybe even an M.P."

His mother had avoided directly answering his question. He made a mental note to have his man of business privately look into Mr. Morrish's prospects.

"Bayard, do stop frowning at Mr. Morrish."

Bayard tried to smooth the tightness in his forehead. "I am not frowning."

"You are staring fiercely. Sir Hermes will think you are attempting to scare away his dearest nephew."

Bayard suspected Sir Hermes, in his usual careless way, would laugh and then give his nephew more tips on how to court Clare, as if it were a huge joke. Sir Hermes did not care about Clare at all—he no doubt craved the further connection with the Terralton family and their money.

Perhaps Bayard was being unfair. Sir Hermes was not as wealthy as Bayard's father had been, but he had a very respectable estate. And while he was attached to his nephew, it seemed he was not malicious in his scheming.

But Bayard did not see Sir Hermes's affability in his nephew. Mr. Morrish seemed more mercenary and deceptive.

Bayard happened to be looking when Mr. Morrish deliberately stepped on his sister's dress, tearing the flounce at the hem. Mr. Morrish had been dancing superbly, which made his gaffe more suspicious. The man appeared contrite in his apologies as he led Clare off the dance floor.

"Whatever is the matter?" Lady Morrish followed his gaze.

"Clare's dress has torn. Perhaps you should help her to the ladies' withdrawing room to repair it."

"No, Mr. Morrish is escorting her. She shall be fine."

Every muscle in Bayard tightened, making his dancing stiff as he watched Mr. Morrish lead Clare out of the room. She looked around, seeking out Bayard, with a look of entreaty on her face, just before she moved out of sight.

"Clare should not be alone with him." Bayard would have led his mother off the dance floor directly, but that would embarrass her and draw attention to his concern.

"She shall be fine. What could anyone do to her in these crowded rooms?"

It was true the Assembly Rooms were especially filled tonight, but that also meant there were more witnesses if Mr. Morrish did anything scandalous. Clare's letter about the boy who had tried to compromise her this past summer still alarmed him. *Lord God, what more can I do to protect my sister?*

When the dance was finally over, Bayard first had to escort his mother to a seat next to her friend, Lady Woolton. Sitting next to her was Lady Whittlesby.

Bayard bowed to the ladies and would have hastened after his sister, but Lady Whittlesby rose and commanded him, "Dommick, it did not occur to me you would be here."

"I did not realize you would be here either, Lady Whittlesby." Normally the dowager avoided the dances at the assembly rooms.

Lady Whittlesby sighed and nodded toward a lively young girl, no more than seventeen, who was dancing. "My youngest granddaughter arrived in Bath yesterday."

At any other time, Bayard would have been pleased to speak to the dowager, who was a celebrated hostess in London. He had hoped to find favour with Lady Whittlesby for her famed annual concert this upcoming season. But he glanced at the open doors to the ballroom, wondering what was keeping Clare so long.

"Come, walk with me," Lady Whittlesby said.

He had no choice, without being rude. He gave the older woman his arm, and she tugged him toward a far corner of the ballroom.

"I intended to call upon you tomorrow morning to ask for your help," Lady Whittlesby said.

"I am at your service, my lady," Bayard said automatically, sneaking a glance at the ballroom doors again.

"I am in need of your expertise in the violin. My friend, Mrs. Garen, approached me today with a curious predicament. Apparently someone has tried to steal her niece's violin. I would like you to assist the gel to discover what is so particular about this instrument."

Why would a genteel woman own a violin? Surely she did not play it? Perhaps, like Lady Whittlesby's violin, it belonged to a male family member.

"I will sweeten the deal," Lady Whittlesby continued. "If you succeed in discovering the provenance of this violin, I will offer to you—and to your three friends in your Quartet—the foremost place in my annual concert this spring."

Bayard's step faltered for an instant, but he recovered quickly. To be featured in Lady Whittlesby's concert would guarantee his social success and the destruction of those damaging rumours spread earlier this year. He desired it not for himself but for his mother and sister—he could not allow his reputation to harm them when they went to London.

Lady Whittlesby smiled. "I assure you I am most sincere. Your sister is a musician as well, is she not? If her performance meets with my approval, she will be featured in my concert. I flatter myself that her presence on my concert bill will bring her to the favourable notice of all the best hostesses in town."

Clare's performance in Lady Whittlesby's concert would ensure his sister's season would be brilliant—she and his mother would be courted and feted by everyone of most importance in the town.

"I thank you with all my heart," he said to her. "May I ask what prompts your generosity?"

"I am not generous," she said with a smirk. "I know the Quartet equals any professional musicians I have heard. And I have heard many, I assure you."

"Thank you, my lady." It wasn't the answer he had been hoping for.

"Mrs. Garen is also a good friend, and her niece a particular favourite of mine."

What was Lady Whittlesby playing at? She had no "particular favourites" in anyone as far as he knew. She loved to gossip and to stir up trouble, and fear of her was the reason why so many of the ladies in town were respectful of her—in public, at least.

"And if I do not discover the provenance of this violin?"

Lady Whittlesby's smile deepened. "Surely there is no doubt? I have utmost confidence in you."

"Enough for you to wager among your friends?"

She laughed outright. "You have caught me out. Yes, I love a good wager, and what is the fun of doing a good deed if I cannot have a friendly wager out of it with my friends? If you do not succeed, why, I will offer my concert to Mr. Kinnier instead of the Quartet."

Bayard had almost been expecting it. "He is a fine musician," Bayard said in a neutral voice.

Lady Whittlesby cackled. "Do not try to convince me that you do not dislike the man heartily."

"I do not dislike him."

"He certainly dislikes you. Perhaps because the two of you were often compared. In fact, my friends and I have argued over which of you were more proficient at the violin."

"That was years ago, when I was playing in London with my friends." Time and war had made him a different man. He hoped he would not feel the same way now about Mr. Kinnier, son of the Viscount Grimslow, as he had when he had been young and foolish.

Lady Whittlesby merely hoped to fire his sense of competition by dangling Mr. Kinnier as his rival. She couldn't know that while Mr. Kinnier was fiercely competitive, Bayard was not. He wanted to play in her concert for the healing of his reputation and the success of his sister's season.

They had finally reached the corner, and Lady Whittlesby gestured to two women who approached. "Ladies, may I present Lord Dommick? Mrs. Garen and Lady Alethea Sutherton."

Bayard bowed to the elderly woman, about Lady Whittlesby's age, and then he met eyes with the dark-haired young woman next to her. She was striking in her beauty. Eyebrows arched over large, almond-shaped dark eyes. She had high cheekbones and creamy skin with a hint of olive, perhaps from some long-ago Roman ancestor, and full red lips that he imagined would spread into a wide smile. She looked familiar to him, but he couldn't remember where he had met her before.

He also could not fathom why she looked at him as if he had just crawled out of the mud.

❧

Alethea stared in horror at Lord Dommick. She hadn't expected that he would remain in Bath. She had not seen him or his friends about the town in the past week, and the arrivals in the paper had not mentioned their names.

She was being ridiculous. She had to put aside one disastrous interaction from eleven years ago. Why should she devote any more space in her brain for him? After all, he wouldn't have remembered her.

"Lady Alethea, have we been introduced before?" Lord Dommick had a politely puzzled expression, probably wondering why she looked as though she desired to run screaming from the ballroom.

For a brief, wild moment, she considered lying to him. Their previous interaction meant nothing to him, and he couldn't have known the effect of his words upon her temper and the direction of her musical study.

But a few people in Bath would remember her horrific London season, and it would seem odd for her to pretend that she and Lord Dommick had never been introduced.

"We met briefly many years ago," Alethea said.

He parted his lips as if about to say something more, but then changed his mind and simply bowed instead.

Lady Whittlesby hadn't missed Alethea's reaction to Dommick and had a curious gleam in her eye. "Lady Alethea is a fine musician. Perhaps you met at one of Dommick's concerts?"

A spasm ran across Alethea's throat before she answered. "Yes. When the Quartet played in London."

"Did we meet perhaps more recently, Lady Alethea?"

She doubted the glimpse on the street, with her dressed like a servant, hardly counted as "meeting."

"I am never in town, my lord." Not by choice, but London had no appeal for her.

"You shall have opportunity to become more acquainted," Lady Whittlesby said. "Lord Dommick has agreed to help you investigate the provenance of your violin."

Why in the world would he agree to that? She cleared her throat rather that blurt out her surprise. "My lord is too kind."

"I have given him incentive. If he is able to solve your little mystery, I will feature the Quartet in my concert this spring."

Ah. Lady Whittlesby's famous concerts featured only gently born musicians, and to be chosen was a high honour. No wonder he'd agreed to help her.

"You're too good, Honora," Aunt Ebena said to her friend.

"Nonsense, Ebena. I hadn't yet decided on the musicians for my concert, and young men enjoy challenges."

Lord Dommick didn't look as though he considered Alethea's problem anything close to a challenge. "I am always at your service, Lady Whittlesby." His eyes strayed to the ballroom doors, which belied his gallant words.

"I do not wish to take up my lord's valuable time." Alethea tried to be gracious but was afraid she sounded peevish. "Lady Whittlesby, I had expected no greater favour than the direction of a shopkeeper or an instrument tuner."

"I had considered that, but Lord Dommick intends to spend the winter in Bath, and there is none more knowledgeable about the violin, with superior contacts in the musical world."

Alethea had to admit her logic was sound. It was hardly Lady Whittlesby's fault that Alethea didn't like the solution.

Lady Whittlesby turned to Lord Dommick. "You will thank me for introducing the two of you, ah, *again*." She tittered. "Lady Alethea is quite accomplished on the violin. You two have much in common."

Alethea almost burst out laughing. She could predict his response to that.

Lord Dommick's dark brows drew together ever so slightly. "You play the violin, Lady Alethea?"

His incredulous tone was exactly the same as when he'd said the same words to her eleven years ago. Whether because of past pain or current pride, she drew herself up and responded with the same words as she had eleven years ago. "Yes, I enjoy it very well." This time, however, her tone was confident and challenging, not meek and eager to impress him. "Tell me, my lord, do you still consider it unfeminine for women to play violin?"

Her question took him aback. Lady Whittlesby was barely holding in her glee at their juicy interchange.

"Alethea!" Aunt Ebena hissed.

Lord Dommick recovered from his surprise and said in an even voice, "Perhaps you would take a turn about the room with me, Lady Alethea?"

She assented grudgingly. She wouldn't embarrass her aunt no matter the low opinion she had of Lord Dommick. Or give Lady Whittlesby more to gossip about.

"I'm sure you have many musical things to discuss," Lady Whittlesby said.

Alethea took Lord Dommick's arm, and he led her toward the ballroom doors. To her great surprise, they approached his mother and his friend, Lord Ian Wynnman.

"Lady Alethea, may I present my mother, Lady Morrish, and Lord Ian Wynnman. Mama, Ian, this is Lady Alethea Sutherton."

Alethea gave him a suspicious glance before she curtseyed. What could be his purpose in introducing her to his mother?

"Lady Alethea, I was acquainted with your aunt when she used to attend the season with her husband," Lady Morrish said.

"She would be pleased to make your acquaintance again, Lady Mor—"

Alethea hadn't quite finished her sentence when Lord Dommick addressed his mother. "Mama, where is Clare? I thought she would be back by now."

Lady Morrish blinked in surprise. "Oh. She hasn't yet returned from the ladies' withdrawing room. She was with Mr. Morrish . . ."

Lord Dommick gave Lord Ian a hard look, and the young man gave a slight nod, his golden-brown hair glinting in the light from the crystal chandelier overhead.

"Lady Morrish, I'll find her. Pleasure to meet you, Lady Alethea." Lord Ian bowed and left the ballroom.

Alethea noticed that it was as though Lord Dommick's insides had been twisted like a knot that suddenly unloosened. His shoulders relaxed their rigid stance, and even his jaw softened. "Mama, if you would excuse us? Lady Whittlesby asked me to help Lady Alethea with her . . . musical problem. I'll return in a few minutes."

"Don't hurry on my account," Lady Morrish said. "I'm sure Ian will bring Clare back soon."

She again sensed that something uncoiled in Lord Dommick at his mother's words. Why was he so concerned about his sister?

She didn't have time to wonder because he led her away toward a quieter corner of the ballroom where several elderly chaperones sat snoozing. "I remember meeting you in London, my lady," he said.

"I hardly expected you to. I'm sure I was one of dozens of women at your concert."

"You were the only one who looked fierce enough to run me through with a sword, had you one at hand, when I mentioned that women should not play the violin."

She gaped at him for a moment. His handsome face was impassive, and she didn't know if he was offended or amused by her. Possibly both. "Rest assured I did not take your words to heart. To be sure, the violin became my favourite instrument."

Especially after he had practically goaded her with his words. *I would never allow a woman to play a violin in one of my concerts, for it would be most unseemly. You would do better to attempt to master the harp or pianoforte.*

"I am not surprised by that information." He cleared his throat. "I would be most interested in hearing more about your violin."

She belatedly remembered that antagonizing him was hardly the way to solicit his help. "It was a gift from a good friend, Lady Arkright, who died three years ago." What a paltry description for their relationship—Calandra had been the mother she'd never known.

"It belonged to her husband?"

The question irritated her. "No, it was hers. She was trained to play many instruments at the orphanage in Venice where she grew up, the Ospedale della Pietà."

Lord Dommick's brows rose. "I have heard of that place."

"It is most famous for training *female* musicians. Calandra— Lady Arkright—trained under Vivaldi himself."

She had his attention now. "Lady Arkright taught you to play?" he asked.

"Violin, pianoforte, and harp, although she was most gifted in violin. She always lamented that it was socially acceptable for women to play the violin on the continent but not in England."

"How did she acquire the violin?"

"Calandra met her husband, Sir William, in Italy. On their wedding journey, he bought the violin from a peddler in Milan."

"A peddler?" Lord Dommick looked pained.

"This is why I need help. If it were a simple matter, I could have made inquiries myself."

"Lady Whittlesby mentioned you thought someone tried to take your violin?"

"A man stopped me on the street and asked if I would sell my violin. I refused, but I was concerned because there is no reason for anyone to know the particular violin I own. I have never played it in public, not even for my relatives, and I practice in private. A few days later my room was torn apart by someone searching for something."

"Was anyone injured? Anything taken?"

"No one was injured, although we were shaken since it occurred while my aunt's niece, the cook, and the housekeeper were all in the kitchen. Nothing was taken." Alethea again thanked the shade of Sir William for crafting such a clever hiding place for it.

"You are certain it was the violin they were looking for?"

"What else could it be? None of my jewels were taken." She did not have many, since Wilfred's wife, Mona, had claimed most of Alethea's mother's jewelry and Alethea's father had never given her gifts, but she did have a fine pearl necklace that Calandra had given to her for her season, which had been at the top of her jewelry case.

"Perhaps the thief was interrupted?"

Alethea stopped and turned to face him. She pitched her voice low, but she said firmly, "Lord Dommick, let us speak plainly. It appears you do not believe me when I say someone wants to steal my violin. And if you doubt me, how can you help me?"

Irritation flashed across his face, quickly masked by politeness. "I apologize if I have made you feel that I am not taking your fears seriously, my lady."

She supposed she could not completely fault him for being irritated—she had verbally challenged him twice now. She should know by now that men did not take kindly to women with opinions, especially if they were different from their own. She absently rubbed the last two knuckles of her left hand.

And the truth was that she needed his help, despite his archaic thoughts about women playing violins and his tendency like others of his sex to be dismissive of women, specifically her. "We should agree upon a time when you will call to see the violin."

"Perhaps next week—"

"I doubt my aunt's temper would survive another intruder in her home. Are you available tomorrow?"

"Tomorrow?" He stared at her for a long moment before sighing. "Yes, I can call in the afternoon."

"Excellent. We are at number six, Queen Square."

He nodded and was silent as he walked her back to her aunt, but the stiff set of his head seemed to indicate he was annoyed at the disruption to his schedule. Lady Whittlesby had thankfully left her aunt. Lord Dommick bowed before marching away.

Alethea sat next to her aunt. The ballroom was hot, for there seemed to be more people than usual attending tonight. Or perhaps she was still upset from her encounter with Lord Dommick.

"What did he say to you when you first met him?" Aunt Ebena asked with a stern look in her eye. "And do not attempt to deceive me. I know something happened momentous on your part, although probably not on his."

Aunt Ebena had a way of aiming for the truth in such a way that it robbed Alethea of any of her dignity. "He treated me as I was then, a silly girl in her first season."

"Lord Dommick does not have a reputation for cruel wit. I cannot believe he would slice you to ribbons simply because you were being silly."

"I *was* silly. It was the end of his concert, the largest that the Quartet had given that season. They were wildly popular, and I was not the first nor the last to speak to him after it ended. I was enthusiastic in my praise of the violin concerto he had composed, and then I mentioned that I played the violin. He expressed the opinion that it was unfeminine for a woman to play the instrument."

"It is unfeminine. The use of your arms is quite excessive."

Alethea remained silent. She had already borne the brunt of

Lord Dommick's disapproval and did not intend to also allow her aunt the pleasure of it.

"I would wager," Aunt Ebena said, "that after that encounter, you returned home from London and worked even harder to master your violin over your other instruments."

Alethea managed to reply in a conversational tone. "I enjoy the violin very much. And Lady Arkright favoured it as an instrument as well."

"But you would perhaps have worked harder at the more socially acceptable instruments had it not been for Lord Dommick. Am I correct?"

"Your friends do not complain when they ask me to play the pianoforte or the harp at their evening gatherings."

"I am not denying your talent. You are better than some of the professional musicians I have heard, which forces me to conclude that you are somewhat gifted."

It seemed Aunt Ebena could never deliver a compliment without trying to spoil it at the same time. But her faint praise made Alethea smile to herself, although she didn't look at her aunt.

Aunt Ebena nodded. "But now I understand your reaction to Lord Dommick."

And his reaction to her had been supremely uninterested, which may have been why she'd spoken so bluntly. She did not care to be the centre of attention, but she also did not appreciate being overlooked.

She had not truly challenged herself on her violin since Calandra died, but perhaps now was the time to push herself to her limits, especially with her newly healed left hand. She did not know how she would accomplish it, but she would find a way to acquire a copy of Lord Dommick's latest composition and learn to play it herself, as well as he did.

He would not overlook her *then*.

CHAPTER FOUR

*T*hat ugly prickle began along the back of her shoulders just as Alethea turned onto Milsom Street.

She took a deep breath, then continued on her way, head erect and eyes forward. She stopped at a print shop with large windows and peered at the reflection in the glass.

The sun was fitful today, peeking out only occasionally from behind heavy grey clouds, so she could not see as clearly as she would have liked. Many people paraded up and down the street, winding in and out of the small shops that lined the road, oblivious to Alethea's unease. She searched the crowds in the reflection of the glass, but no one looked at her, no one loitered nearby.

What had she expected to see in the reflection? A dark hooded figure staring at her from across the street? She continued down Milsom Street.

She didn't know what made her look slightly behind her and across the street. It wasn't a sound, for a carriage was rumbling by and a group of old women chattered in front of her. But she turned and in the brief gap between the horses and the carriage, she saw the same cadaverous man she'd seen in the marketplace, and he was looking directly at her.

This time the prickle was a shiver that shot straight through her spine.

Then the carriage's movement blocked her view for a few seconds, and when it had passed, the man had disappeared. There were two shop doors nearby where he'd been standing, so perhaps he had ducked inside one of them.

And was watching her, unobserved, from behind the shop windows.

She would not give him the satisfaction. She hurried down the street, out of sight of the two shops, and when she had turned the corner, she immediately entered the shop there, which was a bookshop and stationers.

The cool space smelled of paper and leather and ink. Alethea's heartbeat slowed at the familiar scents and the soothing ruffling of pages. She made her way to a bookcase near the large bay window and picked a book at random, pretending to read while studying each person who passed the shop outside.

"Alethea, what a happy meeting."

She started, then turned with real warmth for her sister. After the tension of the last few minutes, her cheeks felt tight as she smiled. "Lucy, happy meeting, indeed." Lucy tried to back away, but Alethea stepped forward to kiss her cheek.

"You shouldn't be seen kissing a maid, Alethea."

"I don't care what people think, and you certainly don't dress like a maid." In fact, she was wearing an amber-coloured dress Alethea had given to her at Christmas that brought out flecks of gold in her dark brown eyes, a slightly lighter shade than Alethea's. "What are you doing here?"

"Running an errand for Mrs. Ramsland." Lucy made a small

gesture with her arms, full of paper and ink. Then her eyes narrowed as she studied Alethea's face. "What has upset you?"

"Nothing."

Lucy glared at her.

Alethea sighed. "It's silly. I thought I saw that man from the marketplace. The thin one whom I thought was watching me *but probably wasn't*," she added emphatically.

"You saw him on Milsom Street?"

"It was only for a second. He disappeared so perhaps he wasn't even there." Alethea glanced outside the shop windows, but the people passing by were few. The tension across her shoulders began to ease.

Lucy's brows crinkled. "Alethea, this is becoming frightful."

"Bath isn't London. It's entirely possible I could have seen the same man from the marketplace if he lives in Bath. I'm simply nervous after what happened with my room."

"What happened to your room?" Lucy asked.

Alethea had forgotten that the incident had been after Lucy's last Sunday visit and before her next one. "Er . . ." Alethea pulled at her earlobe as she frantically thought about how she could tell Lucy the events without causing her to have a fit.

Her sister knew her too well. "Oh, simply tell me, Alethea."

"Someone went through my room Sunday morning when we were at church."

Lucy's mouth opened for several seconds before she remembered to close it. "And after that man at the marketplace and that offensive Mr. Golding . . ."

"I don't know that they're connected, but it is a possibility."

"Did he steal anything?"

"Nothing. Not even jewelry."

"But Margaret and Mrs. Dodd were in the kitchen." Lucy shuddered.

"They heard nothing, but it worries me that someone entered the house during the day, no less, while they were there."

Lucy suddenly looked around. "Alethea, where is your maid?"

"Most of the fashionable set isn't awake yet to see me maidless."

"You are too used to country ways. You cannot go unaccompanied, and after the intruder, it would be safer if you had someone with you."

Alethea had not thought of that. "You are right. I shall take a maid next time."

"Alethea." Lucy juggled the paper and ink she held in order to reach out to take her hand. "Is the violin really worth the possible danger to yourself and your family?"

"You want me to simply hand Mr. Golding my violin?"

"Think of Margaret and your aunt."

Because she'd been left on her own at Trittonstone Park for most of her life, Alethea's actions had rarely affected others' safety. The newly realized responsibility seemed odd to her, settling upon her shoulders almost like a physical weight, forcing her to be stronger. Her life was now more than just her own.

But the image of giving her violin to Mr. Golding sent a wave of nausea up from her stomach and she tightened her throat. When she looked at her violin, she remembered the sunroom at Arkright Manor, the way the morning light would caress the wood of the violin almost reverently as Calandra played, her eyes closed in concentration and adoration of the music. The musical pieces would evoke emotions from Alethea like a bouquet of handpicked flowers—the bright joy of a child's laughter, the cool stillness of the downs at dawn, the warmth and comfort of a crackling fire while rain pelted the windows. Alethea remembered the tenderness in Calandra's hand on her head as she gave the violin to her, saying, "Now you try it, Alethea."

Later, when Calandra grew too ill to play, Alethea would play for her in that sunroom, following her mentor's verbal instructions until she made the music sound almost like tangible emotions. Alethea and Calandra would both be in tears at the end of the piece, and they'd laugh as they reached for their handkerchiefs. "What is music if it does not move you?" Calandra had told her.

Alethea realized she hadn't played that way in a long time, not since Calandra had died. Now she was reduced to bright pieces on pianofortes at evening parties that most people would talk through rather than listen to. No shared tears, no musical pieces of powerful feeling. Her acquaintances in Bath already considered her an oddity for her intense attention during concerts. They would never understand how a concerto could make her cry. She was reminded that she had no one in her life who understood that deepest part of her, and it made her feel desolate.

She was brought out of her sad memories by the squeeze of Lucy's fingers on her hand. "I'm sorry, I didn't intend to cause you to miss her again."

"It's been years. It shouldn't still be so painful."

"It's because no one else understands you as Lady Arkright did."

"I can't sell my violin, Lucy. It would break my heart." Alethea took a deep breath, feeling a little better now that she had acknowledged that fact aloud. "And I will not let a stranger take this last shred of her memory from me. I will stop them."

Lucy nodded as she withdrew her hand. "Now, where are you going? I will accompany you and then see you home before I return to Mrs. Ramsland."

"You oughtn't do that. You might fall into disfavour with your employer."

"You are my sister. You're more important." The look in Lucy's eyes was Alethea's anchor, the one connection in her life that shone brighter than the sun and was stronger than steel.

"I wanted to stop at Porter's bookshop to see if he had any new music, but that can wait for another day."

After Lucy paid for her employer's items, they exited the book-shop. Alethea looked around but didn't see the cadaverous man, so she breathed deeply of the morning air as the sisters walked slowly toward Queen Square.

"Did Lady Whittlesby give you the name of someone to help you with your violin?" Lucy asked.

Lord Dommick's lean, handsome face flashed before her eyes. "Yes," she answered darkly. "He's calling this afternoon, the arro-gant man."

Lucy looked thoughtful. "You may not realize this, but you only ever spoke of one man with that kind of venom."

Oh, no.

"Let me guess. A nobleman, taller than you, for a change. Dark hair, velvety black eyes—"

"He does not have velvety black eyes. And how would you know?"

"Because that's how you described him to me eleven years ago." Lucy grinned at her.

Alethea threw up her hands. "I confess, yes, it's Lord Dommick."

"I knew he would stay in Bath, despite your speculations about it after you saw his carriage."

"He has no reason to winter in a quiet town like Bath when he could be feted in London or attend numerous house parties or just sit and count his violins at his own estate in the country."

"Did you give him a piece of your mind when you met again?"

"It was at the assembly last night and I properly offended him. Twice."

"And he's to help you with your violin?"

"Lady Whittlesby introduced us and dangled her annual con-cert like a carrot in front of him if he helped me. I could have called him a nincompoop, and he'd have smiled and thanked me."

"I think you're disgruntled because you think he wouldn't be induced to help you without Lady Whittlesby's interference."

"Well, he wouldn't."

"Perhaps he's changed."

"Perhaps he hasn't," Alethea muttered. Louder, she said, "I don't have a choice. I can't investigate the provenance of the violin on my own—I don't have the contacts or the resources, and being a woman, I'm less likely to receive answers to any inquiries I send. I need someone to help me. I need Lord Dommick to help me."

"And you certainly look cheerful about it. Positively delighted."

Alethea laughed. "I promise to behave when I see him today."

At that moment, they turned the corner. Alethea happened to look across the street, slightly behind them.

The cadaverous man stood at the corner. Watching her.

She saw him more clearly this time. His skin wasn't as dirty as it had been at the marketplace, but it still had that wrinkled, leathery texture that made him appear very old. Yet he didn't hold his bony body like an old man—his limbs were fluid and comfortable as he slumped against the golden stone wall of a building, his clothing a motley of shades of grey. The colours matched his wiry, thinning hair that floated around his wide ears and his grey, almost colourless, eyes.

He looked directly at her, and then smiled.

It wasn't a pleasant smile. He tilted his knobby chin up and flashed his dirty, crooked teeth—one missing from the front—like a challenge to her.

And this time she was with her *sister*.

She made the mistake of glancing at Lucy, who hadn't seen him, and then back at the man.

He smiled wider, his eyes narrowing.

No. She wouldn't let him intimidate her.

Alethea turned her back and grasped hold of Lucy's elbow in a firm but casual grip. "Tell me, to what heights has Mrs. Ramsland attained in selfish bitterness this week?" She was surprised her voice sounded almost normal, and since a cart rolled past them, Lucy didn't notice the slight tremor.

Lucy shook her head. "Speaking of Mrs. Ramsland would only upset me, and I must be calm when I return to her today."

"Oh, Lucy, surely there is another position to be had in Bath."

"The winter season is starting, so I am hopeful there will be some gentlewoman in need of a new lady's maid. I only wonder how I shall hear of any positions available since I am with Mrs. Ramsland and catering to her complaints all day."

Lucy had told Alethea about those complaints. Things like being quick to accuse Lucy of taking things that she herself had misplaced, and deliberately demanding hip baths late the night before she knew Lucy would need to rise early in order to do her duties before taking her half day off. "I shall keep my ears open," Alethea said.

"And Mrs. Ramsland at least allows me a half day off a week. Some employers conveniently forget."

As her sister rambled on about other employers she had heard about, Alethea walked beside her, her back straight as a fireplace poker and her head held high, while in her chest, her heart thundered.

For the first time, she was glad Lord Dommick was calling this afternoon. The sooner she discovered who was after her violin and why, the sooner she could stop them, and stop the threat to her family.

❧

Bayard had a raging headache. Between the irritation of Mr. Morrish's excessive solicitude toward Clare last night and the dread of his eminent meeting with a woman as prickly as a hedgehog, he felt as if a coach-and-four had run over him.

Lord Ian found it all vastly entertaining.

Ian leaned back against the squabs of the carriage and gave Bayard a wide grin that made his dimples stand out even through the dark gold shadow on his cheeks. "You look like you're heading to a funeral, old man."

Bayard scowled at him. "I look nothing of the sort."

Ian shrugged, raised a hand to flip a lock of hair out of his eyes, and stared out the carriage. Still grinning.

Bayard cleared his throat and said, "Last night, when you went to the ladies' withdrawing room to find Clare, Morrish was waiting for her?"

"When he saw me, Morrish looked as if he'd swallowed a fork," Ian said gleefully. "He told me that I needn't wait for Clare, that he'd knocked on the door and inquired of the maid, but Clare's hem wasn't finished yet."

Bayard frowned. "She could have sewn an entire dress in the time I was speaking to Lady Alethea."

"I said something along those lines—although with much more elegance and wit."

Bayard rolled his eyes.

"I knocked on the door and spoke to the maid, and Clare was out in a trice. When I escorted her back to the ballroom, I must say, Bay, you needn't have been rushing toward us as if she'd been abducted."

"Clare's dowry is seventy-five thousand pounds," Bayard said. "I dare you to walk calmly when that rackety fortune hunter had deliberately arranged to remove her from the room."

"Well, when you put it in those terms . . ."

Bayard suddenly felt the damp coldness of the winter in his bones. He was in Bath for the sake of his mother and sister—he could not fail to protect them. *Lord God, help me to protect them.* He cleared his throat and studied the shine on his Hessian boots. "Thank you for going to her, Ian."

"Wouldn't want the brat getting lost," Ian answered casually, "not with her debut this spring."

At mention of Clare's season, tension squeezed the back of Bayard's neck and shoulders. He needed to repair his reputation after being ruined by his former betrothed, Miss Church-Pratton. While Lady Whittlesby's concert would accomplish that, if he were to be seen associating too often with a woman who played the violin, would people think him an oddity and cast doubts on his sanity, fueled by the old rumours?

Did he have a choice? Lady Whittlesby's concert came with the price of interacting with the brash Lady Alethea Sutherton.

"It's a pity a woman so beautiful is so aggressive and unconventional," Bayard said.

Ian's eyebrows completely disappeared behind that lock of hair over his forehead. "I take it we're no longer speaking about Clare?"

"What?"

Ian gave him a sly smile. "Lady Alethea, eh? Now that's interesting."

"What are you prattling on about?"

"I'm not the one babbling about beautiful women, for once."

Bayard looked out the window. His cravat seemed a trifle tight. With relief he saw Alethea's aunt's home in Queen Square. "Ah, here we are. Thank you for the lift, Ian. I'll walk home later."

"No, we'll both walk back." Ian gave him a wicked grin. "I have a burning desire to further my acquaintance with the fair Lady Alethea now that you've described her as 'aggressive and unconventional.'"

Bayard glowered at him. "What of your call to your mother's friend today?"

"I will visit her tomorrow." Ian exited the carriage. "You don't intend to spend all day in there, do you, old chap?"

Bayard stepped down in front of Mrs. Garen's house. "Lady

Alethea may not appreciate your presence. This is a sensitive matter for her."

"I have never had a woman object to my presence. Unlike you."

Ian instructed his coachman, and Bayard rapped upon the front door.

Suddenly a sound blasted out of the house, putting Bayard in mind of a screeching cat clinging to the back of a runaway horse.

"What was that?" Ian had clapped his hands over his ears.

"Regret joining me?" Bayard said. Accomplished violin player, indeed! Lady Whittlesby was getting on in age to describe Lady Alethea's skill in such lofty terms. The screeching seemed to make the wood of the door rattle against its hinges.

The butler opened the door, cotton stuffed in his ears. "You are expected, gentlemen," he said in a loud voice.

"I am Lord Dommick, and this is Lord Ian Wynnman."

"Very good. If you would follow me?" The butler led them up a carpeted staircase while yet another screech from the floor above echoed off the walls of the high-ceilinged foyer and the marble floor. The butler's shoulders visibly twitched at the cacophony. Then the sound stopped.

However, just as they reached the landing, Bayard heard a new violin sound, a low, throbbing note that seemed to grow from the foundation of the house, soft at first and rising in volume until it hovered in the air like an autumn leaf fallen from a tree and kept aloft by a breeze. Then the note broke into a series of triplets, each sound as delicate as a flower.

Bayard stopped. The player was . . . exquisite. Even more, the instrument had an unusual tone he couldn't quite describe, mellow and smooth like the softest leather, the downy coat of a puppy, the velvety petals of a rose.

Ian had stopped also, his mouth open.

The music transitioned up an octave, and suddenly the sound

became brighter than a sunlit day, more brilliant than a jeweled necklace. The sweet, high notes reminded him of his sister's smile, his mother's laughter, the aching joy in his heart as he rode neck-or-nothing across the fields at Terralton Abbey.

The butler's discreet cough brought him back to his senses. He shook off the spell of the music with difficulty and hurried up the stairs to the drawing room, Ian hot on his heels.

The music stopped like an indrawn breath as soon as the butler opened the door. "Lord Dommick and Lord Ian Wynnman, my lady."

Lady Alethea stood in front of the window, the fitful afternoon light glowing cool and white behind her. Her violin was propped under her chin, her bow poised above the strings. It made Bayard uncomfortable to see her elbow extended so high and the fabric underarm of her sleeve exposed, although she wore a high-necked, long-sleeved blue dress that covered her modestly.

She dropped her arms and set the violin on the table within a moment of their entering the drawing room. Bayard then noticed that a young girl sat in a chair at the round table, her light brown curls a wild riot down her back.

Lady Alethea curtseyed, then gestured to the girl, who promptly stood. "Lord Dommick, Lord Ian, this is my aunt's niece, Miss Garen."

Ian bowed to her. "Miss Garen," he said in a mock-solemn tone that made the girl giggle.

Bayard also bowed, and a smile spread across his lips at the girl's stately curtsey.

"Margaret, go to Aunt Ebena and tell her the gentlemen are here. She'll need to join us."

Bayard usually sighed at the necessity of unmarried women need-ing a chaperone when receiving gentlemen callers, but in this case, he realized it might be better not to be alone with Lady Alethea, con-sidering their arguing last night.

Ian murmured for Bayard's ears alone, "Shall I make sure you and Lady Alethea don't come to blows?"

Bayard glared at him, and Ian gave him an innocent smile.

Luckily, Lady Alethea didn't notice their interaction because Margaret said to her, "Could I take the violin to practice on?"

So, the child had been the cause of the dying cat sounds. Bayard should have known Lady Whittlesby wouldn't have overstated a person's musical skill quite that much.

"No, Lord Dommick is here to see my violin. You can practice more afterward."

Margaret ran out of the drawing room in a swirl of skirts and brown curls flying behind her. The sound of her feet pounding up the stairs made the walls vibrate, but Lady Alethea didn't seem to notice as she gestured to the sofa. "Will you be seated, gentlemen?"

"So, you are teaching Margaret to play violin?" Ian flashed his dimples at Lady Alethea.

Dommick frowned. Could the man ever not flirt with a woman?

"Yes, she prefers it to the pianoforte or the harp."

Clare had also, once. When she was twelve and Bayard had been home briefly on leave, she had begged him to teach her to play the violin, so he'd taught her a few light airs that she picked up with ease. But then she had played the violin after a dinner party when their father was not there. The local women had reduced Clare to tears with their shock and scorn that she played so unfeminine an instrument, and when her father returned home, he forbade her to play again.

"You should teach her the pianoforte or the harp instead," Bayard said in a voice harsher than he had intended.

Lady Alethea's dark brows, so delicately arched, rose in a look of such challenge that it made her seem even taller.

He really should have kept his mouth shut.

"There have been professional female violin players in the last century," she said in a voice that could have frozen the Thames.

"On the continent. In England, women who play the violin would fall under social disdain . . ." He wanted to explain about Clare's painful experience but didn't know how without mentioning specifics that he could not relate in public. In fact, he had never spoken of the incident again with Clare.

And Mrs. Garen chose that moment to enter the drawing room, so he lost the opportunity to soothe Lady Alethea's ruffled feathers.

"Gentlemen." Mrs. Garen greeted them as they rose to their feet. "Pray, be seated. Would you care for tea?"

"No, thank you," Bayard said. "I am anxious to see the violin."

Lady Alethea brought the violin to him and laid it in his hands, although she seemed reluctant to let it out of her possession. The look she shot him clearly said, "Take care, because if you somehow damage this instrument, I shall cause you extreme pain," although she spoke not a word to him.

He studied the shape a moment. "Is this a Stradivarius?"

"Since she bought it from a peddler, Lady Arkright was not certain, but she thought it might be. The shape of the outline, the F-holes and the bridge . . ."

"Yes, and the varnish has this reddish tinge that is very characteristic of his work." Bayard ran his hand over the wood. "What type of wood is this?"

"I don't know." Lady Alethea's dry tone indicated that this was the reason she'd needed his help.

"Bay, I do believe you are at a loss," Ian said. "The wonder of it."

Bayard ignored him and said to Lady Alethea, "The wood is unusual for a Stradivarius. Most are made with spruce and maple, but this one looks like the same wood for both."

"I've always thought it a very ugly wood. Other violins are much more beautiful."

"It doesn't have the distinct, dark vertical graining of normal spruce wood and none of the 'flame,' or the light and dark effect of maple wood. This graining is tight and narrow, the lines muddy and almost indiscernible."

"Calandra nearly didn't buy the violin. Sir William wanted to buy a more beautiful instrument for her. But Calandra said that the peddler slashed the price since he was desperate to get it off his hands, and she liked the weight and feel of it. And although it only had two intact strings, she could discern it was worth much more than the peddler valued it."

"Since the wood is unusual, but it is clearly a Stradivarius, it must have been a custom order," Bayard said. "Likely a nobleman commissioned it."

"I didn't think of that. Will that be easy to track down?"

"Much easier than a violin not custom built, and I have some contacts in Italy, but mail to and from the continent now is slow because of the war. I also will write to a few Italian noblemen in London with whom I am acquainted."

For the first time since he had entered the room, Lady Alethea smiled at him. It transformed her, in her plain, blue gown and her straight, dark hair scraped back from her oval face, to a woman of unearthly radiance and beauty. And even though she only smiled at him because of the contacts he had, the warmth of her gaze seemed to cause a similar warmth in his chest.

Mrs. Garen's words interrupted the look between them. "An Italian noble might know fairly quickly whose initials those are."

"Initials?"

"On the neck," Lady Alethea said.

Bayard was itching to play it, but forced himself to finish his observations first. He turned his attention to the neck and scroll at the end of the violin. "This symbol was on the violin when she bought it?"

"Yes. Calandra and I speculated it might be intertwined initials, but we were in disagreement as to what those initials were."

"It looks like a large elaborate *S* in the middle and then *C* or *G*? And *M* on the left of the *S*, and *A* and *G* or *C* on the right. *GMSAG*?"

"May I?" Ian asked, and Bayard handed the violin to him.

"I do believe it is a *C*." Ian squinted at it. "And the last one is a *G. CMSAG*."

When Bayard received the violin back, he noticed a tuning peg had been replaced, a very good job.

Lady Alethea had followed his gaze. "Lady Arkright had that tuning peg replaced several years ago."

"Where did she send it?"

"I only know she went to London."

"There are only three shops that could replace the tuning peg as well as this was done. I have patronized all three and can write to inquire if any remember this violin."

"How would that help you?" Mrs. Garen asked.

"If they remember this violin, likely they spoke to Lady Arkright about it, and asked questions that might have been different from what musicians would ask. As a consequence, she might have told them information she didn't share even with Lady Alethea."

Mrs. Garen looked suitably impressed. "Unconventional thinking. Now, when are you going to play it?"

He could make more observations later. Bayard shot to his feet as if he were an eager schoolboy, and Lady Alethea handed him her bow. Now that he held it against his shoulder, his chin atop the smoothly varnished wood, he was struck by the fine balance of the instrument. It moulded to him as if an extension of his body.

He paused, considering what to play, and chose a violin concerto in the key of G minor by Vivaldi, in honour of the composer's association with Lady Arkright's former school at the Ospedale della Pietà.

The lush notes almost took him off guard. If he had not heard Lady Alethea playing it earlier, he might have been startled by the smooth, mellow tones of the lower notes, the glittering resonance of the higher ones. The thrumming vibrations of the violin seemed to shake emotions loose from his core, bringing out more fire and warmth from the piece than he had ever played before. He was almost breathless, closing his eyes and letting the music grip his heart, overshadowing his intellect in favour of pure inspiration, pure joy, pure awe.

This was how he felt when kneeling alone at the chapel at Terralton Abbey, when he could almost feel the touch of God upon his head.

When the piece ended, he realized his hands were shaking, his heart beating a frantic tempo. It contrasted with Mrs. Garen, who held a polite expression of pleasure.

Ian, who had heard him play that piece dozens of times, sat with eyes wide and mouth open, for once with no sarcasm or mischief.

But it was Lady Alethea's face that captured Bayard's attention. Her eyes were shining star sapphires, dark against the golden cream of her skin and the rose blush of her parted lips. She stared at him, and the rest of the room fell away. All he saw was her. The beauty of the music didn't compare with the beauty in her expression. She understood how he felt, how the violin had made him feel when he played. She understood perfectly.

Then she smiled at him again. "You played Vivaldi," she said softly.

The moment broke when Mrs. Garen said, "Yes, quite nice."

Suddenly it was as if Bayard could breathe again. He had never played an instrument like this one, and he himself owned a Stradivarius violin. He cleared his throat, taking a few seconds to

compose himself, then sat and handed the instrument back to Lady
Alethea without looking at her.

"I can understand why someone wants to take it from you, my
lady," Ian said, his voice almost back to his normal drawl.

Ian had said that to goad Bayard, who wasn't entirely convinced
the thief had been after Lady Alethea's violin. Although now he
began to doubt.

"Is this instrument so valuable?" Mrs. Garen said. "It has a
remarkable sound, to be sure, but is it old? Rare?"

"That is what Lord Dommick is intending to ascertain," Lady
Alethea said.

"It is a Stradivarius, but I have never heard of any made with
unusual wood," Bayard said. "The famous violins Stradivari made
were of normal spruce and maple."

"And if this is not famous, it isn't as valuable," Ian said.

"But that's even less reason for anyone to want this violin," Lady
Alethea said.

"I don't suppose there might be something hidden inside?"
Mrs. Garen asked.

Bayard, Ian, and Lady Alethea all shook their heads at the
same time. "Any foreign object in the violin would affect its sound.
Its value must lie in its history," Bayard said.

"How did anyone know you owned it?" Mrs. Garen said to
Lady Alethea. "Did you or Lady Arkright perform with it in a
drawing room or for friends?"

"Never. Lady Arkright was well-known for her pianoforte playing and I often played harp. Neither of us played her violin except
with each other or for Sir William."

"Would he have talked about his wife's violin to any in your
social circle?" Bayard asked.

"We were in the country—our social circle was very small.
Sir William knew people would gossip about his wife playing the

violin, so he did not mention it. My governesses and companions never saw it, for I always played with Calandra or alone in the music room at Trittonstone Park."

"Are you certain that the intruder was looking for your violin?" Bayard said. He would likely be bringing Lady Alethea's wrath down upon him again. "The thief wouldn't look in the drawing room after the family had gone to bed?"

Lady Alethea's eyes flattened and she pressed her lips together for a moment before she answered. "No, I do not know that the intruder was looking for the violin. Whoever knows that I own this violin perhaps would also know I do not keep it in the drawing room."

Bayard thought he ought to leave before he made the hedgehog more prickly. He rose. "I will no longer take up your valuable time, Mrs. Garen, Lady Alethea. Have you a case for the violin?"

She stood and looked him squarely in the eye. "I am afraid I cannot allow you to remove the violin from my possession, Lord Dommick."

Irritation rose up like a rash on his skin. "I cannot help you if I cannot examine the violin, my lady," he said in a tight voice.

"You are welcome to examine it here at any time."

"Alethea," Mrs. Garen said, "think of your reputation if he were to call upon you so often."

Her reputation? Bayard was more than a little concerned for his own, and more importantly, any negative repercussions to his sister and his mother. Visiting a spinster who played the violin, already an oddity in society, would not improve people's opinions of his sanity.

"My violin is too valuable." Lady Alethea looked at Bayard, not her aunt, and she was tall enough that her gaze was only a few inches below his own.

"People will talk," Mrs. Garen insisted. "If not of yourself, think of Lord Dommick's reputation."

"Actually," Ian cut in, "we should want people to talk."

"What?" Bayard said.

"We shall tell people that Bayard is helping Lady Alethea investigate the provenance of her violin."

"Provenance?" Mrs. Garen said. "What does that mean?"

"An object's history," Bayard said. "Tracing the proof of an instrument's creation and ownership."

"We shall tell your mother, Bay," Ian said with a grin. "And it'll be all over Bath by nightfall. Then no one will question why you're visiting so often."

But they might still talk about his helping a female violin player. Unless . . . "Are many people aware that you play the violin?" he asked Lady Alethea.

Her eyes glinted and her jaw tightened. She knew why he was asking. He was suddenly ashamed of himself. He could not blame her for being upset, because his question—and his concern for his reputation—was insulting to her. She could not know his worry about how his reputation impacted his sister and mother.

"Only my sister, Lucy," she said.

Ian stood and bowed. "Thank you for your time, ladies."

"I will walk you to the door, gentlemen." Lady Alethea's smile was frosty.

In the entrance foyer, after the butler had returned their greatcoats and hats to them, Lady Alethea turned to Bayard, who immediately steeled himself. Ian was quick to move to a far corner of the foyer so he could not overhear—or, more likely, be swept up in the ire of—Lady Alethea's conversation.

Her voice was low but calm. "I understand your hesitation to believe how anyone could want my violin, but my concern is that since you do not take my assertions seriously, I do not trust you to be as careful with my instrument as you would if you believed me."

He saw her reasoning, although her distrust of him stung. But there was also some emotion throbbing underneath her words that he sensed had nothing to do with him, which fueled her defensiveness. Someone, or perhaps many people, had been the root of her distrust.

However, he was to bear the thrust of it.

She continued, "Your carelessness might allow it to be stolen. You would not deliberately allow that, but I cannot know that you would be as conscientious as I would like you to be."

The hedgehog was forever pricking at him. "I understand your concern, Lady Alethea." His voice was clipped. "I will not undertake this charge lightly."

She hesitated, then stepped back and curtsied. "Thank you for calling."

Bayard could not leave the house quickly enough. Since Ian had sent his carriage back, they walked to the other end of Queen Square to head back to the Crescent.

"Lady Alethea certainly does not think highly of you, my friend," Ian said quite unnecessarily. "What did you do to provoke her?"

"Why is it my fault?" He had only stated the normal societal opinion about women and violins, for goodness' sake.

"Because it's often the man's fault," Ian said sagely.

"But it was eleven years ago."

"Was it, now? You must have made quite an impression on the lady. And she on you, apparently."

"I barely remembered her."

"Indeed," Ian said in a voice that clearly indicated he would be more likely to jump in the Avon than believe Bayard.

Bayard lengthened his stride. The sooner he was able to uncover the provenance of the violin, the better. For his sanity, at least.

❧

"The sooner he uncovers the information about my violin, the better,"

Alethea said as she returned to the drawing room after seeing the gentlemen out. "If only for my sanity."

"And my peace," Aunt Ebena said. "Was it necessary to argue with him?"

"I might have been a bit combative," Alethea said grudgingly, "but he stopped short of calling me a liar about someone trying to steal the violin."

"You are entirely too sensitive," Aunt Ebena said.

Which was ironic since Alethea had needed to become a great deal less sensitive since living with Aunt Ebena.

"I tend to agree with him," Aunt Ebena said. "Why your violin? Surely there are others more famous, or older, or crafted with more—"

They both stopped at the sound of a thump from directly above their heads.

"Is that . . . my bedchamber?" Alethea said.

"You have become overly suspicious," Aunt Ebena said. "It could very well be mine. Although I don't know why Brooks would be there at this time of day."

"Shall I go up to see?" Alethea exited the drawing room before her aunt could object. She had been badly frightened two days ago, but the anxiety of waiting in the kitchen while the butler searched the house had made her feel as though her nerves were on fire. She would not be cowering again while someone else searched the house. "Dodd," she called as she entered the hallway, but then was surprised to see Aunt Ebena's dresser heading toward her. "Mrs. Brooks? But we thought . . ."

"I heard a noise in Mrs. Garen's bedchamber," Mrs. Brooks said, her hand twisting the fabric at her throat. "I was about to go upstairs to look in on her."

"Brooks?" Aunt Ebena appeared in the drawing room doorway. "But if you're here . . ."

Who was in Aunt Ebena's room?

"Dodd!" Alethea called with more urgency, and the butler appeared at the stairs. "With me, please." Alethea hurried upstairs.

"Alethea, don't be foolish," Aunt Ebena called after her.

The corridor was empty, all the bedchamber doors closed. If one of the maids were in a room, the door would have been cracked open. All was quiet but for soft sounds that floated up from the kitchen on the ground floor.

Alethea was no more than two steps down the corridor when she again heard a thump. It wasn't from Aunt Ebena's room.

It was from hers.

Dodd tensed beside her. He took a long stride to place himself between Alethea and her closed bedchamber door.

"How could a stranger have entered the house?" Alethea whispered.

"A window?" Dodd said. "I have made sure all the doors are locked, even during the day."

A stranger in her room, searching for what he did not find the last time?

They slowly approached her door, careful to make no sound on the rug that ran the length of the wooden floor. As they passed a hall table, Dodd grabbed a heavy brass candlestick while Alethea made free with a bud vase from which she removed the flowers.

Dodd laid his hand gently on the door latch without rattling it, hesitated a moment, then swiftly opened the door.

A squeak pierced Alethea's ears as she followed Dodd into her room. Margaret stood near Alethea's dresser. At the sight of the two of them, she dropped the petticoats in her arms, which she had removed from the open drawer.

"Margaret!" Alethea set the vase on a nearby table. "What are you doing in my room?"

"Looking for your treasure."

Alethea sighed. "I told you I didn't have any treasure."

"If you had treasure, of course you'd say you didn't have any."

Dodd cleared his throat. He stood correctly near the open door, the candlestick held in his hands as if he'd picked it up to polish it.

"Dodd, could you please explain to my aunt?"

He nodded and headed back downstairs.

Margaret's eyes gleamed. "Did you think I was an intruder? What were you going to do?"

"If you were an intruder, we wouldn't be having this conversation," Alethea said. "And now, you will pick up everything you have messed up."

"The maids will do it."

"No, they will not. You created this mayhem, so you will clean up."

Alethea was perhaps a touch more exacting in her demands as she directed Margaret to folding and replacing the petticoats she'd dropped, and straightening the bedclothes she'd rummaged around in while searching under the mattress. Margaret grumbled the entire time, and by the time they headed back to the drawing room, Alethea had decided to put the girl on bread and water until she was twenty-five. Or thereabouts.

Aunt Ebena was more sanguine. She had rung for a pot of tea. When Margaret reached for a jam tart, Aunt Ebena gave a decided, "No," and a look that would have curdled milk.

"But I didn't intend to upset anyone," Margaret said.

"You violated your cousin's privacy," Aunt Ebena said.

Margaret sulked and slurped her tea loudly.

Alethea bit into a jam tart with exaggerated relish. "I apologize for alarming you, Aunt, but what was I to think after the frightening events of two days ago?"

"It wasn't *frightening* . . . ," Margaret began, but was stopped by her aunt's *harrumph* as she cleared her throat.

"Indeed." Aunt Ebena, who rarely ate sweets, picked up a jam tart and took a small bite.

Margaret sighed and stared longingly.

"Such a violation to have someone going through my things." Alethea polished off her tart and took another.

"Really, what were you thinking?" Aunt Ebena sipped her tea.

"I'm-sorry-I-won't-do-it-again-could-I-please-have-a-tart-before-Alethea-eats-them-all?" Margaret said in a rush.

Aunt Ebena tilted her head toward Alethea.

"I'm sorry for entering your room and looking for your treasure," Margaret said.

"For the last time, I do not have a treasure." Alethea set a tart on Margaret's plate.

Margaret bit into the tart. "If I had known someone was in your room, I would have used one of Mrs. Dodd's knives and stabbed him through the heart."

"I had no idea you were so bloodthirsty," Alethea murmured.

"That would be extremely foolhardy and dangerous," Aunt Ebena said.

"It would be brave. We have no man to protect us."

"We have male servants and that is quite adequate," Aunt Ebena said.

Was it adequate? "At the time Mr. Golding spoke to me, I did not know I would be putting you and Margaret in danger. If he should approach me again . . ."

"For a moment, let us consider the highly improbable notion that your violin is valuable enough for someone to acquire it by any means necessary." Aunt Ebena sniffed. "When men covet a particular item, possessing it is not always adequate. Could you guarantee that the thief would allow us all to live with the raging injustice of having it stolen from us? Would he not imagine us to be scheming to get it back?"

"Wouldn't he rest in the belief that he has escaped detection?"

"Not if he plays the violin in public."

"So he would try to harm us even after getting the violin?" Margaret licked jam from the corner of her mouth. "I might still get to stab him with Mrs. Dodd's knife."

"You will stab no one. That is not my point. Use your napkin," Aunt Ebena added. "My point is that bullies never stop."

Alethea had never considered Mr. Golding in light of a bully. Her experience with bullies had been the village boys. She had promptly started a fistfight with the largest one, and they had all become fast friends.

Aunt Ebena took a sip of tea, then said to Alethea, "I had never thought you to be so weak that you would allow someone to bully you."

Alethea's neck and ears grew hot.

"We should never allow someone to bully us into doing something against what we know to be right, simply because it is easier to give in." For a moment, there was a tightness around Aunt Ebena's eyes and in her tone, but it was quickly gone, and Alethea did not feel comfortable asking about it.

"Even if my decision puts others in danger?" Alethea said.

"I am not fully convinced we are in danger," Aunt Ebena said. "Was the thief indeed searching for your violin? Even if there were proof, I would advise you not to allow someone as vulgar as Mr. Golding to bully you into doing anything."

Alethea could not see Aunt Ebena allowing anyone to bully her. "Lord Dommick made an observation about the violin belonging to an Italian nobleman because it was a custom order. You would not possibly be acquainted with any Italian noblemen, would you?"

Alethea had been half joking, but Aunt Ebena stared off into the far corner of the room.

"Aunt?"

"Tania, Lady Fairmont, is descended from an Italian count on her mother's side," Aunt Ebena said. "I would not have recalled that were she not holding her ball in a few days' time."

"Would Lady Fairmont be familiar with other Italian noble families and recognize the initials from the violin?"

"You will have to ask her."

"Could we visit her?"

Aunt Ebena frowned. "Tania is planning the ball right now and probably would not be at home to visitors."

"After the ball?"

"Unfortunately, three days after the ball she will be removing to her country estate for a few weeks. If she is preparing to move her household, she may not see me then either. You shall have to speak to her at the ball."

Alethea chewed her lip. "A ball is not an ideal place to have a conversation." She attended very few balls since Aunt Ebena disliked them and Alethea preferred listening to music rather than dancing to it, especially if the musicians were indifferent. However, Aunt Ebena would never miss an event by Lady Fairmont, one of her close friends and one of the most respected residents of Bath, so they were already expected.

"Your only other option would be to write," Aunt Ebena said. "Do you want your answer or not?"

"Yes, you're right."

"You should copy the initials and show it to her," Margaret suggested.

"That's a good idea. I shall send a copy to Lord Dommick as well."

"Tania may not know many Italian noble families or anyone with those initials," Aunt Ebena said. "If she doesn't, do not press her."

"Or she may immediately know whom the initials refer to. Perhaps my problem will be solved before next week." To not see

Lord Dommick again, except for brief, cold exchanges at private parties and the assemblies, should cause her rejoicing and relief, but . . . that was before he'd played Vivaldi for her. And she had to admit that a part of her longed to see the expression on his face when she played a particularly difficult violin piece of his own composition as brilliantly as himself.

"I would not be so hopeful," Aunt Ebena said.

Margaret sighed and swiped her finger through a drop of jam on her dress. "I still would have liked to stab the thief with Mrs. Dodd's knife."

CHAPTER FIVE

*A*lethea walked through the doors to Lady Fairmont's home and immediately felt as if everyone were staring at her.

She surreptitiously studied her dress to make sure mud wasn't splattered across it. The deep lace at the hem was unblemished cream. The rosy-orange colour was perhaps a trifle unusual for an unmarried woman, but Alethea felt her advanced age entitled her to shed insipid whites in favour of colours that suited her better. But surely that wouldn't cause the stares. Was she imagining it?

"Why are people staring at you?" Aunt Ebena demanded in a whisper.

No, not imagining it.

They waited through the receiving line until they reached Lady Fairmont, resplendent in violet satin with an amethyst pendant the size of a walnut at her throat. "Ebena, so good of you to come." Lady Fairmont kissed the air above Aunt Ebena's cheek.

"Tania, you remember my niece, Lady Alethea Sutherton?"

"Of course." Lady Fairmont beamed at Alethea, who curtseyed.

"Lady Fairmont, later in the evening, might I have a word—" Alethea began, but stopped at a look from Aunt Ebena. They continued on and Lady Fairmont greeted the next person in line.

"Tania would forget any meeting you arranged with her in the receiving line," Aunt Ebena said. "Try to find a moment with her later in the evening, when fewer people are attempting to speak to her."

Lady Fairmont's ball was small, limited to the size of her two drawing rooms with the connecting double doors thrown open to expand the dancing area, and a card room and supper room, yet it was one of the largest residences in Bath. The elegant furniture had been removed to make way for the dancers and the musicians in a side alcove, although many chairs in both classical and Egyptian styles graced the walls, several already occupied by guests. The rooms were packed with far more people than could comfortably fit. The musicians had not yet begun, and Alethea wondered how people would clear a space for the dancing.

"I see Mrs. Nanstone," Aunt Ebena said. "She detests me and would be only too happy to tell me why everyone is staring at you as if you've grown tentacles. Go somewhere and be unobtrusive." Her aunt bustled off through the crowd.

The only people not glancing her way were Lord Dommick and his party. His mother and sister sat at chairs speaking to Lord Ian and Lord Ravenhurst while Lord Dommick stood nearby, his posture upright. He did not look tense, but something about him made Alethea think he was not comfortable in the close room with people chatting and occasionally bumping into him. He was all politeness, but there was a stiffness at the edges of his mouth. Alethea realized with a start of surprise that he may not like small rooms and crowds of people. Just like herself.

He happened to glance her way. Alethea did not expect him to notice her in the midst of so many people, but he found her gaze, perhaps because her height set her above most of the women in the room. He froze for a moment as if something had surprised him, then with a tiny shake of his head, he blinked. He nodded his head to her, and she returned his gesture. At least he was not staring and pointing as others were doing.

In her London season, she had been a stone lighter, awkward and insecure. She would have obeyed her aunt's instructions to be unobtrusive by hiding in a dark corner, preferably behind a fern.

But she was not that girl anymore. So, instead, she held her head high, relaxing her shoulders to belie the pounding of her heart, and adopted a polite mask. She decided to emulate Aunt Ebena's excellent strategy and walked toward the cluster of women who appeared to be deriving the most enjoyment from her discomfiture.

Alethea had not been overly impressed with the calibre of Bath misses she'd met this past year while going out in society with her Aunt Ebena. Most of them were daughters, nieces, granddaughters, and grandnieces to Aunt Ebena's friends and acquaintances, and a rather large percentage of them resented being stuck in mouldy Bath with their elders rather than somewhere that possessed more young, single men.

They made Alethea feel rather long in the tooth, because at the advanced age of twenty-eight, she was firmly on the shelf, whereas most of them were still in the fresh, nubile state of mind where dreams of dukes falling madly in love with them still formed the chief of their journal entries. As an earl's daughter who had been introduced to several dukes and marquesses, Alethea had found that many arrogant noblemen lost that gilding painted onto their personalities on account of their rank, so she had even less in common with these young girls.

And the icing on the cake was Alethea's intensity when it came to music. Most of the young women played adequately for social situations, or they found enjoyment in playing, but none of them had Alethea's focus during concerts and her appalling tendency to listen to the music rather than gossiping about the attendees. They did not understand her, and they did not care to.

And so now, Alethea walked straight toward the one girl who embodied all those characteristics—Miss Herrington-Smythe. The bored young woman made no secret of her yearning for the excitement of London rather than being stuck in Bath with her great-aunt, one of Aunt Ebena's friends. She was also confident in her ability to dazzle a duke despite her disparity of funds, and she possessed a rather unfortunate sense of pitch but was convinced she sang as well as the famous soprano Catalani.

Alethea could have chosen any other miss, who would likely flare her nose at Alethea, then give her the cut direct, which wasn't very entertaining.

Miss Herrington-Smythe, on the other hand, would relish Alethea's attention and give her all the information she needed to know, albeit clothed in barbs and insults. An added bonus was that Miss Oakridge, Lady Fairmont's granddaughter, formed part of Miss Herrington-Smythe's retinue, and if Alethea could attain a private second alone with her, she might recognize the initials from the violin.

Alethea approached the two girls. "Good evening, Miss Oakridge, Miss Herrington-Smythe."

"Good evening, Lady Alethea." Miss Herrington-Smythe smiled widely, her crooked teeth emphasizing how pointy her canines were. "What an unusual colour gown you have on. The style for older women is so varied these days, don't you agree? It really does wonders to perk them up."

Miss Oakridge, closest to Alethea's age at twenty-three and embarrassingly desperate to marry, tittered behind a gloved hand while smoothing her white lace gown.

If she wanted any information out of Miss Herrington-Smythe,

Alethea needed to prod her with an insult that was pointed enough to make her vindictive. "I think it a great pity young girls wear white. When they dance, they look like jiggling blancmange puddings."

A strangled noise came from Miss Herrington-Smythe, although Alethea was scanning the room in a casual manner and avoiding her eye. After a moment, Miss Herrington-Smythe said in a voice like candied plums, "Lady Alethea, you must put to rest a most distressing rumour. Have you indeed asked Lord Dommick to discover the original owner of your violin?"

Was this why people were staring? "Yes. Whyever would that distress you, Miss Herrington-Smythe?"

Miss Herrington-Smythe pretended to look shocked. "Lady Alethea, say it isn't so."

Alethea resisted reaching out to shake her. Miss Herrington-Smythe was being vague when Alethea needed information. "I am concerned that you are losing your hearing. I daresay it happens to some of us as we age. I shall repeat my question. Why should the news distress you?"

Miss Herrington-Smythe shrugged off the barb. "I was hoping to have misunderstood you, for I should hate to suspect that you are becoming desperate."

Alethea walked into that verbal trap. "Desperate about what?"

"About your future, of course."

"Miss Herrington-Smythe, I fear the heat has addled your brain. You poor dear."

Miss Oakridge covered a snort with a hand clapped over her mouth.

Alethea continued, "How should anyone think my violin has anything to do with my concerns about my future?"

Miss Herrington-Smythe delivered the crushing blow with relish. "I only have your welfare at heart when I tell you that everyone believes you may have . . . exaggerated the mysterious history of your violin in order to monopolize the time of a certain gentleman."

Alethea almost burst into laughter, but that would ruin Miss Herrington-Smythe's glee in telling Alethea the rumour. "Indeed?" she said in what she hoped were tones of horror.

"I am most sorry to tell you that this is how it appears to everyone in Bath. It's really rather pitiable. Young ladies have no need to resort to ruses to force men to spend time in their company."

"Of course, only a violin would do for your plans," Miss Oakridge added. "How long you must have looked for one old enough to provide a challenge for him."

The comment was like a long, deep scratch on Lady Arkright's violin. "The violin was a bequest," Alethea said through numb lips. These pampered, selfish women would never understand the depth of love that made the violin so precious to her. Their idea of a mother's love was a shopping trip for a new gown.

Alethea didn't like Miss Herrington-Smythe and her friends, so she should not be hurt by the fact that they delighted in society's current disdain of her, but it reminded her once again that the polite world was not a pond she easily swam in.

She had always only depended upon herself, and it was still true. However, she wished her independence was not so isolating at times.

"How fortuitous for you," Miss Herrington-Smythe cooed.

"I am ashamed at the effort some women will undertake to capture the interest of gentlemen," Miss Oakridge added.

"Alethea, there you are." The deep voice behind her seemed to rise up from the murmurings of the crowd and blanket them all with a strange stillness.

Alethea turned and tried not to look astounded. Lord Dommick stood a few steps away, partially screened by the large back of a dowager in masses of black silk and apparently unnoticed by the three of them during their verbal melee. He had a warm smile that he had never directed at her, which made her insides jiggle like the blancmange she had compared the girls to earlier. There was also a sparking in his dark eyes that seemed to hint at some kind of irritation. Was he upset with her?

Then she realized that he had called her familiarly by her first name, which she had not given him permission to do. They were certainly not cordial enough for him to even have asked her for the privilege.

He nodded in a cool fashion toward Miss Herrington-Smythe, who had paled, and Miss Oakridge, who had gone scarlet. "Ladies, I beg you to excuse me and allow me to steal Alethea from you. I hope I was not interrupting anything of import?"

And at that moment, Alethea knew he had overheard a good portion of their altercation. Her stomach clenched. She had walked into this skirmish with the girls of her own accord, expecting the barbs and ready to deliver a few of her own. But once she realized what the rumours were about, she hadn't thought about how it might negatively impact Lord Dommick and his family. Alethea was ready to sink through the floor.

"Alethea, Ravenhurst and Ian told me they had already secured your hand for dances tonight, and they teased me that I had not been faster, so I am come to secure my own dance before it's too late."

Alethea suspected she looked rather like a fish as she gaped at him, but she wasn't sure what his game was.

Lord Dommick then nodded to the two girls and took Alethea by the arm to lead her away.

As it happened, the musicians signaled the start of the first dance. "Are you engaged for this dance?" he asked her.

"No."

"Now you are." The centre of the two connected rooms was being cleared of spectators, and couples began lining up. Lord Dommick led her among them. He said nothing as they waited for the music to start, but his face looked faintly forbidding.

It was fortunate Alethea was not easily intimidated.

The music began and she curtseyed to him. As they drew together in the movement, she whispered to him, "What in the world was that about?"

"Why did you engage in conversation with a vulture like Miss Herrington-Smythe?" Lord Dommick hissed back.

Alethea tried to yank her hand from his, but his fingers bit into her knuckles, and the two healed fingers twinged. "I needed information."

"Don't you realize the girl eats reputations for breakfast and spits them out as the most spurious gossip?"

"Oh, she's harmless."

The movements of the dance separated them, but she could tell Lord Dommick was trying very hard not to scowl at her. As they came together again, he said, "I can't determine if you are simply naive or blind."

She smiled and bared her teeth at him, saying through her tight jaw, "Miss Herrington-Smythe hasn't an original thought in her brain. She only repeats what she hears with great relish, which makes her useful when I need to know why people are staring at me as if I have a peacock roosting on my head."

His face remained stern, but the corner of his mouth twitched. If he weren't so incensed, she was sure he might have cracked a smile. A real one, this time.

"I came to find you as soon as I heard what people were saying," he said.

She blinked at him. "Why?"

"I have seen rumours ruin a person." The ballroom wall suddenly fascinated him. "I thought it very unfair that your simple curiosity about your own violin would expose you to such ugliness."

It had never occurred to her that he would be concerned for her. She had been so busy detesting him and trying not to think about him that she had assumed his heart was an empty shell.

No, that wasn't quite true. From the assembly, she knew he cared deeply for his sister. That he had extended his concern to her . . . she was not certain what it made her feel. "I thank you, my lord."

"You should call me Dommick since I made free with your first name in front of those harpies." He frowned, and at first Alethea thought he was upset about that, but then she realized he frowned because he was embarrassed.

How strange. She had placed him on a pedestal in her season in London, but then later she had set him apart as a cold statue. Yet in both cases, she had made him out to be remote and unfeeling, when in reality, he was . . . human.

Alethea said, "If the rumours only involved myself, I should find it hilariously diverting, but I do regret that the rumour requires people to studiously avoid mentioning your name."

"It's not my name I'm worried about. Miss Herrington-Smythe was doing a bang-up job smearing yours all over the floor."

"Oh, that was nothing to worry about. If you had not extricated me from them, I was going to say something along the lines of, 'Ladies, your conversation has ceased to be entertaining to me, so I bid you good evening.'"

He finally did smile at her. It made his eyes crinkle, and laugh lines deepened in his cheeks. "Can it really be true that you do not care about the rumours?"

Alethea gave a one-shouldered shrug she had picked up from Calandra. "I have had tales told about me my entire life because of living buried in the country. One becomes a figure of curiosity." An oddity. Fodder for ridicule.

The dance separated them and he looked confused.

"Before I even arrived in town for my season, gossip had painted me as a wild hoyden with no table manners simply because I had never been seen in society. Several servants spread tales about how I forsook a regular schedule when I was practicing my music, and so the gossip expanded to say that I was an eccentric."

"I never heard those rumours."

"You probably did, but did not know me at the time and so it meant nothing to you. My Aunt Ingolton was sponsoring my come out and she was appalled, but the tales were so ridiculous I could not help but be amused by it all." Alethea grinned. "I teased my aunt by threatening to pick up my soup bowl and drink directly from it at the next dinner party."

He looked at her as if unsure if he should be amused or appalled himself.

"I no longer credit gossip about anyone else after being the object of such imaginative tales." She could do no less, when the tales had both amused her and hurt her, though she never revealed her pain.

He surprised her with an expression of almost . . . awe. Then his face hardened. "I dislike gossip, but dislike even more being its object."

The dance partnered her briefly with an older gentleman who was a friend of her aunt. "Lady Alethea, how lovely you look tonight."

"Thank you, Mr. Pollwitton."

For the rest of the dance, Alethea and Dommick said nothing to each other, but he did seem to be less disapproving.

And why should she care about that when she didn't care about the disapproval of Miss Herrington-Smythe?

After the dance, he led her not to her aunt but to his mother, sitting with Lord Ravenhurst and Lord Ian. Lady Morrish greeted her with a smile. "Lady Alethea, how lovely to see you. Bayard has told me about your violin. I am relieved you have given him something to occupy his time this winter. He has had nothing to do besides be a trifle overprotective of his sister." She nodded toward the dancers, where Miss Terralton was returning with a ginger-haired man with heavy-lidded eyes. The young lady held herself stiffly and appeared to not want to touch the man's sleeve.

"Lady Alethea, do let me introduce my daughter, Miss Terralton, and my husband's nephew, Mr. Morrish."

Alethea curtseyed, but she didn't like the way Mr. Morrish's eyes lingered on her person as he rose from his bow. She had the childish urge to do what she used to do to the boys in her village and poke at his eyeballs with her fingers. She understood Miss Terralton's distaste.

Mr. Morrish's smile thrust his large front teeth directly at her. "Lady Alethea, how delightful to meet you at last. I have heard so much about your musical abilities."

"I'm sure you have," Alethea murmured before she could stop herself. Possibly things like *absurdly strange* and *such a curiosity*.

"What instrument do you play?" Mr. Morrish asked.

For a man who had heard so much about her, he hadn't apparently paid a great deal of attention. She picked one of the other least acceptable instruments for an Englishwoman of the peerage. "The oboe." Which wasn't a lie, since Calandra had owned an oboe and taught her. Alethea simply hadn't enjoyed playing it very much.

Mr. Morrish blinked at her in surprise. She wondered if he had even heard of an oboe.

Miss Terralton went into a paroxysm of coughing, which also served to distract Mr. Morrish. He seemed overly solicitous for Miss Terralton's health, and Miss Terralton seemed overly annoyed by his attentions, so when the coughing subsided, Alethea cut into one of Mr. Morrish's speeches. "Miss Terralton, I do apologize for taking your brother for the first dance when he should have been dancing with you."

The young woman studied Alethea with bright, intelligent eyes and picked up on Alethea's hint. "I will forgive you if Bay dances with me now." The young woman smiled at her older brother, who cast Alethea a glance before leading his sister away.

Except that Alethea didn't fancy entertaining the lecherous young man, which she realized too late. Mr. Morrish asked her with lubricious gallantry, "Would you do me the honour of dancing with me, Lady Alethea?"

"I am fatigued and wish to sit this dance." She rather abruptly dropped into the chair next to Lady Morrish. "However, I think Miss Herrington-Smythe would be most honoured by a dance with you. Or perhaps Miss Oakridge."

"I am afraid I am unacquainted with the ladies." He smiled as if the omission were the greatest delight of his evening. "Otherwise, I should be most pleased to bestow my hand to your friend."

"I am acquainted with them," Lady Morrish said. "What a good idea, Lady Alethea. Come, Mr. Morrish, I shall introduce you." She rose and drew the man away.

Alethea gave a great exhale as soon as he was out of earshot.

"Nicely played." Lord Ian dropped down to lounge in the chair vacated by Lady Morrish. "How is our dear Miss Herrington-Smythe? Claws recently sharpened?"

"I'm sure I don't know what you mean, sir."

"Ian . . . ," Lord Ravenhurst said in a deep voice.

Lord Ian ignored his friend and turned to Alethea in a confiding manner. "In Miss Herrington-Smythe's first season in London, at a dinner party, she sang abominably after dinner. Other gentlemen paid fulsome compliments. She said, 'La, my performance was but mediocre. Surely Lord Ian can attest to that.' I would not prevaricate in order to indulge her conceit, so I said, 'Yes.'"

"You could have said something polite that would not be a lie."
Lord Ravenhurst frowned at his friend.

"When a woman is fishing for compliments, she must not
expect to be spoiled. Later that evening she sat with a friend, hap-
pily slandering me, unaware I sat behind her, hidden by a potted
palm. But then Raven put an end to my fun when he shouted, 'Ian,
come out from behind that palm!'"

Alethea laughed.

"And thus ended my brief infatuation with Miss Herrington—"
He broke off with a roll of his eyes. "That woman needs to marry
someone like Sir Harold Trout, if only to shorten her name."

Lord Ravenhurst gave him a baleful look. "So it'll be easier for
you to gossip about her?"

"Of course." Lord Ian raised a hand to flip his hair out of his
eyes. "We shall see how disapproving you are in a week. You are the
youngest unmarried marquess in a fifty-mile radius, and so her new
target. Your residence has enlivened Bath for her."

Lord Ravenhurst exhaled with a sound suspiciously like a
moan.

Alethea was surprised. Her experience with men had been
limited to those who were controlling, sadistic, or shallow. Yet here
were two young men obviously fond of each other, able to tease the
way she did with Lucy. She had seen a hint of it when Lord Ian
accompanied Lord Dommick to her aunt's home, but now she saw
the depth of their bond. Almost like brothers. It went beyond their
mutual interest in music, for although they were very different personalities, they accepted each other as they were. It chastised her
for assuming that all men were as selfish and unfeeling as her father
and brother.

"Will you three give a concert this winter?" Alethea asked.

"Yes," Lord Ravenhurst said. "We are each writing new pieces
to perform."

Alethea clasped her hands together. "How wonderful. Will you be publishing your pieces after the concert? When I was at Trittonstone Park, I had difficulty procuring some of your music when the Quartet was still playing in London several years ago."

"What pieces would you like? I would consider it an honour to give them to you." Lord Ian flashed his dimples at her. Even in the depths of the country she had heard about his infamous charm.

"Did you or Lord Dommick ever publish your violin concertos? I should love to learn them."

The smile Lord Ian gave Alethea now had a gleam as if he understood her more than she wanted him to. "Bay has never heard a woman play one of his violin pieces. I am sure it would be highly entertaining to see his reaction."

Lord Ravenhurst glared at his friend. "Are you planning what I think you're planning?"

"A pleasant surprise for our good friend?" Ian said.

"Define 'pleasant.'"

"You haven't heard Lady Alethea play, Raven. And her instrument is truly remarkable."

"So, why wouldn't you simply give her one of your violin compositions to play?"

"Oh, I will give her mine. But she would find Bay's pieces more of a challenge." Lord Ian leveled her a glance that dared her to join in his mischief.

And Alethea was more than willing. "If you give me a piece of violin music, I would be happy to master it."

He grinned at her. "I'm sure you would be."

"I know nothing, I hear nothing," Lord Ravenhurst said with a long-suffering sigh.

Lady Morrish returned at that moment, and Lord Ian relinquished his seat. "Whom did you introduce Mr. Morrish to?" His polite curiosity hid his amusement.

"Miss Herrington-Smythe." Lady Morrish pointed to where Mr. Morrish led the young lady down the dance. "I had hoped Miss Oakridge was available, but she already had a partner."

"Lady Morrish, could you tell me if Miss Oakridge knows much about her grandmother's Italian side of the family?" Alethea asked.

"Oh, I shouldn't think she knows much, but Lady Fairmont is very knowledgeable. Sometimes I wonder if she isn't related to every noble family in Italy."

"I wondered if she knew any Italian nobleman with these initials." Alethea withdrew the scrap of paper she had tucked into her glove and showed it to Lady Morrish.

The two young men peered over her shoulder at the paper. "Ah," Lord Ian said, "you copied it, did you?"

"You will have a difficult time speaking to Lady Fairmont," Lady Morrish said. "This ball is a sad crush."

Lord Ravenhurst cleared his throat. "If I may, I have a dance with Lady Fairmont later and could ask her if she would spare a few minutes to speak to you."

Alethea blinked. She couldn't recall the last time a man had offered to do something for her. But perhaps he was merely assisting his friend. "Thank you, my lord. I would be most grateful."

He bowed, but then added with a half smile, "I would always be at the service of any woman who prefers . . . *challenging* Bayard to fawning over him."

Alethea smiled. "For shame, my lord. Lord Dommick and I have met thrice this winter and have yet to come to fisticuffs."

"Alethea, there you are." Aunt Ebena approached, and Alethea stood.

Lady Morrish said, "Mrs. Garen, how lovely to see you again. It has been many years since I last saw you in London."

Aunt Ebena sat in Alethea's vacated seat. "I am pleased to see you again, Lady Dom—no, you remarried this past year, did you not?"

"I am Lady Morrish now."

Alethea hadn't realized until the two women started chatting that Aunt Ebena had spent every season in London with her husband for several years, until his health failed him. This had all been before Alethea's season. Aunt Ebena was polite to Lady Morrish, who responded with friendliness. By now, Alethea was used to the fact that Aunt Ebena's civility extended to society but not to her niece. But perhaps that was true for all families. It had been Alethea's experience with hers, except with Lucy.

She missed her sister now as she surveyed the room. The stares and whispers and Miss Herrington-Smythe's unkindness had only emphasized how few friends she had. Was she so odd that she could be friendly with no one? It had become clear to her within her first month in Bath that she had very little in common with the people she met. Even the young Bath misses seemed to understand the rules of society better than she did. She only understood the countryside and music, both topics that held little popular interest and only garnered her snide censure.

But that was not true with the two gentlemen standing beside her. She turned to Lord Ian. "I am amazed that the Quartet is resurfacing after all these years, and without Captain Enlow."

"Yes, David's still fighting Boney. We shall have to find someone to take his place, poor chap," Lord Ian said. "Shall you fill in?"

"I doubt Lord Dommick would allow that," she said.

"He's a touch sensitive about his public image at the moment."

Lord Ravenhurst shot Lord Ian a look, and after a moment, looking conscientious, Lord Ian said no more.

She asked, "Have the four of you known each other long?"

"Since Eton," Lord Ravenhurst said.

"Brought together by music?"

"Brought together by a fight, actually." Lord Ian grinned. "No lad will stand for being accused of liking music. Two boys were picking on Bayard and me because they heard us talking about music. No one dared pick on David since even then he was a big, strong fellow, and Raven has that forbidding glare he probably practiced from the womb."

"A contributing factor may be that I outranked all but one of the boys there," Lord Ravenhurst remarked dryly.

"Well, Bayard and I weren't about to let those nodcocks insult our masculinity, so we went at them. But there were six of them and only two of us, and so David and Raven joined in the fight."

"Good gracious." She could picture them as boys, lively and passionate about anything they put their minds to.

"Oh, it was great fun. Those bullies couldn't throw a proper punch if you lined it up for them. But our headmaster wasn't as amused by it."

"Nothing like mutual punishment to bring boys together," Lord Ravenhurst said.

Alethea smiled. "Most young noblemen do not continue their musical training after they enter society, but you four are remarkably accomplished. Your skills rival professional musicians."

Lord Ian bowed. "We had two of the most vicious musical masters in Oxford who whipped us into shape soon enough."

"He exaggerates, my lady," Lord Ravenhurst said. "There were two retired musicians living near Oxford who trained us informally, especially in composition. One was German trained by an Italian master, and the other was French."

"So, that is why your music is so unique. You have had influences from all three," Alethea said. "At the concert I attended in London, Captain Enlow's violin and pianoforte concerto was more lighthearted and complex than any I had heard before, but since then I have heard French compositions with a similar style."

Lord Ravenhurst's white-blond eyebrows rose as he regarded her. "That is very astute of you. When he wrote it, Mr. Enlow was hoping to emulate the atmosphere of French pieces."

"I have not heard much music from other parts of the continent, but I have played several pieces from Mozart," Alethea said. "His music is not very popular here in Bath."

"Have you heard any of Beethoven's pieces?" Lord Ravenhurst asked. "You would enjoy them."

The dance ended, and Dommick returned with his sister. Alethea had not had so enjoyable a conversation in years. Her aunt did not allow her to speak to professional musicians at concerts, who tended to be of the middle class.

"Are you speaking of Beethoven?" Miss Terralton said. "Raven and I adore his music, but Ian pretends to disdain it."

"My dear Clare, I only disdain it because you are in raptures about it," Lord Ian said. "If you only considered it adequate, I would then be Beethoven's greatest proponent."

Miss Terralton gave Lord Ian a disgusted look. He grinned back at her.

"Do you like Beethoven, Lady Alethea?" Miss Terralton asked her.

"I am afraid I have never heard his music."

"I have a trio I can lend to you. Usually Bayard and Raven play the violin and violoncello and I play pianoforte, but you play the violin, do you not?"

"Yes, indeed." Alethea refrained from looking at Lord Dommick.

Lord Ian had no such restraint. "Lady Alethea plays well and has a very fine violin, doesn't she, Bay? A Stradivarius?"

"We are not certain it is a Stradivarius, but I believe so," Lord Dommick said.

"Have you taken it to Quill?" Lord Ravenhurst asked. "He would be able to verify it for a certainty."

"Alethea is understandably hesitant to go traipsing about with her violin in hand."

There was a beat of silence as everyone, including Dommick, realized he had called her by her name only. He had done so in front of Miss Herrington-Smythe to put her in her place, but to do it casually in front of his family shocked Alethea. His face was impassive, but she caught the colour seeping up his neck and realized he must have done so by accident.

Lady Morrish was the first to speak. "Why don't you take your instrument-maker friend to Mrs. Garen's home to look at the violin there?" She turned toward Aunt Ebena. "If you have no objection, of course?"

Aunt Ebena was regarding Lord Dommick with a thoughtful—and not very friendly—eye, but she nodded to Lady Morrish. "I should not mind at all."

"I shall visit Quill tomorrow and arrange a time for us to come by this week," Lord Dommick said.

"You may call tomorrow, if it suits you," Aunt Ebena said. Alethea wondered at her aunt's graciousness until she realized that for several days this week, her aunt had other engagements and Alethea would be home unchaperoned.

"Mr. Quill is a good instrument maker and repairer, and he is considered an expert on instrument forgeries," Lord Dommick said. "He is especially gifted in ferreting out violins purported to be by Stradivari."

"I have never claimed my violin was a Stradivarius," Alethea said hotly. However, she had always suspected it was.

"Don't be ridiculous, Alethea," Aunt Ebena said. "He is only confirming if it is or is not. He is not accusing you of anything."

"Of course not," Lord Dommick said quickly. "I did not mean to imply anything."

"I apologize, Lord Dommick," Alethea said. Why was she so

quick to take offense at everything he said? Something about him put her on edge.

Beside her, Miss Terralton suddenly tensed. Alethea turned to see Mr. Morrish approaching them.

"You both require rescuing," Lord Ian said with a wink. "Raven, take Clare out for this dance, will you?" He grasped Alethea's hand and led her to the dancers forming the new set.

"Thank you for thinking of me, but I have danced with many an unpleasant man," Alethea said.

"While I have only your best interests at heart, Lady Alethea, I am also concerned for Clare." He bowed to her as the music started.

"Miss Terralton?"

"At all the events we have attended since we arrived in Bath, Mr. Morrish has only ever associated with Clare or her female friends."

"Surely he has his own friends?"

"If he does, they all happen to be female and in a close relationship with Clare."

"Oh." Alethea realized she would not like a man like Mr. Morrish around her own sister. Something about him made her feel as if she had butter smeared on her hands and she longed to wipe them.

She spent an enjoyable evening with Lord Dommick and his friends and family. Their stamp of approval appeared to temporarily dampen the whispering about Alethea, and several other men asked her to dance. However, they always returned her to Lady Morrish, since Aunt Ebena sat next to the woman for much of the evening, and neither lady was inclined to move. Alethea didn't know what they spoke of, but neither lady appeared bored.

Finally, Lord Ravenhurst had his dance with Lady Fairmont. Alethea refused a gentleman who asked her to dance and waited for Lord Ravenhurst to return to Lady Morrish.

Lord Ian was dancing, and Miss Terralton had accepted the

hand of a young man with bright blue eyes. Lord Dommick stood at Alethea's side, but his gaze remained on his sister.

"You are very solicitous of your sister, my lord," she said.

"She is very dear to me," he said.

His answer surprised her. Her father and brother had only considered her a duty or an asset to be used, so it was hard for her to picture a man who cared for his family.

He turned to her. "And I asked you to call me Dommick."

His eyes were very near hers. They held a hint of amusement, a hint of uncertainty, a hint of awkwardness. Her blood pounding in her ears made it difficult to gather her thoughts to answer him.

"Or would you prefer to call me Bayard? Raven and Ian do so because we grew up as boys together."

"They told me about the fight."

He smiled then, and it transformed his face from the stern hawk to a much younger man, with laugh lines radiating from his shining eyes and along his mouth. "I trust Ian added much embellishment?"

"I think Lord Ravenhurst would not let him."

He was looking directly at her, so she saw clearly when his expression changed. If he were not always so controlled, so remote, she might have thought he looked at her with a sort of . . . longing.

Then his expression changed again, this time back to his distant, hawklike visage. He did not move a step, yet it seemed to Alethea that he grew farther away from her. He turned back to the dancers.

After several minutes' silence, he said, "We studied together at Oxford under the same music masters."

"Yes, Lord Ian mentioned that. It speaks much of your dedication to continue your music. Most young men do not."

"They are expected to engage in more worthy pursuits than music, but the majority of them frequent gaming halls rather than their estates. I do not think it a bad thing that we spent our time practicing music rather than more unsavory pursuits, and we yet had time for our family duties."

Alethea's brother had certainly spent much of his time gaming. She had not been told the particulars, but she had heard rumours that he had reduced the Trittonstone estate considerably before his death. He had already sold much of the land not under the entail. "You worked hard, then, for your popularity in London," Alethea said. "I am sure many miss your concerts."

"If David and I had not bought our commissions, we would not have continued," Dommick said. "Raven's estates took much of his time, Ian was caring for his mother and sister, and our families . . ." He stopped and seemed self-conscious.

Alethea thought she understood what he had been about to say. "Surely your families were pleased with your popularity?"

Dommick was not looking at her, and his voice was low. "Only for a while."

"They did not understand," she said slowly. "For most, music is something to adequately perform, nothing more. But for some, it rises above mere entertainment." Calandra had understood that in Alethea. What a gift that was. She could not imagine growing up without the support of at least one person.

He looked at her. "Yes," he said in a voice of surprise.

For a moment, it was as if he were touching her. She could almost feel his fingers on her face. His gaze wrapped around her, muting the sounds of the dance and the crowds in the room.

Then he blinked, and she blinked, and they both looked away.

She did not look at him again for the rest of the dance. Their silence was both comfortable and uncomfortable. His presence beside her was a sort of balm, and at the same time, she felt tense and nervous. She did not like not understanding herself, and she could somehow sense that he felt the same way.

The music ended, and Lord Ravenhurst appeared, escorting Lady Fairmont. She looked tired but happy at the success of her ball. One of the violet feathers in her headdress wilted sadly, but her amethyst pendant glittered at her bosom.

"Ebena, Lady Morrish," Lady Fairmont said. "I hope you are enjoying yourselves?"

"A wonderful ball, Tania," Aunt Ebena said.

She turned to Alethea with a polite smile. "And, Lady Alethea, Ravenhurst says you wish to speak with me?"

"It will take but a moment, my lady. My aunt has said you are familiar with many Italian noble families through your mother's side?"

"Oh, yes. My mother was very interested in family trees."

"I came across some initials that may be from an Italian nobleman." Alethea pulled the paper with the initials from her glove and handed it to Lady Fairmont. "I do not know who they refer to, but I wondered if you might perhaps recognize—"

She broke off because Lady Fairmont had turned a glowing crimson that clashed horribly with her gown. The look she gave Alethea was equal parts horrified and enraged. She thrust the paper back at Alethea, then turned to Aunt Ebena. "I don't know what you are about, Ebena, but this is outrageous."

Aunt Ebena's jaw had fallen open, her grey eyes wide.

"My lady, I assure you—" Alethea began, but Lady Fairmont cut her off with a slicing motion of her hand so violent that it made her pendant bounce on her chest.

Then without a word, Lady Fairmont turned and stalked away.

CHAPTER SIX

Alethea paced in her aunt's drawing room. She strained her ears for the sound of her aunt at the front door, but dreaded hearing it too soon, for it would mean that Lady Fairmont had refused to see her.

Why had Lady Fairmont responded with so much anger last night? Alethea's thoughts had been moving sluggishly, unable to grasp what was happening, unable to figure out what to say or how to respond.

And then when Lady Fairmont had stalked away, it was as if all the air had blown out of the room. Aunt Ebena had been white and gasping. They had left the ball immediately. Alethea's last sight had been Dommick's shocked face.

There was the sound of the front door opening. Alethea ran out of the drawing room, down the stairs to the front entrance hall just as Dodd opened the front door to Aunt Ebena.

She handed her cloak and bonnet to the butler. "Tea, Dodd," she snapped, and swept past Alethea to stomp up the stairs to the drawing room.

Alethea followed. "I'm sorry, Aunt."

"If I had not been sitting next to you when you spoke to Tania, I would have thought you had said something inappropriate."

Thank goodness. Aunt Ebena would have been incessant in her complaints about what she imagined Alethea had said.

"Perhaps she did not see you because she was busy packing for her remove to the country?"

"Is that what you believe?" Aunt Ebena shot at her.

"No."

Aunt Ebena swept into the drawing room. "I should hope you were not such a simpleton."

"Lord Dommick sent a note that he would be arriving this morning with his friend, Mr. Quill."

"Perhaps he knows what happened." Aunt Ebena dropped into her usual spot on the sofa and frowned at the cold tea tray in front of her. However, Sally immediately entered the room with a newly set tea tray and steaming pot. She removed the cold tea and scurried out.

Her aunt's ability to frighten the servants was really quite astounding.

"Stop hovering and sit," she ordered Alethea.

Alethea sat.

Aunt Ebena bit angrily into a scone, then tossed it back down onto her plate. "I shall be sure to give Tania a piece of my mind when next I see her."

Alethea realized that this entire event had irreparably altered her aunt's relationship with her friend. "I am sorry to have caused this rift between you."

"Tania is the one to have caused this rift. If she had explained herself instead of flouncing off . . ."

Alethea didn't quite get along with her aunt, but she never wished her harm or to isolate her from her friends. Alethea had few enough friends of her own to want to safeguard those of her aunt. "Would your other friends know why this happened?"

"I shall be lucky if my other friends acknowledge me after this embarrassing—"

She was interrupted by the sound of the door knocker.

"That must be Lord Dommick," Alethea said.

Aunt Ebena straightened, took a deep breath through her nose, and as she released it, moulded her face into a polite mask.

Three men entered the drawing room—Dommick, Lord Ian, and a small, slender man with an intelligent face. Everything about him was quick, short movements—his steps, the idle gestures of his hands, the turning of his head. He bowed to the ladies. "Josiah Quill at your service."

"Thank you for coming, Mr. Quill," Alethea said. "Won't you have some tea?"

"Afraid not, milady. I must be off as quickly as possible."

"Quill has only a few minutes to spare," Dommick said.

Alethea had taken the precaution of fetching her violin as soon as she'd received Dommick's note. She retrieved it from the table and handed it to the instrument maker.

He immediately fell to examining it, his nose bare inches from the smooth wood. He touched it with his long, knobby fingers, poked at the F-holes, even smelled the wood. His brow furrowed deeper the longer he studied it, and he made small noises to himself as he moved from the body to the neck to the pegbox. He also picked up the bow and played a scale. Here, his intent face shifted at the sweet tones.

Alethea didn't realize she'd been digging her nails into the arms of her chair until the pain made her look down at her hands. She relaxed them and her two injured knuckles began to throb.

Mr. Quill handed the violin back to her. "Stradivari. Custom order. Never seen anything like it. One of the tuning pegs was replaced. Good job done on that."

"In London." Alethea's hands curled around the fingerboard, and she felt the strings bite into the skin of her fingertips.

"Have you seen those initials before?" Dommick asked.

Mr. Quill shook his head. "Never seen wood like that either. It's what gives it that unusual tone."

"What type of wood is it?"

"Oh, it's spruce and maple, what you'd expect, but far more solid than anything I've seen."

"How old is it?" Lord Ian asked.

Mr. Quill took a moment to glance at the violin again. "Not one of his early works. Definitely made by Antonio Stradivari and not another one of his family. Seventy or eighty years old. Not more than ninety. Good condition, it doesn't look as if it has been neglected. It would be an expensive custom order or from a very important person. I'm surprised I've never seen any other violin using those woods. Stradivari would have made more violins with them."

"Would they have been from two trees that were unique?" Alethea asked.

"Maybe. Also, Stradivari wouldn't have used an entire tree. He'd have had extra wood."

"Thank you, Quill," Dommick said.

Mr. Quill nodded to them all and bowed to Aunt Ebena. "Good day to you all." He left the room so swiftly that Alethea barely caught the back of his coat as he exited.

"I'll have some of that tea." Lord Ian dropped into a chair as if he lived there. At her aunt's bidding, Alethea poured.

"Lord Dommick," Aunt Ebena said, "I hope your mother is well?"

Alethea did not have the patience for the niceties. "Did you or your mother know why Lady Fairmont responded as she did last night?"

Aunt Ebena shot her a look but did not reprimand her.

"We are baffled," Dommick said. "Lady Morrish begged me to convey her concern for you."

"That is most kind of her," Aunt Ebena said.

"I do not understand what about those initials could have offended her," Alethea said.

"I have known Tania for many years," Aunt Ebena said. "When she spoke of her Italian antecedents, she never hinted at any sort of scandal."

"My mother said the same, although she does not know Lady Fairmont well," Lord Dommick said.

"I shall speak to our friends," Aunt Ebena said, but uncertainty radiated from the edges of her eyes.

"If you permit me, I shall ask my mother to do the same with her acquaintances." Dommick said. "I can assure you of her discretion."

"Yes, and tell her thank you." Aunt Ebena's mood had once again blackened.

Lord Dommick seemed to sense this, for he rose and bowed. "We shan't keep you any longer."

"But I haven't finished my tea," Lord Ian said.

Dommick glared at him, but he simply grinned before downing his cup in one gulp. However, when Dommick turned toward the door, Lord Ian caught Alethea's eye and subtly tilted his head toward the door.

Alethea rose. "I shall see you out."

"Alethea, ring for Brooks before you return." Aunt Ebena looked tired, which would explain why she wanted her lady's maid.

"I regret we did not have more information about Lady Fairmont," Dommick said as they descended the stairs.

"Why should you? This has taken all of us by surprise. My aunt is especially upset because she called on Lady Fairmont this morning and was refused."

"I am sorry to hear that," Dommick said.

"I regret that Mr. Quill did not give us more information on the violin," Alethea said.

Dommick paused. "He gave us a great deal. I had not considered that if Stradivari had had more of the same wood, he might have made more violins with it. It suggests that the wood was given to him for the custom order and that he hadn't acquired it by his normal channels."

"Does that make the violin more valuable, perhaps?"

Dommick and Lord Ian both shook their heads slowly.

Lord Ian said, "There are Stradivari violins much older, which would be more valuable even though this one is unusual."

"It makes me believe that anyone coveting this violin would value it beyond its monetary worth," Dommick said.

"So, it is necessary to discover who commissioned this violin," Alethea said. "Lady Fairmont's reaction must be a clue as to the original owner."

Dommick nodded. "I shall continue to look into this."

Dodd returned the gentlemen's greatcoats and hats, but as Dommick left the house, Lord Ian held back and turned toward Alethea, shielding with his body the sheaf of papers he slipped to her from beneath his coat. He winked at her, then hurried out after his friend.

There were many sheets, folded vertically down the centre. As the door closed, Alethea opened them and saw a handwritten music manuscript. At the top was written: "Copy of Sonata for two violins, by the Lord Dommick. August 1810."

Lord Dommick had just finished writing this piece. Below that in the same handwriting:

"A—Take first violin. Expect practice session in one week.—I"

❧

Bayard thought someone might be following him.

He would never have noticed the thin man in grey clothes if he had not caught the man looking at him from across the street. It had been odd the way he looked away—too quickly for it to have been casual eye contact.

Bayard continued walking back toward the Crescent, but then he was spotted by Mr. Oakridge, an old schoolmate from Oxford who was a few years younger than he.

"Dommick! Didn't know you were in Bath! Staying all winter? M'mother is here with the family until Boxing Day. I daresay you've seen m'sister at all the fancy dos. I say, the cattle in Bath are deplorable. Saw the most spindly-shanked nag I've ever had the misfortune to behold stumbling down Milsom Street . . ."

As Mr. Oakridge pontificated on his favourite subject, with which he had an astounding memory, Bayard angled himself so he could look over the man's shoulder at the street.

And that's when he saw the grey man again.

He wasn't looking at Bayard this time, but he was staring into a shop window and considerably closer than he had been before.

"Er . . . looking for someone?" Mr. Oakridge asked.

"No, I beg your pardon. I thought I was hailed by someone, but I was mistaken."

"Of course, of course. I thought I saw Fanewell's black hunter at a coaching inn the other day, but it wasn't, the haunch was shorter, harder to tell at a distance, what? And did you see that Mr. Nanstone's in Bath? Riding the sweetest chestnut I ever did see. I might induce him to sell it to me. He and m'father were friends, so he might be persuaded, don't you think?"

As Mr. Oakridge paused to draw breath, Bayard interjected, "I'm afraid I must leave you, Oakridge, for my family is expecting me at home."

"Of course, of course, I won't keep you. Compliments to your family." Mr. Oakridge continued down the street.

Bayard walked a few paces, then turned to look behind him. The grey man was following, but he abruptly entered a shop.

Bayard shook his head, then continued up the street. He was not taking heed of his surroundings, however, and he nearly walked into two young women heading in the opposite direction. With a sinking heart, he recognized them as the daughters of one of his mother's friends.

He nodded to them. "Miss Nanstone, Miss Julia Nanstone."

"I declare, Lord Dommick, are you looking for someone?" Miss Nanstone had a high, grating voice that never failed to vibrate down Bayard's spine.

"No, I assure you," Bayard said.

"Why, but we have seen you since we turned onto the top of the street, and you have looked behind you twenty times at least." Miss Nanstone giggled.

"I thought I saw someone I knew, but I was mistaken."

"La, who could that be?" Miss Julia had a lower-pitched voice than her sister, but she also had the habit of batting her eyelashes after every sentence.

Bayard could not immediately think of someone. "Mr. Morrish, my stepfather's nephew," he blurted.

The Misses Nanstone gave each other significant looks before saying at the same time, "How interesting."

"I will not keep you ladies. Good day."

As Bayard escaped, he overheard a grating voice say, "Goodness, I could hardly credit the rumours, but the 'Mad Baron' indeed!"

A tightness settled upon his shoulders and chest, making him feel he was suffocating. He stopped and pretended to look at the prints in a shop window while he forced his lungs to breathe.

The whispers in London this past spring had been incessant and insidious. At first he had ignored them, but then the nightmares frightened some of his servants. Soon the tales were widespread, helped along by Miss Church-Pratton only months after breaking their engagement. His false friends fell by the wayside, and the isolation began to eat at him. It hadn't helped that he feared the return of what he had experienced last year—a fear that still followed in his footsteps closer than that grey man ever could.

And then he had witnessed his mother in tears, shunned by supposed friends who chose to believe the rumours about him. He had whisked her out of town immediately, but not before his mother's heart and spirit were broken. He had vowed to fix this, to ensure that his mother and Clare would not endure the same experience in London the next season.

He did not care about these people, yet it galled him that their opinion had the power to wound his family. It also frustrated him that their whispers stung him. He did not want their gossiping to make him feel anything at all, but he could not seem to subject his emotions to his will.

He forced himself to continue walking toward the Crescent. Things were going according to plan, if he could solve the mystery of Alethea's violin.

He remembered their conversation while dancing. Her outrageous words about Miss Herrington-Smythe, that shrug of her shoulder, the fearlessness in her expression. She was strong, confident.

And thinking about her seemed to pour a drop of her confidence into him. The tightness in his chest eased as he turned the corner into the Crescent.

He immediately saw Clare accompanied by her abigail, walking toward him, several yards away. He couldn't miss her, for her pelisse was a bright yellow trimmed with green ribbons. She smiled and waved. As they drew closer, she said, "I am going to the bookstore."

"Porter's?" It had the largest selection of music.

She nodded.

"I'll accompany you." He turned to walk with her. "I need more of the paper I use for music compositions."

He saw a flash of grey behind him. Cold seeped into his bones. His embarrassment at Miss Nanstone's words had made him forget his grey shadow. *God, help me to protect my sister.*

"You have been writing a great deal of music in the past several months," Clare said. "Is it for your concert?"

"Yes. I had no time to write music while I was fighting Boney, you know." He reached over to tweak her nose as he used to when they were younger.

She swatted his hand away. "Have you set a date yet?"

"Yes, in three weeks."

They walked to Green Street and the small bookstore that, in addition to books, specialized in selling music and parchment. Bayard deliberately did not look for the grey man, but at the door of Porter's, he said to Clare, "Go inside and I shall join you directly."

He strolled up Green Street past two more stores before turning round. The grey man was behind him, and it seemed he had just flicked his eyes away.

Bayard surged toward him, avoiding the occasional shopper ambling along the cobbled street. The grey man froze, blinked once, then turned into the doorway of a fruit shop.

Bayard stepped around a large matron before he could follow him into the shop. The man was discussing the price of a pineapple with the shopkeeper. He glanced up casually at Bayard, then went back to haggling.

"I demand to know what you are about," Bayard said.

He regarded Bayard from almost colourless eyes. "Don't know what you're talking about." His voice floated like a spiderweb on the breeze.

"I saw you on Lansdown Road and the Crescent, and now here. You have followed me across all of Bath."

"'Ere now," the shopkeeper said. "I don't know where you might have seen this gen'lman, but he had an appointment with me about this pineapple. Set it up earlier this morning." The shopkeeper frowned at Bayard, and the grey man did not look smug or sly, simply bewildered.

Bayard swallowed. Was this not the same man? Had this all been pure coincidence?

Had he suspected something more because he was going mad again?

The thought propelled him backward. "I beg your pardon," he muttered and strode from the shop.

He didn't know where he was going. His hands shook. He clenched his fists and walked quickly, keeping his head down lest someone look into his eyes and see his fear, his desperation.

It could not be happening again. He still remembered the living nightmares of summer last year, when reality and memory had exploded together in his mind. He had been able to walk through an English countryside directly onto the shores of Corunna, hearing the crack of gunfire and the keening moans as his friends died. He had smelled the briny scent of the sea, the metallic tang of blood, the screaming of injured horses. And then days, minutes, seconds later, he had returned to the drizzle of English rain, the scent of English earth, the chill of an English wind. He had descended into a pit of chaos and suffering that had been his life back from war.

He had to reassert control over himself. If he did not, he could not take care of his family. It was entirely up to him.

"Lord Dommick."

Alethea. The last person in the world he wanted to meet. He propelled his eyes upward—skimming the brown patterned gown and beaded burgundy spencer to her face.

Her polite expression melted into alarm and concern. She opened her mouth as if to speak, but then her eyes slid sideways to her maid. "Sally, why don't you go home? Lord Dommick will escort me from here."

The maid bobbed a curtsey and headed away.

As soon as she was out of earshot, Alethea stepped close. "Give me your arm. Let us walk." Her voice was low and calm, and as she laid her hand on his arm, he smelled the scent of . . . roses in the rain. Her composure soothed him, and he was able to walk slowly with her beside him. His heartbeat gradually slowed to the pace of their steps.

Still in that low voice, Alethea said, "May I assist you in any way?"

He was about to say no, but took a breath or two instead. "You have already done so."

"Please tell me what has upset you."

"It is nothing."

"Dommick, I did not think you a man who would lie to me."

The use of his name on her lips in that familiar manner eased something inside of him that had been painfully tight, which he had not noticed until it unwound. "I thought I saw a man following me, but I was mistaken."

Her fingers on his arm clenched. "A man? Is he still behind you?" Her head jerked to the side as she almost turned to look.

He had expected soothing platitudes, not this immediate belief. "I . . . do not think so. I haven't looked."

"What did he look like? Thin? Dirty-faced? Grey?"

He stopped to stare at her. She faced him, her burgundy bonnet framing her oval face, almond-shaped eyes, full red lips. She was completely serious.

"You have been followed as well," he said.

"Twice."

The concise answer and clipped tone revealed more than a multitude of words. He moved closer to her. "You did not tell me."

"I didn't think to. I wasn't certain if it had anything to do with
the violin. And you . . ." She turned her head until her profile was
partially screened by the side of her bonnet. "You didn't appear to
seriously consider someone was trying to steal the violin."

He didn't know how to answer her, so he continued walking.
She kept pace beside him, but he missed being able to see her eyes,
hidden by the dip of her bonnet. He only saw the smooth curve of
her cheek and chin.

He had not believed her, yet she had believed him immediately
without knowing what the man had looked like. It shamed him.
For the past year, everyone around him told him that what he saw
was not real.

Alethea was different. Perhaps God had been trying to show
this to him all along and he had been too stubborn to see it.

"I am sorry," he said.

"It is understandable. Although to be sure, I could not have said
that to you a week ago. I do hope you will be escorting me home,
since I have dismissed my maid."

"Of course." It was not mere gallantry. If someone were indeed
following her, he would not allow her to walk anywhere alone.
"We must first stop by Porter's bookshop. My sister is there." He
directed their steps back to Green Street.

"Excellent. I had wanted to look for new music."

"Clare will convince you to purchase Beethoven."

Alethea laughed, a rich sound that reminded him of the velvety
lower tones of her violin.

However, just as they turned the corner to Green Street,
Bayard caught sight of Mr. Morrish, looking smug as he adjusted
his high-pointed collar and entered Porter's bookshop.

Alethea recognized him also. "Is that . . . ?"

"Hurry." Bayard pulled her with him. He had to protect Clare.
There was no one else who would care for her as he did.

It seemed the street was suddenly full of people blocking their way. He did not want to move too quickly lest it bring more attention to himself, but he could not seem to politely dodge as nimbly as he wished.

"Surely he will not harm her in the time it takes us to reach them," Alethea said as they waited for a rumbling vegetable cart to move out of the way.

"No, you are right." But he still felt alarm at the sight of the man's confident, sly face. Bayard was certain Mr. Morrish knew Clare would be in the shop. Also, Mr. Morrish was not musical, and while Porter's sold books, there were other, larger bookstores frequented by the fashionable set in Bath.

They finally reached the shop door and entered. The first thing Bayard saw was Clare's maid near the front of the store, flirting with a shop boy.

"Betty, where is your mistress?" Bayard demanded.

The girl went pink, her eyes wide, but she managed to answer in a sulky voice, "I'm sure I don't know, milord. She bid me stay here."

The shop boy frowned at her. "She did?"

Betty's mouth pinched as she glared at him. "A'course she did."

Bayard gave her a hard look, then moved past her deeper into the busy shop. Alethea followed. They wound their way through the bookcases and around tables laden with stacked leather-bound books and paper booklets of music.

"Dommick." Alethea moved toward the far corner of the shop, where he caught a flash of yellow. He also heard the sound of Clare's voice in a low, harsh whisper.

"I demand that you release me." There was anger and fear in her tone.

Bayard rushed forward. He heard the sounds of a scuffle, some books falling, the rocking of a bookcase that had been knocked into. Was she being attacked?

Then Mr. Morrish's loud, smooth voice saying, "Oh, Mrs. Herrington-Smythe, I fear you have caught us out." And Clare's loud gasp.

They turned the corner and came upon the short, beady-eyed matron looking avidly upon the sight of Mr. Morrish with his arms around Clare, who was obviously trying to push him away. It looked like a lover's tryst had Clare not been glaring daggers at Mr. Morrish, and had the young man not looked so triumphant.

Clare would be ruined.

CHAPTER SEVEN

✦

*B*ayard froze, unable to think quickly enough of something to do to curb Mrs. Herrington-Smythe's gossiping tongue. He was helpless again, as he had been this past spring, to stop the storytelling that would spread like a disease.

"Mr. Morrish!" Alethea said in tragic tones quite unlike her normal sensible voice. She crushed her hand to her chest. "I am ashamed of you!"

Mrs. Herrington-Smythe now turned to Alethea with curious, bulging eyes. She looked rather like a pug dog anxious for a treat.

Alethea continued, "And after you had assured me last night that you were anxious to confer your attentions upon Miss Herrington-Smythe!"

Bayard thought back to last night. Actually, Mr. Morrish had said something like that while being gallant about asking Miss Herrington-Smythe to dance.

Mrs. Herrington-Smythe started, making the fruit dangling from her hat jump and sway. The woman regarded first Alethea, then Mr. Morrish with narrow eyes.

The young man stiffened, giving Clare the opportunity to shove him away and hurry to Bayard's side.

Alethea marched up to Mr. Morrish. "Miss Herrington-Smythe will be most upset." She turned to Mrs. Herrington-Smythe. "Ma'am, I shall be sure to tell *everyone* of this man's dastardly conduct in regards to your lovely daughter."

At Alethea's words, the pink circles of rouge on the older woman's cheeks stood out against her pale skin. There was silence among them all, and Bayard could almost see Mrs. Herrington-Smythe debating her course of action. Would the whisper of scandal spread by Lady Alethea Sutherton about her daughter outweigh the whisper of scandal she could spread about Miss Clare Terralton?

She cleared her throat and said with reluctance, "Surely, Lady Alethea, my daughter does not deserve to be exposed to more pain."

Alethea affected contrition. "You are right. Forgive me, ma'am. I allowed my righteous anger for your daughter's sake to overrule my good sense. We must not speak of this, in order to spare her feelings."

Mrs. Herrington-Smythe pressed her lips together. Alethea had outwitted her. The gossipy matron would not speak of this incident about Clare for fear Alethea would then speak about her daughter. Checkmate.

Mrs. Herrington-Smythe cast them all a disdainful glance, then said through tight lips, "I bid you all good day." She swept away.

"He did this on purpose, Bay," Clare whispered. "He cornered me. He was simply talking until he heard someone approaching. Then he embraced me before I could see what he was about."

"I did no such thing." Mr. Morrish's voice was full of injury. "I steadied Miss Terralton when she stumbled."

"I did stumble as I tried to get away from you," Clare hissed.

"Miss Terralton, what happened to your maid?" Alethea's voice was soft with a root of iron.

Clare hesitated. "She was with me, but when Mr. Morrish arrived, she had disappeared and I hadn't noticed."

"How much did you pay her?" Alethea demanded of Mr. Morrish.

He sniffed. "I'm sure I don't know what you're talking about."

"Sir Hermes will hear of this," Bayard said.

"Bay, he will only think it a good joke," Clare told him.

She was right. And neither Sir Hermes nor Bayard's mother were averse to an alliance between Mr. Morrish and Clare.

"At the very least, Miss Terralton, you can hire a new maid," Alethea said.

"Come, Clare." Bayard also held his arm out to Alethea. "Shall we depart?" He pulled both ladies away without another word to Mr. Morrish.

As they reached the front of the shop, Betty moved toward Clare with an expression of contrition. "There you are, miss. I wasn't sure where you were."

"Betty, return to the house immediately," Bayard said. When she hesitated, he barked, "Now."

She scuttled out of the shop.

"When we get home, I shall turn her off," he said.

Clare sighed. "I shall have to find a new lady's maid."

The air outside the shop seemed crisp and clean, as if he had been breathing something foul but hadn't realized it.

"I am not a disinterested observer," Alethea said, "for I know of an excellent lady's maid who will never be bribed or distracted from her charge."

"How can you be certain of her loyalty?" Bayard asked.

"I know and love her better than any other creature in the world. She is my half sister, Lucy Purcell."

"How could your sister be a lady's maid?" Clare asked.

"She and I grew up in the same village, but not in the same household," Alethea said delicately.

An illegitimate daughter of the Earl of Trittonstone? Clare seemed to understand without needing further clarification, but she did venture to ask, "How is it that you are so intimate?"

"Clare," Bayard said in warning. The conversation was becoming indelicate.

"I assure you, it is nothing scandalous," Alethea said. "She is older than I by a few months. Her mother married before Lucy was born, giving her respectability, but I grew up always knowing Lucy was my half sister. The matrons of the village wanted to dictate to me whom I could not associate with." Alethea quirked an eyebrow. "So naturally, I sought Lucy out and we became fast friends."

Clare looked both astounded and admiring.

"I would trust Lucy with my life." Alethea's eyes were dark and serious as they looked to Bayard. "I would have hired her myself had my financial circumstances been different. She has served as a lady's maid for several gentlewomen in Bath. Right now, she is working for Mrs. Ramsland but would be pleased to move to a different situation."

"What do you think, Bay?" Clare said.

"Certainly, we should be happy to hire your sister." After what had just occurred, he did not care if the woman dressed Clare in sackcloth, so long as she could be depended upon to protect her.

"Splendid." To Alethea, she asked, "Do you attend the concert tomorrow night?"

"Yes, but I have never heard of the soprano who will be singing."

"I heard that she is very new and supposedly descended from Italian royalty."

Bayard listened with only half an ear since they had discussed this last night. Now that it was over, he could feel the relief he had suppressed in the bookshop. If Alethea had not thought quickly, Mrs. Herrington-Smythe's poisonous tongue could have ensured that Clare would be ruined or engaged to Mr. Morrish.

Alethea had risen to protect his sister. Her actions hinted at a self-sufficiency he admired. Things she had said gave him the impression that she had not had many people to rely upon in her life. And for some reason, that thought bothered him a great deal.

≪✤≫

The soprano's piercing high C was like both ice and fire poured down Alethea's back as she squirmed in her seat in Lady Rollingwood's concert. She had already suffered through two songs, and the soprano was nearing the end of butchering a third. However, it seemed that no one around her noticed the woman's sad sense of pitch, for as usual, many of the fashionable set of society chatted with each other rather than listened to the music. If she did not intend to speak to the singer after the concert, Alethea might have been tempted to leave for the quieter air in the other room.

Thankfully, Signora D'Angelo finished the song with a flourish and a toss of her magnificent head. The applause was more enthusiastic than her performance warranted, perhaps due to her magnificent bosom threatening to fall out of her gold-and-blue gown.

Sitting next to her, Aunt Ebena muttered something that sounded like, "Thank goodness."

Lady Rollingwood announced a brief intermission, and Aunt Ebena went to visit with friends sitting in another part of the room. Signora D'Angelo held court near the front, flashing white teeth framed by red-stained lips. Her eyes, heavily made up with kohl, flirted with the gentlemen flocking about her. Alethea was not hopeful that she would be able to speak to her before the concert resumed. However, the soprano was likely to use the ladies' withdrawing room after the concert, and Alethea could speak to her then.

When Alethea fetched glasses of lemonade for herself and her aunt, she met with Miss Terralton.

"Lady Alethea, may I sit with you?" Miss Terralton asked without preamble. "Mr. Morrish is of our party tonight."

"How can your stepfather allow him to pay such attentions to you after what happened?"

"You must understand. Sir Hermes is of a jovial and complacent disposition. His nephew said that he meant no disrespect to me, and Sir Hermes believed him."

Privately, Alethea thought Sir Hermes an idiot. At least Miss Terralton now had Lucy ensconced in their home to protect her. "Of course you may sit with us. Tell me, Miss Terralton, how do you like Lucy as your maid?"

"She is very like you. And you must call me Clare."

They chatted until the intermission was over, and Signora D'Angelo sang another three songs, quite as badly as the first three. Then Lady Rollingwood introduced a young German violinist, Mr. Dohman, who would be performing a new violin concerto of his own composition.

From the first measure, Alethea was entranced. Dohman played with fire and speed, nothing staid or stately. He played as if the music burned in him, and its power pervaded the room. The notes swelled in her heart and ears, and she closed her eyes. The music brought up memories of the hot, bright sun against her skin and the overpowering scent of lilacs in bloom, a mad dash across the downs on her horse in a storm with the sting of the rain against her face and the bite of the wind through her riding habit, the horrible darkness of sorrow at the death of her dog, Sheltie, a stray whom she had raised since she was ten years old.

When the music ended, she realized there were tears on her cheeks. She felt drained, as if she'd run across the park without stopping. She gulped in air, then rummaged in her reticule for a handkerchief.

Aunt Ebena thrust one into her hands, snapping at her, "Compose yourself."

She couldn't help it. Music had always had the power to move her, to play her emotions the way she played her violin.

Why must she be so different from everyone around her? She supposed she could restrain herself and hide who she was, but that would be a prison. She would rather be alone and free.

She cleared her eyes to find Clare staring at her, brows knit. She tentatively said, "You enjoy your music with . . . fervor."

"I live my life with fervor. Music is a large part of my life."

"The way you listen to music . . . it makes me feel as if I am missing something in my life."

"Missing something? In not showing proper decorum in a concert?"

"Sometimes, especially when I am playing music, I want to express myself fully without concern about whether it is proper or not, but I am always afraid of making a fool of myself."

Alethea studied Clare, taking in the earnest dark eyes, the droop of insecurity about the soft rosebud mouth. "As you grow older, you will gain more confidence," Alethea said. "You will learn when to be sensible and when to have sensibility."

Clare took several moments to think on her words. Finally, she reached out to squeeze Alethea's hand.

Mr. Dohman and the pianoforte player who had been accompanying the soprano began an instrumental piece by Pergolesi that Alethea recognized, although she had not heard it in a long time. It had a simple, lovely repeating melody line that was easily recognizable and lent itself well to the poignant tones of Dohman's violin. However, she realized that Dohman must have added and embellished, for it differed from the short, simple piece she and Calandra had played together. She listened with delight, remembering the smell of woodsmoke in Calandra's music room, the patter of rain against the window, the vibrations of the pianoforte on the wooden floor as Alethea played the moody piece with feeling.

Clare exhaled softly as the piece ended. "How beautiful."

"One of my favourites," Alethea said.

"Do you know it?"

"It is by Pergolesi."

"Who?"

"He wrote mostly opera and vocal works, but this was an instrumental piece that Calandra—my neighbor, Lady Arkright, especially liked. I have the music—would you like to borrow it?"

"Oh, yes, please. It was such a beautiful, pensive piece. It reminded me of Terralton Abbey in the rain."

The concert was over. Clare glanced toward her family. "Mama is signaling to me."

Alethea saw Signora D'Angelo heading into the ladies' withdrawing room. She said to Clare, "I will escort you back to your party." Afterward, she would waylay the soprano. Hopefully the woman would not be too quick to return to the drawing room.

As they approached where Clare's family was seated, Alethea noticed Dommick standing next to a well-built man with curly blond hair. He looked familiar, and as they drew near, she recognized Mr. Kinnier.

He was a nobleman, an accomplished violin player and well-known. She had often seen him at concerts and parties during her season. She had had the unfortunate experience of overhearing Mr. Kinnier after the ladies in a dinner party had performed for the guests. He spoke to the hostess and disdained Alethea's harp playing but praised the indifferent pianoforte playing of the daughter of the house. She suspected his intention was to cozy up to the hostess, and she had despised him for such toadying. She had heard him play at several concerts, and while he was of superior skill to most amateurs, he had not been as skillful as Dommick.

"Oh," Clare said in a low voice. "It is Mr. Kinnier." Her tone indicated that Clare might care for Mr. Kinnier's company as little as she did. "I cannot think what Lady Whittlesby is about, for she knows Mama does not care for him."

Lord Dommick held himself stiffly, but Lady Whittlesby had wicked amusement in her eyes as she stood and chatted with the two men. She caught sight of Alethea and Clare and waved them over. "Lady Alethea, you have met Mr. Kinnier, have you not?"

"Indeed, my lady."

She curtseyed to him, and he pretended to remember her. "I am pleased to see you again, Lady Alethea." He surveyed her with his small, dark eyes, which looked even smaller because his eyelashes were so fair.

Alethea noticed that Clare had swiftly pulled her brother away to speak to him, leaving Alethea with Mr. Kinnier and Lady Whittlesby.

Mr. Kinnier did not seem to notice Miss Terralton's defection. "How do you enjoy Bath, my lady?"

It was the normal chit chat she expected from evenings such as this, but Alethea wanted to speak to Signora D'Angelo, so tonight it seemed interminable. She said in a slightly rushed voice, "It is very enjoyable. Are you just arrived?"

"Indeed. And already I find friends among the society here." He nodded toward her.

Mr. Kinnier was a hostess's dream with his excellent manners, but Alethea wished instead for Dommick's strong opinions—even if he was wrong—and stronger feelings. Mr. Kinnier's bland good taste bored her, and she could not trust his affable mask since she had witnessed his tendency to say whatever was pleasing to the listener.

Her question was more pointed than polite. "You have not held a concert in two or three years, I believe. Do you intend to hold one in Bath?" She had read in the London newspapers three years ago that his last concert had been a dismal failure. He had not held one since.

His mouth quirked in what could be taken for a smile, but the skin around his eyes tightened. "How kind of you to recall my musical aspirations. Alas, I have no plans for a concert. There are already fine artists to be had, such as at tonight's event."

Alethea was impressed that he could say such a thing without a single wince or indication that the principle musician had been akin to an exuberant parrot. His self-depreciating comment would normally require some flattery in response, but Alethea did not feel like indulging his vanity. She smiled serenely and remained silent. She suspected he had no idea who she was. In finding himself at a loss with a reticent partner, he would probably excuse himself and she would be free to find Signora D'Angelo.

Clearly she underestimated a charming man's ability to fawn over a woman. "I look forward to participating in spontaneous musical evenings. Lady Whittlesby informs me that you often play to entertain your hostesses."

"Indeed, Lady Alethea, your harp playing at Mrs. Isherton's card party was exquisite," Lady Whittlesby said.

"You would be a welcome addition to our amateur performances," she said to him. "Perhaps you could compose something, such as an aria for our Signora D'Angelo."

His polite mask subtly hardened. He was aware of her goading him. She did not care. She had no patience with frauds who would speak one thing to one person and the opposite to another.

"I'm afraid I have not the skill to compose vocal pieces, especially any that would properly flatter the lovely soprano."

Alethea took this opportunity to escape him. "I was hoping to claim a few minutes of her time to praise her performance tonight. I beg you both will excuse me." She curtseyed and headed toward the ladies' withdrawing room.

She had just entered the hallway when a hard hand grabbed her elbow. "A word, if you please, Lady Alethea," Mr. Morrish hissed in her ear.

She yanked her elbow but could not dislodge his fingers, which bit into her skin. The only way to extricate herself would have been to physically push him, but it would draw attention, and she did not want to cause a stir in the home of Lady Rollingwood, a good friend of her aunt. Alethea had already caused Aunt Ebena to lose her friendship with Lady Fairmont.

She planted her feet, staring Mr. Morrish into his serpentlike eyes since they were of a height.

"You will stop interfering in my business or I shall shred your good name and that of your aunt."

"My aunt is one of the most respected women in Bath. What do you suppose people will believe—her word or yours? You are a stranger, Mr. Morrish, and the Bath residents are very loyal to each other." Alethea wasn't certain that was true, but she was reasonably sure her aunt's friends would stand by her over a fortune-hunter.

His rosy cheeks grew dark and blotchy, and his sneer emphasized his protruding front teeth. "You dare threaten me? You are merely a weak woman."

"You are merely an ineffectual bully."

His grip on her elbow clenched, crushing her bones. She could not school her expression against the pain, and she turned away as tears sprang into her eyes and she grit her teeth.

"Do not underestimate what I would do to anyone who stands in my way."

She was about to tell him not to underestimate a woman who knew exactly where to place a well-aimed kick when a voice called, "Mr. Morrish, your uncle is in immediate need of you."

Dommick stood a few feet away. His gaze was stormy, but

Alethea immediately felt a steadiness under her feet as though she had found a rock to stand upon.

Several people milling around nodded to Dommick and looked curiously at Mr. Morrish. Mr. Morrish's grip spasmed even tighter, causing her to hiss with pain.

Dommick stepped between them and forced Mr. Morrish to break his hold on her. Mr. Morrish stumbled to prevent falling down on his elegantly clothed behind.

Dommick's tall figure shielded her from Mr. Morrish, and she clung to his arm with trembling fingers, trying to slow her breathing.

Dommick cast a scornful glance over his shoulder. "Your uncle seemed most urgent in requiring your services, Mr. Morrish. I suggest you make your way to him posthaste."

Alethea raised her head to look at Mr. Morrish. He stood with his hands fisted low at his sides and cheeks sullen, which made his weak chin almost disappear into his cravat. He gave Dommick's broad back a stiff bow and left them.

She gripped his arm tightly and closed her eyes, concentrating on her rapid heartbeat. His warm hand covered hers, the fingers gently massaging her knuckles.

After several moments, she opened her eyes to find his face very near. He smelled of soap, and something that brought to mind walking in the oak wood at Trittonstone Park on a cool autumn day. Mr. Morrish melted away, and she felt as if she were home again, safe.

But suddenly his mouth firmed and he jerked his head away. The moment broke as if a crystal goblet had shattered.

She pulled her hand from his arm and stepped back. The noise of the party swept in around her. Thankfully, no one noticed them for there were more important and interesting people to gossip about than a spinster and a once-popular nobleman musician, and none of them had known Mr. Morrish.

"Thank you, my lord. I beg you will excuse me." She turned

to go but he reached out to clasp her elbow. When Mr. Morrish had done so, her arm had shrunk from his touch, but Dommick's gloved hand was gentle. She stopped.

It seemed he had reached out to her without consciously thinking of it, for he dropped her elbow like a hot coal. He cleared his throat. "Where are you going?"

"I wanted to speak to Signora D'Angelo about the initials."

Dommick gave a wince. "I shall spare you the effort. I spoke to her before the concert."

"Was she able to identify them?"

"I didn't ask her. It would have been of no use."

"No use?"

"Did you know that I speak Italian?"

Alethea blinked at him. "What?"

"For I can assure you that 'Signora D'Angelo' does not."

"You mean—?"

Dommick nodded. "She isn't Italian."

CHAPTER EIGHT

When Alethea knocked on the door to the Marquess of Ravenhurst's home the next day, she was surprised to find it opened by Clare herself, with the butler hovering behind her. "Miss Clare...," he said in a pained voice.

The girl pulled Alethea inside. "Thank goodness you've come."

Alethea said to her maid, "Sally, feel free to have a cup of tea in the kitchen."

"You may send your maid home after she has her tea, if you prefer," Clare said. "When Bayard returns, he can accompany you home."

Alethea nodded to Sally, who curtseyed and headed to the kitchen. The butler moved to accept Alethea's cloak.

Clare led Alethea toward the drawing room. "Mr. Morrish arrived half an hour ago. Bayard is on some errand, Ravenhurst is attending to estate business, and Ian is paying a call on a friend of his mother who lives outside of Bath. Mother is complacent about allowing Mr. Morrish to sit beside me, and quiz me about my embroidery, and comment on my dress. Next he shall ask to see my teeth." Clare stomped up the last few steps.

"I shall pay my respects to your mother, and then we can remove into the music room." Alethea handed Clare the sheaf of music she had brought. "Here is the Andantino, for violin and piano, by Pergolesi."

"That melancholy song from last night? Oh, thank you." Clare riffled through the music as she walked.

Lady Morrish lounged on a chaise in the drawing room, her embroidery a tangled mess about her but her face revealing only a languid contentment. "How lovely to see you, Lady Alethea. Do sit and have a cup of tea."

Mr. Morrish had risen to his feet, and the smile he gave to Alethea was wide and cold.

"Thank you, my lady." Alethea positioned herself next to Mr. Morrish so that Clare sat next to her mother instead.

"How is your aunt, Lady Alethea?" Lady Morrish asked.

Clare handed Alethea a cup of tea. "Quite well," Alethea said.

"I am so distressed by what happened at Lady Fairmont's ball," Lady Morrish said. "I have asked among my acquaintance, but I cannot find out why she would have behaved so."

"She has removed to her country house for the winter, I believe."

"Yes, more's the pity. But I am likely to see her in town this spring when Clare has her come out, so if I have an opportunity, I shall speak to her for you."

"Thank you, that is very kind of you."

"Indeed, Aunt." Mr. Morrish flashed a toothy smile at the lady. "I was not present when Lady Fairmont spoke to Lady Alethea, but I heard about the incident and it grieves me greatly."

Alethea was sure it did, about as much as a tickle in his toe.

She had taken her second sip of tea when Clare jumped to her feet. "Mama, Alethea and I shall be in the music room. She has brought some new music for me."

"Certainly." Lady Morrish returned to picking at the tangle of her embroidery silks. "Mr. Morrish, will you assist me? I cannot seem to . . ."

Mr. Morrish's pained expression was the last thing Alethea saw before she left the room.

"You have made it clear that you do not wish to entertain Mr. Morrish's suit, have you not?" Alethea asked as they made their way down the hallway to the music room.

"Yes, but Sir Hermes simply laughs and says I am yet too young to know my mind firmly. Mother goes along with everything he says."

"Has he no respect for your wishes?"

"Sir Hermes desires the match. Bayard would have refused Mr. Morrish entry into the house, but Mama prevailed upon him, saying it would cause too much talk to deny Mr. Morrish his uncle." Clare huffed. "And so nothing prevents Mr. Morrish from inflicting his presence upon me."

Alethea's opinion of Clare's stepfather sunk lower. The man may be a jovial personality, but he was also thoughtless of others and selfish. He reminded her of her father and brother, although with less cruelty. But unlike herself, Clare had a brother and his friends to protect her. Alethea had only had Calandra and Lucy and, most of all, herself to depend upon.

Clare threw open the double doors, and a bright shaft of light nearly blinded Alethea. The Ravenhurst music room was even grander than the drawing room. Tall windows drenching the room in light flanked bookcases of sheet music. She was immediately engulfed in the spicy aroma of hothouse flowers, which sat on tables set against the walls in front of large oval mirrors that reflected the sunlight, making the room even brighter. A large, impressive pianoforte sat in the far corner next to a large harp, and Lord Ravenhurst's violoncello rested next to it on a stand.

Some movement caught her eye. She turned to look, but saw

nothing except the two tables set up in the other corner of the room with instruments scattered across them, and next to those a heavy wooden desk piled high with paper, both blank and manuscript music. The blotter was heavily dotted with ink. Dust motes floated in the air, illuminated by the window behind the desk. All the windows had their curtains drawn back so that as much light as possible filled the room.

"Did you see that?" Alethea asked.

"See what?"

She stared out the window, then shook her head. "I must have seen a bird outside."

Clare sat at the pianoforte. "Should you like to play the violin portion?"

Alethea scanned the violins on the tables. "Will Lord Ravenhurst object if I use one of his instruments?"

"Oh, those are Bayard's. Choose any one."

While Clare picked out the piece on the pianoforte, Alethea studied the violins and spotted the Stradivarius immediately. It was older than hers. She could tell by the feel of the wood. There was another violin even older, which she thought might be a Guarnerius. She played a few measures on each and chose the possibly-Guarnerius since it had the more beautiful tone. But she felt her own violin had more velvety depths to the lower notes and more jewel-like brightness to the higher ones.

They practiced together for nearly half an hour. Clare was quite accomplished at the pianoforte and picked up the music quickly, and Alethea had played the piece many times with Calandra.

There was a gentle tap at the music room door. Clare stopped playing. "Come."

Lucy entered the room and shut the door behind her, then drew close to the two women. Her dark eyes were somber. "Miss Terralton, Mr. Morrish has just left the house, but I have been in your bedroom for the past three-quarters of an hour. I came upon Mr. Morrish's servant in your bedchamber."

"What?" Alethea exploded. The violin bow slipped through her fingers, and she grabbed at it quickly before it fell to the rug. She set the instrument upon the table.

Clare's face was frighteningly pale in the light from the windows.

"I confronted him and he left," Lucy said, "but I thought it prudent to remain in your bedchamber while Mr. Morrish was in the house."

Clare was still silent and shocked. "Was anything taken?" Alethea asked.

"I don't believe so." Lucy laid a hand on Clare's shoulder and said in a gentle voice, "Do you feel quite able to come upstairs with me to make sure?"

Clare inhaled a short breath, then firmed her chin. "Yes, let us go up." She took Alethea's hand to pull her along, and Alethea could feel the girl's fingers trembling.

Clare's room had been a guest room decorated in shades of pink and red, but the girl's personal items were easy to spot because they were all in what appeared to be her favourite colour of blue. "Lucy, where was Mr. Morrish's servant when you saw him?" Clare asked.

Lucy pointed to the dressing table. "He had opened the top middle drawer, miss."

"That would be the first place I would look," Alethea said. "Perhaps Lucy interrupted him before he had time to search."

Clare said nothing, but she went through all her drawers at the dressing table, then through her clothespress, although Lucy said she had checked and nothing seemed to be missing.

Finally Clare sank onto the sofa in front of the fireplace. "Lucy, you may go. I know you have much to do before this evening."

Lucy bobbed a curtsey, but as she passed her, Alethea reached out to squeeze her hand. Lucy gave her a smile and squeezed back, then left the room and closed the door behind her.

Alethea sat next to Clare on the sofa. "What will you do?"

Clare lifted her chin. "I will speak to my mother and Sir Hermes. But I fear he will simply tell his nephew to reprimand his servant." Clare stared at the closed door. "You are so close to your sister."

"We grew up together. She is my best friend."

"But you are so far apart in station. What did your neighbors think?"

"Oh, they were disapproving, just as they disapproved of my friendship with Lady Arkright, who was Italian, never mind that her deceased husband had been English through and through. Even the rector would drop nasty hints about 'low company.' I simply replied with 'love thy neighbor.'"

Clare stifled a laugh. "How could the rector say such a thing?"

"Oh, he wasn't the worst one. The pious women in the village—the ones who were forever going on about their good works for the Lord and then mistreating their servants—would cross the street rather than meet with me when I was with Lucy." Alethea attended church every Sunday, but she listened to the reverend with a very cynical ear. She had little respect for the religious. They were all hypocrites, and they served a God who had abandoned her in her hour of need.

"And you didn't care."

"Of course not. Lucy and Calandra loved me more than my family. I never heed public opinion if it goes against what I believe to be right and good." Alethea added, "Think of your brother. He loves you deeply. Would he forsake you? I could no more forsake Lucy."

At the tail end of her words, there came a loud crash from downstairs, the sound of a door slamming against the wall. Then another crash, something heavy and wooden dropping to the floor, accompanied by a tinkling descant of shattered pottery.

Alethea and Clare jumped to their feet and raced out of the room.

⁂

Bayard should have paid attention to the prickle of unease he felt as he read the letter he received that morning. It was from Jones Brothers, an instrument shop in Chippenham. They had heard of his inquiries about a violin and may have some information for him, if he would be so good as to visit the shop.

He had called for his gig and set off directly after breakfast, but just as he passed the outer edge of Bath, he realized he had forgotten the copy of the initials that Alethea had made for him. He turned around immediately.

He drove up before the house and dashed to the front door, opened by the butler. "Have someone hold my horse, Chapman. I shan't be a moment." He bounded up the stairs two at a time and passed the closed drawing room door, where he heard his mother's faint voice on his way to the music room.

He thrust open the music room door and froze.

A slender man sat at the desk, rummaging through a bottom drawer. He shot to his feet at the sight of Bayard.

It was the grey man from the street.

Bayard rushed forward just as the man leapt over the desk and launched himself at him.

The man caught Bayard's shoulder and collarbone when he crashed into him. Bayard staggered backward, landing hard against the closed door, and it whipped open to slam against the wall. Bayard toppled to the floor, the man on top of him.

The intruder was whipcord lean and strong, and Bayard grabbed his arms as the man lashed out at his head. He prevented two blows but a third landed above his left ear and made stars twinkle in front of his eyes for a moment. He grabbed at the man's torso, but the grey, dingy coat was in the way. The pockets were stuffed with cloth or paper.

Bayard kicked out to shove the man off of him. The thief rolled along the carpet and bounded to his feet with agility. Bayard was slower, and the man kicked him solidly in the side while he was still on his hands and knees

The pain thrust the air from his lungs, but he managed to whip out with one leg and land a blow against the man's knee. The man grunted and lurched into a table against the wall. The table tipped over, and the vase atop the smooth surface slid down in a graceful dive, shattering against the floor.

Air flooded into Bayard's lungs in a rush, and he thrust himself to his feet. The man was limping rapidly down the hallway toward the stairs.

At that moment, Clare rushed out from the short side passage that led from the stairs from the bedchambers above. Bayard drew breath to yell, but it was too late.

The man found himself facing Clare, who inadvertently blocked the main stairs. He pushed at her, his legs unsteady and causing him to stumble.

Clare flew into a hallway table in a wild tangle of skirts, knocked against it, and slid to the floor.

"Clare!" he shouted. *Lord, let her be uninjured.*

"Clare!" It was Alethea's voice. She ran out from the same short passage and dropped to her knees at his sister's side.

The grey man staggered down the main stairs. Bayard reached the top of the staircase in time to see the man leap down the last few steps, landing awkwardly on his injured knee. He pushed past the startled butler, yanked open the front door, and was gone.

"Good gracious!" His mother stood in the drawing room doorway, her face bloodless as she saw Clare on the floor. She kneeled next to Clare as Alethea rose, running downstairs calling for Lucy. Bayard crouched beside his sister.

Clare had landed on her stomach, but she now rolled over and was trying to sit up. Bayard tried to stop her. "Do not rise."

"I'm well," she insisted. When she sat upright, she swayed slightly, but it soon passed and she looked at them with clear eyes.

"I shall send for a doctor," Bayard said, but Clare shook her head.

At that moment, Alethea arrived with both Lucy and his mother's maid, and the three women helped Clare and Lady Morrish to their feet and into the drawing room. "I also sent for tea," Alethea told him. In a low voice she added, "What happened?"

Bayard explained briefly, and Alethea looked puzzled. "What was he looking for? Did he find it?"

"I don't know." Bayard headed back to the music room, Alethea following.

He saw immediately that all his notes on her violin were gone, including the drawing of the initials. "He stole all the information I had gathered on your violin, little as it was."

Alethea stood by the table. "Your instruments have been moved. Clare and I were here but a few minutes ago. I had thought I saw movement by the window . . ." She shuddered. "He must have been here the entire time we were practicing."

He looked over the violins, which brought him closer to her. He wanted to wrap his arms around her, offer her comfort. He closed his eyes, hands clenched, jaw tight, as he breathed in her faint scent of rain and roses. Then he scanned the table and moved quickly away from her. "He did not take any violins."

"It is fortuitous you interrupted him."

"Yes." Bayard drew out the letter from his coat pocket and frowned down at it. "I should not have been here." He handed her the letter.

She shook her head as she read. "How could they have heard about your inquiries? Did you write to them?"

"No, I have only written to the instrument shops in London, since that was where Lady Arkright had the tuning peg replaced."

"And those shops would not have idly chatted with an instrument shop in Chippenham."

"I did not feel it prudent to ignore the letter, for they may have had a legitimate reason to speak to me."

"Of course." She gave the letter back to him. "But this note conveniently would have taken you from home for several hours. The man could have observed you leaving on a day trip and then entered the house."

"It was the same man who had followed me."

Alethea exhaled and rubbed her forehead. "I should not have asked for your help. I have put you and your family in harm's way. I am sorry."

"I am the one to apologize. I did not believe you when you insisted the intruder in your bedroom had been looking for your violin. I did not take precautions when making inquiries into the violin. I was so confident I could have the answer quickly." Bayard turned his back, ashamed to face her. "I have been so arrogant."

He heard the rustle of her dress, smelled a rose-scented waft of air, and felt the soft touch of her hand upon his cuff. She was not wearing gloves and her fingers brushed the bare skin of his hand.

"You could not know," she said.

"I should have expected it. He invaded your home in broad daylight, with servants and your niece in the house."

She fully clasped his hand. Her touch was warm, her fingers strong, and his skin tingled where she touched him.

"We suspected, but we had no proof. We do now," she said.

Then she slipped her hand from his. He immediately felt the loss, like a cold draft.

The sound of her dress was a sigh in the air, an echo of her presence after she had left the music room.

※

"An unlocked window? But surely it would have been too small for anyone but a child to fit through," Lady Morrish said to Bayard at breakfast the next morning.

"The man was very slender and agile." Bayard sipped his coffee. "I have ordered all windows locked from now on."

"It is very cold," Clare said. "I can't imagine why the window would have been unlocked in the first place."

Bayard shot her a warning look, which she understood and promptly stopped speculating. He had thought of that yesterday when he discovered the storeroom window, wide but shallow, had been left open. He had asked Lucy privately if she knew if the window was usually left open, but she had not been working in the household long enough to know.

"How could he have made his way from the storeroom to the music room?" Lady Morrish fretted. "Surely someone would have seen him."

"It isn't as though the servants were on the watch for a stranger in the house," Clare said.

"He did not find what he wanted," Bayard said. "He took my notes on the violin, but that is little enough, and he did not take any of my instruments, although I am unsure that he would recognize Lady Alethea's violin if it had been among mine."

"This violin . . . Much as I like Lady Alethea, could you not simply stop investigating this affair?" Lady Morrish asked. "Would it not solve everything?"

"But how would the thief know that Bayard had stopped investigating?" Clare asked.

"Surely if we spread it about that he has withdrawn his help? After all, is that not how the thief came to know Bayard was involved with Lady Alethea's violin?"

Bayard and Clare were both silent. He could see the wisdom behind her worry.

"But, Mama," Clare said after a moment, "Lady Whittlesby has told Bay that if he discovers the truth behind Alethea's violin, she will feature the Quartet—and me too—at her concert. It would be the cachet of the season."

"But your safety is surely more important than a concert," Bayard said.

"It is not the concert, but the mark the concert will have," Clare said reasonably. "All the premier hostesses in London will invite us to their events."

"Yes, I did not receive as many invitations this past spring," Lady Morrish said slowly.

Clare bit her lip and glanced at Bayard. His jaw tightened, and he stared at the buttered eggs congealing on his plate. The rumours of the "Mad Baron" had caused several of his mother's friends to withdraw from her. Only her wedding to Sir Hermes this past summer had revived her spirits.

"Without the concert," Bayard said, "Clare could still have a good season and none of you would be in danger now."

"This is all very distressing." Lady Morrish crumbled her toast into her plate.

"I know, Mama." Bayard placed his hand over hers. "I will keep you safe."

"Dear boy, I know you shall." His mother gave him a tenuous smile and grasped his hand with hers, smearing butter over his knuckles.

At that moment, the butler entered with the post. Bayard wiped his hands and sorted through his letters. He immediately opened one from an instrument shop in London to which he had written.

Dear Lord Dommick,

In response to your inquiry of the violin previously belonging to Lady Arkright and currently in the possession of Lady Alethea Sutherton, we do recall the instrument in question. Lady Arkright brought us the violin twice. Once many years ago upon her return to England from Italy, she entrusted the violin to my father to sand down scratches on the body and replace the strings. Secondly, six years ago to replace a tuning peg. The violin's extraordinary tone has made it memorable to my father and to myself. On both occasions, we inquired of Lady Arkright about it, for while we suspected it was crafted by the incomparable Stradivari, we had never seen an instrument of its like. She described buying it from a peddler in Milan, Italy, on her wedding trip. It had been sold to the peddler, along with other inexpensive household items from a man who had recently departed of this life, by his family who had been eager to sell off the last of his possessions. Lady Arkright described the violin as the most valuable of all the peddler's wares, for the deceased man had not been wealthy. We wish Lady Alethea all the pleasure of many years of performance and wish you to convey our readiness to attend to any of her needs for her instrument.

Your obedient servants,
Samuel and Jacob Swithers
Swithers Instrument Shop, London

Bayard read the letter through two more times. While it did not convey much more information than Alethea had given to him, there was something about the story that teased at him. Something that he could use in his research. He would need to meditate upon it further.

He turned to the next letter, and it caused a tightening in his chest.

There was no postmark, so it had been delivered by hand. The handwriting was uneven, perhaps written with the left hand or by someone not well versed in his letters. It read:

> I require Lady Alethea Sutherton's violin and the sum of five hundred pounds in exchange for the safety of your sister and mother. If amenable to this transaction, hang a red cord in the front drawing room window and await instructions.

At first, he felt as cold as if entering a room with an unlit fireplace. Then his body burst into flame. He almost expected the note to turn to ashes where he crinkled it in his hand.

He wanted to ram his fist into a man's face. He wanted to smash the coffeepot. He would not stand for this.

"Is anything the matter, Bay?" Clare looked at him warily.

He smoothed the note on the table and schooled his features into a more neutral visage. "A problematic business concern."

"I do hope it will not take you from Bath," his mother said. "Ravenhurst mentioned that his mother has written. She intends to arrive within the fortnight, and you must be here to greet her and thank her for the use of her home."

"I shall make every effort."

At that moment, Raven and Ian came down to breakfast, and Bayard stood. "May I have a word with both of you in the library?"

Ian gave a sorrowful look toward the sideboard, laden with food, and Raven impatiently said, "Bring your breakfast with us, you greedy guts."

In the library, the three men gathered around a small round

table near the window. Bayard handed Raven the note, and Ian read over his shoulder while shoveling food from his piled plate into his mouth.

Raven fingered the paper. "Very fine quality. It is from someone of means." He held it up to the light. "Pity there's no watermark."

"I had suspected the grey man had been hired," Bayard said. "And Alethea mentioned that Mr. Golding, who approached her about selling the violin, had spoken of a wealthy client."

"What shall you do about this, Bay?"

"I shall certainly not submit," Bayard growled. "How dare he threaten my family? It is as good as a glove in the face."

"Not quite so honourable, for he neglected to sign his name," Ian drawled.

"While this man is alive and able to threaten me, I shall never feel secure and never be able to keep my family safe."

"If you give him the violin, he might go away." Ian flittered his fingers, although his cynical expression belied his words.

"Right now he wants the violin and five hundred pounds," Raven said. "But men like this will always push an advantage if they have one. After you give in, next he will demand something else. He will continue to endanger your family."

"He must be a very stupid person to think this would work." Ian flipped the note between his fingers.

"I don't know what to make of him," Bayard admitted. "I'm sure there are other violins less protected."

"The violin is not valuable to him," Raven said. "The violin is *precious* to him."

"That is why I need to know who the instrument belonged to. It must point to who would want it so desperately." Bayard looked at his friends. "In the meantime, may I count on you both to guard Clare and Mother?"

Raven nodded gravely, but Ian ran his fingers through his tousled hair. "Your sister will be even more annoyed by my presence than normal. And if she complains, I will tell her that you ordered it."

Raven gave Ian a sour look, then said to Bayard, "You should do your best to find the answers quickly, else your sister might do bodily harm to your friend."

Bayard remembered the letter from the instrument maker and passed that to them. "Alethea said that the peddler had wanted to be rid of the violin. The letter adds that he had bought it with other items from the household of a recently deceased man. All of low value. All unusual company for a violin that was a custom-ordered Stradivarius."

"How did the dead man acquire the violin?" Raven said. "Was he the one who ordered it, or did he buy it from the man who did?"

"Why should a nobleman's family have need to sell the man's common household items?" Ian asked. "Would not the entire estate become the property of the heir?"

"I am becoming convinced that a merchant or middle-class family somehow obtained the violin," Bayard said. "It would be something a nobleman could sell for a significant amount, if he had pressing gaming debts."

"And then our merchant died and the violin passed to our estimable peddler," Ian said.

"Have you heard yet from London about the initials?" Raven asked.

Bayard shook his head. "I wrote to the Count of Casafuori and also to Lord Mabrey to inquire of his wife, but have not heard from either as yet. Should I inquire of Italian merchants about the violin?"

"Would you really expect one Italian merchant to happen to know of another Italian merchant who died decades ago who used to play the violin? Your better course of action would be to trap this fellow." Ian tapped the extortion note on the table.

Raven's light blue eyes glittered like ice. "That sounds much more profitable."

They discussed a plan for the better part of the morning, and then Bayard found a red tapestry cord and hung it from a corner of the front window. He had misgivings, but they were overruled by his frustration and confusion as to the man he was dealing with. Why did he need this particular instrument? What sort of man would resort to these measures for a violin? He could not understand, and even worse, he could not control the situation.

The only way to ensure the protection of his family would be to stop this villain. Permanently.

CHAPTER NINE

Alethea would not have picked such a day for a walk in the park, but the house seemed too close and Margaret was restless, so she bundled them both in long, wool cloaks and sturdy half boots, commandeered one of the footmen to accompany them, and headed out into the fitful drizzle.

Aunt Ebena was positively gleeful they were both leaving. "Do not hurry back. I have no use for your brooding and her screeching," she said, referring to Margaret's fledgling efforts on the violin.

The rain did not bother Margaret, who skipped through puddles and caught drops on her tongue, but Alethea pulled her cloak around her more tightly as occasional gusts dampened her pelisse. Aunt Ebena had been correct, Alethea had been brooding. She had been trying to think of other ways she could find clues about her violin. So far, her efforts seemed pathetic and trite.

She wanted to stop reacting to things. She wanted to lash out at her enemy.

Perhaps not lash out. Perhaps . . . lure him in. With the one thing he desired, her violin. Like a rat in a trap. But what kind of trap?

The park was more occupied than Alethea would have expected, but perhaps other children had been annoying their nursery maids and governesses. As they crossed the street, Alethea happened to see a familiar figure walking toward the shopping district of town.

"Hello, John," Alethea greeted the farmer from whom she had bought vegetables at the market.

"Why, miss, how nice to see you somewhere b'sides the market-place." John tipped his hat to her, then cast a curious eye on the bored footman tailing her. "Haven't seen you lately."

"My aunt's cook has been sending one of the maids to do her shopping instead." In reality, Alethea hadn't felt safe going by herself. Aunt Ebena had preferred sending a maid or a footman to market while Alethea supervised Margaret's schooling. "How is your family? Did your youngest daughter recover from her cough?"

"Oh, aye, and shouting to bring down the rafters."

"You are doing your own shopping today?" It was not market day, but in addition, John was dressed in a finer coat than he normally wore at the marketplace.

"Going to the jeweler's. It's my wife's birthday tomorrow and I had a ring made for her."

"How lovely. I pray you will give her my compliments."

Margaret, bored with the conversation, tugged at Alethea's cloak, and the footman, slightly scandalized to witness his mistress fraternizing with a farmer, had sidled a little ways away from them.

"Good day, John."

"To you too, miss." John continued on his way, whistling and heedless of the spitting rain.

They followed a path in the park. Margaret pointed to a small girl with flyaway strawberry curls. "Look, it's Elizabeth." She ran over the wet grass toward her friend.

Mrs. Isherton, Elizabeth's mother, was with her daughter along with her maid. Mrs. Isherton's aunt was Lady Rollingwood, Aunt

Ebena's friend, but Alethea had not known her well until Margaret had joined the household. Mrs. Isherton heard of it and suggested her daughter as a suitable playmate, as they were of an age.

"I see the rain has not kept you indoors either," Mrs. Isherton said.

"The scamp was driving Aunt Ebena to distraction with her scraping on my violin."

"She will either grow bored with the instrument and lay it down, or she will master it. Your eardrums will be spared."

"But not quite *yet*."

It was awkward to Alethea to speak of raising children. She hadn't thought to ever have the duty since she had her own plans for her inheritance, and she'd always felt ashamed that she cared not for the normal things other women wanted, a husband and family. Her own examples of family love had been defective, so she couldn't imagine wanting one of her own. She had wondered if there was something wrong with her. She had avoided mothers and neighborly relationships in the country surrounding Trittonstone Park so that people would not realize how different she was.

But caring for Margaret was nothing like she had expected. Perhaps Alethea's plans for her inheritance were not because she did not want a family, but because none of the men she had met had induced her to want to change her goals.

Lord Dommick's face flashed in her mind as she had seen him yesterday after escorting her home from her visit with Clare, his dark eyes intent on hers as he bowed over her hand at the door to her home. It had been odd to her how a man's gaze had somehow given her value, like turning a stone into gold.

No, she needed no one but herself.

Mrs. Isherton nodded to where Margaret and Elizabeth chattered like magpies. "She is outgrowing her dress. She may grow as tall as yourself or Mrs. Garen."

"Oh, no. I had not noticed." Now Alethea could see that Margaret's sleeves were short for her long, wiry arms. "I just had that gown made for her."

"It is that way with them until they are grown. When you next take her to the seamstress, have the woman make the sleeves a trifle longer, and put a deeper hem in the gown so that you can let it down."

"I had not thought of that." Alethea felt woefully inadequate. "I am certainly much obliged to you for your help."

Mrs. Isherton lowered her voice. "I have learned much from the governesses and maids I have spoken with here in the park. Most mothers leave the raising of their children to servants, but I have never desired that. I want to mould my child myself and have a hand in all that concerns her."

Certainly, Alethea's own father had left her to governesses and maids, but in that case, perhaps it was just as well. Her father had been incapable of loving anyone but himself. He had had some small amusement in the companionship of his son, but no tenderness for him.

Alethea had relied on Calandra for motherly love and Lucy for sibling affection, but against her logic and reason, a part of her had insisted upon longing for some sort of approval from her father. She had scolded herself into gratitude for what she possessed. God had not been kind enough to give her a loving family, so she would accept it and rely on herself.

They continued to chat until Elizabeth, running after Margaret, fell upon the slick grass with a sound of fabric renting.

"Good gracious." Mrs. Isherton brushed at the mud on Elizabeth's dress and examined the gaping hole where a section of the skirt had come detached from her bodice. "We must return home, my dear."

"But we just arrived," Elizabeth cried.

"And there are many people here to whom I do not wish you to reveal your petticoat. Come. I bid you good day, Lady Alethea." Mrs. Isherton nodded to her, then carted her daughter and maid away.

"Must we leave?" Margaret pleaded. "I promise not to tear my dress."

Alethea eyed Margaret's dress askance. "It matters not, for you have dirtied it beyond belief. And how did you get mud in your hair?"

"Lady Alethea, if I may have a word?"

The oily voice had the power to freeze her to the spot. Heedless of the mud, she pulled Margaret close to her and turned to face Mr. Golding.

He wore a bright blue cloak today, which kept the rain from the purple ensemble peeking through its folds. He smiled that odd V-shaped smile, but his eyes were colder than the gusts of wind. He made a pretense of civility as he doffed his hat at her.

Where was the footman who had accompanied them? She turned to look but could not see him. He had wandered off while she spoke with Mrs. Isherton. She considered sending Margaret to find him, in order to get her away from Mr. Golding, but decided against allowing her to wander alone in the park.

"Mayhap you have changed your mind about selling your violin?" His pudgy hands smoothed over his wide, round belly. "Some instruments can be quite . . . dangerous to own."

The rain grew icy. Alethea's hands dug into Margaret's shoulders. The girl was silent and stiff, picking up on Alethea's tension.

She remembered the horrible sense of violation as she stared at her disheveled room. She remembered the horror of seeing Clare's limp body on the floor of the hallway.

"Money is no object," he said.

If she took his offer, she would not have to wait for her inheritance. She could find a small house in which to live with Lucy.

Once the war ended, they would go to Italy. She would seek out the music masters and be accepted into the circles of people who understood how music drew emotions from the listeners, fed emotions into warm hearts.

But it was Calandra's violin she was bargaining with. Taking it to Italy would be like bringing Calandra with her. When Alethea's life had been darkness, Calandra had been light. Only when Calandra had died had Alethea's brother been able to hurt her. The last two knuckles of her left hand throbbed once, painfully.

And as she stared into Mr. Golding's brown eyes, she saw the malice lurking there like a dragon. She thought of what Calandra would want her to do.

The passionate Italian woman would have told her, *Fight! Fight for what is important to you. When you give in to evil, you give up a piece of yourself to them.*

"I do not surrender to bullies," Alethea spat.

His eyes narrowed and his smile disappeared. "This is a simple business transaction, milady. You must be reasonable."

"It is a business transaction if both parties are willing to negotiate. I am not. The violin is not for sale."

His voice grew less polished, more animallike. "I can make your life very unpleasant if you don't comply." His eyes drifted to Margaret. "Your life, and everyone you care about."

Margaret tore herself from Alethea's hands. "You don't frighten me. I won't let you hurt me or Cousin Alethea. Now leave us alone."

"I'll leave you alone when your cousin sees reason."

"My answer is still no. I can protect my family." Alethea feigned a firmness she did not feel.

"You foolish girl." He stepped forward and grabbed her shoulders, his fingers digging so deep that it felt like two pokers had driven into her flesh. "How can you protect them when you cannot even protect yourself?"

"Let go of her!" Margaret grabbed his hand and hung off of it.

"Margaret, find Bill!" The footman had to be nearby.

But instead, Margaret sank her teeth into the exposed flesh of Mr. Golding's wrist.

He gave a hoarse cry and released Alethea, jerking his hand away from Margaret.

The girl never did anything by halves. Bright blood dripped from a deep half circle of teeth marks on the back of his wrist.

With a snarl, Mr. Golding drew back a meaty paw and back-handed Margaret across the face. She twirled for a moment like a leaf, then crumpled to the muddy ground.

"Margaret!"

Mr. Golding lifted a foot as if to kick her, but Alethea launched herself at him, pulling his hair and jerking at his cravat. He twisted back and forth, shoving her away. She fell hard on the ground, the back of her head bouncing against the dirt.

"Oy!" The shout sounded like the growl of a large dog. Then John filled her vision, planting a facer upon Mr. Golding's jaw.

The man staggered back, hands grabbing his face, leaving streaks of blood upon his skin from Margaret's bite.

John was a head taller than Mr. Golding and with his stout physique and the fire in his eyes, he seemed quite intimidating to Alethea.

He apparently seemed that way to Mr. Golding as well, for the round man turned and ran, his blue cloak billowing behind him.

John knelt beside her. "Are you hurt, miss?"

"I don't think so." The back of her head ached, but that was the worst of her pains. "Is Margaret injured?"

"I wish I'd kicked him in the shins too!" Margaret's voice was full of ire.

Alethea sat up and saw Margaret already halfway to her feet. John helped Alethea to stand while Margaret picked leaves out of her brown curls.

"Did he hurt you?" Alethea touched Margaret's face, and the cheek he had hit was warm to the touch and swollen.

Margaret pulled her head away with a slight wince. "Stop fussing."

"Ye'll have a beautiful black eye come tomorrow," John said cheerfully.

"Will I?" Margaret grinned. "I shall have to show Elizabeth."

Alethea turned to the farmer. "Thank you, John. I do not know what we should have done without you."

"I did what any decent man would."

"You did more than Bill," Margaret said darkly.

"Where is he?" Alethea's jaw hardened as she looked around.

"The footman 'oo was with you earlier?" John jerked a thumb over his shoulder. "I passed him back there, flirting with a maid-servant. 'Ere he is now."

Bill came wandering back to them from between the trees. The sight of Alethea and Margaret covered in mud made him goggle.

"Fine job you've done," John growled. "While you were dallying with that tart, your mistress was attacked."

"Wot?" Bill's mouth became as round as his eyes.

"I'll escort you home, shall I?" John said to Alethea.

She shook her head. "Go home to your wife. We are not far. And thank you, John, with all my heart."

"Only too glad to be of service to you, miss."

"Thank you, sir." Margaret waved to him as he strode away.

"I, uh . . . I'm sorry fer being distracted, milady," Bill said.

She speared him with her gaze but said nothing. She turned to Margaret. "Come. We must get out of our wet things."

She didn't know what induced her to look back over her shoulder, but as they passed out of the park, she turned in the direction Mr. Golding had gone.

And saw the cadaverous man.

He leaned bonelessly against a tree. In his grey clothes, he almost blended into the background, his figure smudged by the falling rain. He was looking directly at her.

Then he smiled. And as before, it was not a nice smile.

He turned and sauntered away, following in the footsteps of the departed Mr. Golding.

❧

The second note was hand delivered like the first. Bayard questioned the servants, but the maid simply said that a scruffy boy at the backdoor shoved the note into her hand and raced off.

"Was it the same boy as before?" Bayard asked. She had been the maid to accept the first note.

"No, milord. I've never seen him in my life."

He also received a note from Alethea asking him to call today as she had something to discuss, but the trap Bayard and his friends had set required them to be engaged for most of the morning. And perhaps by this evening there would be an end to this business, and he could bring her the happy news.

Bayard had sent his valet, Ord, to buy a violin yesterday, and between the two of them, managed to stain it to approximate the colour of Alethea's instrument. It had been Ian who drew the initials upon the neck. From a distance it would look like the coveted violin, although if anyone knowledgeable enough played it, the jig was over.

The note instructed Bayard to be at the Fairy Grotto near the Chinese bridge in Sydney Gardens at eleven o'clock, so Ian and Raven left at half past nine. Bayard impatiently paced his rooms while Ord sat at a table finishing the touches on the faux violin.

"Pacing won't bring the battle sooner, milord," Ord said as he set the violin in its case and closed the cover. He had been Bayard's batman during his days on the Peninsula; he had a strict sense of honour and correctness.

"I don't wish to think of this as a battle, Ord," Bayard said softly.

His friend grew grave.

Bayard finally said, "Are you certain you do not wish me to drive you partway to the gardens?"

Ord gave him a look that clearly indicated he was aware Bayard was talking out of nervousness, for they had arranged yesterday for Ord to walk to the rendezvous point. It would be too simple for the grey man or someone else to be watching Bayard's carriage and follow it. The follower would see him dropping his servant off at some point and suspect some scheme to interrupt the business transaction.

Ord finally glanced at the clock and stood. "I'll be off, milord. Do pace around the room so as not to wear the carpet in one spot."

"I had better not see you or recognize you at the gardens," Bayard growled.

"Do not worry, milord, I shall be careful," Ord replied, for that was what Bayard had really meant.

He spent a painful half hour waiting until it was time to leave. He conspicuously carried the violin in its case and a large sack of pound notes through the front door to his carriage, which had been pulled up before the house.

It was bitterly cold today, and while there was no snow, the air burned his nose. He instructed his coachman to drive slowly so that anyone following him would have no trouble.

He exited the coach before the Sydney Hotel and walked into the Gardens. He was not certain where the Fairy Grotto was, but he was familiar with the bridge in the Chinese style that spanned the canal. He met few people on his way because of the weather, and he worried that the lack of crowds would make Ord stand out. Would the man after the violin recognize Bayard's valet?

He crossed the bridge and came across a bower shaded by

sparse tree limbs with a seat carved with a winged fairy along the side. He sat down and looked around.

A maid strolled with a young man, who looked by his clothing to be a groom. A man on horseback who looked vaguely familiar to Bayard nodded to him as he rode down a nearby path. Two young women in warm spencers walked briskly down another gravel path, chatting with each other. There was no one else.

Then from behind him, in the foliage at the foot of the trees, a rustling and a hissed, "Ow! That was my foot."

"Be quiet, you two," Bayard said under his breath.

"You haven't been crouching here in the cold for the past hour," groused Ian.

"Nor has he had to listen to you complain the entire time," Raven said.

"You weren't seen?" Bayard asked.

"Not as far as we could tell. We took the punt down the canal and climbed up at the rough stairs cut in the stones at the south end of the gardens," Raven said.

"Didn't see Ord," Ian said.

"Then he's doing his job," Bayard said.

They waited in silence for ten minutes, then a whistling broke through the cold winter air like ice being shattered. The bright peacock colour of a waistcoat flitted through the trees, coming toward him. As the person drew nearer, Bayard saw it was not a peacock-coloured waistcoat, but a peacock-coloured coat, with a claret-coloured waistcoat straining over a large, round belly. From Alethea's description, it appeared Bayard was about to meet the infamous Mr. Golding.

The man sat casually next to Bayard as though they were good friends. He smiled, a strange V-shaped smile that made his eyes glitter rather like a snake's. "Good morning, Lord Dommick." Mr. Golding's jaw was swollen and bruised.

"Had a brush with someone?"

The smile flattened, and his gloved hand reached up to touch the swollen skin.

"Let us hope it was not a woman." Bayard gave him a bland smile.

"You have the violin?" the man snapped.

Bayard gestured to the case on the seat beside him.

Mr. Golding pursed his full lips and studied Bayard. "Play it," he said in a honeyed voice.

Bayard kept his face relaxed, but his stomach clenched. He should have listened to Ian, who had brought up this possibility. "The cold has affected the strings."

"Play it, or I will send a message to my man watching your home to enter into your sister's room this time."

Bayard's entire body grew taut.

Mr. Golding stiffened, but then lifted his chin against the expression in Bayard's eyes. "Play the violin, Lord Dommick, if you please."

The violin was a badly made practice violin, and he wasn't certain how the staining they'd done would affect the sound. Was Mr. Golding experienced enough to notice?

Bayard stood and took his time removing the cover. At that moment, he saw the bushes behind the bench shift and Ian's face appeared.

Bayard quickly glanced to Mr. Golding, but the man sat on the bench, facing forward, and did not notice.

Ian mouthed, *Bach Adagio.* Bayard knew immediately he meant Bach's violin concerto in G minor, the first movement, adagio. They had played it often in university, and it had a slightly discordant opening that would work perfectly for the imperfect violin.

He positioned the instrument, then struck the first double-stop. The violin had a tinny sound, but the melancholy music hid some of its worst tones. He did not tempt fate for long and stopped within a few measures. As he dropped the bow away, he exhaled a low, shaky breath.

Mr. Golding gave mocking applause. "Well, at least you have not tricked me on that score. Have you the money as well?"

Bayard noticed the slight tremor of his hand as he reached for the sack of pound notes and shook it, but he did not give it to Mr. Golding.

"That is very satisfactory. You may—"

He was interrupted by rustling in the bushes behind Bayard, then a violent scuffling of earth and leaves, punctuated by grunts. Mr. Golding shot off the bench. There was the thud of a fist impacting flesh, then another. Then a man was flung through the foliage, who landed hard against the back of the seat and flipped over it.

The man was a stranger, with a face like a roughly cut stone. He had hands the size of small boulders and a solidly built torso under the dirty woolen tunic.

Ian and Raven burst out of the trees, but the man lumbered to his feet and moved away from them. Raven's knuckles blushed red.

Bayard turned to Mr. Golding. "What is the meaning of this?"

Mr. Golding was already backing away. "I should say the same of you, Lord Dommick. You never would have known my associate was present if you had not also had compatriots hidden."

"Did you think I would meet with you alone?" Bayard tried to sound reasonable.

"You would if you were serious about trading the violin." Mr. Golding was now several yards away. "I will consider this a definitive answer to my inquiry and assume you have no interest in completing our transaction." The man turned and ran.

Bayard hastened after him, but while he had the advantage of height and stride length, Mr. Golding obviously knew the gardens better and had slipped out of sight before Bayard was winded. Ian was only a few steps behind him when he stopped.

"Slippery fellow," Ian said.

"Raven?"

"He's after the man with the granite fists." Ian rolled his shoulder. "He got a solid blow on me before Raven gave him a nice poke in the eye."

"I am all astonishment," Bayard said dryly.

"I wouldn't have been surprised by him sneaking up on us if I hadn't been saving your bacon."

"I owe you for that."

"Too right, you do."

They returned to the grotto to find Raven there, looking grim. "A great beast such as that should not have been able to catch us unawares. We knew there was a possibility the man would have had his own associate sneaking around."

"Can a plan be more botched than this?" Bayard muttered.

As Bayard gathered the sack of pound notes and the faux violin, Ian said, "I didn't see Ord."

"It will be excellent as long as we don't see him." Bayard headed down the gravel walk, flanked by his two friends. "It will mean he is still following Mr. Golding."

CHAPTER TEN

*T*he card party was an insipid affair, although Alethea admitted her foul mood made it especially less enjoyable for herself.

Seated at the hostess's pianoforte, Alethea pounded out a Bach sinfonia in F minor at a funereal pace. It suited her frustrations, which had plagued her since speaking to Dommick earlier today.

"I believe you are playing that too fast," Lord Ian said as he came up behind her.

She ignored him and embellished a note into a particularly dismal chord.

"I take it you did not agree with Bayard's decision?" Lord Ravenhurst appeared on the other side of her.

"Why is it *his* decision?" she snapped. "It was *my* idea."

"You fired it at him rather suddenly," Lord Ian said. "You must give him time to think it over."

"He doesn't want to go through with it because he won't perform with a woman." She finished the sinfonia and switched to the fugue in a Bach Toccata in the key of C minor so she could pound out a smashing minor chord.

Lord Ian rattled his finger in his ear. "I believe that piece is supposed to be melancholy, not angry."

"He didn't wish to pursue your idea because he felt it would be too dangerous," Lord Ravenhurst said over the thunderous chords she was producing. "Only consider, we had called upon you bare hours after our trap in Sydney Gardens had failed and Ord had lost Mr. Golding, only to be met with your aunt's niece sporting a purple eye. And then you suggested playing in our concert in order to display yourself and your violin as bait. You must excuse him for being alarmed."

"If he truly wishes to protect me and my family, our best course of action is to be on the attack. And after *your* trap had failed, all the better reason to attempt *my* trap."

"I do not understand why you two are working separately rather than together," Lord Ravenhurst muttered.

"My point exactly. Which is why I should play in your concert in a few weeks with my violin to lure the villain out."

"Bayard might be more amenable to the suggestion if he were to play the violin instead of yourself."

"Many men would hesitate to attack another man who might overpower him, whereas the villain would be overly confident in attacking a woman, who is physically inferior. And all of you will be there to protect me."

"There will also be dozens of people and servants, any one of whom may be hired to kidnap you or harm you."

"The point is that it is a *trap*. We shall be tricking him into doing precisely what we want."

Lord Ian sighed. "You are quite as stubborn as Bayard."

Alethea thought it prudent to change the topic of conversation. "Have you heard any news about Count Escalari? Someone mentioned he may attend tonight." Alethea peeked up to glance around the room before she had to look back down at her hands on the keyboard.

"Is he expected in Bath?" Lord Ravenhurst asked.

Alethea finished the fugue on a mistaken chord, quickly corrected. She winced. "I attended tonight specifically because the rumour was that he would be here."

"From whom did you hear that?" Lord Ravenhurst asked.

"One of the maids, who had heard it from a maid from Lady Eaglen's house, who had got it from—"

"Never mind," Lord Ian said with a groan.

"Why do you wish to see him?" Lord Ravenhurst asked.

"To ask about the initials on the violin, of course. Assuming he is Italian," she said, remembering Signora D'Angelo.

"He is," Lord Ravenhurst said. "He is acquainted with my mother."

"How fortuitous. Would you be so kind as to introduce me?"

"Lord Ravenhurst, Lord Ian." The hostess, Mrs. Penning, approached the pianoforte with Mr. Kinnier in tow. "I insist you two accompany me. There are two young ladies I wish you to meet."

Lord Ravenhurst bowed with his usual politeness, although there were tight lines around his mouth. Lord Ian, however, gave Mr. Kinnier an icy stare.

Mrs. Penning continued, "I have brought Mr. Kinnier to turn Lady Alethea's pages for her."

Lord Ian glanced at Alethea. She gave him a subtle nod. What in the world about Mr. Kinnier so offended Lord Ian?

As Mrs. Penning led the two men away, Mr. Kinnier turned to her with a very correct bow. "What shall you play next, Lady Alethea? I am at your service."

"I have been playing from memory, sir." She nodded toward the card tables. "I wouldn't wish to deprive you of tonight's entertainment."

He leaned closer. "In truth, you have rescued me. I am an indifferent card player, and I easily frustrate my partners. If you would allow me to keep you company here at this fine instrument, I should be most grateful."

She could hardly refuse him. She distrusted his smooth speeches, and yet she had only one overheard conversation to base her opinions upon. Was she being too harsh upon him?

Continuing in her Bach mood, she started a partita in the key of E minor. "How have you enjoyed Bath so far, Mr. Kinnier?"

"It is quite lively. I have heard that you have had some excitement."

Her fingers twitched, causing her to miss a note, but she picked up immediately and it was hardly noticeable. "Excitement? I assure you, my life is hardly exciting." Could he have somehow found out about Mr. Golding and Margaret in the park?

"Why, the mystery about your violin is quite intriguing."

"How so? It is a fine instrument, and I would naturally wish to know more of its history."

"Many instruments have quite treacherous histories, full of theft, extortion, and violence."

Her fingers crashed into a chord that Bach had never intended to be played in his piano piece. What did Mr. Kinnier know? What was he insinuating? What did he want?

"Oh, forgive me, Lady Alethea, I did not mean to alarm you. I was not serious. I am sure Lord Dommick will discover that your violin has a quite innocuous history."

She was overreacting, surely. And yet, why would he use those particular words to describe her violin? She could not read his mood or his thoughts, for his face was as pleasant as ever. She continued with the partita.

Mr. Kinnier added, "And Lord Dommick is . . . creative in his ideas."

"What do you mean, sir?"

"His unorthodox methods certainly give the *impression* of competence."

She flared with resentment at his implication. "It is my understanding that Lord Dommick is quite knowledgeable about the violin."

"That is indeed what was said about him. But he has yet to discover anything about your violin, is that not so?"

"This case is quite difficult."

"Is it?" He gave her a significant look.

What was he saying? She wished the annoying man would speak plainly. "Mr. Kinnier, are you suggesting I find another investigator for my violin?"

"I assure you, I am not suggesting myself."

His words confused her, but they also made the tightness in her chest ease slightly.

"But are you certain Lord Dommick is capable enough to find the answers to your questions?"

His tone was reasonable, although Alethea did not care for his words. She could hardly accuse him of being self-serving since he did not volunteer his own services to her. She strove for a polite tone, but was afraid she only sounded petulant as she said, "My affairs are my own, sir."

"You are right. Forgive me." He looked sincerely contrite. "You must allow me a concern for you and your investigation, which prompted my rash words."

Alethea added an extra embellishment to the Bach piece. Not exactly a humble apology. She also did not feel the need to accept it. "You are always ever a model of polite behaviour, Mr. Kinnier. You could never say anything rude or insulting."

He appeared to take it as the forgiveness it was not. He smiled that perfect, glassy smile that made him seem less trustworthy than Dommick's stern frowns.

She rushed the Bach piece to end it quickly, then stood. "If you will excuse me, Mr. Kinnier?"

He bowed to her, and she walked away, feeling as if she had been attempting to breathe through a piece of wool and only now pulled it from her face.

Alethea hid in the cloak room for a few moments, then headed
to the dining parlour where a buffet had been set out. She didn't
care to return to the card room and risk enduring more of Mr.
Kinnier's innuendoes, whether innocent or deliberate, but she
hoped to find guests who might know when Count Escalari would
arrive in Bath.

She was in luck. There were two groups of women in the room,
one with Mrs. Isherton and Mrs. Layston, an older lady who was a
friend of Aunt Ebena, and also Miss Oakridge and Miss Nanstone
standing in front of the buffet, picking at the lobster patties and cold
tongue. The girls stopped chattering as soon as they saw Alethea,
then burst into a fit of giggles.

Alethea approached Mrs. Isherton and Mrs. Layston with a
smile. "Good evening."

"We heard your lovely playing," Mrs. Isherton said.

"I was just telling Mrs. Isherton about my granddaughters' love
for the pianoforte," Mrs. Layston said and went into a monologue
about each granddaughter's proficiency in the instrument.

However, Alethea could not help overhearing Miss Nanstone's
nasal voice. "People have claimed that her violin is nothing more
than a cheap instrument with a dark stain and a painted symbol
upon it to give it a more interesting appearance."

Alethea kept her smile in place as she strained to hear more.
Dommick had bought a cheap violin and stained it to fool the
extortioner in Sydney Gardens. How had those facts been spread
abroad?

"But would not Lord Dommick have recognized the inferior
instrument immediately?" Miss Oakridge asked.

"That is what is most astounding. People are speculating that
Lord Dommick's supposed expertise in the violin is all a sham.
Otherwise he would have recognized that it was a forgery and
would not be continuing his investigation."

So, it was not the story of the forged violin that had reached their ears, but aspersions were being cast upon her own instrument. Alethea wondered if people would be speaking of Dommick in such a manner were he in attendance tonight.

"People have said that since she may have embellished the mystery of her violin, there may be other things she has not been entirely truthful about," Miss Nanstone said.

The prickle of thousands of needles poked her neck and back. It was the same feeling from eleven years ago during her season, when she had first heard the outrageous stories that she was a wild woman with no table manners. A part of her wanted to lash out, to defend herself, and another part of her wanted to laugh. That she, a pitied spinster, was accused of lying about her violin in order to trap Lord Dommick was nearly as ridiculous as the stories about her eating her fish with her dessert spoon.

But she did worry about the effect the gossip would have on Lord Dommick's reputation, and by extension, Clare's.

She was not entirely certain why the young ladies of Bath did not like her. She knew it was partly because they despised her for being out of the normal way. They disliked independence of any sort and so would not care for hers.

However, especially at moments like these, she felt lonely. She was not married or a mother like Mrs. Isherton, yet she was not quite acceptable to the younger unmarried women. She was her own person. While that should have pleased her, it made her realize how isolated her life had been, both here in Bath and at Trittonstone Park.

No one understood her. No one cared for her and no one cared to know her. They treated her as though something were wrong with her . . .

No, she was being melancholy. She had confidence in who she was, no matter what others said about her. She shook off her dark mood and remembered her initial intention for seeking Mrs. Isherton. Mrs. Layston had finally reached her last granddaughter, and even Mrs. Isherton's eyes looked slightly glazed.

Alethea interrupted before Mrs. Layston could launch into her grandsons as well. "Ladies, have you heard ought of Count Escalari? Will he arrive tonight?"

"Oh, not tonight," Mrs. Layston said. "He is expected tomorrow."

Excellent. Alethea might meet him this week. "He will be a refreshing addition to our society."

"Indeed," Mrs. Isherton said. "I believe he enjoys music a great deal, so you may have much to speak about with him."

Alethea stayed to hear Mrs. Layston as she indeed spoke of each of her grandsons, then excused herself. The pianoforte was still abandoned, so she returned to her spot. She was almost immediately joined again by Lord Ravenhurst and Lord Ian.

"I had wondered where you were," Lord Ian said. "If I am not mistaken, Raven was most desperate for you to come and tell us that Lady Morrish had need of us or something or other."

"I was nothing of the sort." Lord Ravenhurst jerkily adjusted his cravat and turned his back to the general direction of the two ladies they had been speaking to.

Lord Ian's face grew hard as he said, "I congratulate you in that you managed to escape Mr. Kinnier."

"I would think you and the gentleman have much in common," she said carefully.

Lord Ian looked offended. "Not likely."

She didn't wish to pry. "I left him in order to find out more about Count Escalari. He is expected in Bath tomorrow."

"In answer to your previous question, I would be honoured to introduce you to him," Lord Ravenhurst said.

"Thank you, my lord." She hesitated. "I heard gossip about Lord Dommick that concerned me."

Lord Ravenhurst and Lord Ian looked more worried than she would have expected about an idle rumour. "What was it?"

She repeated what she had heard about the false violin and Dommick's inability to see through the ruse. "I would not have thought much of it if Mr. Kinnier had not mentioned the same slur earlier."

Lord Ravenhurst looked grave. "He will be distressed over the repercussions of the gossip upon Clare and his mother."

Alethea could envision how the rumours might harm Clare's debut. "The way to counter people's opinions would be to quickly capture the violin thief."

Lord Ravenhurst looked to Ian. "Perhaps these new rumours will cause Bayard to revisit his earlier objections to having Alethea play her violin at our concert."

Lord Ian winked at Alethea. "Have you been practicing?"

"Of course." In addition to Dommick's concerto, Lord Ian had given her music for concertos he and Lord Ravenhurst had recently completed as well as two popular pieces the Quartet had played in London years ago. She diligently practiced second violin for all five pieces, but Dommick's violin concerto was her favourite. Something about it made her almost uncomfortable, as though it exposed some vulnerability of the composer that she was not meant to see, but perhaps she was feeling guilty that Dommick did not know she had a copy of his music.

"Practicing what?" Lord Ravenhurst demanded.

"I sent her copies of the two concertos you and I recently finished writing."

Lord Ravenhurst's eyebrows rose, although he did not look unduly upset to hear this.

Lord Ian flipped his hair away from his forehead as he continued, "And I sent her a copy of Bay's newest violin piece."

Lord Ravenhurst did not quite roll his eyes, but he did look up at the moulding on the ceiling. "He will kill you."

"I didn't give the pieces to Lady Alethea with the intention of featuring her in the concert, but I'm beginning to believe it to be a good idea."

Alethea smiled at him. "I shall wait for you both to speak to

Lord Dommick. In the meantime, what will be the harm in practicing ahead of time?"

⤞⧫⤝

"I am sorry, milord, but Lord Ravenhurst is not in," Raven's valet told Bayard.

"Where did he go?" Bayard asked.

"I believe he and Lord Ian were intending to call upon Mrs. Garen."

Bayard hurried out of the house and walked toward Queen Square. He had heard this morning that the Count of Escalari had arrived in Bath, and Bayard wanted Raven to arrange an interview with him so he could show him the initials from the violin.

It was barely ten o'clock in the morning, and it seemed odd for Raven and Ian to visit Alethea. Or perhaps they had some errand to run for his mother that involved Mrs. Garen.

He did not want to ponder the suspicion that perhaps one or both of his friends were romantically inclined toward Alethea. After all, what would it be to him? He could not become intimate with any woman, not while the nightmares still plagued him. He must first conquer his problems before he could risk letting anyone close to him.

The day was cold, so he walked quickly, but his mind returned to the two letters he had received this morning, both from his contacts in London with connections to the Italian nobility. Neither had known of any Italian nobles with those initials. His investigation was at an impasse.

He was forced to consider Alethea's suggestion of using her and the violin as bait in their concert in two weeks. Everything within himself rejected the notion of putting her in such a dangerous situation, but he saw the wisdom of her plan, and a part of him even applauded her courage.

Was it courage or foolhardiness? He didn't know.

He was approaching the house when he heard strains of music. The sound was faint, so at first he believed it was only a single violin, but as he drew nearer, he realized it was two. Was Ian playing with Alethea? Perhaps she had wanted more instruction in the instrument. Was she so much more comfortable with Ian that she would ask him for help and not Bayard?

It was after he had knocked on the door that he recognized the piece they were playing.

It was his.

It was untitled. He had started it the morning after meeting Alethea again in Bath. He had poured more of himself into that composition than he had felt in a long time. She was in every line, every measure. His frustrations, his attraction to her, even the nebulous intensity stirring deep inside had been written into that piece. It was a private part of him. It was a real part of him, which he hadn't had the courage to show to anyone else. Even Ian and Raven did not quite understand him in this inner place, but he had written the piece because somehow he knew, from that first short, tense conversation, that Alethea would understand him. And it made him afraid.

And she was playing it.

The butler opened the door, but Bayard could only stare in shock. Bayard looked down at his waistcoat. He had been ripped open. He should be bleeding.

"My lord?"

Somehow she had gotten possession of it and was playing it.

He suddenly saw only a red, blazing haze before his eyes. He pushed past the startled butler, and before he knew it, he was at the drawing room door and slamming it open.

Mrs. Garen started in her seat near the fireplace. Bayard's gaze swung around the room and came to rest on Alethea and Ian standing in front of two music stands, with Raven sitting at the table nearby.

"How dare you?" he demanded.

Ian hastily put down his violin. "Bay, listen—"

He suddenly understood how she had acquired that particular piece of music. Ian must have taken it from the music room, made a copy for her, and then replaced it before Bayard knew it had been missing. Why that music? Of all the pieces he could have taken?

"How could you take it and give it to *her*?" It was coming out all wrong but he couldn't stop himself.

"Lord Dommick!" Mrs. Garen's strident tones sliced through his pain, his shock. She had risen and stood tall and magnificent, horrified by this spectacle, ready to instill order.

He did not want order. He wanted to be rid of this feeling that Alethea had somehow seen inside him.

Dommick turned and left, pounding down the stairs and out the front door.

He didn't remember the walk back to the Crescent. He remembered the cold wind, which at some point swept away his hat so that he arrived at the front door hatless.

That piece of music. He had wondered what he would do with it, if he would ever have the courage to show it to her. He had wondered what it would sound like if she played it, and yet a part of him had not wanted to think about it. She could never see it. No one could see it, or they would immediately know his confusion and weakness.

Oh, God, how could you let this happen?

The butler gave him a startled look when he entered the house, but quickly dissolved his curiosity into an unobservant mask. Bayard didn't remember him removing his greatcoat. He suddenly found himself in the drawing room. He had come here out of habit, but he did not want to be here. He needed to be alone. He turned almost immediately to leave when the nearly inaudible sobs stopped him.

Mama sat alone upon the sofa, face buried in her handkerchief, trying not to cry out loud.

"Mama," he whispered.

Her hand flew to her mouth. She turned her face away, trying to staunch the tears still falling. Her shoulders were hunched and shaking.

He was by her side in a moment, arm around her, pushing her face into his shoulder. He had held her like this earlier this year, in London, when he had come across her after the visit of some of her "friends" who had relayed the vicious rumours about the "Mad Baron."

Last night at the dinner party he had attended, he had heard new rumours. People were disparaging his abilities, and the remembrances of the "Mad Baron" had been resurrected.

"All will be well, Mama."

"It will not." She sobbed even more. He caught her cries in the superfine of his coat, wiped her tears with his cravat.

She calmed enough for her breath to no longer come in gasps. "Bayard, Mr. Morrish attempted to kiss Clare, and she slapped him."

His hand on her back clenched into a fist. In a low voice he said, "When did this happen?"

"Today, upstairs in the hallway outside her bedchamber. He should not have been there." Her voice rose at the end of her sentence. "I ordered him out of the house. Sir Hermes is to return from the hot baths soon. I don't know what I shall tell him."

"I will speak to him."

"No." She inhaled a shaky breath. "I will speak to him. Clare is my daughter. It must come from me." She sobbed once, then said, "I should have listened to you."

"Don't think that, Mama."

"I did not like Mr. Morrish's behaviour no matter what he said to Sir Hermes, but I did not want to displease him." She began crying again.

He tightened his arms around her. All his life, he remembered his mother nervously wanting to please his exacting father and hurt by his cold reaction when she did not. His father never publicly humiliated his mother, but the servants knew he berated her behind closed doors. His children knew how he had insulted her.

Bayard had shown his father respect, but they never spoke of his father's behaviour toward his mother. When he died last summer, Bayard could not say he missed him.

He wanted to always protect his mother, but he had been able to do nothing about his father's treatment of her. He had been able to do nothing as his mother agreed with everything Sir Hermes decided about his nephew.

He could do nothing now, but he would not leave her alone.

༄

"You are no longer welcome in my house."

Sir Hermes's pronouncement was not said in a loud voice, but Bayard heard it echoing off the high ceiling of the front entrance foyer. Mr. Morrish had not yet even divested himself of his hat or coat.

Sir Hermes stood before his nephew, his round face no longer jovial. He looked like a wild boar, small but dangerous. His expression did not change as Mr. Morrish attempted to explain.

"Uncle, I assure you—"

"You can say nothing that would induce me to change my mind."

Watching this scene from the first landing of the stairs, Bayard tightened his arms around his mother on one side and Clare on the other. His sister had buried her face in his shoulder, but his mother watched her husband with eyes wide despite the tears falling from them. Her arm around Bayard's waist tightened.

"I wanted to believe you," Sir Hermes said. "I thought you were like your mother, who was always misunderstood, who was lighthearted and loved a good joke. But you have caused pain to my wife and insulted my stepdaughter."

"Uncle—"

"You made Lady Morrish cry, you cad!"

And Bayard then understood how he had misjudged his stepfather. Sir Hermes was a bit of a fool, but it sprang from his tendency to only see the good in people, even though they would deceive him. And despite his faults, Sir Hermes did truly love his mother and would do anything to keep her happy.

Sir Hermes signaled to the butler, who stood like a statue against the wall during this exchange. The servant opened the door, letting in a freezing column of air that swirled around Bayard's legs and made his sister's muslin dress flap around her ankles.

Mr. Morrish stood in a state of indecision, unsure if he ought to try to cajole his uncle or give in to the anger simmering behind his pale eyes. Then his gaze fell on Bayard and Clare, and a sneer settled upon his mouth.

He turned and left, and the butler shut the door with a snap.

Sir Hermes seemed to deflate. Lady Morrish rushed down the stairs and embraced him, acting as a crutch as she stumbled up the stairs with him. Bayard approached them to help, but Mama waved him away. They continued up the staircase to their bedchamber.

Clare took Bayard's hand, just as she used to do when they were children. He drew her to the music room and sat her down in a chair. "How are you feeling?"

"I am well. He frightened me at first, but he was so shocked when I struck him that I was able to run back into my room."

"Where was your maid?" He had hired Lucy specifically to protect his sister.

"Don't blame her, Bay. She was in my bedchamber, putting away my clothes. I chose to go downstairs on my own. I did not know Mr. Morrish was in the house or that he would dare venture to the second floor."

"He should have been watched more carefully."

"You could hardly order a footman to shadow him, Bay. And he would not have heeded a servant. He tried to prevent Lucy from informing Mama, but she evaded him. When Mama ordered him from the house, he said the most horrid things about spreading rumours about me."

Bayard paced the floor. Rumours and lies had become the invisible enemy he could not vanquish. He could not shoot a lie or run his sword through an innuendo. And the worst of it was that he could not protect his family from them either.

He felt so helpless. Of what use was he if not to protect them?

He had to bring an end to all this, to solve the mystery of the violin. It would accomplish everything—the danger to his family and to Alethea would cease, it would bring him and Clare the éclat of Lady Whittlesby's concert in the spring, and that would counter any rumours Mr. Morrish might spread so that they wouldn't impact Clare's season or hurt his mother.

Alethea had been right. He would have to be more aggressive.

He paused, his throat tightening at the memory of this morning, hearing his music played by her violin. He was aware that he had hurt her, although not intentionally. He had been lashing out at Ian and the words came out wrong. He could apologize, but he didn't know what would make her understand his hurt, his frustration, this feeling that he was raw and bleeding.

His father would mock him. Men were not to feel hurt. They were to fight through the pain. And Bayard had done so, all through the Peninsula until Corunna, where he had seen the gates of hell.

Now he was a weak shell of who he had once been, trying to hide the fact that he had returned from war with something broken in his mind.

"Bay, what should we do?" Clare's voice brought him back to the music room, to the slight chill in the air not dispelled by the numerous fireplaces.

"Act on the offensive."

CHAPTER ELEVEN

*A*lethea had opened the front door to head to the park with Margaret when she came face-to-face with the one face she'd seen in her head all night.

"Dommick." The name came out strangled.

He lowered his hand from where he'd been about to raise the door knocker. He looked as if coal had been smudged under his eyes, and his normally immaculate dark hair had been twisted by the breeze, for he had removed his hat. "You are going out?"

"To the park."

"May I . . ." He swallowed. "May I accompany you?"

She swallowed also. "Yes." She busied herself in ordering the new footman to return to his duties rather than accompany them. Bill had been turned off by an irate Aunt Ebena after what had happened to Margaret.

Margaret was studying Dommick with a critical eye. "I do not know that I wish him to come with us."

"Margaret," Alethea said. "Pray do not be rude."

"He was rude yesterday."

"He was not rude to *you*."

Dommick gave Margaret a formal bow. "I am come to apologize. Will you allow me to do so?"

Margaret pretended to think about it, then gave a regal nod.

Alethea wished all would be well with so simple a gesture, but her heart was bruised and her emotions stormy. And the worst of it was that she did not really understand what she was feeling.

She closed the door and they all headed to the park. "You may apologize to Alethea now," Margaret said grandly to Dommick.

"May I apologize to you first for upsetting your household?"

A gleam appeared in Margaret's eye. "I will if you will buy me my own violin to practice on."

"Margaret!" Alethea was mortified.

"Alethea is always practicing on hers and I am only allowed to borrow it, and then only when Aunt Ebena is out of the house since she says the sound causes her indigestion. Although I don't understand how violin music can affect one's stomach."

Perhaps when the "music" sounds like a dozen shrieking fishwives, Alethea reflected.

"I would be most happy to procure a violin for you," Dommick said.

"Dommick, no," Alethea said. "Margaret, your response to him was highly inappropriate."

"My response to you was highly inappropriate." He turned to her, and the expression in his eyes caused the storm in her stomach to rumble and bluster. "I beg you will allow me this small token."

"Oh, please, Alethea." Margaret tugged at her sleeve.

Alethea used Margaret as an excuse to break eye contact with Dommick. "I shall consider it if you behave. You were a veritable hoyden all morning. And don't for a moment think that I have forgotten the vase you broke with the fireplace poker."

"I was only trying to act out the lesson to make it more interesting. Reading Shakespeare is quite boring."

"What were you reading?" Dommick asked Margaret.

For the rest of the walk, he managed to draw out all the most bloodthirsty portions of *Henry IV*, which delighted Margaret to no end. Alethea huddled in her pelisse and muff and tried to decide if she wanted to listen to his apology or simply deliver a stunning set down and walk away from him. Except, of course, that she couldn't think of a suitably stunning set down, and she couldn't abandon Margaret into his care either.

At the park, Margaret wandered off to annoy any wildlife to be found, and Dommick turned to Alethea. "Let me explain—"

"No, I should like to speak first." Her hands were shaking where they pressed into her churning belly. "Your behaviour was shocking yesterday. You embarrassed me in front of my aunt and your friends, and your reaction was inappropriate."

"All true." His face was grave.

"Stop being agreeable. I am not finished." She huffed in a breath. "I asked Lord Ian for a copy of your violin music since I had had difficulty procuring it, and I certainly did not realize he would copy an unpublished piece. I am quite offended at your disapproval of the fact that I was playing it. Why should not a woman play your music? Your objection is preposterous—"

He stopped her speech by reaching out to grab hold of her shoulders. He leaned his head closer to hers, his eyes intense. She realized, in astonishment, that behind his embarrassment and contrition, he was in great pain.

"I did not object to your playing my music because you are a woman." His voice was low with a slight tremor. "I started writing that piece the day after I met you again in Bath."

She inhaled . . . and could not exhale. She suddenly saw his anger in a completely different light.

"I was embarrassed that you heard the piece, much less played it," he continued. "When I was writing it, it was a very . . . consuming composition."

She had known this, even as she practiced it, even in only hearing her own instrument and not the full effect of both violins. There had been something aching in the music. She had been anticipating practicing with Lord Ian so that she could hear and feel it fully. And now she knew why it had called to her.

Dommick's hands dropped from her shoulders, and he took a half step back. "It does not excuse my behaviour. I deeply apologize for what I said. I was upset and disconcerted because, in many ways . . . the piece was for you."

She stood there, unable to speak, unable to move. Something about this man made her want to cry, made her want to throw herself into his arms. She simply stared at his downturned profile, the hawklike nose, the dark winging brows, the firm jawline.

He straightened, seemed to collect himself. He was the old Dommick, slightly more handsome and slightly more aloof than she liked. "I have no right to ask this of you, but would you consider entering into your original plan with me?"

"Using me and the violin as bait in your concert? Will you be quite resigned to playing in a public concert with a woman on a violin?" She lifted her eyebrows in challenge to him.

"My objections were for the sake of my sister. I could not allow any slur to my reputation to reflect poorly upon her, and unconventionality is one thing polite society does not make light of."

"I had not thought of the impact upon your sister." She had been only too ready to battle him for her right to play. "This concert will do exactly what you fear."

"I no longer fear it, for the outcome will outweigh any momentary discomfort. You were right. We have been reacting to this man's schemes. We need to act on one of our own."

She watched Margaret chasing ducks and tried to sort through what she was feeling, but it was no use. She was feeling a multitude of things at once. "What do you wish me to do?"

"The concert has been set for tomorrow, fortnight. There is not much time to prepare. Can you come to Raven's house this afternoon to practice?"

"With my violin? Will that be quite safe?"

"I shall call with my carriage, but you would need to conceal it as you left the house."

"I could hide it under my cloak."

"Shall I call for you at three o'clock?"

She pursed her lips as she regarded him. "I have not yet said that I forgive you."

Then he rattled her with that devastating smile that brought out the laugh lines radiating from the corners of his eyes and deepening the creases alongside his mouth. "Perhaps you will consider it when I tell you that I have a new composition."

"What sort of composition?"

"For two violins, a violoncello, and pianoforte." He bowed to her. "I am asking you to make up the fourth of the Quartet."

❧

Alethea scurried into Dommick's carriage rather awkwardly since she had the violin in a case hidden under her cloak and it banged against her knees. Once she was inside, she set it on the seat next to her. Her heart pounded so hard she thought it might be seen against her dress bodice.

Across from her, Clare grinned. "How exciting this all is!"

Dommick scowled at her. "I would not have included you, brat, if propriety had not necessitated it."

"No one knows Alethea is transporting her violin, so why should there be any danger?"

"No one in your household saw you with the violin?"

Alethea shook her head. "I keep it in my bedchamber, and I hid it under my cloak while inside."

She did not like exposing the violin in this way. But her aunt's drawing room, filled with tables and chairs, did not have the spaciousness of Lord Ravenhurst's music room, which was necessary to accommodate both violinists and a violoncello player.

At the marquess's house, she thought she would need to keep her cloak until she reached the music room, which would look exceedingly odd, but as the carriage pulled up, Lord Ian met them outside. He opened the carriage door, smoothly took her violin case, and carried it into the house under his greatcoat. As the butler and maids removed their outer garments, Lord Ian casually handled the violin case as though it were his own.

"Such subterfuge," Clare said to Alethea as they headed toward the music room.

"I would prefer it were not necessary," she said.

"But think, we should not have met had you not needed Bayard's expertise."

"How do you know that Lady Alethea's existence has been enriched by your acquaintance and not the opposite?" Lord Ian asked Clare.

Clare glared at him.

"I assure you, your acquaintance has been a delight to me," Alethea said while shooting Lord Ian an exasperated look. He grinned at her.

At the music room door, Clare said, "I must attend to Mama, so Lucy will sit with you. I shall return later to hear you play." She headed toward the drawing room.

As she entered the music room, Alethea saw Lucy, for propriety's sake, seated in a corner with some mending. Her sister gave her a quick smile, then returned to her work.

The music room had been set up with three chairs and three

music stands ranged around the magnificent Broadwood piano-forte. Lord Ian handed her violin to her, and it was both strange and exhilarating when he held out her chair for her, which was not at the pianoforte.

He procured that seat for himself with a sigh. "I miss David exceedingly. Pianoforte is not my forte."

Lord Ravenhurst grunted as he took up his violoncello, a beautiful instrument with a deep golden glow in the wood. "If David were here, you would not be playing at all. I much prefer Lady Alethea to your ugly mug."

"Alethea, please take second violin." There was a speculative gleam in Dommick's eyes as he handed her the music manuscript, and her stomach tensed. In the concert, they would play the pieces she had already been practicing with Ian, but today they would play something new that he had just finished composing. She opened the manuscript.

The breath eased out of her chest as she looked it over. It was beautiful and challenging, but not extraordinarily difficult, even with her two injured fingers, which she had stretched earlier. She massaged them to warm them.

"Are you injured?" Dommick's brows lowered.

"An old injury. It is nothing." She was almost grateful to her cousin for forcing her to Bath, for only here could she have found a physician to help her regain the use of her left fingers.

She began her normal warm-up on her violin, exercises to stretch the stiff tendons in the last two fingers of her left hand, build finger speed, and increase the flexibility of her bow hand. She ran through some intonation and vibrato exercises, then skimmed through Dommick's music to finger passages that might be tricky.

She finished as the other men completed their own warm-ups. She flipped to the first page.

"We shall take the first page at a decreased tempo," Bayard said.

Lord Ian interrupted him. "Let us do a straight run-through instead."

Dommick frowned, and Alethea thought he might have glanced quickly to her.

"Try it and see," Lord Ian said cryptically.

After a moment's hesitation, Dommick nodded. "Then, from the beginning." He set the time with his bow, and with a firm nod, indicated for them to begin.

The music blasted into existence like a choir of angels, grabbing her heart and squeezing tightly. She had never before played with more than one other musician. The sound roared through her in powerful waves, chords and runs in unison that echoed from the high ceiling of the room.

The piece diverged as each instrument carried the primary melodic line in turn, weaving from one to the other in a tapestry more colourful than any hangings on the walls of Trittonstone Park. The complexity fascinated and excited her, and she eagerly played, barely aware of herself as she gloried in the rich sounds produced.

Then the music softened like the stillness of early morning on the downs, and each instrument became a bird welcoming the day, a rabbit rising up to sniff new scents on the air, the hawk soaring on the high winds above the world.

The music built like a storm, first with the pitter of raindrops, then the blustering wind, then the crashing thunder and blistering sheets of water flattening the grass. The instruments again wove into each other, one at the forefront and then the other, each carrying a storyline of the music until they all converged into a climax of nature's fury. The piece ended as if on a sigh.

Alethea was breathing heavily as she lowered her bow. Her heart felt filled with simmering emotions that spilled over—awe, sadness, tenderness, ecstasy. She closed her eyes, trying to recapture the rush of euphoria of those last measures.

"I told you," Lord Ian said in a smug voice.

She opened her eyes to find Dommick staring at her in complete astonishment. "Good Lord," he said.

She didn't know what he was referring to. The potency of his gaze made her anxiety begin to rise. "What is it?" Her voice was weaker than normal, and she cleared her throat. "What is wrong?" she demanded in a stronger tone.

"You are . . . magnificent." Dommick's voice was filled with wonder, and the yearning in his eyes was suddenly all she could see. And she knew he could see the fullness of her heart, the fragility exposed whenever she played because she played with all her being.

Dommick had heard brief strains from her violin, but unlike Lord Ian and Lord Ravenhurst, he had not seen her perform before now.

"Lady Alethea, you see Bayard flabbergasted," Lord Ian said. "I do believe you are even better than I on the violin."

"I never doubted your ability, but I had never seen you challenged." Dommick broke eye contact and looked at his music, but Alethea saw the faint flush of colour at his jawline. It was endearing to see him embarrassed.

Alethea glanced at Lucy. Her sister gave her a wink and a smile as if to say, "Well done, you have bested them." It buoyed her spirits as she returned her attention to the men.

"Now that we are aware that Lady Alethea can outplay all of us, shall we continue?" Lord Ravenhurst said.

It was the most enjoyable two hours she had spent in many years. Alethea forgot about Lucy, sitting in the corner as her chaperone. Dommick had the ability to write music that sounded elaborate, yet was straightforward to master. Lord Ravenhurst had uncanny intuition about tweaking passages to create more emotional impact. Lord Ian suggested changes that enhanced the strengths of the individual instruments.

Clare and Lady Morrish entered the music room to sit and listen to the final product of their practice session. Lady Morrish expressed pleasure at the piece, but Clare sat immobile for a full minute after they had finished, her mouth in an O and her eyes darting at the musicians, landing most often upon Alethea. Finally she gasped, "Bayard, that piece is your most commanding composition yet. And, Alethea, your talent is . . . staggering."

"Yes, she is brilliant," Lord Ian agreed.

"I thank you." Their praise should have made Alethea feel vindicated after her interest in the violin had been denigrated by so many people. Yet she felt uncomfortable. She did not want to stand out from the other musicians—she realized she wanted to belong to them. They never made her feel like an intruder to their circle, but she nonetheless was not quite one of them. And she longed to be. She longed to call them her intimate friends.

"I should return to my aunt," Alethea said reluctantly.

"We shall see you and your aunt tonight at Mrs. Pollwitton's rout?" Lady Morrish asked.

"Of course."

Alethea replaced the violin in its case and gave it to Lord Ian to carry downstairs for her. Lucy had gathered her mending and waited to follow them all out, but Alethea held back to reach for her hand.

"I have never heard you play so well," Lucy said.

"I am glad you were here." Alethea left the room and Clare fell in beside her.

"I knew you would be remarkable. The entire household could hear all of you practicing and it sounded wonderful," Clare said.

Something about Clare's comment caused a tickle of unease in her stomach, but it was forgotten as she retrieved her coat and bonnet from the butler. This time Lord Ian joined them on the drive back to Queen Square.

Dommick said, "For our next practice—"

There was the sudden *crack!* of a gunshot. Alethea's heart tried to shoot out of her chest.

"What—" Lord Ian looked out the window, then was flung backward as the carriage jerked forward.

They rattled along the cobblestones as the horses raced down the street. Alethea heard cries as people darted out of the way of the runaway horses. The street was short, and as the horses skidded and tried to turn, the carriage slid and flipped onto its side.

The sound of wood crashing and sliding along the pebbles filled the carriage. Clare landed atop Alethea, and she grabbed the girl and held on tightly, curling them both into a ball. A gentleman bounced atop her legs.

Then the carriage stopped moving. The frantic cries of the horses filtered through the fuzziness in Alethea's brain, along with screams and the babbling of bystanders. She cast an eye upward where the window of the carriage opened to the sky.

A shadow passed through the light, and then the carriage door was wrenched open. The face of the cadaverous man peered inside.

Alethea screamed.

His grey eyes darted around the carriage, and he reached in to grab the violin case. Dommick kicked at him and hurled himself out of the overturned carriage at the man, and they disappeared from sight. Ian clambered out after him.

Alethea smoothed the dark hair from Clare's pale face. "Are you injured? Are you in pain?"

"I am well," she said in a squeak.

Alethea struggled to a sitting position, but her heavy woolen skirts hampered her. She pulled herself upright by grasping the edges of the carriage door and peered outside.

The cadaverous man was fleeing, jostling through the crowd. Dommick gave chase, but Lord Ian turned back to them. He reached for Alethea's arms and helped her out of the carriage. "Are you hurt?"

"No."

He assisted Clare, wrapping his arm around her waist to carry her out of the carriage and set her upon her feet. He then went to help the coachman with the panicked horses. After they had unhitched them from the broken carriage shafts, he helped the coachman sit down on the side of the street, for there was blood running from a gash on his head.

Alethea lent him her handkerchief to staunch the worst of it. "What happened?"

The coachman nodded in the direction the cadaverous man had taken. "He was at the side of the street on horseback, and he shot a pistol right near the horses. They bolted."

"He followed the runaway coach?"

"Must have. Next thing I know, I sees him opening the carriage. That's his horse, methinks." The coachman pointed to where a saddled horse stood with trailing reins, unable to do more than circle nervously because of the crowd.

Ian was holding the carriage horses, so Alethea grabbed the lone horse to calm it before it trampled someone. It looked to be a hired hack.

Dommick returned soon, breathing heavily. Strangely, he hesitated before he took the bridle from Alethea. "Is Clare unharmed?"

"Yes."

"Whose horse is this?"

"The coachman believes it belonged to the cadaverous man."

Dommick's face was white and angry. "How could he have known you had the violin? You didn't know until this morning that we had a practice session, and none of the servants saw you carrying it."

Alethea remembered Clare's remark, and now understood why

it had caused a feeling of misgiving. "The servants heard us playing. Lord Ian walked into the house carrying it, and I was in the music room with you all. It could not be difficult to hazard a guess that the violin was mine and I was playing it."

Tension radiated from Dommick, which began to affect the horse. Alethea reached out to pat its neck and speak soothingly, and it quieted.

Dommick turned to her with burning eyes. "There is a spy in my household."

CHAPTER TWELVE

*B*ayard walked with Raven toward New Sydney Place the next day. His friend looked like the vengeful Roman god Apollo with his stern face, flashing ice-blue eyes, and white-blond hair as he marched along.

"It is through no fault of yours," Bayard said again.

"Half of those servants are mine," Raven said through his clenched jaw. "Of course it is my responsibility."

"We shall uncover the informer in due time. I asked Lucy Purcell to discover who among the staff may have informed the cadaverous man about Alethea's violin."

"You are certain no one knows Lucy is Lady Alethea's sister? They look remarkably alike."

"Miss Purcell assures me she has not told anyone she has a sister, and she has not visited Alethea on her half day as she normally would. The other servants rarely see her in the same room with Alethea."

"This is a wretched situation." Raven scowled.

They arrived at New Sydney Place, near the gardens, where the Count of Escalari had taken a house for the winter. Ravenhurst gave the butler his card, and within moments the two gentlemen were being ushered upstairs to a grand drawing room furnished with copious pieces of Egyptian-style furniture.

"Ravenhurst, it is good to see you." The count entered with a limp and arms outstretched in welcome. "Your mother is well?"

"She is with my sister at Windmarch's estate in Devonshire. You may congratulate her when next you see her, for she has a new grandson."

"A boy! She mentioned to me her hopes."

"May I present Lord Dommick?"

"I am acquainted with your mother, Lord Dommick," the count said. "She and I met at parties in London while you were off fighting Napoleon."

"It is a pleasure to make your acquaintance." Bayard bowed.

"You returned with no injury?"

"A mere scratch, I assure you." And the hellish hole in his sanity.

"I have my own injury." The count gestured to his leg as he sat heavily upon a delicate-looking chaise lounge. "Not from war, but from a battle with my horse. The doctor has prescribed the waters of Bath."

Bayard and Raven sat in chairs across from him. "My stepfather is here for his gout," Bayard said.

"Bath is full of we who are infirm." The count's smile crinkled his small black eyes into merry twinkling stars. "The warmth of the waters remind me of Italy, and I grow homesick."

Bayard drew the paper from his pocket. Alethea had made him another copy of the initials on her violin. "I hope I might draw upon your reminisces of your homeland. I believe these may be the initials of an Italian nobleman."

The count took one look at the initials and his grey-spiked eyebrows rose. "I have not thought of Sondrono in many years."

Bayard's heartbeat stuttered. "You know who that is?"

"It is Camillo Michele Antonio Giustinani, Count of Sondrono. The *S* in the middle is his title, and the other initials are his name."

Bayard had not thought that the enlarged *S* was separate from the other letters. "How do you know of him?"

"He and my grandfather had estates in the north of Italy, in the Alps near Livigno, but they did not see each other often except by chance in Milan or Turin. Where did you get this?"

"The initials were painted on the neck of a violin."

"Ah, yes. Sondrono and his wife were musical patrons. They performed for close friends on rare occasions."

"What instruments did they play?" Bayard asked.

The count shrugged. "I never heard. But his wife sponsored many musicians until she grew ill and the count's gambling grew severe. Sondrono was infamous for his reckless gambling, which grew worse after his wife died, according to my grandfather."

"We had suspected gambling debts would induce the owner to sell the violin."

"I do not doubt it. He died in penury at his estate, with no children. His estate passed to his nephew, who had to sell much of it to pay Sondrono's debts. There was not much left, according to my grandfather, because Sondrono had sold most of his family's treasures to fund his gambling."

"Did you hear of any musical instruments he sold?"

"No. My grandfather mentioned Sondrono's vast art collection, but not musical instruments. However, those are Sondrono's initials, so the violin probably belonged to him."

"Do you know of the count's living relatives?"

"All in Italy, I imagine. I know none of them personally."

A servant tapped upon the door and entered. Escalari nodded to him. "Yes, yes, I am coming. I beg leave you will excuse me, gentlemen. I am expected in the hot baths. I must follow my doctor's instructions."

"Of course. Thank you for seeing us." Raven stood.

Bayard also stood. "May I ask one more question? Are you acquainted with Lady Fairmont?"

Escalari's face immediately lit up. "Yes, her mother's uncle was Count Inizinesso. I see why you ask. Inizinesso was also a reckless gambler. He lost his estate to Sondrono in an infamous card game, but Sondrono then lost the estate to some other man, I do not recall, who would not allow Inizinesso to buy it back. Inizinesso blamed Sondrono for the loss. Me?" Escalari gave a one-shoulder shrug. "I say Inizinesso should not have gambled with his estate in the first place."

That explained Lady Fairmont's outrage over Sondrono's initials. It did not appear to be related to the violin. "Thank you." Bayard bowed.

As they headed back toward the Crescent, Raven said, "If Sondrono sold his violin, it does not explain why someone would want the violin now. If Sondrono was about the same age as Count Escalari's grandfather, then Sondrono died over fifty years ago. How long did Lady Arkright own the violin?"

Bayard tried to recall. "I will need to ask Alethea. Perhaps one of the count's family believes the violin rightfully belongs to him, and it took until now to track the instrument to Alethea."

"In that case, he may be an older gentleman, somehow connected to Sondrono."

Bayard bent his head against a cold gust of wind. "We have not fully investigated if there were other Stradivarius violins made with this unusual wood. Alethea's instrument may not be unique, and the violin may have profound sentimental value to the villain."

Raven gave him a long look. "And that would make him a very dangerous villain."

They walked in silence for the length of a street, then Bayard said, "Do you know anyone who may be able to tell us about Sondrono's living relatives?"

"I have one or two I can write."

They arrived at the house, but as they divested themselves of their hats and greatcoats, Clare appeared at the top of the stairs. "Bay, may I speak to you?"

He gave her a curious look, but she simply thinned her mouth and widened her eyes at him in exasperation. Shrugging, he followed her up to her bedchamber.

Lucy curtseyed from where she stood beside the fireplace. Clare closed the door. "We could not allow anyone in the house to know Lucy was speaking to you."

"Milord, about the carriage accident yesterday . . . I have discovered who in this house informed the thief about my sister's violin."

⁂

"This gig is decrepit. Where in the world did you get it?" Bayard's neck jostled as the carriage bumped over yet another rut in the road.

Ian, at the reins, gave him a pained look. "I would think you would be more grateful that I managed to acquire this nondescript equipage in such little time."

"We could have used your carriage if you had not sent it back to your estate," Bayard said.

"In Bath, there was no need for mine. And you cannot be certain the bounder would not have recognized my carriage."

The bounder in question rode almost a quarter mile ahead of them on a hired horse. Lucy had discovered that a footman, Simon, had inexplicably come into a large sum of money after the carriage accident. He insisted it was from gambling, but the other servants confided that Simon had no head for cards.

As a test, Bayard had mentioned loudly in Simon's presence that Alethea would be arriving with her violin the following day at three o'clock. They had watched and waited, and sure enough,

Simon had snuck out of the house, hired a horse, and headed out of Bath.

Following a man while posing as two unremarkable gentlemen had not been as difficult as Bayard would have supposed, once Ian had procured the ancient gig and even more aged horse. They dressed in their most shabby coats and hats, and if Bayard's neck did not snap in half from the rough and tumble motion of the unsprung carriage, all was going smoothly.

Then the footman's horse threw a shoe.

Ian groaned. "Do you think he would notice if we hung back and waited for him to continue?"

"If we travel too close to him, he will recognize us." Would they be forced to abandon this plan when they were so close to seeing the footman's contact?

"I have an idea." Ian turned the gig onto a side road, and they left the footman cursing his horse in the middle of the main road.

This side road was pitted with more ruts than the other, and then it began to climb. From their vantage height, they could see the main road and the footman walking, leading the lamed horse. Ian paused the gig near the top. "He can't travel much farther with that horse."

"Let us hope he does not hire another one, or we shall lose him."

He stopped at a shabby inn down the road. Ian continued along the side road until they could turn onto another path and meander back to the main road. However, he drove the horse along the side, hiding them amongst a stand of trees with the inn in sight. The footman loitered in the inn yard, waiting for someone.

They hadn't long to wait. A landau pulled into the inn yard, and the footman immediately stepped up to the window. The angle of the vehicle gave them an excellent view of the two horses, well-matched dappled greys, but not a good view of the interior of the carriage.

"Can't see inside," Bayard muttered. "Can we get clos—"

The landau pulled out of the inn yard after stopping for barely a minute. It turned and barreled down the road away from them.

"We'll lose him!" Bayard half rose in his seat.

Ian whipped up the poor horse, and they pulled out of the trees onto the main road. Bayard caught sight of the footman's startled expression as they sped past the inn yard.

However, the landau, with its two horses, was much faster, and the distance between them widened.

"They are heading to Chippenham," Ian said through chattering teeth. The day was too cold for a long-distance trip in the open gig, and the horse was flagging.

They lost sight of them at a bend in the road. When they reached the bend, there was a fork with no indication as to which they'd taken.

Bayard slapped the side of the gig in frustration.

"Should we pick a fork and go along for a ways?" Ian asked.

"They were too far ahead of us. And the horse would strenuously object." It was lathered and its sides heaved.

"Poor creature couldn't do anything strenuously."

But the horse did not mind turning around and heading back to Bath at a more sedate pace. They were chilled by the time they turned the horse and gig over to the groom.

"At the very least, we can dismiss Simon," Ian said as they dragged themselves into Raven's house.

"My lord."

Bayard recognized the soft voice as Lucy Purcell's. She stood in the shadow of the staircase, kneading her hands.

Bayard quickly gave his greatcoat to the butler and approached Lucy. "Is Clare safe?" He sensed Ian close at his shoulder.

"Yes . . . now."

That one qualifying word was like a gunshot that sent his heart beating rapidly against his throat. "What happened?"

Lucy swallowed, and in that moment she looked exactly like her sister. But when she spoke, she had a softness and diffidence that was missing in Alethea. "She asks that you meet her in the music room."

He and Ian hurried upstairs, Lucy trailing behind. Clare seemed remarkably unaffected, sitting at the pianoforte and practicing the piece Ian had written for her to perform at their concert in less than two weeks' time.

"What happened?" Bayard strode into the music room. Lucy closed the door.

Clare stopped playing and raised her chin. "It was nothing serious."

Not a propitious beginning to the conversation.

"Good Lord, Clare, just tell us," Ian demanded.

"Lucy thought she saw something."

"While Miss Terralton and I were out, she stopped to speak to Lady Whittlesby while I waited a few feet away," Lucy said. "I thought I saw the same grey man seen by you and Alethea."

Bayard swung his gaze back to Clare. "That is not nothing," he ground out.

"I did not see him," Clare said, "and Lucy only saw him the once."

"I glanced at Clare, then back where I had seen the man, but he was gone. I am not certain if he had been there at all," Lucy said.

The thought of the grey man watching his sister, shadowing her every step, nearly sent him into a rage. "Clare, you are not playing in the concert," Bayard said.

"Bay, I have to."

"No, you do not," Ian said, his face nearly as stern as Bayard felt.

"Today, Lady Whittlesby said she was looking forward to hearing me at the concert," Clare pleaded.

If Clare performed to Lady Whittlesby's standards, she would feature Clare in her concert in London this spring. "Our concert will be dangerous. You of all people know that."

"It will be dangerous for Alethea, but not for me. And I will have Lucy with me at all times."

Lucy had paled at the comment about the danger to her sister, but she gave Clare a firm nod.

"I heard rumours while we were at the milliner's shop today," Clare said. "Mr. Morrish is saying terrible things about me."

"You shouldn't listen to the likes of Miss Herrington-Smythe—"

"It was Mama's friends. They did not tell me to distress me, but they were concerned."

Bayard snorted. "I'm certain they were." The way they were distressed for Mama this past spring and raced to tell her the rumours about her son.

"I *need* to perform for Lady Whittlesby," Clare said. "You cannot control what others say about us. Lady Whittlesby's concert will counteract all those lies, not just about me, but about you as well. You know this."

Silence settled amongst them. Bayard shuddered. All he had ever wanted to do was protect his family, yet no matter what he did, things worsened day by day.

"I'll watch over Clare," Ian said in a low voice. "You and Raven and Ord can keep watch over Lady Alethea."

"There, you see? I shall be well protected," Clare said.

Bayard rubbed his hand over his forehead. "Very well," he said reluctantly.

"I take it you were not able to follow the footman?" Clare asked.

Ian related what had happened.

"Simon may not bother to return," Bayard said. "He clearly saw us as we passed the inn."

"Then you needn't dismiss him," Ian said. "One less thing to do."

"One less servant to worry about," Bayard said.

There was a sudden commotion from downstairs, and the sound of a familiar voice floated up to the music room.

"Is that—?" Clare headed out of the music room.

Bayard and Ian followed her down to the entrance foyer, where new, unfamiliar servants in the livery of the Marquess of Ravenhurst carried in parcels, trunks, and portmanteaus. In the midst of the chaos stood a tall woman with fine, flyaway brown hair in a loose style that framed her fine-boned face. Her lady's maid was removing her hat, a grand affair with copious flowers and trailing ribbons. She caught sight of the three of them as they descended the staircase.

"Clare, how lovely you look, dear," she said in her low, musical voice. "You have grown since I last saw you, I declare. And, Bay and Ian, what odd costumes you two are wearing, to be sure. Whatever have you been about?"

The Marchioness of Ravenhurst looked about her home with a happy sigh. "How lovely to be back in Bath again. Where is my son?"

Just when Bayard had been worried about the number of servants, the Marchioness of Ravenhurst had returned, with her entire retinue, earlier than expected. Simon may be one less servant to worry about, but now he had an entire houseful of strangers.

CHAPTER THIRTEEN

Six days later

Alethea's hands were sweating within her gloves, and yet her fingers were cold. She fussed with the lace at the throat of Margaret's gown until the twelve-year-old pushed her hands away. "You're choking me."

Aunt Ebena entered the drawing room, regal in a dark brown gown with rich beading along the collar, cuffs, and hem. She studied Margaret in her white gown, then straightened the lace at her neckline.

She turned to Alethea and swept her eyes from the embroidery edging the hem of her green gown, up to the embroidery at her square neckline and edging her puffed sleeves. Aunt Ebena tugged at the embroidered sash just under Alethea's bodice, smoothing it into place. "Where is your shawl?"

Alethea grabbed the shawl from the chair, a large silk affair in a lighter shade of green but with the same detailed embroidery at each end.

"Your sleeves are too loose," Aunt Ebena said.

"I had the gown made with more ease in the shoulders so that I could play my violin." Before now, she had practiced with her old gowns, which were already cut loosely at the shoulder. She'd never had cause to play while wearing an evening gown, and so had this one specially made.

Aunt Ebena sniffed. "It looks odd."

"It will not be noticeable once I am playing." Alethea added dryly, "If it pleases you, I shall contrive not to turn my back to anyone."

"Do not be ridiculous." Aunt Ebena turned to the door. "I believe I hear Lord Dommick at last."

Within minutes, Dommick had entered the drawing room. He looked magnificent in evening wear, the severe black coat and white linen a stark contrast to his square jawline and raven-black hair. His shoulders seemed wider and he filled Aunt Ebena's drawing room.

He blinked rapidly in surprise at the sight of Alethea. He had seen her in evening dress before, but perhaps her nervousness made her more wan and scrawny than normal. She resisted the urge to slouch. Calandra had scolded her, saying that it made her look gawky rather than more petite.

Dommick bowed to Aunt Ebena, but to Margaret he took her hand and bowed over it. "Miss Margaret, you look enchanting."

Margaret giggled and gave a creditable curtsey.

"Lady Alethea." When he took Alethea's hand, his fingers pressed into her palm and his thumb caressed her knuckles in an intimate touch. It was as if they were alone in the room, and her breath came faster. He held her a moment longer than necessary, but Aunt Ebena did not seem to notice.

"Your violin arrived safely at the house earlier today," Dommick said, although she already knew for he had sent a servant with the same message. "Ladies, shall we?"

Aunt Ebena led the way from the drawing room, her shoulders stiffly set.

Dommick murmured to Alethea, "Your aunt still does not approve of your participation in this concert?"

"She does not approve of my choice of instrument. She says that news of my violin playing has already caused a stir."

"That is precisely what we desire, in order to lure the villain out."

"Aunt Ebena says the gossip has reflected negatively upon her, although I have not heard so, even from such knowledgeable sources as Miss Herrington-Smythe and Miss Nanstone."

They arranged themselves in their cloaks, and once outside, Alethea noted a man on horseback beside the carriage.

"My man, Ord," Dommick said. "I thought it safest."

As she stood and waited for Aunt Ebena to settle herself in the carriage, Alethea glanced down the street of the square and caught sight of another man on horseback before another house. A single forefoot on the horse was white, which seemed to glow in the twilight.

Aunt Ebena's forbidding expression made Alethea choose the opposite seat, facing backward. Dommick sat beside her, and she caught the faint scent of oaks in wintertime. She breathed deeply and the tightness in her chest eased.

The streets of Bath were busy in the early evening as people travelled to and from engagements. But as the carriage turned a corner, she looked out the window and caught a flash of white.

It was the horse with the white forefoot that she had seen in the square. Her stomach clenched. "Dommick," she whispered, "I thought I saw—"

"I saw that horse in the square." His voice was tight. He stuck his head out the window and said something to Ord. In a moment, Ord had wheeled his horse around and headed back in a clattering of hooves.

Alethea tried to stick her own head out the window to look behind them, but Aunt Ebena scolded, "Alethea, your hair will become a mass of tangles."

"What's amiss?" Margaret sounded excited. "Is it bandits?"

"Do not be absurd," Aunt Ebena said.

She wasn't certain how long she sat in the carriage, jostled to and fro while her insides churned. She could sense the tension radiating from Dommick's stiff limbs.

Then came the drumming of horse's hooves. Heedless of *his* hair, Dommick looked outside the coach. Ord appeared in the carriage window and shook his head. Where Dommick's legs touched her skirts, Alethea felt his muscles relax.

"I am overly apprehensive about tonight, I daresay," she said.

"Yes, be sure you do not make a glaring mistake," Aunt Ebena sniped.

Alethea's pulse beat rapidly at the base of her throat. However, she felt Dommick's hand reach for hers under the cover of her cloak.

They soon arrived at the Ravenhursts' home on the Crescent, ablaze with lights. It was too soon for guests to arrive, and servants bustled about with last-minute preparations—carrying a chair, or a vase of flowers, or with a dustcloth in hand. Lady Ravenhurst stood in the entrance foyer directing the servants, and she smiled as they entered.

"Mrs. Garen, Miss Garen, thank you for arriving early. Please forgive the disorder. We shall have a cozy tea amongst ourselves while the young people practice. A maid will escort you to Lady Morrish in the sitting room, for the drawing room is not yet fit to be seen, I assure you. I shall join you in a trice, after I have organized these flowers." She bent to Margaret. "Cook has made her very best cakes for us tonight."

Margaret grinned, displaying her protruding front tooth that made her look as angelic as she was not.

"Lady Alethea, we are still at sixes and sevens, as you can see. Clare, Raven, and Ian are awaiting you in the music room."

Dommick led Alethea up the staircase, and Lady Ravenhurst called, "I have had a cold collation laid out for you. Do be sure to eat something."

"I couldn't eat a crumb," Alethea said in an undertone.

"We shall practice, and that will settle your nerves. It is always that way with me before a performance."

"You? But you have performed in numerous concerts."

He shrugged. "Ian and Raven are very cool about it, but David and I were always pacing."

"I shall need new handkerchiefs. I shredded three of them this afternoon alone."

They had reached the closed music room door, and she could hear the pianoforte. Rather than opening the door, Dommick touched her elbow and smiled at her, and a bolt of something more radiant than nervousness coursed from her head to her toes. He reached into his coat and withdrew a folded piece of white linen, then grasped her hand and pressed it to her. "I am sure my handkerchief will be slightly sturdier than your lace ones."

Even through their gloves, his fingers were warm and strong. She should thank him and withdraw her hand, but she could not. His touch and his nearness caused a fluttering and dancing in her ribcage.

He swallowed, and his dark eyes gleamed with something that made her pulse leap.

Then suddenly he was leaning away from her, drawing in a shaky breath that matched her own. He turned and opened the door.

Alethea took a second to compose herself before following him into the room. He was a man. She must always remember he was a man. The men in her life who had held closest ties to her had only hurt her. She ought not to trust any of them, no matter how handsome, no matter how talented and arrogant and kind and distant.

The music room had already been prepared for the evening's entertainment. Chairs were set up for the guests, with the musicians' seats ranged around the pianoforte, their music stands set before them. Later, the grand double doors that led from the drawing room would be opened so guests could enter the music room and arrange themselves to listen.

Clare left the pianoforte and clasped Alethea's hands. "I can't stop shaking."

"Keep your anxiety to yourself, for I have ample enough of my own."

"You are both escalating your hysteria," Lord Ian drawled. "You have performed at evening parties. This is nothing different."

For Clare's sake, Alethea smiled. "You are correct."

"Shall we begin?" Lord Ravenhurst sat with his violoncello.

They practiced the pieces to be performed—to start, the Quartet with Alethea would play a composition each by Dommick, Lord Ian, and Lord Ravenhurst. After a short break, Clare would play two of Captain Enlow's older pianoforte pieces, and then a duet between Clare and Ian on violin. Lastly, Alethea and the gentlemen would play two of their most popular concertos from their years in London.

As she played, Alethea's hands and fingers remembered the music, but the buzzing in her head and the churning in her stomach seemed to worsen as the hour drew near.

As they concluded, Clare said to Alethea, "The embroidery on your sleeve is awry."

She saw the trailing end of a thread on the backside of her left sleeve. "I shall go to the cloak room to have a maid attend to it."

She exited through a small door into the connected library, which was where the performers would congregate. Lady Ravenhurst had sent up a tray of cold meats, but the smell made Alethea's stomach heave. She hurried out to the hallway. She saw, farther down, guests already making their way into the drawing room, greeting Lady Ravenhurst.

Alethea turned the corner and entered the small room set apart for the ladies, with mirrors, small dressing tables, and combs and cosmetics set out for any emergency. The maid there looked at her embroidery. "The pulled thread has caused the sleeve to pucker. I shall need to slip the shoulder off to fix it, milady."

Alethea and the maid went behind the screen, and the maid undid the hooks on her gown, pulling the shoulder down. She busied herself with loosening the offending thread from the puckered fabric and refurbishing the embroidery design.

The door to the room opened, and Alethea recognized Mrs. Nanstone's voice, high and grating like her eldest daughter. "What a crush. I do not know how we shall fit in the music room. Oh, good, here is some rouge."

Alethea remained silent. Mrs. Nanstone heartily disliked Aunt Ebena and by extension, Alethea.

"I believe the concert shall be quite . . . interesting," said Lady Rollingwood in an uncertain voice. "I have not heard the gentlemen perform in many years."

"I have never heard them, Aunt, but people say they are excellent," said the soft voice of Mrs. Isherton, mother to Margaret's playmate.

"People are more influenced by their money, rank, and handsome faces than their talent." Mrs. Nanstone had a sneer in her voice.

"Yes, Mr. Kinnier is superior in address and in talent, and yet the Quartet was all the rage in London those years ago," Lady Rollingwood said.

"Wasn't there some scandal attached to Mr. Kinnier?" Mrs. Isherton said, but she was interrupted by Mrs. Nanstone.

"And what of Lady Alethea playing a violin? I am ashamed for her aunt, to be sure. It is most unseemly for her to draw attention to her body in such a way."

Alethea waited, but Mrs. Isherton did not reply to this, and it sent a pang through her. Did Mrs. Isherton believe, as did many others, that Alethea's violin playing was scandalous?

"She must not be very talented," Lady Rollingwood said. "She would not have had the music masters available to a man."

"Her pianoforte and harp playing are most pleasing," Mrs. Isherton said.

"But she will be playing violin," Mrs. Nanstone said. "If she is so amazing in her skill, why has she not performed before? There, how does that look?"

"The rouge has done wonders," Lady Rollingwood said.

"I cannot think how it could have been wiped off between my bedchamber and this house."

There was the rustle of fabric as the women bustled out, but before the door closed, Lady Rollingwood said, "I have heard that Lord Dommick is helping Lady Alethea with her violin simply because he does not wish Lady Whittlesby's London concert to go to Mr. Kinnier. Oh, goodness, the concert is about to start." The door closed with a click.

Alethea stood in silence with the maid for several minutes. A wildness grew in her stomach from the seed of doubt planted with Mrs. Nanstone's and Lady Rollingwood's words, and watered by Mrs. Isherton's silent embarrassment. How could she do this? She would make a horrible mistake and fulfill all the tabbies' predictions for her downfall.

Finally the maid said, "It is fixed, milady." She helped Alethea rearrange her gown and did up the hooks again. "You look quite beautiful. And . . . if I may be so bold . . ."

"Yes?"

"Your violin playing is quite lovely. All the servants have enjoyed your practices this past week."

Alethea smiled at the maid, although her mouth felt tight. "Thank you. You are very kind."

She opened the door to the room with hands so cold that the door felt warm. She took a step outside and thought she might stumble. She leaned against the wall and staggered to the corner. She must perform. She must make it to the library.

Everything within her quailed. She could not. She could not do this.

The door to the library opened, and Dommick appeared. He took one look at her face and came to her. "What is it?"

She shook her head, unable to speak.

He took her hands and drew her back along the side corridor, away from the prying eyes of guests entering the drawing room down the hallway. "What is it?"

"I can't do this," she whispered.

"Yes, you can."

She gasped in a few more breaths. "I need ... a moment ..." But it seemed the more she breathed, the more lightheaded she became.

He drew closer and grabbed her shoulders. "You can do this. I believe in you."

Her entire body trembled. She wanted to explain about the women's words, about the fear and pain, about feeling so alone with no one to understand her now that Calandra was gone. But she couldn't speak. Her mouth was dry, her heart rate faster than a galloping horse.

His hands tightened on her shoulders. And then his head blocked out the light as he swooped in to kiss her.

She had never been kissed before, and he was not simply touching her. She could feel him all around her. She could somehow feel his heart beating with hers, she could hear it in her ears. His lips were warm and firm, and the knot inside her slowly unwound. Her hands touched the silk of his waistcoat, and he was solid and dependable. His very presence was sheltering like an oak tree.

He ended the kiss and looked into her eyes. She could breathe again, and she filled her lungs with the tang of lime, the woody scent of oak, the sharp, warm musk scent that rose from his skin.

In his eyes was something avid and yet wishful. She caught a glimpse of the vulnerable part of him that he seemed never to show.

And then he retreated behind an invisible wall. He took a deep breath, which seemed to wipe the yearning from his eyes, and he straightened, although his hands remained on her shoulders.

She should not have lost control. Not in front of anyone, not in front of a man, and not in front of *this* man. Especially because of how he made her feel so alive.

"I am sorry." She strived for a steady voice. "I was quite . . . out of my mind. I daresay we both were."

He dropped his hands from her. "Yes."

It was not necessary for him to be quite so quick to agree.

She straightened, stiffened her shoulders, steadied her knees. "I am ready."

He offered his arm, for which she was grateful, because she was not as strong as she pretended to be. They entered the library, and as soon as they opened the door, Lord Ian said, "They're ready for us."

Clare appeared at her side. Lucy was there also to keep Clare company while the four of them performed, and she took Alethea's clammy hand in a soothing touch. She did not look like an abigail tonight—she had a new gown in rich blue, a gift from Clare, and she looked as elegant as any woman who would be in the music room.

Alethea gathered her violin from the table and Lord Ravenhurst escorted her into the music room, which had been filled with people.

Fans fluttered, waving a rainbow of feather plumes, while the chandelier above and the wall sconces illuminated glittering jewels like stars fallen to earth. Alethea kept her head high, her shoulders back, but as her gaze swept the room, she could not see any of the faces.

She sat in her seat, but the sheet music on the stand swam in front of her eyes. Then Dommick was sitting beside her, and his leg gave her a not-so-gentle kick in the shin.

She blinked at him. He gave her a firm nod, and a look filled with all the strength and confidence she did not feel.

She positioned her violin.

Her contribution to the first chord was tentative. But her second note sounded stronger, and by the end of the first page, her heart was soaring with the music. She had forgotten the audience, forgotten the men playing alongside her, only knew the sounds echoing in her ears.

They had chosen to start with Dommick's composition, which flew her on sweetly harmonious chords to the mountains of Italy, as she imagined them to be in her mind, to the solid castles built into the rock, rising above snow-white mist and the multicoloured hues of the turning leaves in autumn. The music sang of crashing waterfalls, the mist spraying up like tears on her face, the water rushing down and over rocks in a dancing swirl, to slow at last into a tranquil pool that spoke of the cold, still kiss of morning light, of leaves drifting down from dreaming trees, of whispered lovers' vows.

The concerto ended with a delicate, winsome air of two violins chasing each other round and round until they met in a rapturous chord that died into the silent room.

The applause was thunderous. Even at other concerts Alethea had attended in the past year, she had never heard such a response. She came to herself and realized there were tears on her cheeks.

Dommick had an exultant smile. "I would give you my hand-kerchief, but I seem to have misplaced it."

She laughed and dug his handkerchief from her reticule. She dabbed her cheeks and met the triumphant look from Lord Ian, the proud expression from Lord Ravenhurst.

As the applause quieted, Lord Ravenhurst flipped the page on his music stand. "Ready?"

They completed the next two pieces flawlessly. While Lord Dommick's piece had been evocative, Lord Ravenhurst's concerto was the most technically challenging, and Lord Ian's quartet clev-erly highlighted the unique tone of her violin in the measures where it soared above the other instruments or resonated with power in the melodic line.

They stood to more applause and exited the room back into the library. Alethea's hands now began to shake as if she had a fever. She touched her forehead, but it was cool and damp.

Lord Ian grabbed Alethea's hand and kissed it with a smack. "Quite amazing, my lady."

Lord Ravenhurst gave her a regal bow, then a blinding smile. "Indeed."

But it was Dommick's gaze that made the room spin about her until he clasped her elbow. Then the world righted itself, and all she saw were the dark stars of his eyes. A breath or two, and she was herself again.

Clare and Lucy were beside her. "You were wonderful. You did not even look nervous," Clare said.

"You could see us?"

"We watched through the open library door," Lucy said. "The angle is perfect. If we stand behind the closed one, no one can see us."

The door was closed now and murmuring had erupted in the music room as the guests mingled during the short intermission.

After intermission, Clare's three pieces were not long, and then the Quartet would play the last two compositions.

Alethea took a deep breath as Lord Ravenhurst escorted her into the music room. She was surrounded by people, some she knew only as casual acquaintances, who were fervent in their praises. Cynically, she wondered which of them were speaking truthfully in their compliments.

But the most meaningful words were from Aunt Ebena, who waited for a break in the people around Alethea before she approached. "Your practice has been to good purpose," she said severely.

"Yes, Aunt."

She hesitated, her face impassive, then said in a low voice, "You were quite good, Alethea."

Those words, more than the most fulsome praises, made satisfaction well up in her heart.

As intermission ended, Alethea and the performers returned to the library. She took Clare's hand, which pressed hers almost painfully, before Lord Ian escorted her into the music room.

Lord Ian and Dommick had decided upon a slow, sweet tune to help calm Clare's nerves. It worked, for Clare's performance was without error, if a bit wooden. But then for her second solo, she added fire to a quick tempo and created thunder with crashing chords, ending in a gale of sound and power. And for her duet with Lord Ian, she was smiling, as Alethea could see as she watched from the library. The two of them created a playground where the pianoforte and violin played tag like laughing children.

Lucy stood beside Alethea, their arms about each other's waists as they had done as children. Lucy whispered, "The song reminds me of our games on the downs."

"It reminds me of happy times."

"After our final performance, you must circulate around the room with Clare," Dommick said near her ear.

"It will not put Clare in danger?"

"Leave your violin here, in the library. We shall be watching you and the violin at all times."

Lord Ravenhurst added, "If you are not with the violin, you shall not be in harm's way."

"I shall stay in the library with Clare while you play your last two pieces with the gentlemen," Lucy said. "Then you and Clare can go forth among your guests."

Clare and Lord Ian finished with a flourish, and after they had bowed to the loud acclaim, she returned to the library with cheeks flushed and eyes brilliant.

Alethea was not as nervous during the last two songs. The Quartet was most famous for these particular concertos, and to be part of them made her feel as if she possessed a true, close-knit family. For those minutes, she pretended they were the brothers she had never had, ones who would support her rather than sell her to the highest bidder.

They ended to magnanimous applause, and after bowing, returned to the library.

Unaccountably, a chill swept through Alethea as if a draft had shot through an open window. She did not understand. She should be relieved, for it was over and she had not been drowned in censure.

Then suddenly she realized what was missing. "Where are Clare and Lucy?"

They all grew still.

Alethea ventured further into the room and checked in corners where she knew the two women would have no reason to be. Her ribcage began to ache. "Where are they?"

And then near the door that led into the hallway, she spotted an object on the floor. She picked it up.

It was a woman's cloth slipper in a rich blue colour. It had been ripped from the ribbons attaching it to the wearer's ankle.

"What is that?" Dommick's voice was urgent.

She held it out to him, and her legs began to tremble. She nearly fell as she whispered, "This is Lucy's slipper."

CHAPTER FOURTEEN

*B*ayard tried to convince himself that Lucy's slipper did not necessarily indicate that Clare and Lucy were in danger, but as he headed into the bowels of the house, he knew he was lying to himself.

The two women had not been in any bedchamber. Raven and Ian searched among the guests, but Clare was not there, nor had anyone seen her.

Alethea trailed behind him. He had delivered her violin to Ord to hide it away. Bayard had trusted him with his life at Corunna and knew he could trust him now.

Bayard found the butler in the kitchen, about to oversee the laying out of the cold light supper in the dining room. "Chapman." His voice was harsher than he intended.

The butler snapped to attention. "Yes, my lord?"

He was about to blurt out about Clare, but a small voice of caution made him amend his question to, "Have you seen Miss Terralton's maid?"

"No, sir."

"Have any of the servants seen her?"

Chapman clapped his hands and the kitchen noise dropped in volume. "Has anyone see Purcell?"

Silence. Bayard pressed his fists into his thighs, but they still shook. "Where else would the servants be?"

"They should be here or in the dining hall, but they could be where they should not." Chapman's mouth was grim.

Alethea said, "Are there any servants whom you have not seen within the past fifteen minutes?" It had been that long since they had discovered the women were missing.

A maid said, "George and Anna?"

Chapman shook his head. "I saw them a few minutes ago in the dining room."

"Jack and Mays?" a footman said.

A hitch of silence, then Chapman barked, "Who saw them last?"

"I sent Mays to the storeroom for a platter," the cook said, "but I don't recall when that was."

Chapman's grey brows drew low. "I sent Jack to the storeroom for a different epergne for the dining room half an hour ago."

Bayard, Alethea, and the housekeeper followed Chapman to the storeroom at the back of the house. The heavy wooden door was shut, but it opened when Chapman touched the latch.

Two young men lay on the stone floor, stripped of their livery, their hands and feet tied and gags stuffed into their mouths. As the door creaked open, one lifted his head and feebly tried to rise.

Alethea gasped. The housekeeper pushed past to bend over the man. "They've been knocked in the head." She untied his gag.

"Send for a doctor," Bayard said. Alethea turned to go, but Bayard grabbed her wrist. He would not allow her out of his sight. He sent the housekeeper upstairs, and she bustled away.

Chapman said, "With the marchioness's new servants in the household, it has been difficult for all the staff to remember each other."

Bayard ground his teeth. An under-servant might see two footmen in livery and not realize they were impostors. He knelt beside one of the men and untied his bindings while Chapman untied the other man. "Do not get up. What is your name?"

"Jack," he said in a hoarse voice. "Milord, I didn't expect—"

"I would be surprised if you did. Did you see them? Was there one man or more than one?"

"They hit me from behind. I woke up here, tied up, and two men was tying up Mays. I kept me peepers shut, so I didn't see their faces, but I heard them. One was cursing fit to be tied 'cause they were late. He said they was supposed to be in position a'fore the concert started."

"Did you recognize their voices?"

"No, milord. Sorry, milord."

"Did you hear anything else?"

"I heard footsteps going out back toward the carriage house." He nodded toward the back door of the house, which lay near the storeroom door.

"Good man. Thank you." Bayard said to Alethea, "Follow me." But she stood her ground, her mouth in a mulish cast. "No."

He frowned. "Alethea, I cannot be worrying for you—"

She lowered her voice so that only he could hear. "It is ridiculous for you to be concerned for me when your sister is missing." She raised her voice. "Chapman and I shall find Lord Ian and Lord Ravenhurst and send them to the carriage house after you." And with that, she spun around in a swirl of green skirts and hastened up the passage toward the upper levels of the house.

Chapman gave him a quick look, and at Bayard's nod, rushed after her.

Bayard opened the backdoor, whose hinges had been recently oiled. He dashed across the backyard of the house, a long, narrow strip of gardens and walks, to the carriage house that formed the back wall of the garden. His evening shoes slipped on the grass, and he felt the bite of the evening frost through the superfine of his coat, but he ran on. Surely the coachman in the carriage house saw something. But if he had seen Clare, wouldn't he have gone to the house to inform someone?

The door to the carriage house lay in the right corner of the garden wall and opened into a narrow corridor that ran through the structure to the street behind, with a door into the space where the carriages were kept. Bayard hurried into the large room, calling for the coachman.

The old man came down the narrow stairs from his quarters above. He was dressed in his working garb and not his nightshirt, so he had been awake in the past hour.

"Did you see anyone? Two footmen in livery?" Bayard demanded.

After a moment of confusion, the coachman shook his head. "I've been upstairs, milord."

"Were any other grooms here tonight?"

"They're all helping at the house, on account o' the concert." The staff at the house would have depended on all hands to help with the event. "I was out front directing the carriages and holding horses earlier, when the guests was arriving, but I returned here during the concert until I might be needed again."

"You heard nothing? Miss Terralton's maid has disappeared and two footmen were attacked and stripped of their livery."

"I did hear a carriage on the street, and a few minutes later I thot I heard someone in the passageway. Then the carriage moved off. I'm sorry, milord, I had s'posed it to be the neighbors."

"When did you hear this?"

"No more'n fifteen minutes ago."

They were not so far ahead of him. "Lend me your cloak, man. I shall run to the stables to procure a horse."

"We'll both ride." Ian walked into the room, his greatcoat swirling about his shoulders. "Raven's with Lady Alethea."

The news eased some of the constriction in his chest. "Let's go." The Ravenhurst horses were not stabled far from the carriage house, but he and Ian dashed down the street and were heaving when they arrived.

Bayard had not ridden a horse since returning from war. He had not replaced Champion despite the suggestions put forth by Raven and Bayard's own head groom. He simply could not bear it. He could not bear the thought of touching a horse, as if the contamination of what had happened in Corunna would infect it.

But now he saddled the fastest horse with a quickness honed from years of war. The movements came to him without thought. The animal caught his desperation and leapt forward as soon as he had mounted. He and Ian galloped out, following the likely path of the mysterious carriage.

Bayard rode and knew a sense of hopelessness. How could they catch up with a carriage for which they had no description? He could only guess on where the carriage would take Clare—out of Bath, where the villain could have time and space and few neighbors. Why had he taken her? Could Bayard expect a ransom note on the morrow? Wouldn't it have been more effective to steal away Margaret or Mrs. Garen, to force Alethea to turn over her violin?

Lord, help me! I have no one else to guide me in this. The prayer came up as a despairing cry from the depths of his soul.

They passed the carriage house and rode down the street to the end. Bayard caught sight of a familiar figure—Mr. Oakridge, his horse-mad schoolfellow.

And he suddenly knew the Lord God had answered his prayer. He pulled up beside Oakridge, walking along the road in evening clothes, apparently headed to some event. "Oakridge, well met."

Ian pulled up beside him, his face tense with confusion. "Bay?"

Bayard ignored him and addressed Oakridge. "This is of utmost urgency. Were you in position to see a carriage come from this lane in the past twenty minutes?"

"This lane? No, I've just come from your concert, my lord—"

"Did you see a carriage pass you, going quickly, which may have come from this direction?"

"I saw two," Oakridge said, and Bayard's stomach dropped. But Oakridge continued, "One was old Mrs. Ramsland's carriage, going at barely a jogg-trot with a tired old queer prancer that the most bungling thief'd be able to bite. The other carriage had the nicest pair of matched dappled greys I ever saw. Didn't see the vehicle, it was going too fast and I was distracted by those gallopers, but it was low-slung, I believe."

Bayard inhaled sharply, and Ian straightened in his saddle. They remembered the matched dappled grey horses pulling the landau—a low-slung vehicle—which stopped at that inn outside of Bath the day they followed the footman. "Which direction did the greys go?"

"Turned there." Oakridge pointed. "Wouldn't be surprised if it were headed out of Bath. Fine horses," he said on a longing sigh.

"Much obliged to you, Oakridge." Bayard kicked at his horse's sides and took off.

They galloped out of Bath. Bayard knew the Lord had heard his prayer and was leading them to Clare. He had to believe it. He had no other clue to follow.

They followed the same road they had taken in the decrepit gig, but this time they flew over the earth. Moonlight lit the ruts so they could avoid them.

As they clattered into the yard of the inn, Bayard realized they should have ridden in stealth, for the men who stole Clare and Lucy would surely know they had arrived. Just being led away by a groom were the matched dappled grey horses and the landau. A thunderbolt of relief and elation sent him hurdling from his saddle and into the inn.

"Where is she?" he demanded of the innkeeper, a round man with a filthy apron and blackened fingernails.

"I'm sure I don't know—"

"Whatever they promised to pay you, I shall pay double." Bayard slammed his purse upon the pitted wooden counter.

His bloodshot eyes grew round, and without taking his gaze from the money, he jerked a fat thumb toward the stairs. "First door on the right."

Bayard and Ian bounded up the stairs two at a time. The door was locked, but several solid blows by their shoulders made the rickety wood give way.

They were in time to see the bottom of a shoe as a man tumbled out of the open window to the ground below.

"Bay!" Clare and Lucy sat on the bed, hands tied but otherwise unharmed. When Bayard turned to Clare, she threw him a fierce look. "Never mind us, go get him!"

Ian rushed back down the stairs to head the men off in the inn yard. Bayard hurried to the window, which was only ten feet from the ground. The man had landed without injury, for two figures darted away toward the back of the inn. Without hesitating, Bayard leapt over the windowsill and dropped to the ground.

The landing jolted through his feet, clad only in evening shoes, but he quickly gave chase. As he circled round to the back of the inn, Ian came hurtling from the other side, and the two of them raced over weed-choked ground to the forested area behind the building.

They wove in and out of the trees, guided by the darting shadows of the two men ahead of them. Then Ian fell with a muffled

"Oof!" Bayard slowed, but Ian waved him on, his face crumpled in pain. "Go!"

Bayard ran on, bushes catching in the cloak flying around him, low-hanging branches slapping at his face. His lungs heaved, but still he ran. He stumbled once, but righted himself. Then he stumbled a second time and pitched forward, hands outstretched to break his fall. The sticks from a bush splintered in his face, and his palms slid through mouldy leaves and freezing mud.

He was up before he drew another breath. He staggered a step or two, then continued running.

Except he could no longer see the figures ahead of him.

He searched the dark and light between the trees for movement, the flap of a coat, a wildly swinging arm. He saw nothing.

He paused and heard nothing. An owl hooted and then was silent.

The cold bit at his neck and jaw, and bitterness lingered on his tongue. He'd lost them.

❧

"This will not happen again," Bayard ground out.

"You shouldn't blame yourself, Bay." Clare wore a long-sleeved morning gown, but he could see the redness of her wrists from the rope that had bound her last night. "They were after Alethea, just as you had intended. They simply made a mistake."

Alethea sat on a chair, her sister sitting beside her. In the light streaming from the music room windows, the two looked remarkably alike. Lucy had lighter eyes and a softer face than Alethea's determined one.

"It was clever of Clare to step on my slipper so that I could slip my foot out and rip the ribbons off," Lucy said.

"If anything, it is my fault," Clare said. "It was I who insisted

Lucy wear a more elegant gown and dress up her hair for last night's event. If I had not, the two men would not have mistaken her for Alethea, and they would not have taken me simply because I was with her."

Bayard turned away from her to control the wild anxiety that still rose up in him when he remembered his helplessness last night. They had found Clare solely by the grace of God.

He never wanted to feel so powerless again.

Ian looked deceptively casual where he sat at the pianoforte, but Bayard could see his clenched fist as he said, "Bath is too full of strangers. There were too many ways the carriage could have taken. I thank God for whatever made you stop to ask Oakridge. I would not have thought of that."

Raven spoke from where he leaned against the front of the desk. "You are guests in my house, your servants mingling with mine. Two strangers in Ravenhurst livery were easily overlooked."

"You did not recognize either of them?" Bayard asked.

Clare shook her head. Lucy said, "Neither of them was the grey man, nor Mr. Golding from Alethea's description of him."

"I doubt it was the grey man," Ian said. "You injured his knee, and the blighters last night weren't limping."

"One of them could have been the man from Sydney Gardens," Raven said.

"I didn't get close enough to see their faces."

"We never saw the man in Sydney Gardens," Clare said, "but the two men who took us were large fellows. I should have noticed their livery fitted them ill when they entered the library last night, but I was watching the performance. They were strong enough to hold us and put their hands over our mouths so we could not call out."

"That one fellow in Sydney Gardens was like a mountain." Raven rubbed his knuckles in remembrance.

"Even if you had seen them, Mr. Golding could simply hire new men next time," Alethea said.

"I am tired of Mr. Golding's client hiring underlings to do his bidding," Bayard said. "It is time the scoundrel came out into the open."

"We must force him to do so," Raven said. "He will not be tricked into it."

"Which is why I think we must move to Terralton Abbey."

"Leave Bath?" Clare said. "Mama will not like it."

"I need you to convince her, for she must act as hostess for our 'house party.'"

"I am assuming you mean myself and my aunt as guests?" Alethea said. "Aunt Ebena will not like it overmuch either."

"You must convince her, in light of the danger."

"But you will need to include Margaret as well," Alethea added.

"I intended to."

"My mother will not like me to leave her alone in Bath," Raven said.

"Would she join us? Without her retinue of servants," Bayard qualified.

Raven's light blue eyes surveyed Alethea, then Bayard. "I believe so," he said.

"At Terralton Abbey, the servants will be all ours," Bayard said. "The countryside is known to us, the neighbors are friends. Any strangers will attract attention where they would not in Bath."

"The villain may not follow us to such a dangerous situation for him," Alethea said.

"He will if he has incentive to do so. We fooled Mr. Golding into believing the fake violin was real. In the country, we will have time to create a more credible forgery. If you show it around the village, and let it become known that it is being stored in the Terralton Abbey music room, he will try to take it."

"And if he hired local men to do his bidding, he or Mr. Golding would still need to arrive in the area to do so," Ian said.

"I doubt he would hire men," Alethea said. "They would not know which violin was the true one. He would need to reveal himself in order to have opportunity to see if the violin is the one he seeks."

"And we shall be watching," Bayard said.

"If we can seize Mr. Golding, we may induce him to reveal the name of his client," Raven said. "We could offer him more money than the man who has hired him."

Lucy said tentatively, "His client may have more caution than you assign to him. He may not follow us at all."

"If he does not, it will enable me to continue my investigations into the violin," Bayard said. "I have received a letter this morning from Lord Hazardfield. He is a prodigious art collector, especially pieces acquired from Italy. I wrote to him and asked for any information on the Count of Sondrono's descendants, since he is familiar with Italian noble families. He writes that he does not know, but it happens that his father bought three paintings commissioned by Sondrono, and he has given me the direction of the man who acted as the agent in selling the pieces. The agent's name is Guido Manco, and he is in London."

"Very Italian name," Ian murmured.

"I have written to him. Since he or his employer somehow acquired Sondrono's family treasures, he may know more about the family, or who we may contact, or even about the violin. I asked him to reply to me at Terralton."

"When do you wish to leave?" Clare asked.

He glanced to Alethea. "It will depend upon your aunt agreeing to this scheme. We shall convey you all to Terralton Abbey. I believe that would be safest."

Clare stood. "I shall convince Mama. After the events of last night, she may be eager to leave Bath."

The threat to his family and to Alethea plagued him. It was an enemy he could not touch. He could not simply knock the bounder down with a solid blow to the chin. "The sooner we can stop this man, the sooner everything will return as it was before."

There was a sadness and also a firmness to Alethea's face and figure as she also stood. "Yes. The sooner this is over, the better for us all."

CHAPTER FIFTEEN

*M*argaret was thriving in the country. If alienating every child between the ages of ten and fourteen within a twenty-mile radius could be considered thriving.

Just returned from visits to Dommick's neighbors with Lucy, Alethea sighed at the sight of Margaret, the scruff of her dress held in the firm hand of one of Dommick's grooms, her lip bloodied, her skirt torn, and a long twig sticking straight out of her tangled brown curls like a feather in a lady's headdress. She also had enough mud upon her face and dress to create her own flower garden.

Before Alethea could say anything, Margaret said, "I did as you said, I didn't provoke them. This was entirely unprovoked. They . . . *besieged* me."

"A *siege* typically involves waiting, not attacking."

Margaret thought a moment. "It was a very aggressive siege. Much like . . . the Vikings. Do you see, I am learning something from my history book."

"I cannot recall that the Vikings besieged anyone. I rather think they attacked without mercy."

"That is exactly what happened to me," Margaret declared.

Alethea sighed, too tired to follow the circular logic of a twelve-year-old. She looked to the long-suffering groom, who had apparently seen the melee and waded into the fray to rescue Margaret. "Thank you. I shall take her."

"Alethea! Did you see the child?" Aunt Ebena's strident voice carried down the main stairs of Terralton Abbey to echo in the entrance hall. Her aunt appeared at the top of the staircase, and the sight of Margaret in her miry glory sent her hands and eyes into the air.

"I shall take Margaret to be cleaned," Lucy said. "You should calm your aunt."

Alethea hastened up the staircase, removing her bonnet as she met Aunt Ebena on the landing. Below, Lucy marched Margaret toward the back of the house.

"Where have you been?" Aunt Ebena walked with her toward the drawing room.

"I have been visiting Mrs. McDonald and Mrs. Wyatt."

"Did you not call upon them with Miss Terralton only a few days ago?"

"Mrs. McDonald's daughter favours the pianoforte and Mrs. Wyatt's daughter enjoys the harp, and they both asked for new music to play, so I lent them some of mine."

Aunt Ebena snorted. "All this socializing and visiting you are doing."

Alethea refrained from answering until they were alone in the drawing room, away from the servants. "I am being seen, which will hopefully draw the thief to this area to attempt to steal the violin. And once he is revealed, we may return to Bath, ma'am."

She could not blame Dommick for wishing his life to return to normal as soon as possible. He had a happy family and good friends. He did not need a knotty spinster, her prickly aunt, and her ramshackle young cousin in his life threatening the safety of his sister.

Aunt Ebena sat upon the sofa and reverted to her original grievance. "You must do more to control that child."

"I have spoken to her numerous times about fighting with the rector's daughters."

"I told her the same only hours ago, and you see how she returned to the house. I should think that the offspring of a clergyman would be more agreeable."

"I fear that Margaret is overly sensitive to their remarks."

"But fighting! I should hope the rector is properly disciplining his children."

"I shall go to speak to his wife today or tomorrow," Alethea said. "Margaret must learn to be more amiable. She cannot pick a fight simply because she does not agree with what her playmates propose to do for the afternoon. That appears to be the common theme of all her altercations."

Aunt Ebena's brows suddenly lowered, and she regarded Alethea in consternation. "Oh, surely not," she muttered.

"What is it?"

"Perhaps I am to blame. When Margaret first complained that the girls at the rectory would browbeat her into submission to their games, I insisted that one must never give in to bullies."

"You said something similar to me once, as I recall."

"I told you that you must never allow someone to induce you to do something against what you knew to be right. It was quite a different thing, but I am afraid I did not differentiate it for Margaret. She probably took my meaning to be that she should never allow anyone to coerce her to their will."

"How did she get that impression? Surely you did not use those exact terms."

"I did not, but . . ." Aunt Ebena's eyes seemed to have the weight of years behind them—painful, heavy years. "I was quite adamant about standing up to those who would intimidate us."

Alethea stared. She wanted to ask who had attempted to intimidate her aunt, but she did not dare. She did not want to jeopardize their current truce with probing, possibly impertinent questions.

Aunt Ebena said in a tired voice, "How shall you discipline Margaret?"

"She shall have only bread and water today, and tomorrow I shall have her apologize to the rector's daughters." Alethea hoped that would be enough.

"If only we could somehow force those obstinate children to become friends." Aunt Ebena was silent a long moment, then she rose to her feet. "I feel the need for solitude. I shall see you at dinner."

Alethea sat in solitude herself in the drawing room for several minutes. Her aunt's strange mood made her thoughtful and melancholy herself. And yet, today's short conversation had been the most intimate she had had with her aunt since coming to live with her. The two of them had drawn closer, and she was sure that was what enabled Aunt Ebena to reveal this glimpse of herself. Alethea wondered what had put that pain behind her words.

She was soon interrupted by Lady Ravenhurst. "Good day, Lady Alethea. Am I disturbing you?"

"Of course not, my lady. Shall I ring for tea?"

"Yes, please. I feel as though breakfast was days ago." She gave a light laugh in her low, soothing voice, which put Alethea in mind of warm treacle.

After the maid had brought the tea and Alethea had poured, Lady Ravenhurst set her cup down and said in a confiding tone, "I do hope you will forgive me if I impose too much, but when I entered the room, you seemed despondent. Is there anything I can do for you?"

"I apologize, my lady, I did not intend to cause you concern."

"I would not have remarked upon it had I not seen your aunt leave the drawing room to walk upstairs, and she also looked quite downcast. And from my bedroom window, I spotted Miss Margaret with a terrific split lip."

"We are unsure what to do about Margaret. She refuses to get along with the girls at the rectory."

"Ah, yes, that can be a difficult situation. Raven's sister did not often play with the squire's daughter for that reason. You have spoken to Margaret about being accommodating to new playmates?"

It reminded Alethea of the strange pain in her aunt's eyes, the sense that someone had tried to intimidate Aunt Ebena at some point in the past. "Yes. However, she misunderstood when Aunt Ebena spoke of not allowing others to intimate us."

Lady Ravenhurst tilted her head and leaned closer. "Are you well, my dear? You again have that despondent air about you. You are quite worrying me."

"I assure you, I am well," Alethea said quickly. They were silent a moment, and Alethea worried that her remark had seemed cold, which was ungrateful in the face of Lady Ravenhurst's warm concern. Alethea said tentatively, "I was thoughtful because my aunt had been earnest in advising Margaret not to allow others to bully her. She gave me the same advice when Mr. Golding approached me to sell my violin. There was a . . . heaviness in my aunt's countenance as we spoke earlier. It made me wonder if perhaps someone in her past had intimidated her."

There was a look of consciousness in Lady Ravenhurst's face, and she stared at her teacup. Alethea worried she had been imprudent, and was about to apologize and excuse herself when Lady Ravenhurst said in a softer voice, "What your aunt advised can be a good piece of wisdom, especially when a woman's life has been altered by the plans of others."

Alethea was confused, which her face must have revealed, for

Lady Ravenhurst reached out to touch the back of her hand with gentle fingers. "And now I am the one who is despondent. But I will explain, for I believe I understand your aunt and . . ." She searched Alethea's face. ". . . I do not think anyone else will be able to tell you this confidence."

"Confidence?"

"Your aunt is older than I, but our husbands were of an age. Mr. Garen was twenty years older than your aunt when he married her, and there were thirty years between myself and my husband. Raven does not remember his father." Something in Lady Ravenhurst's eyes made Alethea suspect that the marchioness believed that to be an advantage. "He came into the title when he was six years old."

From Lady Ravenhurst's tone, Alethea suspected she had not been in love with her husband, and Aunt Ebena had not been in love with Mr. Garen.

"Before my husband died, we would spend every season in town, just as Mr. and Mrs. Garen did. I did not know her well, but my husband was acquainted with Mr. Garen. There are not many in town now who remember that your aunt's father, Lord Winterscomb, had not been very wealthy. However, he received a generous settlement upon your aunt's marriage to Mr. Garen."

The air solidified in Alethea's lungs, and she could not breathe. She heard the hated rise and fall of her brother's voice as he explained the betrothal arrangements he had made on her behalf. She remembered his vitriol and anger. She remembered the searing pain of him breaking the last two fingers of her left hand because she had defied him. The knuckles, healed for over a year now, began to throb.

Lady Ravenhurst was not looking at Alethea. "You must understand that in those times, it was not so unusual for a woman to be sold in marriage by her father. But it can be very damaging to a woman's heart to know she has had no authority over the direction of her own life."

"Yes," Alethea whispered. She rubbed the fingers of her left hand. "I understand. Margaret may have misunderstood my aunt, but women have so few choices that when able, we must not allow others to tyrannize us."

"You must not think your aunt had an unhappy marriage. She greatly enjoyed the culture of the city—the concerts, private art exhibitions, museums, literary circles—and her husband enabled her to indulge her passions."

"She still does." Alethea understood, now, her aunt's love for Bath and all the events she could attend there, where she could live within her means as opposed to London.

Lady Ravenhurst took a sip of her lukewarm tea and grimaced. She warmed her cup with more from the pot and did the same to Alethea's. In a more cheerful voice, she said, "I fear we have wandered far afield from the original lesson to be taught to your young cousin. What shall you do, then?"

The discussion moved to the trials of being a parent, until Lady Morrish wandered into the drawing room.

"My lady, allow me to ring for a fresh pot of tea," Lady Ravenhurst said.

Alethea rose. "I beg you will both excuse me, for I must speak to Margaret, and then I must call upon the rector's wife."

She found Margaret sulking near the Monk's pond—or perhaps skulking was the better word, for she was avoiding the nursery maid who had been assigned to her. Lucy had cleaned Margaret's face and removed the twig and any other gifts of nature from her hair, which was now somewhat tamed. She had put Margaret in a fresh dress, but the girl had run outside with only a light spencer against the cold. Her stubbornness had refused to allow her to return inside for a cloak, and her lips were beginning to turn blue.

Alethea pulled Margaret close to wrap them both in her cloak and directed their steps toward the small, walled garden on the other side of the house, with its narrow walks and stone benches along the perimeter. Margaret had not spoken but leveled her with a look not in the least bit subordinate. Alethea had not spoken either, and they passed under the archway into the sheltering arms of the garden. They sat upon a stone bench, and the stillness wrapped around them.

The garden would be beautiful in the spring, with flowers bordering the paths and the arches of trained pear trees in full blossom. In winter it was more bleak but still beautiful.

"I will not apologize to them," Margaret said.

"What started the squabble this time?"

It involved some game of Robin Hood with roles that Margaret had objected to. "I don't like it here. I want to return to Bath."

"There will always be people we do not perfectly sympathize with. But we must learn to be amiable and polite."

"One cannot be amiable with girls like that."

Alethea thought of all she had learned about her aunt this morning and how, a year ago, the two of them would never have had the conversation they did in the drawing room. "When I first came to live with Aunt Ebena, we did not comprehend each other well. But I worked to understand her personality, and now I know for a certainty that she loves me and you very much."

"How can I understand their personalities when they are so overbearing?"

"Sometimes we must simply be silent. Eventually, they may realize they are in the wrong and apologize."

"That is what Mrs. Coon says," Margaret said, referring to the rector's wife. "She said that God would speak to our hearts and convict us to do what is right."

Alethea was not so certain of that. Where had that God been when her brother had broken her fingers?

Margaret continued, "And I told her that God told me to give Maria a slap."

Alethea tried not to smile. "That was very wrong," she said.

"Mrs. Coon said that if we are not listening to God, he cannot speak to our hearts, which is why people are often disagreeable to each other."

That simplistic observation sobered Alethea. Her family had been very disagreeable to her, but had she not been disagreeable to Aunt Ebena and Dommick? The thought that she had behaved like her father or brother was disturbing.

"You should try to understand Maria and Louisa better," Alethea said. "Perhaps they have a reason for why they are so forceful in their opinions. And you yourself are not very pliant in your own ideas."

Margaret grimaced. "Oh, very well."

"Now." Alethea stood, forcing Margaret to her feet also. "We shall go to your room, and I am going to ask you to do something courageous, involving great skill and strength."

"What?" Margaret looked eager.

"You will spend the rest of the day in your room—"

"But, Alethea—"

"—reflecting on what I have told you, and thinking of ideas of how you may implement them."

"Of understanding Maria and Louisa?"

"Yes. And then you will gather your might so that tomorrow you may apologize to them—"

Margaret groaned.

"—and even somewhat *mean* it."

⁓⁂⁓

After depositing Margaret in her room with the nursery maid, Alethea turned her steps toward the rectory, feeling apprehensive.

Mrs. Coon was a kind, gentle woman, but her two daughters were absolute terrors. They had much more energy than Mrs. Coon could spare to them out of her full days.

Alethea was crossing the stretch of gravel in front of the abbey when she came in sight of Dommick, a shooting rifle over his shoulder and his gamekeeper walking beside him. Two dogs pranced about his feet, then raced to Alethea as they caught sight of her.

She knelt and gave them her hands to sniff and lick, and when she rose again, Dommick stood before her. He had given his gun to the gamekeeper, and he now offered her his arm. "Have you a moment to walk with me?"

"Of course." Alethea was more than willing to interrupt her visit to the rectory.

The dogs followed the gamekeeper toward the house. Dommick led her through the grass around the lake. They entered the forest edging part of the lake, tramping deeper through the trees toward the far side.

They came upon a stream that emptied into the body of water and followed it back to where it flowed in several fingers of trickles. Reeds grew at the water's edge, and a path beside it had been constructed of flat rocks pressed into the soil. Trees overshadowed the path, and the brown fingers of ferns curled alongside. There was a wildness to the place that appealed to her.

"May we stop here?"

"There is a bench farther upstream."

They continued until they came upon a tiny gazebo of dark painted wood tucked under the trees and trailing vines. Moss covered the shingled roof, which protected the wooden seats and stone floor from the falling leaves and rain, although the benches were a little damp from the last storm. Alethea did not mind and promptly sat, drawing her cloak about her to protect from the chill in the shadows of the trees.

Dommick drew a letter from his coat pocket. "I have been pleasantly surprised by the result of my letter to Guido Manco. His father, who was also named Guido Manco, was in fact Count Sondrono's secretary. He was the intermediary who sold Sondrono's paintings to Lord Hazardfield's father."

"Does he know of the count's living relations?"

"He has sent me the names of two of Sondrono's brothers who lived in Italy, but Manco's father left the country before Manco was born and he does not know more. I can inquire, but correspondence to the continent is slow."

"This is not promising news."

"That is not what was promising about his letter. Manco's father kept meticulous records of each item he sold for the count, which included the names of the men who bought them. He also had records of where and how the count acquired the item."

Alethea stared in disbelief. "He has a record of the violin, although it was sold so long ago?"

"He may. When he received my letter, he looked through his father's records and found that his father sold three violins as well as other instruments."

"So we can determine which of those violins is mine. We will know where the count obtained it and to whom it was sold."

"The thief could be related to Sondrono, or to the man who commissioned the violin, if it was not the count, or to the man to whom the violin was sold."

"You are thorough in your distrust. I would not have considered those suspected persons."

Dommick gave a half smile, and this time Alethea's breath caught for a different reason.

"Manco is employed by the Duchess of Meyrick, managing her private art collection. He writes that he is travelling to several of the duchess's estates to inventory new acquisitions and will be passing near this part of the country in a few days. Rather than waiting for my reply, he will call upon me to view the violin and compare it to his father's records."

"A few days and we may know all." And soon after that, if Dommick could uncover the identity of the thief, she would return to Bath. She pushed aside the lowering thought. "Has anyone approached the music room to look at our forged violin?"

He shook his head. "Ord watches from the hidden gallery, and Raven, Ian, and I take our turns."

"I have been doing as you asked and calling on your neighbors and speaking to the local shopkeepers. They all now know that I am a guest at Terralton Abbey and the owner of a particularly fine and mysterious violin."

"I'm sure Clare was able to direct you to the ones most likely to spread news of your arrival all throughout the country."

"Oh, yes. However, your mother is still ill from the effects of travelling from Bath, and so Clare has been reading to her. I have taken Lucy with me on my visits." She hesitated, then confessed, "Several people have remarked on our similar features. I did not wish to deceive them, but I have no desire to cause gossip—the neighbors of Trittonstone Park knew of Lucy's parentage from the moment of her birth, and my association with her was what they objected to. But here, people know nothing of her and she is Clare's abigail. I have attempted to turn the conversation, but I am afraid many have guessed she is a baseborn relation of mine."

"It cannot be helped. Clare will determine the tone of the gossip. She has but to bat her eyelashes and the neighbors quite spoil her."

"You should show your support of Clare and Lucy. One of the reasons my neighbors disapproved of my friendship with Lucy was because my father had been vocal in his disapprobation."

"Probably because it was an embarrassment to him."

"Oh, no doubt." She gave a harsh bark of laughter. "He did not appreciate his indiscretion being flung into his face. And I fully knew it. He could not know his blustering would make me fight harder to be close to her."

"You must admit that your friendship is unusual."

"It is part of the reason why I value it so highly. Lucy wants nothing from me, because like me, the men in her life have been nothing but disappointments." The bitter words hung in the air between them. She immediately regretted saying so much. "I apologize, my comments were indiscreet."

"I think I understand you better." He looked abashed. "When I first met you in London, my words must have seemed an echo of your father's treatment of you."

She had never consciously connected the two events, but he was right, of course. "I assure you, I was childish and willful. But the violin has always been my favoured instrument. Its music touched me in ways the music of other instruments did not."

"I have felt that about the violin. I had more time to practice when I was in school. After university, I spent much time with my father learning to manage the estate, and then I went to war." His voice dropped, and she sensed a darkness had settled upon his mood.

"You have a lovely estate. In Bath, I missed the freedom of the countryside. I am happy to be here." And when she left it, she would leave both Dommick and Lucy. The thought made her feel empty, and she stared out at the stream, the reeds waving in the motion from the water.

The sight of the reeds reminded her of happier days and one of her favourite pastimes. "Have you a knife?" she asked.

Looking confused, he reached into his coat and withdrew a small folding penknife. "This belonged to my father."

"I shall be careful with it." She rose from the bench and

approached the water. The mossy ground was soggy, but she managed to nick several reeds at the waterline with the knife.

"What will you do with those?" Dommick asked as she returned to her seat.

"Pipes. Did you never make them yourself?"

His smile appeared like sunlight through the mist. "No. You must show me."

She removed her bonnet to better see the reeds, and he placed it on the bench next to his hat. She measured the proper length, then formed holes at appropriate intervals. She handed him the knife and guided him in making his own pipe, although she widened a few of the holes he had made. "I shall clean your knife for you." She folded it and tucked it into her pocket.

She formed her fingers over the holes and blew. The sound was breathy and soft, matching the gurgle of the water over the stones and the green shade of the trees.

With very little instruction, he had mastered the notes, and soon they were playing duets. The music was challenging but fun, and they laughed at some of the horrible runs of intervals they made.

Alethea's heart returned to the golden glow of days playing the pipe with Calandra beside the lake at Trittonstone Park. She had been young and carefree. Her brother had been only a bratty boy, cosseted by the nurse and her father, and not interesting enough to play with. Lucy had not played the pipe but had danced in the glade as they made music. Alethea had been so happy.

She was happy now, and not just in the remembrance of fonder days. She was enjoying music again with a skilled musician. Playing with Dommick made her feel as close to him as an embrace.

"I am not surprised you know how to play a pipe," Dommick said. "Wind instruments are even more scandalous for women to play than violin. I expected no less from you."

"I was not very skilled at the flute. Calandra compared my playing to a mournful owl with a very poor sense of pitch."

"When I first learned to play the flute, Ian said that he would rather muck out the stables than listen to me."

"Cruel friend." Alethea smiled.

Dommick frowned at his pipe. "He would say so today. Half the time my G sharps were flat."

"You must angle your fingers differently." She reached for his hands and positioned his fingers over the holes in the pipe.

They had removed their gloves to play. His fingers were supple and strong, with rough calluses from violin playing. This close to him, she could smell the scent of lime from his skin, mingled with the green smell of the trees and the spicy warmth of his musk. She avoided looking at his face, for he would see in her eyes how he affected her. She hoped he did not notice her shortness of breath.

After she had positioned his fingers, she was about to remove her hands when he suddenly took hold of them. His palm felt hot against her cooled fingertips. He tugged, and she leaned closer.

Then his warm palm was on the skin of her neck, just over her racing pulse, just as his mouth touched hers.

He did not kiss her as desperately as he had the night of the concert. At first, his lips moved softly, as if hesitant to touch, to taste. Then he pressed closer, and she felt as if he had pressed her against his soul. His kiss was like the comforting wood of her violin, like Calandra's touch on her head, like the scent of a rose in summer, like the sweetness of a trembling violin note. He felt like home.

She had fallen in love with him.

The thought frightened her, sent her heartbeat galloping. Or perhaps that was because his hand cupped her cheek, her jaw, while the other buried itself in her hair.

She had thought she would never meet a man deserving of

her trust. But this man had shown his concern for her safety, his love for his sister, his passion in music, his courage in danger. He had shown his own stubbornness, his own flaws, his willingness to argue with her, his ability to apologize. He was not perfect. He was Dommick.

She loved him. She never wanted to leave him. She would give all she possessed if only to be with him.

It was just as she realized this, just as she was pressing closer to him, that he suddenly stiffened. His hands left her face, her hair. He drew back, looking down at her with a mix of longing and unhappiness.

What did it mean? He didn't seem the sort of man to blithely steal kisses. Yet he wasn't looking at her as a lover might. He had said nothing of his feelings.

And what of her feelings? What of her determination not to marry, her plans for Italy, her love for Lucy? What of her love for music that had motivated her for so much of her life?

She pulled away and shot to her feet. She didn't like the look in his eyes, and she was afraid of the words that would arise out of his conflicted feelings. They would be more wounding than the words other men had inflicted upon her, because these words would come from Dommick.

"I must go," she said.

"Alethea—"

"Say nothing," she said fiercely. "I have no wish to hear it. I could not bear . . ." She took a breath to try to calm herself. "We may both say things we will later regret."

He rose to his feet now, his eyes burning into hers. There was confusion, and still that yearning, that pain, that terror in his eyes. She did not know what to make of it all, and it cut her to the quick.

She turned and walked away before the tears began to fall.

CHAPTER SIXTEEN

lethea could not avoid the visit any longer. She should have gone yesterday, but she had been too troubled by what had happened with Dommick to be able to speak rationally to any creature. She had pleaded a headache and asked for a dinner tray in her room, which she had devoured. She'd then shocked the maid by requesting an extra serving of dessert.

The poets who waxed eloquent upon the starvation of love were full of rot.

This morning she dabbed her eyes with water so they didn't look quite so much like two welts on her face, but she had eaten early to escape the rest of the house, and now she wore her closest bonnet to shade her countenance. She went upstairs to the schoolroom where Margaret was picking sulkily at the remains of her breakfast. Alethea removed her from her half-eaten toast and cold tea with difficulty.

"You look terrible," Margaret said nastily as they walked to the rectory.

"Since I must speak to the rector's wife about your behaviour with her daughters, is it any wonder? Or should I have left *you* to speak to the rector's wife?"

Margaret's first reaction was excitement at the prospect, but as she imagined the tenor of the conversation, she grew sullen again. "I suppose not."

"Have you meditated upon my advice to you yesterday?"

Margaret kicked at a stone on the path.

Alethea continued, "It might help you to understand Maria and Louisa better. And if it does not, then you shall use the opportunity to learn to be polite."

"I am polite."

"Polite behaviour is responding indifferently to what we do not like."

"Why must I be polite to them?"

"Why must you play with them?"

Margaret knotted the strings on her bonnet. "There aren't any other girls to play with. The squire's boys are very stupid."

"Then if you will choose the girls' company, you must learn to be polite."

Margaret heaved a sigh, but her sullen expression softened. Alethea hoped she had made some progress toward mutual felicity between the two houses.

The rectory was a snug cottage but rather bleak in the flower gardens, as it appeared Mrs. Coon was not a great gardener. As Alethea and Margaret walked up the path to the front door, the squire's wife was just departing.

"Mrs. Coon, Lord bless you for sending your maid to us with the squire ailing so," the woman said.

"I should come myself if I could," Mrs. Coon said. "Do let us know if there is aught else we may do to assist you." Her eyes alighted on Alethea and Margaret, and although Alethea had expected some exasperation upon seeing Margaret, she instead smiled broadly and invited them inside.

"You will pardon the dirty tea things," she said cheerfully, "but the squire's wife has been here for the past hour. Poor woman, her husband has a horrid cough. Indeed, he had a horrid cough last month." She frowned and tilted her head at the thought. "The man gets them curiously often."

"We have certainly not arrived for tea, Mrs. Coon. Margaret wishes to apologize to your daughters."

"As to that, they wish to apologize to her."

"Whatever for?" Alethea did not miss the fleeting look of satisfaction on Margaret's face and gave her arm a discreet pinch. The girl winced, and her look of long-suffering returned.

"Apparently Maria had made an inappropriate comment about Margaret's deceased parents, which was what precipitated the altercation." Mrs. Coon sat on the settee, and Margaret and Alethea took the sofa opposite.

"I told you—" Margaret whispered to Alethea, but she stepped on her young cousin's foot to silence her.

Mrs. Coon continued as if she had not heard. "I have spoken most severely with her on the matter."

"Be that as it may, Margaret should not have responded so," Alethea said.

"The girls are out back, helping the old gardener with the vegetables. Mr. Coon really should pension the poor man off, for he can barely keep up the kitchen garden and I am no gardener, but we don't have the heart to do it to him. Margaret, you may join the girls in their toils or inform them that they are allowed a reprieve."

Margaret bounded up, but Alethea grabbed her wrist and ventured to Mrs. Coon, "Is that altogether wise?"

"Fear not, Lady Alethea. I have instructed the girls in what they should say and do. For this afternoon, at least," she qualified.

Alethea said to Margaret, "I expect you to apologize, miss."

"Yes, Alethea." And Margaret was gone in a swirl of skirts.

"With willful girls, Lady Alethea, allow me to guide you, as I possess two of them." Mrs. Coon smiled. "Instruct them in proper behaviour and then allow them to find their own way. If you dictate to them, they will invariably do the opposite."

Alethea squirmed on the sofa, reminded of her own childhood. "I see your point."

Mrs. Coon sighed. "I admit I have been indulgent to Maria and Louisa for several weeks. I believe I know the cause of the girls' rude behaviour toward Margaret."

"I assure you, Margaret is not blameless. She misunderstands their comments and responds inappropriately."

"But of course she would misunderstand when she doesn't know what has occurred recently. You see, Lady Alethea, the girls' playmate, Daphne, died quite suddenly two months ago."

Alethea drew in a breath. "How tragic."

"Daphne was a retiring creature, sweet and helpful. The girls were devastated. I assure you, the fight yesterday was unwonted behaviour from them. They have been combative not only with Margaret but with other children in the neighborhood since Daphne died. After the fight yesterday, I suspected that my girls were still grieving for their friend. When I forced Maria and Louisa to repeat the conversation prior to the exchange, it appeared to me they were attempting to mould Margaret into Daphne's role."

"Which Margaret would not take kindly to. She is very willful."

"The three of them are peas in a pod, I am afraid. I spoke to them about Daphne and their behaviour toward Margaret, and the girls were truly contrite, especially after they had spent some time in prayer."

Alethea could not understand how prayer would benefit a ten- and a thirteen-year-old girl. When Alethea had been Margaret's age, prayer had been a chore and opportunity to consider where she would ride her horse after service ended.

Mrs. Coon laughed. "I see you are not convinced. Here is another piece of advice for the raising of willful girls. Nothing you could say would have greater impact than the Lord convicting their hearts. They will obey you out of principle, but they would obey God out of true feeling."

Still doubtful, Alethea said, "Margaret mentioned that you had spoken to her about God speaking to our hearts and guiding us in doing what is right."

"Then let us hope that Margaret will also listen to God. You smile, Lady Alethea."

"In my experience, that is not what people will most often do."

"No, it is not," Mrs. Coon said candidly. "But in those cases, we must allow God to comfort us in our troubles."

The words were what the Trittonstone Park clergyman had preached at the pulpit, a tired intonation of the trite and hackneyed. Yet Mrs. Coon's expression was far more discerning and kind than any clergyman Alethea had known, and from her lips, the words had a stronger, deeper meaning.

But Alethea's spirit wrangled with the notion. Where had God been when her brother hurt her? Why had God taken Calandra just when Alethea needed her most? Why had God allowed Wilfred to kick her out of her home? Why would she desire comfort from such a God?

"We most often base our experience with God upon the actions of others. But you must not mistake human frailty for divine relationship," Mrs. Coon said.

"Divine relationship? I do not comprehend."

"God's love for us."

"Oh." Yes, the parson had preached of God's love, but it had always been a vague thing that had to do with words such as *salvation* and *sanctification* and *justification*.

"I beg your pardon." Mrs. Coon rang the bell, and the maid removed the old tea things. "Fresh tea, please, Daisy."

"There is no need."

"Of course there is a need. While you remain here, the girls will not dare descend to bickering or, worse, fisticuffs." Mrs. Coon winked.

"I am mortified by Margaret's behaviour. She has not responded well to discipline in this matter. Speaking to her, scolding her, punishing her have all come to naught."

"I have raised many children. Maria and Louisa are my youngest of seven. So you may trust my advice in this matter. If you discipline with love, Margaret will respond to that. We all only want someone to love us."

Who had ever loved Alethea besides Calandra and Lucy? Would Dommick be able to love her? She shied from that thought.

Yes, Alethea could say she loved Margaret. She, who had never wanted children. She had felt so ashamed of who she was, assuming something was wrong with her for not desiring a family. But her bias had been because she had never found a man whom she would consider for the candidate of father and husband.

Until Dommick.

But in caring for Margaret, she had changed, and she could now see the possibility of having her own family, if she found a man whom she could love. Who would love her.

Her solitary life felt desolate. Her violin and her sister used to comfort her, but that was before she had done the foolish business of falling in love.

Could Dommick love her?

Dare she find out?

❧

He was a cad. A fool.

Bayard stood at his study window looking at the courtyard

garden, grey and brown beneath the heavy clouds. Beyond them lay the square pool and the grassy terraced areas of the Great Garden where Margaret was running, her cloak long discarded, her brown curls flying behind her. Slower but no less exuberant, Alethea gave chase, her dark hair falling loose from its pins and tumbling down her shoulders.

He could not condemn a woman with such a love of life to living with a man in his condition. He could not expose her to his constant fear.

He was a coward. Alethea would not treat him as his former betrothed had done, and yet he feared what her reaction would be if she discovered the truth, the horror, the ugliness, the utter monstrosities in his mind. He could not even face them himself.

All the men in her life had only hurt her. He could not do that to her as well.

He had been happy yesterday by the stream, playing reed pipes. What other woman would delight in something so simple? What other woman would revel in the musical challenge of the duets? What other woman could have stirred him to forget his scruples and kiss her the way he knew he should not? But the music, her voice, her touch had been like awakening from a nightmare, a sunlit day from a stormy night. He wanted that awakening, that sunlight. He wanted Alethea.

He could never have her. He could never have any woman while he was . . . like this.

A tap at the study door, and then his butler, Forrow, appeared. "My lord, Lady Whittlesby has arrived and wishes to speak to you."

Here? Now? Before he could speak, the lady pushed past Forrow. The butler withdrew and closed the study door.

"Lady Whittlesby, my mother—"

"I have not come to speak to your mother, but to you." Her

carriage dress brushed the Turkish carpet as she sat in the solid oak chair before the desk.

"May I ring for tea?"

"No, I shan't be a few minutes. I have stopped while on my way to London." She thumped her palm against the heavy armrest of the chair. "What is this I hear of Miss Terralton's kidnapping?"

He stiffened. How had the news been spread abroad? "I am grieved that it has reached so many ears," he said slowly.

"Oh, don't get into a bother, it's a well-kept secret. Everyone is tittering about the maid running off with a footpad, who attacked two footmen, or some such nonsense."

"How did you hear of it?"

"I did not. I guessed. My groom happened to mention that on the night of the concert, he saw a hired hack pull up before Ravenhurst's home, and the two women who emerged looked remarkably like Lady Alethea and Miss Terralton, although rather disheveled. I recalled I had been speaking to Lady Alethea at that moment and knew it could not have been her. But later I remembered that when I stopped Miss Terralton on Milsom Street the other day, I had noticed her maid because of her striking resemblance to Lady Alethea. When I heard the wild stories, I pieced the information together. Miss Terralton is well?"

"She is."

"Why was she taken? Ransom?"

"No." Bayard did not want to say more, but Lady Whittlesby heaved an exasperated sigh.

"I have puzzled out this much, Dommick, so you may as well tell me the rest."

He supposed Lady Whittlesby had some right to know since she had involved herself in Alethea's violin. "The kidnappers were working for a man who wanted Lady Alethea, not Clare. They mistook the maid for Alethea and took Clare since she was with her."

"But Lady Alethea's dowry is not . . ." Lady Whittlesby gasped. "Never say it is because of her violin? I never would have suspected the threat to be so violent."

"I thought it safest to remove them all here, to Terralton Abbey."

Lady Whittlesby leaned forward. "I assure you, Dommick, I had no idea my request would put your family or Lady Alethea in danger."

"I am working to discover who is pursuing Lady Alethea's violin, but I have nothing definitive for you."

Lady Whittlesby sat back in the chair. "After the concert, had you not left Bath so precipitously, I would have told you that I was sufficiently impressed by Miss Terralton's performance and the renewed Quartet. I have decided to feature you all in my concert this spring, regardless of your inquiries into Lady Alethea's violin." She gave him a pleased smile.

But Bayard could not return it. London now seemed full of dangers and menace. Alethea was safer here, at Terralton. She would probably say he did not have the right to be concerned for her, but he was determined not to be like the other men in her life who'd had no care for her at all.

He spared a pang for Clare and his mother. He had agreed to Lady Whittlesby's scheme for their sakes, but he would hope they would agree that Alethea's safety precluded a brilliant social opportunity.

Lady Whittlesby's smile faded, and she gave him a piercing look. "You do not seem pleased."

"London is too dangerous for Lady Alethea until I can uncover who is threatening her life."

"Do you intend to hold her hostage here?"

Alethea would kill him. "If need be, until the danger is dissipated."

"But think of the opportunity for your sister."

"If something dreadful happened to Lady Alethea for the sake of a debut season, what would that say about me as a man?"

Lady Whittlesby was silent. She looked disgruntled, but there were also traces of respect.

"I apologize for disappointing you, but it would better serve you to engage Mr. Kinnier."

"Mr. Kinnier does not have the Quartet's flare or Miss Terralton's pretty charm," Lady Whittlesby groused. "However, I quite see your point. I shall not press you further." She stood. "Should you change your mind, you have until the beginning of the new year."

"Thank you, although I could not guarantee the danger would be passed by then."

He walked her to her travelling coach, which had been kept waiting before the house. As he watched the coach disappear down the gravel drive, Ian appeared at his shoulder. "So, Lady Whittlesby arrived."

"She stopped by on the way to London. She wanted to know the progress about the violin. Made some noise about her spring concert and Mr. Kinnier."

"I hope that spurred you to mention some brilliant clue and assurance you'd have the answer for her by next week."

"Unfortunately, I told her I have nothing as yet." Bayard turned to him. "Aren't you supposed to be watching the violin?"

"Raven is there. We were in the hidden gallery playing cards, but I came down for refreshment."

"I do wish our friend would make some sort of play for it."

"We have made it quite difficult for him. He must resort to being clever about it."

Bayard decided not to tell Alethea he had refused Lady Whittlesby's concert. She would not understand why he so desperately wanted to protect her. He had no wish for her to guess how much he cared for her.

Slowly, against his inclinations, she had grown around his heart like ivy, but he must work harder to undo their closeness, to push her away. For her own sake, and for his.

⁓❦⁓

Bayard awoke with a start, with the echoes of his scream reverberating around him. His heartbeat was the rapid blows of a hammer cracking his breastbone from inside out. He gasped in air, trying to remember how to breathe. He then noticed the hard floor beneath his knees. His hands scrabbled at cold stone, blood streaking from his scraped fingertips.

He was in the family chapel.

His body felt as if he'd been walking coatless in a snowstorm. His arms and legs trembled violently and his stomach cramped. His eyes burned as if his tears had been as bitter as wormwood, as acrid as vinegar.

The images of the nightmare still passed before his eyes in wisps like shades of the dead. There was recrimination, and crushing guilt, and pain. And blood.

A footstep echoed against the bare stone walls of the chamber. Raven, come to help him back to bed, to dose him with a bottle of whiskey so that the shrieks of the dying receded into a pit of oblivion and blinding headaches.

"Dommick?" The whisper was soft, like a cobweb on his ear.

No. No, it could not be her. Not here, not now.

"Are you unwell? How can I help you?"

Into the line of his vision crept her feet in bed slippers. Then the rounded shape of her knees beneath her green dressing gown as she knelt beside him. A flash of white, then the touch of her hand against his forehead, his cheek.

"Dommick, let me help you—"

"Go away!" He pushed with his hands and scrambled backward away from her until his back hit the edge of a pew.

Her eyes were wide and dark in a ghostly white face. Her hair had been tied back and braided, but locks had come loose to wave around her face. She reached toward him.

He slapped her hand away with a blow that must have stung. She jerked her hand to her chest, and there were drops of blood on her skin from the scrapes on his fingers.

Still she would not go away, still she would not become angry or disgusted or afraid and run away.

And at that moment he realized that Alethea would never run away. She ran from nothing.

"I don't want you," he lashed out. "How could anyone ever want you?"

His words repelled her as his blow had not. She shrank within the dressing gown. He knew the pain in her eyes because he felt that pain scored across his soul. He needed her to go away, to forget she saw him like this. Right now, he was only wounded and bleeding. With her here, he would be exposed and raw.

And still she was not afraid. She rose to her feet, trembling, but with anger and not horror. "You truly are a mad baron," she said in a voice awful and horrible, and then she ran away, the sounds of her slippers soft against the stone floor.

Before the sound of her retreat died to nothingness, he heard a heavier tread, then an astonished, "Lady Alethea."

Raven, come minutes too late.

His friend approached him, also clad in bed slippers and a dressing gown. "You're only in your nightshirt, Bay. You must be freezing."

"I feel nothing and everything," he murmured.

"I am sorry. I did not know anyone would be awake to hear you."

Perhaps this was better. She had come too close. She had seeped into him when he had needed to be impenetrable. Now she would avoid him.

Now she would hate him.

～❦～

It was time to become more tantalizing bait.

Alethea hoisted her violin case in her arms and marched down the main street of Chippenham with Lord Ian beside her and Lucy behind.

"You needn't look quite as though you were going to execute someone," Ian murmured to her.

"Don't be ridiculous," she snapped.

In truth, she wanted to finish this business and be gone from Terralton Abbey. The best way she knew how was to lure the villain out with a show of foolish vulnerability, but her present frame of mind was hardly vulnerable. She sighed and tried to relax her expression. "There, do I look approachable?"

He flipped his hair out of his eyes. "As a growling bear."

She shot him a sour look.

Lucy said loudly, "My lady, the instrument shop is just there."

Recalled to her purpose in travelling to Chippenham, she headed toward the shop on the outskirts of the marketplace on High Street. She said in a low voice to Lord Ian, "I do not see Ord."

"You're not supposed to see him."

Yes, that would make sense.

Her brain felt as cluttered as a lady's workbag. She had not slept even before encountering Dommick in the chapel. She had been in the library looking for a book when she heard him scream, and after he shouted at her, she had spent the rest of the night crying.

The sight of his face had frightened her more than his scream, more than his ghostly appearance in the chapel in his nightclothes, more than the blood on his hands where the stone floor had cut his skin to ribbons. He had looked as if his inner pain had stolen his reason, his strength, his courage, leaving only black terror, red agony.

He had looked mad.

She should not have said that to him. Just as he should not have said his cruel words, which still heaved under her ribcage like a pair of wild dogs, tussling about, clawing and biting.

Strangely, a portion of her mind knew he had said such terrible things to force her away. She still felt the pain and anger, but in the light of day, her soul did not feel so desolate.

They reached the instrument shop. Lord Ian murmured to Alethea, "There's a man who has been following us. Enter the shop without me."

Her heartbeat jumped, and it took an effort of will not to turn and look. She nodded and entered the dark, dusty shop with Lucy behind her. Lucy looked back at Lord Ian but said nothing.

The shopkeeper had bulging eyes that appraised Alethea with shrewdness while his loose lips formed into an ingratiating smile. "How may I help you, my lady?"

"I need a string replaced in my violin." She placed the instrument in its case upon the counter. She had hated removing the string earlier today but had no other excuse to bring the violin into Chippenham.

The shopkeeper's bushy yellow eyebrows rose as he regarded the violin. Alethea had the suspicion that he recognized it as a Stradivarius. "A string, eh?"

The man took infuriatingly long about the business, and the string he used to replace the missing one was of inferior quality. When he named an exorbitant price, she speared him with a look until he named a lower one.

Her visit today was to taunt the villain, to fan the flames of his covetousness. However, if the villain hired someone to follow them, and if Lord Ian captured him, they may discover his employer.

As Alethea and Lucy left the shop, she hesitated, for Lord Ian was nowhere in sight. Was it wise for them to wander about Chippenham alone? Had something happened to him? "Let us go to a tea shop to wait." They started down High Street, Alethea looking about her with caution.

They suddenly heard a man's raised voice. "You're mistaken. I'm telling you the truth."

Lucy stiffened. "Richard?"

"Who is Richard?"

"He was head groom in Mrs. Ramsland's household when I worked for her. But surely he would not be here all the way from Bath."

The sound came from an alleyway running perpendicular to High Street, whose mouth lay several feet ahead of them. Alethea took the precaution of peeking around the corner into the narrow, dim passage.

She first saw the broad back of a man in a greatcoat with many capes, with Hessian boots below the edge of his cloak. He appeared to be struggling with something. In the shadows beyond she saw Ord's round, rugged face, his hand rubbing his jaw as if in pain.

"Let me go!" said the man in the greatcoat.

"Richard!" Lucy cried out.

The man turned, and Alethea saw that it was Lord Ian. The man who had spoken had not been him, but the lean, wiry man struggling in his grip.

"Lucy, tell them to let me go. What's going on?" Richard twisted violently.

"Do you know this man, Miss Purcell?" Lord Ian grunted as he strained against Richard.

"That is Richard Collum, the head groom for Mrs. Ramsland."

"And why are you in Chippenham?" Ord's voice was muffled from his hand rubbing his lower face.

"I've quit the old harridan, and good riddance to her. Let me go." Mr. Collum lashed out with his boot.

"That doesn't explain why you were following Lady Alethea," Lord Ian said through gritted teeth. He was three or four inches taller than Mr. Collum, but the man was sinewy and strong from his job handling horses.

"I told you already, I wasn't following her."

"Please let him go," Lucy pleaded. "He is no threat to Alethea."

With obvious reluctance, Lord Ian loosened his hold and Mr. Collum wrenched himself free. He immediately went to Lucy. "What's to do, my girl? Are you in danger?"

Alethea suddenly felt as though her boat had lost its mooring. It still drifted near the dock, but it was starting to move away.

"I am in no danger, Richard," Lucy said. "Why are you here?"

"What am I to think when the rumour in Bath is that Miss Terralton's maid has run off with a highwayman who popped off two footmen?"

"Shot them?" Lucy's voice rose. "They weren't shot."

"Well, you haven't run off with a highwayman either."

"Mr. Collum," Alethea said, "why were you following us?"

"I beg your pardon, milady, but I was hoping for a private word with Lucy."

"With me?" Lucy's dark eyes widened in surprise.

"Of course. How could you leave Bath with only a note to me?"

She gave him a look of gentle rebuke. "You gave me no reason for anything else."

"Well, I'm giving you a reason now." He grabbed her hands in his. "Lucy, say you'll marry me."

CHAPTER SEVENTEEN

✦

*I*t was apparent Lucy had been influenced by Alethea, for her sister delivered a hard blow to Mr. Collum's arm for a proposal notably unromantic. "How can you ask me like this?"

"When can I ask you when you have bodyguards jumping me in an alleyway?"

"If you had come to me at Terralton Abbey rather than skulking..."

"I arrived the moment you'd left for Chippenham. I couldn't wait to see you."

Alethea had to admit this was quite romantic. Lucy pursed her lips as she regarded him, but she seemed a trifle more mollified by his explanation.

"Perhaps it's best we return?" Lord Ian suggested dryly.

The carriage ride back to the abbey was silent, although Alethea was dying to speak to Lucy about Mr. Collum. Lucy's countenance was bland and professional despite the recent scene. They let Mr. Collum down at the inn nearest Terralton Abbey, then continued on to the house.

"Miss Terralton desires your services as soon as you returned," the butler informed Lucy as they entered the house.

Lord Ian said, "I'll waylay Clare and tell Bayard what happened today, shall I?"

Alethea and Lucy went to the music room where the faux violin had been displayed on a table. Alethea locked the music room door and went to her wooden chest, shoved into the corner behind a harp and a violoncello as if forgotten. "Lucy, you must tell me all."

"I am as surprised as you. Richard and I became friends at Mrs. Ramsland's home. He is quite educated. His father was a merchant who lost his fortune, and Richard took a job as a groom since he preferred horses to a job as a clerk. I have known him since I began working for Mrs. Ramsland."

"You said nothing of this to me." Alethea pulled from the chest the blankets folded inside.

"There was nothing to tell. We spoke often, for Mrs. Ramsland's stable and carriage house is behind her home, and she keeps but one horse and her gig. If there was not much to do, he would come to the house to help. I thought perhaps he had a preference for my company, but he was friendly and helpful to everyone."

"You had no indication he desired to marry you?" After emptying the chest, Alethea pressed the spring-loaded joint that would open the false bottom to reveal the cavity where she had hidden her violin.

"Goodness, is that where it has been hiding all this time?" Lucy asked. "I had no idea."

"Calandra's husband made this chest for her as a joke, since she prized the violin so highly," Alethea said.

"Lady Arkright always had the violin in her music room on the table, as did you."

"I could not leave the violin on Aunt Ebena's drawing room

table." Alethea removed the fake violin from the cavity in the chest and replaced it with hers. "So I stored it in my room in the chest."

"I had assumed you stored it in a case."

"No, the cavity in the chest acts as an instrument case."

"That is why the thief could not find it. A clever storage spot."

Alethea closed the hidden compartment and replaced the blankets in the chest. "You have conveniently forgotten my question."

Lucy sighed and walked to the wide windows. Alethea followed her. The view overlooked the courtyard garden and beyond that, the square pool.

"I was not certain his intentions had progressed to such a point," Lucy said slowly, "but I did wonder . . ."

Alethea swallowed and asked through a dry throat, "Lucy, were you afraid to tell me?"

"No, of course not—"

"Lucy."

She fussed with the heavy burgundy curtains swept back from the window. "Perhaps I was, a little."

"I would never begrudge you happiness for the sake of my plans, which are far off and unsettled."

"There really was nothing definitive. If he had asked me when I was at Mrs. Ramsland's house, I do not know what I would have answered. I still do not."

"Do you love him?"

"I like him. I feel I know the essence of his character. Is that love?"

Alethea thought of her feelings for Dommick. She esteemed his character, and she felt as though he understood her in ways no one else had. "When you left Bath, did you miss him? Did you regret the fact that you may never see him again?"

Lucy's face grew drawn and tired. "Yes."

"Do you wish to marry?"

"I do not wish to hurt you." Lucy took Alethea's hands. "We have had these plans since we were girls together. They have sustained me through my most difficult trials."

"Would you be happy in Italy? It has been my dream, but is it yours? Or would you be happier in England with Mr. Collum?"

"I do not wish to leave you. I love you."

"Lucy, I would not force you to choose between Mr. Collum and me. Your happiness means more to me than your company. I love you, and I want your happiness."

"You cannot afford to hire a paid companion."

"Then I shall find a travelling companion to share the costs. Lucy . . ." She took her sister's hand. Although her heart was breaking, Alethea said, "If you love him, then marry him."

~❧~

Alethea did not know what drew her to the chapel. She had thought it would be a place she would avoid since the incident with Dommick, but there was a peaceful silence here that she had not found in her empty bedchamber or even in the bleak gardens, smothered by the deep cold of approaching winter.

Her heart felt like those gardens, and she was ashamed. Lucy's happiness was important to her, but she worried now about her plans for living in Italy, her dreams of independence. She could not move to the continent until the war ended, but surely it would not last more than two years? When it ended, perhaps it may not be difficult to find a travelling companion.

But that companion would not be her dear sister.

She was ashamed that her dependence upon Lucy could have cost her sister a family and children. Alethea had been thoughtless and selfish, assuming Lucy would always fall into her plans for them both.

She sat in a pew and studied the altar at the front, standing atop the small raised platform. The altar's rich wooden carving had been smoothed by time and perhaps industrious tools in the hands of little Lord Dommicks in earlier centuries. Light glowed in the low vaulted ceiling arches and draped across the embroidered cloth on the altar's surface, but the chapel was dim because of the narrow windows, which had perhaps once had stained glass, but now only held diamond-cut panes.

It was a place of past grandeur. Dommick's grandfather had stopped the practice of daily prayers, and so the chapel lay empty and forgotten much of the time, an abandoned mother longing for her grown-up children.

Perhaps that was the reason for Alethea's affinity with the chapel, the air of desertion. She knew logically that Lucy had not deserted her, but the loneliness settled in her bones like an early frost.

Loneliness should be an old friend to her, but Lucy had always been her shield against lowness and pain. Lucy had always been her comfort. Now she fought the stirrings of betrayal and an unsteadiness in the foundations of her life that frightened her. There was no comfort for her now.

It may have been the chapel that caused the words of the rector's wife to come in a whisper: *divine relationship.* It meant nothing to her, and yet there was a promise of comfort if she could understand its meaning and take hold of it. Yet what kind of comfort could God offer to her? He had not comforted her before.

Or perhaps, like Margaret, Alethea had simply not heard him.

It was absurd to think that God would want to comfort her. Did he not control circumstances as he willed? Why should he cause suffering in order to bestow comfort?

No, she was being unfair. God did not cause suffering. Her father had caused her suffering. Her brother had caused her great pain. Dommick had lashed out in fear. Her sister . . .

But where was comfort? Where was the surcease of burdens? It was not here, in this lonely room, amongst relics and cobwebs.

Light footsteps sounded outside the chapel doors, then the creak of a door centuries old. Alethea turned to see Aunt Ebena in the doorway.

"Good gracious, you certainly are acquainted with the most unlikely places. If a servant had not happened to see you, I never should have found you." Aunt Ebena stopped at the pew where she sat. "Well? Be so good as to allow me to sit."

Alethea moved over.

"I had not known you intended to travel with your inheritance." Aunt Ebena scowled at her.

"You knew about my inheritance? I thought only my father and brother knew of it. And Wilfred now, if the lawyer has informed him."

"Of course I knew of it. My sister's husband set it up to form the dowry of any of his granddaughters, since he did not trust the prudence of his eldest son and did not wish shame to come upon the house of Trittonstone should the girls have no portions. Your father was freely able to squander what was not tied up in trust for you."

"Why should it surprise you that I wish to use my inheritance? My marriage prospects are highly unlikely."

"I suspected you would want your independence, but I had not thought that you would travel."

"I have read that in Italy one may live on very little expense. And there are music masters I wish to study under." Of course, it may all come to naught now.

"But now that Lucy will not travel with you, you will need a paid companion, which may be a financial hardship," Aunt Ebena said.

"I had thought that when the war ended, I might find a travelling companion to share the expense."

"That is very wise of you." Aunt Ebena hesitated, her face as stern as always, but faint apprehension in her grey eyes. "It was my thought to offer myself."

Alethea could not speak for nearly a full minute. She realized her mouth had dropped open and closed it with a snap. "You would . . . want to . . . travel? With me?"

"I have always desired to travel, but . . . it did not appeal to Mr. Garen."

Now that Alethea knew her aunt's history, the reticence of her comment spoke volumes. "You enjoy travel?"

"I have not travelled at all. But I desire to partake of foreign culture."

Alethea recalled her aunt's avid attendance at concerts, art exhibitions, lectures. What must it have been like to marry a man much like Aunt Ebena's father, in control of all her actions and decisions? How had she borne the frustration of wanting something dear to her heart, knowing her husband had the funds for it, but being unable to attain it?

Alethea also knew her aunt's income. "May I ask an impertinent question?"

"When have you ever asked permission?"

"After Mr. Garen died, you never wished to sell your house and travel?"

Aunt Ebena said in a halting voice, "I had thought my age and respectability a deterrent. But I flatter myself that I have come to understand you in this past year. You will not allow such a setback to forestall you."

"No." Not while Italy beckoned.

"Then I cannot allow my notions to forestall me. Our combined income will enable a very comfortable housekeeping, more so than independently of each other."

It was true. But her aunt's abrasiveness had caused no small discomfort to this past year.

However, she now understood Aunt Ebena better. And might some of that abrasiveness have been a reaction to Alethea's carefree spirit, her determination to pursue her desires, whether befriending her illegitimate half sister or playing an instrument scandalous for genteel ladies? Weren't all those things against what her aunt had upheld for most of her very correct, upright life?

"Are you certain you could live with *me*, ma'am?" Alethea asked with uncertainty.

"I have lived with you for the past year," she snapped, then seemed to regret her tone. "You are sensible, and while you can be headstrong, you are not foolish. We shall rub along tolerably well, I fancy."

Aunt Ebena, for all her faults, was strong and confident. Alethea needed her confidence now, for she felt very alone and unsure. "I should be glad of your company, Aunt Ebena."

Her aunt nodded as though she had known all along that Alethea would agree. "We can make no plans until you have received your inheritance and the war with France is ended, but you may know that I will remain committed to our schemes."

"Thank you, Aunt."

What an unexpected turn her life had taken in less than a day. Yet out of this, all three of them would achieve their dreams. Aunt Ebena would travel, Lucy would marry, and Alethea would still go to Italy.

But in the depths of her heart, deeper than she wanted to scrutinize, was the doubt that Italy was still the focus of her dreams. Yet what else did she have? She would do better to forget what was not directly before her and instead embrace this new opportunity.

❧

Bayard was certain Richard Collum was involved somehow in the intrigue surrounding Alethea's violin.

Verifying it, however, was a different matter.

Bayard wrapped himself against the freezing wind, damp and smelling of a brewing storm, and rattled the knocker at a small, respectable house in Chippenham. It had the look of former affluence, but had fallen into disrepair and neglect. The widow of an attorney lived here, but he had no wish to speak to her.

Mr. Collum's appearance was too convenient. He was a stranger, but his presence was excused by his engagement with Lucy. No one would note the doings of Lucy's betrothed.

Clare was disappointed to lose Lucy as her maid, for she would leave as soon as Mr. Collum found a new position. Clare had dropped broad hints that Bayard should hire Mr. Collum as a groom, for their head groom was getting on in years, but Bayard had rather doggedly pretended not to hear her. He would not hire a man he could not trust.

He hadn't spoken to Alethea in days. He had never realized how effortless it would be for a woman to avoid speaking to him in the confines of the abbey. He wasn't certain what he would say if she did speak to him. It was better by far that she avoided him and believed him to be a blackguard.

Bayard had spent the majority of the day in Bath, speaking to Mrs. Ramsland's butler about the letter of reference Richard Collum had produced upon being hired as head groom, then following the trail backward to two other homes in Bath where Mr. Collum had worked, and finally here in Chippenham, where Mr. Collum had supposedly worked for five years.

The butler who opened the door was aged, with wispy, white hair and a stoop to his shoulders. "I regret that Mrs. Boane is unavailable."

"I have come to speak to Mr. Keable."

The butler's thin, white brows climbed toward his balding pate. "Me, sir? Please do come in."

Bayard entered the house but remained in the gloomy foyer, which was lit only by tapers on the entrance table. "I am Lord Dommick. I was given your name in order to ask about a groom who worked here ten years ago."

"I am afraid you are mistaken, my lord, for Mrs. Boane keeps no horses."

This was the inconsistency Bayard had been hoping for. "You have been with her long?"

"For ten years."

"And there was no groom when you started?"

"There had been no groom since Mr. Boane died."

"There has been no servant named Richard Collum in Mrs. Boane's employ? Whether as groom or footman?"

Mr. Keable stiffened. "Mr. Collum? I beg your pardon, my lord, but I was mistaken. Yes, Mr. Collum was Mrs. Boane's groom ten years ago."

Bayard found himself nonplussed. "He was?"

"Indeed. He was a good lad, very bright and amiable."

Bayard was confused and frustrated at the same time. "How long did Mr. Collum work here?"

"Several years."

"For whom had he worked before?"

"He was hired based on the recommendation of a former servant in this house. Mr. Collum proved to be an excellent worker."

For a man who had professed not to know anything about a groom ten years ago, Mr. Keable suddenly knew a great deal about Mr. Collum. "You knew him well?"

"Mr. Collum left soon after I began my employ with Mrs. Boane, but he impressed me during the period I knew him, and the other servants spoke highly of him. Mrs. Boane herself wrote his references quite willingly."

Bayard was at a loss. There was something havey-cavey going

on, but Mr. Keable seemed most earnest in his estimation of Mr. Collum's character. Yet what could Bayard do, short of accusing the man of lying. "Thank you, Mr. Keable."

"If it is not impertinent for me to ask, I hope Mr. Collum is well, my lord?"

The butler's question struck Bayard as rather odd for a fellow servant and Mr. Collum's supervisor. "Yes. He is at Terralton Abbey."

"Mrs. Boane will be glad to hear of it."

"Mrs. Boane would remember a groom from ten years ago?"

Mr. Keable looked confused, then said, "Mrs. Boane is most solicitous of her servants." Which was an even more bewildering answer. "May I help you in any other way, my lord?"

"No. Good day, Mr. Keable." He exited the house and hurried through the rising wind toward his carriage.

Bayard drove home disgruntled, aided by a cold rain that worsened into a downpour. Perhaps he would need to hire someone else to look into Mr. Collum's background.

The travelling coach in the gravel sweep before his house was unknown to him. He ran through the rain and up the steps to the front door.

The butler took his wet greatcoat from him. "Lord and Lady Trittonstone have arrived, my lord, along with Mr. Kinnier."

The rain had not seeped through his coat, but Bayard was suddenly chilled. Why would Alethea's cousin and his wife be here with Mr. Kinnier, of all people? Was Bayard unreasonably suspicious to jump to the conclusion it had to do with the violin? The timing of their visit was too coincidental.

"I prefer to announce myself, Forrow." Bayard headed to the drawing room.

As he opened the door, he heard an unfamiliar male voice say, "The papers have been signed."

Alethea stood opposite the door, and the expression on her face caused every vein in his body to pulse with fear, anger, protectiveness. He had never seen her so white. He had never seen her with such a look of vulnerability, devastation, terror. He knew that whatever had just occurred, her entire world had gone up in flames. Her hand went to her mouth, and she swayed on her feet.

A man standing with his back to the door turned and saw him. "Who the devil are you?" His thin voice was just shy of a whine.

Bayard shot him a look that made him flinch. In a low, snarling voice he said, "I should ask the same, as it is my house and you have upset my guest."

The man's brow cleared. "Oh. I am Trittonstone, Alethea's cousin." He bowed.

Bayard refused to return it. "What have you done?"

Movement to Bayard's left had him twisting in alarm. Mr. Kinnier stood a few feet away, his dark eyes gleaming in triumph. He looked like a pale snake about to strike. "Congratulate me, Lord Dommick," he said. "I have become betrothed to Lady Alethea."

She had been sold. Again.

She was going to be sick.

Alethea rushed forward, pushing past Wilfred, past Dommick, out the drawing room door. She stumbled on the staircase and nearly fell, but she grabbed the bannister and regained her footing, only to hurtle herself down the last flight.

"My lady!" Forrow cried as she sprinted across the entrance hall, throwing herself against the front door. "My lady, it is raining—"

She unlatched the door and plunged into the dark.

The rain drenched her, shocking her with its cold. The wind sliced through her like an icy bayonet to her stomach, and still she ran into the teeth of the gale, running away and yet feeling as though she were not moving. The gravel of the sweep bit through her thin slippers, and then she was sliding on the half-frozen grass, mud oozing between her toes. She ran on, across the vast lawn, heedless of direction until a faulty step sent her tumbling face-first.

The cold ground bit into her cheek like a serpent's kiss. She dug her fingers into the mud and pushed herself upright, but could not rise from her knees. She knelt in the grass and pooling water, rain falling upon her shoulders.

She had been sold.

She heard her brother's voice through the moaning of the wind. *Signed the papers this morning. You'll marry my friend by special license tomorrow and he'll give me a nice cut of your dowry.*

Wilfred had said almost the same words tonight, and with them, had taken away everything. He had the power to force her to his will because she was not yet come of age and he had authority over her. She was twenty-eight years old, and he controlled her life as if she were eighteen. She squeezed her eyes shut and dug her fingers into the dirt.

If she ran away again, there was no certainty in her ability to hide from him until she reached her majority. He had the resources to find her.

She had built her dream like an oasis in a desert. She had clung to Italy as the only way she could be happy. And now it was gone.

She was helpless, and hopeless. The dark storm without was the same as the dark storm within.

A sound behind her made her jump and twist around, but it was Lucy with a cloak.

"How did you know I was here?" Alethea's teeth chattered.

"Forrow found me and sent me. Come inside."

"Lucy, Wilfred has sold me."

Her sister's hands, which had been draping the cloak around her

wet figure, tightened in the folds of cloth. "Like . . . your brother?"
She did not need an answer, for Alethea's face said enough. She
threw her arms about Alethea and squeezed tightly.

Her sister's fervent embrace opened the floodgates, and Alethea
wept tears that felt like shards of glass slicing her skin. She wept for
all she had lost. She wept for all that men had done to her. She wept
for the life she would never know.

"Who is it?" Lucy whispered.

"Mr. Kinnier."

Lucy jerked away, her hands tight on Alethea's shoulders. "No.
No. Alethea, you must run away again."

"What?" Alethea had never seen her sister look so terrified.

"You must run away. You cannot marry him."

"I escaped my brother last year because of the accident. I could
not hope for something similar again. Wilfred would find me."

"You will have me with you this time."

"Richard—?"

"I won't marry him. Alethea, I won't leave you alone. We will
escape. I will keep you safe from him."

"What is it about Mr. Kinnier? You must tell me."

Lucy pressed her hand to her mouth. Her eyes were wide and
stark white in the darkness. "Alethea," she said, her voice thick with
tears, "Mr. Kinnier killed his first wife."

CHAPTER EIGHTEEN

*M*r. Kinnier knew about her violin. Alethea was certain of it.

She didn't know if he was the villain himself, or if he happened to uncover the truth about it and now coveted it. Regardless, he knew. She had seen it last night. While Wilfred pronounced the betrothal agreement with his usual indifference to sensibilities, Mr. Kinnier had regarded her with those small dark eyes, and a nasty smile had curled his perfect lips.

A cat, about to pounce. A snake, preparing to strike.

What did he know about the violin that they did not? She had heard from her aunt's friends that Mr. Kinnier's fortune was substantial enough that he would not need her dowry, which may be why he was willing to pay a significant bride-price for her. And after he married her? Would he kill her as he had killed his first wife?

She wandered through the wet grass, flattened by the storm last night, and followed the edge of the lake. The morning was grey and bitterly cold, and she wrapped her cloak more tightly about her and trudged through the mud. A ball of ice lay in the centre of her body, numbing everything inside her, and so she did not mind the weather.

What did Dommick think of all this? She had not seen him, and he had not sought her out. It was not his affair, and he could do nothing. It would be laughable for a woman to insist on any legal rights in this matter.

Lucy was determined for Alethea to run away. Mr. Collum said he would assist them. He confirmed the rumours Lucy had heard about Mr. Kinnier.

"At my last position before Mrs. Ramsland," he'd said, "I'd been hired with two other new grooms who had left Mr. Kinnier's employ after Mrs. Kinnier died. The local magistrate turned a blind eye, but all the servants knew Mr. Kinnier had struck her—and not for the first time—and then pushed her down the staircase. The two grooms said they couldn't work for a murderer."

Alethea found herself in the wilderness garden, following the rushing stream to the gazebo. She brushed damp leaves from the bench and sat. The sound of the water flowing past made her feel as if she were being left behind.

Here in the stillness, with only the stream to speak to her, she gave in to the stabbing pain in her stomach. She doubled over, sobbing. She was so alone.

Why had such a thing happened to her? Why was she at the mercy of men such as her cousin and Mr. Kinnier? Why were men so determined to hurt her? Who in this entire world would ever not hurt her?

A divine relationship.

She did not know what that meant. The God she had known in her church had been condemning, and his people had been judgmental and hypocritical.

But hadn't Mrs. Coon shown her that there was something more? Hadn't she told Alethea not to base her impression of God upon the people in her life?

Well then, who was God? How could Alethea discover who he was? Was this divine relationship real?

She did not know how long she sat there, staring at the water, when she suddenly became aware of a splashing out of rhythm with the ripple of the stream. Within moments, Margaret appeared.

"Margaret, get out of the water! You'll catch your death of cold." Alethea rushed to the bank.

"I can't feel my feet. It's quite a curious sensation." Margaret clambered onto the wet grass, clutching a long tree limb in her hand. She'd had the foresight to tuck her skirts into her sash so only her stockings and shoes were wet. In addition to her spencer, she wore a heavy wool shawl.

"What were you doing in the water? You are supposed to be at Mrs. Coon's home." A most alarming thought occurred to her. "Margaret, what happened?"

Margaret untucked her skirts and cloak and they fell to slap against her wet ankles. "We got into another argument."

"Again? Oh, Margaret."

"It wasn't bad this time, I promise. We were playing Knights of the Round Table when Mr. Hokes came by. He was quite boosey."

"This early in the morning? How unfortunate. And how did you come to hear such cant?"

"It was Maria who said he was boosey. I was shocked, but Louisa said he came by often in this condition to see their mother for food, and that we ought to love him because he was a sinner. And I said that the rector in my Aunt Nancy's village said that God hates all sinners and only loves the good Christians. But Maria said that God loves sinners if they are remorseful. And then Louisa said that God loves sinners if they give a lot of money into the poor box.

So, we argued about it until Mrs. Coon sent Mr. Hokes away and caught us quarreling."

"Margaret, could you ever play with those girls and not quarrel about something?"

"I played with them yesterday and we didn't argue once." Margaret blinked. "Well, sort of." She rushed on, "Mrs. Coon said that God loves everyone even if they do not love him back."

The divine relationship.

Margaret continued, "And then, for quarreling, she made us write out some passages from the Bible about God's love. I finished before Maria and Louisa. Their copperplate was so bad that Mrs. Coon made them rewrite it." She dug into her pocket and pulled out a rock and a folded piece of paper.

Alethea found herself interested in reading the passages, although she noted that the rock, smooth and flat, was quite perfect for skipping across the lake. "Margaret, I hope you don't intend to throw this through a window."

"Of course not." Margaret regarded her with raised eyebrows. "It's a perfect skipping stone." She then proceeded to slash about with her stick, narrowly missing Alethea's elbow. "I only came to the river to find a new sword. Maria broke my other one."

"For Knights of the Round Table?" Alethea stepped out of the path of the swinging "blade."

"I shall go back to the rectory now, for Maria and Louisa will be finished copying passages. Will you keep my skipping stone safe? Louisa wanted it very badly."

"I shall guard it with my life."

Margaret was gone in a whirl of muddied skirts and squishing half-boots.

Alethea returned to the bench in the gazebo. She did not immediately open the paper Margaret had handed her. The wilderness seemed more loquacious now, with the wind rustling the tree leaves and the peep of an occasional bird. The stream rushed on, heedless and winding.

She had sat there only moments before the storm that was Margaret, and she had been wondering, perhaps even asking God, about the divine relationship. And now she held Bible verses in her hand. She felt a little afraid, as if she had been poking a bear, thinking it was stuffed, only to find that it was very much alive and she had awakened it.

She opened the paper.

"But God commendeth his love toward us, in that, while we were yet sinners, Christ died for us."—Romans 5:8

"For I am persuaded, that neither death, nor life, nor angels, nor principalities, nor powers, nor things present, nor things to come,

Nor height, nor depth, nor any other creature, shall be able to separate us from the love of God, which is in Christ Jesus our Lord."—Romans 8:38–39

"The Lord hath appeared of old unto me, saying, Yea, I have loved thee with an everlasting love: therefore with lovingkindness have I drawn thee."—Jeremiah 31:3

"The Lord thy God in the midst of thee is mighty; he will save, he will rejoice over thee with joy; he will rest in his love, he will joy over thee with singing."—Zephaniah 3:17

Alethea had been taught the death of Christ upon the cross for the sins of the world, but she had not before drawn the connection that he had done so out of love. That the God who would die for her loved her.

Loved *her*.

She, who had known the intolerance of her neighbors, the whispers of her peers. She, who had believed there must be something wrong with her, that she was an oddity compared to the people around her. She, who had felt isolated and misunderstood. She had felt so alone, but perhaps she had never been alone.

The paper trembled in her hands as she read the verses again in Margaret's very correct handwriting. There was a rousing in herself, deeper than her heart, deeper than her soul. There was a place deeper than knowing, and a Presence there stirred her and soothed her all at once.

She was not alone.

God *loved* her.

God would take care of her.

The words blurred before her eyes as the tears fell, but not the bitter, hot tears of earlier. These tears were like the stream, cascading, cleansing, releasing.

She was not alone.

God *loved* her.

God would take care of her.

She surrendered something inside of herself, and there was an uncoiling of tension. God was with her. He would never abandon her as her father had. He would never abuse her as her brother had. He would never leave her as Calandra did. He would never reject her as her peers had done.

In that green space in the wilderness, she felt that Presence all around her and inside her. She was comforted. She was at peace.

❧

What did Mr. Kinnier know about the violin that they did not?

Bayard paced his study until, unsatisfied with the small space, he flung open the double doors to his music room. Where the study had been dim, the music room was bright despite the cloudy day. In the far corner, upon an inlaid table, the fake violin lay as though carelessly set aside, while above the room in a hidden gallery, Ord sat watching.

He had not seen Alethea since that one horrifying glimpse of her face before she ran out of the drawing room last night. He had searched the house for her after breakfast, and he would have searched the grounds but for the meeting with his steward this morning.

Mr. Kinnier's superior expression last night had fueled Bayard's frustration that his inquiries had not produced information in a timely enough fashion.

But even more than the violin, the thought of Alethea being Mr. Kinnier's wife—being any other man's wife—felt like an old, venerable oak tree being violently uprooted from his gut. He was undone. He was distraught. He knew that his world was about to change forever.

He simply didn't know exactly how it would change.

He paced the length of the music room, growing more and more agitated. A germ of an idea formed, but it was so absurd, so imprudent, he could not even voice the idea to his own mind.

A tap at the music room door, and Forrow appeared. "Forgive the intrusion, my lord, but there is a Mr. Guido Manco to see you."

The Italian art steward whose father had worked for the Count of Sondrono. Bayard realized he was not in the most propitious emotional and mental state to receive him, but here may be the solution to all their troubles. "Please bring him in."

Guido Manco was older than Bayard's mother by at least two decades, a short man with a light step, a shrewd eye, and jet-black hair liberally sprinkled with grey. He carried a packet of papers under his arm, and he looked very smart in his London-tailored clothes.

"Thank you for stopping by," Bayard said.

"I regret I have but a few moments, my lord. We started late this morning on account of a broken axle, and Lady Mayrick expects me at her home this evening."

Bayard had to remove Alethea's violin from its hiding place in the presence of Mr. Manco. He laid the violin on the desk near the window.

At the sight of it, Mr. Manco's expression showed surprise and confusion. He set his papers on the desk and shuffled through them. "According to my father's records, he sold three violins for the count, a Stradivarius, a valuable Amati, and a Guarnerius. This looks to be a Stradivarius?"

"We believe so."

Mr. Manco shook his head as he found the paper he sought. "This is not the Stradivarius my father sold."

Bayard was so shocked he could not speak for a moment. When he exhaled shortly, he realized he had stopped breathing as well. "Are you certain?"

"The Stradivarius had a distinctive scroll pattern atop the pegbox with a carving of the Sondrono coat of arms. My father described it exactly."

"There was no mention of initials painted upon the neck?"

Mr. Manco's brows knit. "No, I am afraid not. I reviewed all the records of the count's musical instruments during the journey here, so my memory is fresh." He traced the design on the violin's neck. "The Sondrono family favoured the family crest rather than initials."

"Is there any chance that your father's records are incomplete? Or that the violin was sold before his employ with the count?"

"My father was the only agent Count Sondrono utilized when his debts began to require him to sell his family's possessions, and there are no holes in his records. He was turned off mere months before the count died, and at that time, there were no items left in the count's possession to sell. However, my father was not required to inventory the count's collection. He simply recorded what was sold. If the count owned anything that was not sold before my father's termination or the count's death, it would not be in the records." He sighed. "I am sorry, my lord. I cannot even verify this instrument belonged to Count Sondrono."

Nothing. Bayard had nothing. "Do you know of anyone I could contact about this instrument?"

"If I may borrow a pen and paper? I have the address of an instrument shop in Turin, where my father sold two instruments— a flute and an oboe. They may have arranged the sale of this violin rather than my father, unknown to him."

"Thank you, Mr. Manco."

After Mr. Manco left, Bayard returned to pacing the music room. He had always been able to find solutions to his problems, but now he had no other ideas on where to turn. What did Mr. Kinnier know about the violin that Bayard did not?

How could Bayard keep Alethea from marrying him?

He forced himself to sit at the desk to begin drafting a letter to the instrument shop in Italy. What else could he do?

The door abruptly opening made him blot his paper. When he spied his mother's and Clare's drawn faces, he leapt to his feet. "What is it?"

His mother flew to the desk, leaving Clare to close the door behind them. "Bayard, you cannot allow Alethea to marry Mr. Kinnier."

"I do not know what I could do to stop it."

"You can marry her yourself."

Her words solidified the vague, ethereal idea that had been forming in his head. His heart pulsed at the thought, but then he remembered the chapel, and all that he would need to hide from her. "Mama, that is a very drastic suggestion."

"You must listen to what Mama knows about Mr. Kinnier," Clare said.

"You know I have never cared for him, but I have never told you why, for I did not wish to spread gossip. However, my abigail, Ingle, knows the lady's maid who served the late Mrs. Kinnier."

"Mama, I have heard the rumours and there is nothing substantial."

"I thought so as well, but the maid saw Mrs. Kinnier's death from behind a cracked door. She was afraid to tell the magistrate for fear of Mr. Kinnier. He was enraged and he pushed his wife down the stairs, Bayard. He is a murderer."

"Are you certain?"

"All of Mr. Kinnier's servants knew the truth. Some had witnessed it, others had heard the commotion. It was not an accident. She was killed."

"Mama, this is all the word of servants."

Lady Morrish drew herself up and looked him squarely in the eye. "Bayard, mere months after it happened, I spoke personally to Mrs. Kinnier's maid, and I assure you, she is not exaggerating." His mother reached out to grab both of his hands in hers. "I have come to know Lady Alethea these past weeks and esteem her greatly. And I would not wish the daughter of my worst enemy to marry Mr. Kinnier. Please do not allow this to happen. You must marry her yourself, before Lord Trittonstone can take her away from here."

"And she would keep her violin, Bayard," Clare said. "You cannot allow him to possess it."

"I would need a special license—"

"I have already spoken to Sir Hermes," Lady Morrish said. "You know that he has many friends, and among them is an official representative of the archbishop. He is willing to ride to his friend to get a special license for you."

Bayard would never have imagined the type of service his stepfather would be doing for him now, thanks to Sir Hermes's extraordinary talent for forming friends wherever he went.

He nodded. "Please ask him to do so. I will speak to Lady Alethea."

⚜

"You what?" Alethea looked at him as though he were stark raving mad.

This was not the most propitious opening to a proposal.

Bayard cleared his throat. "I wish to marry you."

Alethea exhaled a shaky breath, then turned to walk the length of the music room. It took her some time, as the room was so large, and by the time she returned to him, she looked more composed. Bayard, on the other hand, had grown more tightly wound with each step she took, and he could not understand why.

She said, "Tell me why *you* wish to marry *me*."

He was not certain, from the way she said it, if she had insulted himself or herself. "It is the solution to your troubles. You were very upset last night," he said lamely.

Rather than falling at his feet in gratitude, she threw up her hands. "This is as extreme a measure to acquire my violin as Mr. Kinnier's."

"This has nothing to do with the violin," he said hotly. "There is no other way I can protect you."

She stilled. Something about her look seemed to shine, seemed hopeful, waiting for him to say something else . . . but he didn't know what.

She dropped her head and turned away from him. "My cousin has signed the betrothal agreement with Mr. Kinnier."

"It doesn't matter what they have signed if you are already

married. It will be on Lord Trittonstone's head that he cannot honour the agreement."

She whispered, "Why do you care?"

He swallowed. He had avoided examining his feelings because he hadn't wanted to draw close to any woman, and especially not Alethea. But he could not remain silent and inactive in the face of this injustice to her. "I have heard . . . things about Mr. Kinnier's character."

"He killed his first wife." Her voice was dead, with an undercurrent of anger.

"I cannot stand by and allow you to marry a man whom I know is a monster."

"But why do you care?" She spoke with frustration, but she looked at him with a glimmer of longing.

"If something were to happen to you, I could not live with myself, knowing I could have stopped it." Bayard could not tolerate the thought of Mr. Kinnier touching her, possessing her, hurting her. "Please, Alethea, allow me to protect you."

He saw the moment she relented. There was a softness about her mouth, colour that rose back into pale cheeks, a relaxing of the stress lines around her dark eyes.

"Thank you, Dommick. I will marry you." And then she burst into beauty. It was as if he had never seen her before. Her look was grateful, but there was also a radiance, an intimacy that drew him, dazzled him.

And even as he took a step toward her, pulled by the promise in her smile, his fear stopped him as firmly as a blow to his gut. She had seen a glimpse of his madness, but she only knew about the nightmares. She did not know about the rest of it, the episodes that had him gasping and weeping, the weakness and helplessness.

He did not want to offer that man to her. He did not want that man to fall in love with her. He did not want to expose her to all his pain and misery. He was afraid of the expression that would be in her eyes when she discovered his shameful secret. He wanted to care for her. He did not want her to have to shoulder his burden.

He cleared his throat and clenched his hands behind his back. "I apologize for the indelicacy, but I wish to assure you that due to the unusual circumstances of our arrangement, you need not fear that I would impose myself upon you."

The light went out in her face. "What do you mean?"

"Ours would be a marriage of convenience only." The words grated.

A spasm passed across her throat and the colour drained from her cheeks. But then she straightened her shoulders. "I understand," she said softly. "I am most grateful for your sacrifice for me, Dommick."

He did not want her gratitude. But what he wanted, he could never have.

CHAPTER NINETEEN

*M*ona, Wilfred's wife, sat perched on the edge of Alethea's bed, ostensibly "helping" Alethea to pack her trunks in preparation for her removal from Terralton Abbey, but in reality watching to ensure she did not pack a smaller valise she could run away with. Alethea's task was to distract Mona and allay Wilfred's fears of her fleeing another betrothal agreement—he had heard of Alethea's last interaction with her brother, when she had escaped a locked room rather than falling into her brother's plans.

"Really, Alethea," Mona said in an affected simper, "I declare I did not see you all day yesterday."

According to Clare, Dommick had reluctantly offered hospitality to Wilfred, Mona, and Mr. Kinnier. His mother had insisted that it would reflect poorly upon the Terralton family's reputation if he forced them to go to the inn. At dinner last night, Lord Ravenhurst muttered about the wisdom of keeping the vipers where they could be closely watched.

"In fact, I have not seen you since we arrived two evenings ago," Mona said. "One might almost think you had *run away*."

Alethea tried to affect a dejected, capitulating attitude, but her hands trembled as she folded her petticoats. "And why should I do that, Mona?"

Mona's mouth pinched. Alethea knew she would prefer Alethea call her Lady Trittonstone but couldn't very well demand it. "That is what I told Trittonstone, and he was confident that if you *should* run away, he would spare no expense to find you."

Anger flared, but Alethea doused it. She must not allow Mona to suspect the plan in place for today. Sir Hermes, always up for a lark and believing Dommick's hasty, clandestine marriage to Alethea to be the greatest adventure, had driven off last night to visit the representative of the archbishop to acquire the special license. It was only as he left that he admitted that, in truth, he was friends with the man's brother, and not the representative himself, but Sir Hermes did not believe it would cause any hindrance to his task.

Alethea had been alarmed, but Dommick had been sanguine. "Sir Hermes could convince bees to buy honey from him."

Alethea dropped a shoe and rooted under the bed for it. "Mona, running away would be foolish. I have no wish to live in hiding like a French spy for two years."

"That is exactly what I said to Trittonstone. And he said that he would tie up the legalities of everything to ensure that you would never get your inheritance, even should you appear on the lawyer's doorstep the morning of your thirtieth birthday." Mona gave a nasally titter.

Alethea's hand clenched tightly over the shoe before she regained mastery of herself and rose to her feet.

When Sir Hermes returned today with the special license, they would gather at the rectory for the wedding. The rector, under the tender influence of his wife, had agreed to perform the service. It all now depended upon Sir Hermes.

"I wonder that I have not seen Lord Dommick today." There was a thread of suspicion in Mona's tone.

"I have not spoken to him since yesterday." Alethea began sorting through her stockings. "No doubt he is unhappy that his house party is being disrupted." Dommick had driven to his attorney early this morning to consult about her inheritance and her marriage. After the wedding, his attorney would contact the lawyer in charge of the Trittonstone estate. Dommick had said that even if Wilfred had the power to withhold her dowry, Dommick did not need her money. All that mattered would be that she would be safely married so that Wilfred could not sell her to Mr. Kinnier.

"I did invite him to the wedding," Mona said. "He declined for himself but said his sister and mother would be glad to attend."

Mona seemed convinced of Dommick's indifference to Alethea. She doubted her cousin and his wife suspected their specific plans, but they certainly suspected something may be afoot.

"I expected you to have more fashionable gowns," Mona said as Alethea shook out the green gown she had worn to the concert.

"I expect Kinnier will buy more for me in London." Alethea slid a sidelong look at Mona, who predictably looked sour at Alethea's change in fortunes. "Will you and Wilfred be in London this spring?"

"No," Mona snapped.

"Ah, well. Unfortunately, Wilfred did not inherit the estate as enriched as it had been before my father's time."

"We have had a great many expenses associated with his new title," Mona said irritably.

"It is perhaps just as well Mr. Kinnier has no title. Since I will be returning to town for the first time in years, no expense will be spared."

"You certainly seem pleased now about the marriage. When Trittonstone told you, I thought you would vomit," Mona said nastily.

"You yourself know that my cousin has no great skill in delivering momentous news."

Mona nodded reluctantly.

"At the time, I was unaware of the pecuniary advantages of the match," Alethea said. "However, Lady Morrish had more information as to Mr. Kinnier's prospects."

Mona's eyes narrowed. "Did she?"

"Did Wilfred not inform you? It is close to ten thousand pounds a year."

Mona's watery blue eyes goggled at her. "Good gracious."

Alethea knew that Wilfred's income was no more than four thousand and possibly less since he had been forced to sell some land in order to honour her brother's gambling debts. "When did Mr. Kinnier approach Wilfred about this marriage?" Alethea asked casually.

"How should I know? At least two weeks ago."

After the concert and her remove from Bath? Did the timing indicate Mr. Kinnier might be the villain? Was this his next move when his hired men failed to kidnap Alethea? She supposed that kidnapping her was a great deal easier than marrying her. "Do you know much about Mr. Kinnier?"

Mona looked conscious for a fleeting moment.

So, her cousin had heard the rumour about Mrs. Kinnier's death and yet moved forward to contract the marriage. Bile rose in her throat and her limbs felt stiff. She turned away from Mona.

"He is very gentlemanlike and amiable," Mona said.

Alethea didn't respond.

"Really, could you hope for better at your age?" Mona said.

"I suppose not," Alethea replied mildly.

Mona rose. "Assisting you has made me excessively tired," she said. "I need to lie down."

It was late afternoon. Surely Sir Hermes had returned by now? Alethea wondered when Lord Ian would come to fetch her.

"Where is your violin?" Mona said.

"Why is it important?" Alethea asked slowly.

"Oh, Mr. Kinnier most specifically desired to make sure you brought the violin with you into the marriage. He had it mentioned in the marriage agreement."

"My violin is not part of the Trittonstone estate," Alethea said through clenched teeth. "It was personally bequeathed to me in a legal document by Lady Arkright upon her death."

"All that can hardly matter since all your possessions become his," Mona said. "Where is it?"

"In the music room."

"Be sure to pack it." Mona exited her bedchamber.

Alethea slumped upon her bed. Mona's company was nearly as exhausting as the pretense of packing.

She glanced at the clock. She could no longer sit about and wait. Since Mona intended to nap, she would make her way to the rectory.

Because Mona had mentioned her violin, Alethea went first to the music room, ostensibly to fetch it. She could use a door that opened onto the terrace to make her way to the grounds and across the park to the rectory.

When she entered the music room, however, she saw a man standing before the fake violin on the table. He turned.

"Mr. Kinnier." Alethea stood rooted to the floor.

His smile was smooth and pleasant as always, but there was a spark of exultation in his small dark eyes. "My dear. Have you come to practice?"

"I have come to pack my violin."

"Do not let me hinder you." However, he stood directly in front of the fake violin. Alethea was forced to walk close to him in order to reach behind him.

His hand whipped out and clenched hard on her wrist. He leaned close and said, still in that pleasant voice, "Do not offer me an insult by attempting to deceive me."

His hand would leave a bruise, but she refused to wince. He wore some sort of perfume, but it did not quite mask the scent of tree rot about him.

She looked at him with cold eyes. "Pray, why does my violin interest you? Surely you have several of your own more valuable."

He did not respond, but his gaze drifted down from her eyes to her lips.

Her stomach wrenched. She jerked at her wrist, but he held her fast. His head moved, and she twisted her body violently, planting one foot and kicking out with the other. His other hand grabbed hard around her waist and hauled her up against him.

She flailed at him, her captured arm moving stiffly but her other hand lashing at his shoulders, chest, and neck, with blows as hard as she could deliver. He responded by clenching his fingers into a crushing grip on her wrist, his other fingers digging into her spine.

And suddenly it was not Mr. Kinnier but Alethea's brother, his grip painful on her left hand. The edges of her vision darkened, and she could smell the tallow smoke from the candles in her brother's study as he savagely wrenched at her fingers, breaking first one, then the other.

She screamed.

Abruptly, she was released and she fell backward. She unconsciously braced herself with her injured hand and cried out again.

Lord Ian had filled his fists with the cloth of Mr. Kinnier's coat. Mr. Kinnier grabbed Ian's shoulders, and the two of them wrestled in small, jerking movements, circling about. They slammed against the edge of the desk near the window, dislodging pens and an ink stand, and pieces of music drifted to the floor.

Then Lord Ian shoved hard against Mr. Kinnier, and the man lurched backward several steps before regaining his footing. Both men glared daggers at each other, breathing heavily.

"You will leave her alone while she remains in this house," Lord Ian said.

Mr. Kinnier straightened and yanked his coat into place. But then he looked at Alethea and his eyes narrowed, making them almost disappear in his face. "Very well," he said through stiff lips. He turned and strode from the music room, closing the door behind him with a snap.

Lord Ian helped Alethea to her feet. "Are you injured?"

"No." She rubbed her wrist, but no bones were broken.

"I'm sorry I didn't arrive sooner. Ord was watching the violin and ran to fetch me as soon as he saw you enter the room."

"I should not have antagonized him."

"He will be a nuisance to you no longer. Sir Hermes is at the church."

They gathered servants' cloaks from just inside the small door that led from the house into the kitchen gardens and hurried across the park. Alethea's heart pounded. "Mona is in her bedchamber. Where is Wilfred?"

"He was in the stables."

The twenty minutes' walk to the church seemed to take hours. The wind had risen, pressing the cloaks tightly against them and hampering her legs. The wind died as they entered the forest at the edge of the park, but the undergrowth tugged at Alethea's hem and the wet leaves clung to her slippers, the damp chilling her toes.

They reached the church just as rain splattered the roof. After they rushed inside, Mrs. Coon helped them remove their cloaks. Her normally merry eyes were grave. "How I could wish this was a more festive wedding for you, my lady."

Alethea touched her hand. "I am marrying a good man, surrounded by the people I care about. I need nothing else."

Mrs. Coon squeezed her fingers, which made Alethea's injured wrist twinge, and then they were in the sanctuary, with a small group of people gathered near the front.

Lucy and Mr. Collum were there, and her sister came up the aisle to hug her and kiss her cheek.

"We must hurry," Lord Ian said. "We met Mr. Kinnier before leaving the house, and he may suspect something."

"Then let us begin," Lady Morrish said. Sir Hermes had a grin on his face, his cheeks cherry red with excitement.

Lord Ravenhurst offered her his arm. "If you will allow me to give you away?"

"Wait." Clare handed her a bouquet of hothouse flowers from the Terralton Abbey greenhouses.

"Put this in your hair." Margaret gave her a blue ribbon.

Lucy tied it into her coiled braids while Aunt Ebena fastened a pearl bracelet to her wrist. "Old and borrowed."

"And this is new—my gift to my future daughter." Lady Morrish fastened pearl eardrops to her ears.

"You needn't do this," Alethea said.

"It is a legal wedding, your family is here—almost all your family—and you are suitably decked out," Aunt Ebena said. "We can say it was all that was proper."

Alethea took Lord Ravenhurst's arm and walked down the aisle to stand before Mr. Coon, who had dressed in his robes.

Dommick took her hand. He was pale, his face a mask.

Alethea turned away from him and faced Mr. Coon.

The ceremony was short and efficient, until the marriage vows. Dommick stumbled, not upon the words "to love and to cherish," but upon "in sickness and in health." As Mr. Coon pronounced them man and wife, she realized she had married a man who had spoken his wedding vows as a complete lie.

Empty. She felt so empty.

But she was not alone. There was a Presence, small and beautiful, in a space deep inside her. She knew it was there with a knowing deeper than knowledge.

Mr. Coon finished the ceremony, and the two of them had signed the registry when the door burst open. Wilfred rushed inside, his narrow face flushed, his pale grey eyes bloodshot, with Mr. Kinnier and Mona behind him. "What are you doing?"

Dommick faced him, placing his body between Wilfred and Alethea. "It is done."

Wilfred stood stock-still in the aisle, rainwater dripping from the brim of his hat, his mouth contorting in a series of grimaces. "No. You had no license—"

"Didn't you know, my lord, that I am friends with a man who represents the archbishop of Canterbury? We are quite close," Sir Hermes said.

"I signed a betrothal agreement—"

"You did not sign one with me," Dommick said. "It is now your own affair that you could not fulfill your side of the contract with Mr. Kinnier."

Wilfred stood in furious disbelief, then wrenched off his hat. "Do you realize what you have done to me?" He began to roar his complaints, the sound reverberating from the church's ceiling.

Mr. Kinnier stood slightly behind Wilfred. On the surface, his face was impassive, but an anger glittered in his eyes that made Alethea's throat burn and a shiver course across her shoulders. Mr. Kinnier whirled around, his greatcoat capes flicking water in a graceful arc, and exited the church. Mona watched him leave with wide eyes.

When Wilfred's language grew more colourful, Mr. Coon reacted with righteous censure. "You will not speak so in the house of God."

Wilfred stormed out of the church, but Mona remained. Her skin seemed to tremble, and Alethea realized the woman was holding in a fury like nothing she had ever seen before.

When Mona opened her mouth, her voice was far different than Alethea had heard from her before, sibilant and awful. "You think you've won, but no one crosses us without repayment in kind."

"You will leave my house within the half hour," Dommick said.

As if he hadn't spoken, Mona moved closer to Dommick. "I have been in the highest society in London for the past decade and have far more dangerous acquaintances than your idiot mother."

"Get out!" Dommick shouted.

"I will ensure that your sister's season is *ruined*."

And with that terrible pronouncement, Mona stalked out of the church.

⁕

It was the most awkward, frightening, exciting night of Alethea's life. But mostly it was simply awkward.

She sat before the mirror at her dressing table and brushed her long, dark hair. A maid had brushed it earlier, but it was something to occupy her hands.

She had been moved from the guest bedroom to the one connected to Dommick's bedchamber via a small sitting room. The furnishings had been redone by Lady Morrish a few years ago, so they were not old or unfashionable, but the pinks and yellows of the wallpaper and upholstery were more feminine than Alethea was accustomed to.

The connecting door taunted her. Should she retire to the canopied bed or stay awake in case Dommick came through? Either option promised embarrassment and pain.

Her stomach growled. She had not eaten much of the wedding dinner prepared by Dommick's surprised staff. There had been both an air of festivity and also a current of anxiety among the guests. Most had exulted in successfully routing Wilfred and

Mr. Kinnier, but it was obvious that Clare and Lady Morrish, especially, were deeply affected by Mona's threat and attempting not to show it.

At that moment, the connecting door opened.

Dommick wore a blue brocade dressing gown. The white of his nightshirt blazed at his throat, which made it more apparent when he blushed in embarrassment at the sight of her.

She looked away from him. "I had not expected you."

He swallowed. "I do not wish to mortify you, but there are things . . . I do not wish the servants to gossip." He flushed even darker than before and crossed to her bed. She saw the flash of a small knife, and he did something to the sheets and mussed her bedding.

He walked back to her, binding a small cut he had made on his forearm. "I apologize. I do not wish anything about this to embarrass you."

Except that his presence here, doing what he had done, was embarrassing her. She could not answer him. She laid her brush down on the dressing table. Her body and her heart reacted to his presence so near to her, in so intimate a situation. Yet the three feet separating them may as well have been the lake in front of the house. She felt adrift, forsaken. She fought the tears pricking her eyes.

Then she felt the warmth of his fingers touching her hand. His touch was strong and tender, as she imagined it might be if he had come to her in love rather than this deception for the servants. He cradled her hand between both of his own, and then he raised it to his lips and kissed the back of her wrist. His lips seemed to linger, or perhaps she imagined it because she desired it to be so.

But then he turned her hand over, and she felt a warm puff of breath just before his lips touched her palm. His mouth seemed to heat her skin like a stream of hot tea, pooling in her hand, running down her fingers and across her forearm.

And then he dropped her hand. She drew it to her lap, cradling it with the other.

"Good night, Alethea."

"Good night, Dommick."

He left, closing the connecting door behind him.

This, then, was what her marriage was. This was what it would be to love him—this pain, this desiring more but afraid to ask for it, knowing the answer would only slice her deeply.

The soft Presence as bright and comforting as a candle flame that had sustained her throughout the wedding ceremony, throughout dinner, now flickered out.

She had never felt so alone.

❧

Alethea woke with a start. She had not realized she'd fallen asleep. How long had it been since Dommick had left her? She rubbed at one eye while searching the darkness for the fireplace and saw the embers of the coals. Not long, then.

The low keening carried through the closed door, making her skin prickle. Was that Dommick? What was amiss? Was he injured?

She was through the door and into the sitting room before she could think further. She hesitated at the closed door to Dommick's room, but then a hoarse cry from within made her scrabble to open it.

"No, I am able to fight, I tell you." The earnest, frustrated voice came from the bed at the far side of the room, lit by the low-burning fireplace. Then he shouted, "David!" with the dragging desperation of a man full of terror.

She approached the bed. He appeared to be having a nightmare. Should she wake him?

Then he began to sob, deep, wracking sobs that shook the entire bed. "Champion . . . God, please . . . I can't . . ."

She recognized the pain in his voice. It was utter despair, drowning condemnation, arid helplessness. She had felt it the night her brother sold her. Tears filled her eyes at the torment in his voice, in the sight of the curled figure on the bed, shaking with sobs.

Just as she was reaching to wake him, he spoke again, still sobbing, but this time with a small voice full of fear.

"Raven, they can't know about this, about Bedlam . . ."

Bedlam. What had happened to him to have placed him in that asylum for the insane?

"I have to do something . . ." He broke into bitter tears. Sounding like a petrified child, he said, "Raven, I don't want to go mad again."

She gasped. She had not credited the rumours, assuming they were designed to inflict hurt by questioning his sanity. But this . . .

"Oh, Dommick." She touched his shoulder.

He jerked upright, striking at her hand. He did not recognize her for a moment, his eyes wide and white in the darkness. He panted, quick and shallow like a dog.

She knew when he had woken because his breath calmed. "Alethea?"

Slowly, as though with a wild animal, she reached her hand to him. She touched his cheek in a soft, gentle stroke. His skin was cold and slick with sweat. "I am here. You are safe."

His hand covered hers, pressed it to his face. Then he turned his head, and he kissed her palm again, his fingers tightening around hers.

He remained thus for long minutes, his breath fanning against her skin while his breathing slowed and his skin warmed. Then he looked at her. "You are cold."

She had not noticed. She had rushed from her bedchamber

without a wrapper, and now she felt the numbness creeping into her bare toes, the shivering in her torso. She saw his dressing gown thrown over the foot of the bed, and she pulled it on. The fabric was cool, but she was warmed by the scent of his musk that wrapped around her throat.

She sat on his bed and tucked her cold feet under her. "You were dreaming of war," she said.

He stared toward the fireplace. His eyes had become dead. "Of Corunna."

She had read about the retreat in the newspapers, and the casualties. "Captain Enlow was there with you?"

"He saved my life." He began to rub his shoulder, although he did not seem conscious of it. "I had been injured during the retreat and lost a great deal of blood. David helped me to the port and onto a rowboat to the medical transport ship."

His other hand, resting on the covers, suddenly clenched the bedclothes, and the pain of his memories seemed almost like a physical blow to him. His eyes squeezed shut and he bowed his head.

She touched his cheek and stroked his fisted hand, caressing him until he had calmed again. "What happened?" she whispered.

"The retreat had been . . . blood and bodies and chaos. When we finally reached Corunna, the majority of the transport ships hadn't arrived. They ordered us to kill our horses . . ." His voice hitched. He couldn't continue for a few minutes, but when he did, his voice was broken. "I couldn't do it. When I was on that rowboat, Champion plunged into the water after me. He swam alongside . . ." She felt hot tears flowing down her fingers. His voice thick, he said, "Even as the transport ship was leaving the bay, he swam after us. He was trying to follow me . . ." He could no longer speak.

Neither could she. She cried with him, for his guilt and remorse, for the loyalty and bravery of an animal who did not understand why his master was leaving without him.

When his tears had run their course, she wiped them from his face with her fingers, smoothed his hair back from his forehead. He enfolded her hands in his, their skin wet with tears.

"I awoke in a London hospital crying out for him. I didn't understand I was no longer in Spain. The battle was before my eyes as if it were happening again. I thought I was *there*."

"What did the doctors do?"

"They sent me home. I hadn't known until then that my father had died while I was recovering in London. The nightmares—the ones at night and the waking ones during the day—frightened my mother and my betrothed. They sent me to Bedlam."

She tightened her hands around his.

"I don't remember my time there, except that it was horrible. Then Raven came and took me away."

Thank God. What would have happened if Ravenhurst had not saved him? She remembered Dommick's anguished cry, *I don't want to go mad again*. She now understood fully the panic behind those words. "You will never go back there. I give you my word."

Even in the dim firelight, she saw his sadness, the vulnerability . . . and the tenderness. "I don't want to frighten you if it happens again. The waking nightmares."

"They will pass. They will become less frequent, and then they will become less powerful, and you will be able to break their hold over you more quickly."

He shook his head. "It has been over a year."

"It may take longer, I suppose. But I do think it will pass." She hesitated, then said in a whisper, "I had them."

His brows drew low over his eyes. "Why did you have them?"

For an instant, she smelled the smoking tallow from her brother's study, but then the warmth and scent of Dommick's dressing gown brought her back to the firelight. "My brother had gaming debts. He had a friend who needed to marry for some reason—he never told me. They signed a betrothal agreement—I would marry his friend, and my brother would receive half of my dowry."

There was a grim, taut line at the edges of Dommick's mouth as he heard this.

"I refused," Alethea said. "So my brother sought to . . . coerce me." She swallowed, and her left hand began to throb, faster with her increasing heartbeat. "He broke two fingers of my left hand."

Dommick jerked in surprise, then he looked down and touched her hand. His fingertips gently massaged the two knuckles obviously more swollen than the others.

"He locked me in my room until he could procure a special license and force me to marry his friend, but I ran away. I don't know what I thought it would accomplish, for I had no funds. My brother chased after me, but he had always been a reckless driver. His high-perch phaeton tipped over and he was thrown. He broke his neck and died instantly."

Dommick looked astounded. "I heard about his carriage accident."

"I had managed to get to Bath and Lucy, and then discovered my brother was dead. Two weeks later Wilfred forced me to leave my home and move to Bath, and the nightmares followed me."

"Your Aunt Ebena knows about them?"

"Oh, yes. She ignored them and let me be, gave me time and space. And . . . she rented a pianoforte for me." At the time, Alethea had not truly appreciated her aunt's gesture, but a year later, with a broader perspective, she saw her aunt's wisdom. "Then she began taking me out into society, forcing me to exert control over myself. She did not give me opportunity to be afraid."

"And they went away?"

"Mostly. My last nightmare was this summer."

He shook his head again, and frustration grated in his voice. "It's been over a *year* . . ."

"You have friends and family around you. My family, your family, your friends and neighbors—they have changed me. They have made me stronger and brought me closer to God. They will help you heal."

She released one of his hands to stroke his hair, his cheek, his jaw. It felt comforting to touch him, to press her fingertip to the pulse at his throat and feel the life coursing through him.

Then his hand was touching her hair, her cheek, her jaw. But his palm against her neck was far from comforting—his touch was strong and sure, different from hers, and his skin felt hot and rough against hers. Her breathing became shallow gasps, her heartbeat throbbed harder in her chest. She became acutely aware of the darkness broken only by the firelight, the unfamiliar intimacy of his bedchamber, the feel of his dressing gown around her, and the sight of his own pulse rapidly beating at the base of his exposed throat.

When he leaned forward to kiss her, she felt complete and then filled to overflowing. There was a roaring in her ears. Her hand on his throat felt the vibrations as he murmured her name. She tasted the remnants of his fear and doubt, and she sought to wash them away with the strength of her promise to never allow anyone to harm him. She would keep him safe, even from his fears of himself. She sought to convey that to him as his lips softly pressed against hers, gentle movements that at once revealed his strength and his vulnerability.

He drew back far enough to rest his forehead against hers, his hands cupping her cheeks. "Alethea, you have made a bad bargain."

"I was about to say the same for you."

When he laughed, she felt the rounding of his cheeks, the warmth of his breath, the shaking of his shoulders. Then he said, so softly it was almost like a thought, "I am still afraid."

"I will protect you, Dommick."

"Stay with me."

Without hesitation, she let the heavy dressing gown fall to the floor and climbed under his covers beside her husband. She wrapped her arms around him.

"I want you to call me Bayard." His voice rumbled next to her cheek.

The way they had addressed each other had been a topsy-turvy business, a mix of embarrassment and deception. But this request was more intimate than anything else that had passed between them. "Bayard," she whispered.

His arms tightened around her.

"Bayard, I will keep the nightmares away."

CHAPTER TWENTY

$\mathcal{F}$or the first time since returning from Corunna, he had slept without fear. He had felt protected and cherished. He had been vulnerable, but he had been held like a precious treasure. And when he had awoken, the anxiety of his madness that had been like a millstone around his neck seemed a lighter burden.

He awoke alone, but the knowledge that she was close, that she was in his house, that she was his wife, was an assurance like a salve over his raw soul. She had done more than she realized in listening to him, in her sympathy and empathy, her lack of fear. His mother had been afraid, his friends had been wary. Alethea had been beside him, supporting him, accepting him. He knew that even were he to be mad the rest of his life, she would be there with him.

However, the reality of Lady Trittonstone's threat reared its head the very next day. Bayard had just finished with his steward, and the man was leaving his study when his mother burst in, handkerchief aflutter, followed closely by Clare.

Bayard stood. "What is amiss? Is Alethea well?"

Clare paused and gave him a speculative look. "Alethea is well."

"I am here." Alethea entered the study carrying a full tea tray.

"You should not be doing that," Lady Morrish said, scandalized. "You are Lady Dommick now."

"I have been Lady Alethea all my life. June has a sore wrist and nearly dropped it, so I told her I would bring it to Bayard." She looked at him as she said it, and he noted the change in her voice as she said his name.

"Mama, do stop being so high in the instep," Clare said. "Since when is it a crime to be kind to the maids?"

"Since our reputation is in shreds!" Lady Morrish dropped into a chair before the desk, and her face crumpled like her handkerchief.

"It is not so bad as all that," Clare said, but Bayard heard the note of uncertainty in her voice.

"Yes, it is," she moaned.

"Which is the reason I asked cook to prepare tea." Alethea set it on a clear corner of his desk and began pouring. She handed Lady Morrish her teacup first.

"Will someone please tell me what has happened?" Bayard asked.

"You have been with your steward, so you are unaware Mrs. McDonald and Mrs. Wyatt called?" Clare said.

"I sent the announcement to the papers only this morning," Bayard said.

"They did not call about our marriage, although they offer their sincere congratulations," Alethea said.

"They met at the rectory this morning with Mrs. Amsden," Clare said. "The three of them are organizing the church bazaar this year. Mrs. Amsden's good friend, Lady Trittonstone, arrived last night with the most scandalous stories about me."

Bayard slammed his hand down on his desk, rattling the china. "That poisonous woman."

"First of all is the story that my lady's maid is the Earl of

Trittonstone's natural daughter and a . . . er, prostitute." Clare coloured at the scandalous word. "She has apparently corrupted my moral character."

"You will recall, when I first came into the neighborhood, people noted that Lucy and I look alike, and we both resemble our father," Alethea said.

"I'm sure I don't know how she would assume an illegitimate daughter would be a . . . that sort of woman," Lady Morrish said.

Unfortunately, since many illegitimate children were born in poverty, Bayard could easily see the connection. "What else?"

"Under the influence of my maid, I have been engaging in scandalous evening activities and have often been seen returning in the wee hours of morning with my gown mussed. Obviously a liberal retelling of my kidnapping."

"How did she know about it?" Lady Morrish wailed.

"If Lady Whittlesby's groom saw Clare returning with Lucy that evening, another servant might have also spied them," Bayard said grimly.

"If that were the case, the story would have been widely spread long before this, for Mona would not have been the first to whom the servant told it," Alethea said.

"I think that Lady Trittonstone heard the rumours regarding my maid and simply embellished them," Clare said. "She couldn't know she would touch upon a thread of truth."

"Mrs. McDonald and Mrs. Wyatt were quick to show their disapprobation," Lady Morrish said, "and they assure me they will do all they can to show that the rumours are unfounded. But to whom else will Lady Trittonstone speak?"

"Mama, the rumours are patently ridiculous," Clare said.

"It matters not how ridiculous they are. It will be ruinous for your season. Especially after . . ." She stopped with a conscious look at Bayard.

Alethea quickly turned the conversation. "More than ever, we must uncover the truth about the violin and win Lady Whittlesby's concert."

Now it was Bayard's turn to feel self-conscious. He had done the right thing in refusing the concert, but with the specter of Lady Trittonstone's malicious influence already hovering over the coming spring, Bayard felt squeezed, as though a heavy rock lay over him, holding him down. "I have sent out inquiries to Mr. Kinnier. I cannot think that his betrothal was anything but an attempt at the violin."

"Was it he who arranged Clare's kidnapping?" Lady Morrish pressed her handkerchief to her throat.

"Clare is in no danger, my lady," Alethea said. "The kidnapping targeted me, and they will not make the same mistake again."

"They will simply ruin Clare's season." Lady Morrish gave a great sob.

"Mama, your tears are distressing Bayard." Clare removed her teacup from her hand and took her by the shoulders. "Let us go upstairs and I shall put some lavender water on your temples." Behind her mother's back, Clare shot Bayard a look that clearly said, *Do something.* His sister walked their mother out of the room.

Bayard slumped in his chair. "I cannot do this to her again."

"Your mother?" Alethea sat down. "Until now I had not fully understood how the rumours would hurt your mother's feelings."

"Miss Church-Pratton broke our engagement when I was recovering in the hospital after Corunna. Thinking to be clever, she spread stories of the Mad Baron this past spring. My mother lost a great many friends because they feared associating with a woman with a mad son."

"Why would your former betrothed do that?" The colour had risen in Alethea's cheeks.

"Our betrothal had been arranged by our fathers. I knew she

had wanted a man of higher rank, and then my nightmares only heightened her disgust of me. It pleased her to slander me."

She sipped her lukewarm tea. "I had been coming to speak to you when Aunt Ebena drew me into the ladies' visit in the drawing room. Earlier this morning I was going over Margaret's geography lesson—"

"You are Lady Dommick now. You can hire a governess for that, you know."

She tilted her head. "By jove, you are correct. I had not thought of that. Thank goodness." She smiled at him, and his world tilted for a moment. "But you will be glad I was her tutor today. She is obsessed with Count Sondrono, and since lessons with her have been a chore, I have been indulging her. I had her look up the flora and fauna of the Alps, and today she gave me this." Alethea passed him a slip of paper with a small flower drawn upon it. "This is a 'cat's paw' or 'wool-flower,' which grows in the area of the Alps where the count's estate is. She immediately recognized it as a flower carved upon my jewelry box."

"How did she know that?"

"She ransacked my room once—I shall tell you the story another time. Calandra gave the jewelry box to me when Sir William made her a new, larger one. She only mentioned it was from Italy, nothing more. After Margaret pointed out the flower, I looked more closely at my jewelry box, and I believe it is made from the same wood as the back plate of my violin."

"Are you certain?"

"I was going to fetch my violin to be sure."

Bayard and Alethea removed the violin from its chest in the music room and headed upstairs to her bedchamber. It was an unfamiliar but comforting feeling to be allowed in her private quarters, to know that as his wife, she shared herself with him in this way.

Except that she would share in his disgrace as well, especially if Lady Trittonstone's rumours found their targets in London. The thought depressed his spirits.

The jewelry box was of a narrow-grained wood that appeared to be similar to the violin, although it was difficult to be certain even in the light from the window.

"If this is the same wood as the violin, then this box also belonged to the count," Alethea said.

"And if Lady Arkright bought this box from the peddler with the violin, then perhaps the peddler received all his wares from the count's home directly, not from some deceased merchant as we have been supposing. It would explain why Mr. Manco had no records of selling this particular violin, for the count never sold it."

"Calandra said that the peddler's wares were cheap things, and so perhaps the count's heirs sold his violin with other objects, thinking it to be worthless."

"But why did the count not sell this violin if he was so in debt?"

"I would not sell my violin to Mr. Golding because of my emotional attachment to it," Alethea said. "Perhaps the count had a strong sentimental attachment to it."

"And the family assumed it was worthless because he had already sold off everything else of value."

"It is an ugly violin, to be sure, and it had been damaged."

Bayard ran his hand down the smooth neck of the instrument. "If one of the count's family discovered the violin had been mistakenly sold to the peddler, he would pursue it, believing it rightfully belongs to his family."

"That is a strong incentive."

"My previous inquiries have turned up naught, but I must redouble my investigation into the count's living relatives and look into Mr. Kinnier's family tree."

She replaced her jewelry box and sat in her chair. "For your family's sake, we must win the spot in Lady Whittlesby's concert."

He was silent.

"I heard Lady Whittlesby called upon you last week, but I hadn't found opportunity to speak to you about it."

"She stopped on her way to London." Bayard opened his mouth to repeat what he had told the others, but he could not lie to her. "Alethea, she offered me her concert, even without the information on your violin, and I refused."

"What? But . . . Clare's season."

"It would be too dangerous for you to be in London."

"Then leave me here."

"I will not leave you alone."

She gave him a small smile, but then sobered. "Bayard, think of Clare and your mother, especially now."

"I love my family, and I am . . . very fond of you." He did not perfectly understand his feelings for her, and he had not had time to meditate upon them. Everything was unfamiliar to him.

She looked down at her lap and did not respond.

He continued, "But you are my wife now, Alethea. I will not place you in a dangerous situation."

"We may yet discover the villain."

"I have until the first of the year to change my mind."

"Bayard." Alethea laid her hand over his, and her fingers were cool. He reveled in the feel of her skin on his. "You must write to Lady Whittlesby. You must do this for Clare and your mother. There is such éclat attached to the concert, it will do everything to counteract the rumours."

He laid his hand over hers. "I will do everything in my power to eliminate this threat to you. I wish I had more than a few tidbits about an Italian count's family. After Mr. Manco said the violin hadn't been sold, that he couldn't even verify it belonged to Sondrono . . ." He hated feeling so powerless. "I have nothing. I only desire some guidance . . ."

She drew him to sit in a chair near her. "I do not know how to advise you," she said hesitantly, "but I can tell you that I have felt comforted and refreshed in your family chapel. I have been reading your family Bible on the altar, since I have no Bible of my own."

"You do not?" He was shocked.

"My father left me at Trittonstone Park with nannies and governesses. If I owned a Bible, it is probably still there, gathering dust on a shelf."

"I shall procure one for you directly."

"I would like that. But I enjoy your family Bible, reading your family tree. And the text is . . . piercing at times."

Piercing. Yes, he understood that. Bayard realized that he had not spent time in prayer for several weeks, since that one frantic prayer the night Clare was taken. He had drawn away from a faith that had always comforted him in the past.

There was a knock on the door, and a maid appeared. "The cook wishes to speak to you, milady."

"I shall be down directly." She rose, and in answer to his questioning look said, "The servants were quite shocked at our marriage, more from the fact that they were not able to throw us a proper wedding breakfast. The cook has asked for permission to provide a festive dinner tonight to remedy that."

He rose to his feet. "I had not thought of that."

"There have been many things I have had to learn as mistress of this house, the first of which is that your cook is not to be argued with." She smiled at him.

On impulse, he leaned down to kiss her. Her presence here at Terralton Abbey was soothing to him, fulfilling his life in a way he had not realized he needed.

She touched his cheek and left.

Instead of going to the music room, he found himself standing outside the family chapel. The wooden door creaked as he opened it, but the utter stillness within settled upon him like the first snowfall. He sat in one of the pews and let the light from the windows fall upon him, highlighting the dust motes floating in the air.

His worry over the rumours and Clare's season seemed like childish things, here in this place, and yet the anxiety gnawed at him like rot overtaking a log. He was nothing in the face of the troubles outside these walls. There was nothing he could do about them that would give peace to his family.

He rose to his feet. The chapel had only emphasized his helplessness and heightened his apprehension. Here was a place where the stillness enabled a man to count his troubles one by one and see how he was lacking.

He strode up the aisle ... and hesitated. Alethea had mentioned the family Bible, and although he'd had no intention of looking at it, something turned his feet around and drew him up the three short steps to the altar.

The Bible lay open, perhaps where Alethea had been reading it. The print was small, so his eyes skimmed over the page without really seeing it.

But then a verse seemed to leap up and slap him across the face.

"Trust in the LORD with all thine heart; and lean not unto thine own understanding."

Piercing, she had called it. Yes, he felt pierced.

"In all thy ways acknowledge him, and he shall direct thy paths."

He knew these verses, had memorized them as a boy. He had known their meaning like a rock skipping across the surface of the lake, but now they held a deeper meaning he had never known before.

In all his fears for his sanity, for his sister, his mother, Alethea, his reputation—he had depended upon himself and not upon the Lord. He had only thought about the next steps he could take, the precautions he could establish. But his attitude had been a disbelief in the power of God to work for him, to help him solve his problems.

He leaned against the altar, head bowed. *Lord, forgive me.*

The silence gathered around him like a crowd of witnesses, invisible hands resting upon his head.

I will trust in thee to heal my mind. I will trust in thee to care for Clare, my mother, and our reputation. I will trust in thee with my marriage . . .

He did not know what else to pray. His feelings were a jumble of impressions and confusion. And yet even there, perhaps the Lord would help him to untangle the strings.

I will trust in thee to teach me to love.

❧

Today, Alethea would tell Bayard that she loved him.

She had gathered her courage. She had received enough encouragement to know he would not reject her. She would tell him that she did not expect him to love her, but she hoped they might draw closer. And she wanted children. She wanted *his* children.

She thought a moment. Mayhap she should not quite mention children just yet.

Yesterday, when she had first looked inside her jewelry box, after Margaret had shown her the flower drawing, she had seen Bayard's handkerchief, the reed pipe, and Bayard's penknife, which she had intended to return to him, but hadn't. All precious treasures. Embarrassed, she'd placed them in a drawer before going to look for him to tell him about the jewelry box.

This morning she slipped all three into the pocket in her old-fashioned morning gown. When she found him, perhaps they could go to the gazebo to talk. Playing pipes with her had lifted his spirits, so he might be cheered by them again today.

As she descended the stairs, she heard a curious sound from

the morning room. Women's laughter, loud and raucous, hooting with mirth.

She entered the room to the sight of her Aunt Ebena, Lady Morrish, and Lady Ravenhurst gathered around the table, laughing so hard that tears streamed down the faces of Lady Morrish and Lady Ravenhurst. Gone was the anxiety that had lined Lady Morrish's face yesterday, and Alethea could not help smiling.

"I can scarce believe she did such a thing," gasped Lady Morrish. "Good morning, Alethea."

"You three are quite disturbing the household."

"Shall you tattle on us to Lady Dommick?" Lady Ravenhurst said cheekily.

"Your aunt has the most amusing tales of London," Lady Morrish said.

Aunt Ebena looked pleased. "When you have the number of acquaintances that I do, you collect a vast number of stories about them, for they are each gossiping about each other. Lady Jersey is an especially voluble letter-writer."

"Lady Jersey?" One of the most feared and powerful society hostesses in London?

"Oh, yes. We have known each other many years. I no longer see her in London, but she visits me in Bath once every two or three years, and we write frequently."

"Your aunt was writing to Lady Jersey for us," Lady Morrish said. "We owe her a debt of gratitude."

"It is nothing," Aunt Ebena said gruffly. "Sally owes me a favour."

While Lady Morrish and Lady Ravenhurst had their embroidery work before them on the table, Aunt Ebena had a half-finished letter. "What are you writing?"

"I am writing ostensibly to give the *on dit* about Dommick's hasty wedding. You needn't worry, miss, I am writing of how he could not be torn from your side in Bath, which culminated in his invitation to his house party."

Alethea realized that Bayard's actions indeed would appear to be a besotted swain. No wonder the misses in Bath had seemed jealous—she, an aged spinster, capturing a wealthy nobleman? Of course they were gnashing their collective teeth over it.

"Sally will appreciate the firsthand account of all the details, and the haste with which she will receive it ahead of anyone else," Aunt Ebena said. "But I am also writing to request her influence in town for Clare's come out and to refute any nasty stories put about by Lady Trittonstone."

"She will do this?" Alethea asked.

"Oh, yes." Aunt Ebena looked smug, but did not embellish her comment.

"And your aunt has agreed to come stay with me and Sir Hermes at Morrish House after the new year," Lady Morrish said. "Ebena, you must stay with us in London this spring as well."

Aunt Ebena's cheeks glowed peach. "I shouldn't wish to discommode you—"

"We should love to have you."

"I think that would be lovely, Aunt," Alethea said. "I shall keep Margaret with me, if you like."

Her aunt gave her a small nod. "Thank you."

Alethea left the morning room with a bounce to her step. This good deed of her aunt would alleviate Bayard's concerns as they had lifted Lady Morrish's anxiety. She couldn't wait to tell him.

She also reflected that now that she was Lady Dommick, she needn't give up her dreams of Italy after all. Perhaps a family trip with Aunt Ebena and Margaret?

First she needed to find him.

As she was about to head down the more deserted corridor

toward his study, she heard footsteps behind her. "My lady?" It was Forrow.

"Yes?"

"Mrs. Coon is here to see you. She said it is quite urgent."

"Where is she?"

"In the drawing room."

Before heading there, Alethea asked him, "Where is Lord Dommick?"

"He received a letter, and after reading it, set off for Chippenham, I believe, not more than half an hour ago."

"Did he indicate when he would return?"

"He said he would return in time for tea."

Alethea entered the drawing room and was startled to see Mrs. Coon pacing in front of the fire. "Mrs. Coon, whatever is the matter?"

"Lady Dommick, I do hope I am not alarming you unnecessarily," Mrs. Coon said. "I have just seen your sister, Lucy, with a strange man in the woods."

"Mr. Collum, her betrothed?" But then she remembered Mrs. Coon had met Mr. Collum at Alethea's wedding.

"No. Lucy was without her cloak, my lady, and she looked frightened."

"Where was this? What did the man look like? When did you see them?"

"As soon as I saw them, I came here directly. The man was very slender, with grey clothes. He had grey hair and he walked . . . loosely."

Alethea's heart stopped. Pain radiated from her chest, across her shoulders, down her arms.

"I saw them in the woods, but I know of an old gamekeeper's hut nearby. If you have a map of the estate, I can show you where it is."

"I'm sure there is a map in Lord Dommick's study."

Her limbs felt leaden but she forced them to move. As they headed toward the study, she repeated to herself as though afraid to forget, *Find Ravenhurst, Ian, or Ord. Find Ravenhurst, Ian, or Ord.* They would know how to find Bayard.

She scanned the orderly top of the desk, then began opening drawers. A bottom one held rolls of paper and she removed them, dropping them all onto the desk. She and Mrs. Coon fell to unrolling each one until Mrs. Coon said, "This one."

They spread it out upon the desk, anchoring the edges with paperweights and the ink stand. Mrs. Coon pointed to a place in the forest. "When I saw them, they were here. They were heading in the direction of the hut, which is here." She pointed to another place nearby.

Alethea nodded, her neck stiff. "I will tell Bayard. Thank you."

"I shall be praying, my dear. I am afraid I must return—I left the girls home alone in order to come to tell you."

"Yes, of course."

Mrs. Coon departed, leaving the door open. Alethea heard her footsteps retreating down the corridor.

She studied the map, then grasped a pen and opened the ink stand. Footsteps approached the study. She hoped it was one of Bayard's friends. She drew an X where the hut was.

A voice like rancid butter spoke from the doorway. "Might I have a word, milady?"

She looked up.

Mr. Golding stood just inside the doorway.

CHAPTER TWENTY-ONE

t first, her mind could not grasp that he was here in her house. It was so bizarre that she could only blink at him.

Mr. Golding stepped into the study and shut the door. "And before you think of calling for the servants, your sister will die if I do not deliver you within fifteen minutes."

She gasped, trying to pull air into her lungs. She gripped the edge of the desk.

He said in a bored voice, "I do hope you will not faint. Your sister's life is still forfeit."

She had to regain control of herself. She took in one breath. Then another. "I will come with you."

"You will come now," Mr. Golding said in a flat voice. "You will leave no messages for anyone."

Surely they would be seen by a servant as they left the house. Alethea nodded in acquiescence, but then under cover of gathering her skirts, she reached into her pocket and grasped the reed pipe. She slipped it onto the map with a flick of her hand and walked around the desk toward Mr. Golding.

He had not noticed her movements. "Come, milady." He grasped her arm and opened the study door.

"How did you get into my house?" she asked.

"It was quite easy while the servants were eating."

"That was half an hour ago."

"I had to wait for you to be alone, naturally, so I hid in the coat room. I thought I would have to wait longer."

She looked about. Where were the servants? They were nearing the side door that opened into the park, and she had not seen anyone.

He smiled. "A few burning rags tossed into the kitchen garden creates a marvelous diversion."

"How did you accomplish that while in the coat room?"

"There are always local boys to be bought for pranks such as that. They only need a signal from a window to be set in motion. I would quicken my step, if I were you, milady. That fire is also a sign to my associate. If I do not deliver you, your sister dies."

Her stomach clenched. His cleverness appalled her. "What do you want with me? Don't you want my violin? The music room is that direction."

"We know your violin is in the music room for you've played it there, but we also know the one on the table is not the true instrument. That being the case, we know the music room is somehow being watched. So, for now, you and I shall simply walk out of your house."

Dear Lord . . . please help Bayard find us in time.

⌘

Bayard knocked on the door to the home outside of Chippenham, burrowing in his greatcoat and hat.

"You picked a fine day to visit," Ian remarked, also shivering in his outer garments.

"I cannot waste time," Bayard said. "I wrote to Doctor Meredith weeks ago about Lady Fairmont's Italian connections, and I received his response only today. If I write again, I may need to wait another month." In addition to his parish duties, the reverend had become well known for his study of the family branches of the peerage.

The housekeeper let them in out of the biting wind. After giving her their cards, they were ushered into a large library stuffed with books. Bookcases lined the walls, but others stood perpendicular from the walls, forming alcoves and leaving only a space in the centre of the room for a long table reminiscent of the ones he remembered from university.

Doctor Meredith stepped forward to greet them, skirting stacks of books on the floor. "Lord Dommick, this is an unexpected pleasure."

"I hope you will excuse the intrusion, but the information I require has an urgent nature."

"That is distressing. I hope I may be of assistance." Doctor Meredith gestured to the table, half hidden by the books and papers scattered atop it. He cleared a space by sweeping his arm across the surface and shoving his books aside. "My housekeeper will bring tea presently. Pray, be seated."

"I had written to you about Lady Fairmont's Italian relations, but I have since discovered that she is related to the Count of Inizinesso."

"Have you now? I must write that down." Doctor Meredith rummaged among the papers and discovered a pencil and a piece of foolscap. "How is he related to her?"

"Er . . . her mother's uncle, I believe. Doctor Meredith, I am now interested in any relations of the Count of Sondrono whom you may know about."

Doctor Meredith studied the haphazard piles of paper and

decided to stick the foolscap between the pages of a large blue book.
"Sondrono, you say? While I have done extensive research into our
English noble families, my records of their foreign connections are
incomplete." He went to the far end of the table, rummaging about
until he found a stack of papers. He returned and paged through
the stack. "Sondrono hails from which region of Italy?"

"North, in the Alps."

"Ah, that narrows the field." Doctor Meredith finally found
several pages that he removed. "I have only one small reference to
Sondrono, I am afraid."

Bayard saw the short line:

> Giovanni Accatino, great-grandson of the Count of Sondrono,
> and his family to London, 1715.

Bayard's hopes began to rise. "Have you information on this
man's family in England?"

"Of course." Doctor Meredith disappeared behind a bookcase and returned with three books. He opened one to a page and
pointed to a reference. "According to this, his daughter married Sir
John Mande in 1720."

Doctor Meredith flipped through another book and pointed to
a second reference. "Sir John and Lady Mande had one boy, James,
born 1721. He married Miss Catherine Beggston, eldest daughter
of Baron Venerton, in 1740. They had two daughters, Elizabeth in
1745 and Louisa in 1750. The eldest died unmarried in 1767. The
younger married Viscount Grimslow in 1770."

Cold shocked through Bayard. "Grimslow?"

Doctor Meredith was becoming quite excited, as though
embarking upon a treasure hunt. He opened another volume.
"Viscount Grimslow has three children: William born in 1775,
Grace in 1777, and Charity in 1778."

A frantic knock at the library door brought the housekeeper

looking aggrieved. "I'm sure I don't know what the world is coming
to, but they insisted upon seeing you at once, sir."

Bayard and Ian rose as Ord and Mr. Collum appeared in the
doorway, both breathing hard and wearing the mud of the road on
their coats. Ord said in a rush, "I'm sorry to interrupt you, my lord,
but in the village, Mr. Collum here has seen—"

"Kinnier," Bayard interrupted. "You've seen Mr. Kinnier."

❧

"Kinnier is related to Count Sondrono." Bayard turned to Ian. "I
should have trusted your instincts. You have never liked him."

"But when he appeared in Bath, I had no idea he was connected
to the violin."

"Ord, you were following Mr. Collum?" Bayard said.

"Although I am a stranger to you, I demand to know why you
suspected me," Mr. Collum said in a tight voice.

"I visited Mrs. Boane, and there was some discrepancy in your
employment . . . What is so amusing?"

Mr. Collum made a valiant effort to wipe the smile from his face
and failed. "Mrs. Boane is my aunt. She wrote a reference for me for
my first employer in Bath. I assume you spoke to Mr. Keable? He
was my father's butler before he went to work for my aunt."

Bayard felt foolish.

"You did not speak to your wife about me?" Mr. Collum asked.

"I did not wish to upset her by confessing I suspected her sister's betrothed."

"I suppose I could understand that," Mr. Collum admitted.

Ord said, "I was watching Mr. Collum at the inn where he is
staying when we both saw Mr. Kinnier arrive at the inn yard and
speak to Mr. Golding."

"I recognized Mr. Kinnier," Mr. Collum said. "I did not realize
Ord was following me, or I would have suggested we split up."

"I wouldn't have agreed," Ord shot back.

"Regardless, I chose to follow Mr. Kinnier as the better choice, but in the woods, he attacked me," Mr. Collum said.

"I was too far behind Mr. Collum to catch up to Mr. Kinnier when he ran," Ord said. "I lost him in the woods."

"I suppose I should be grateful you came back to help me," Mr. Collum said dryly.

"You only got a wee bump in the head," Ord said. "My lord, we went to Terralton Abbey and informed Lord Ravenhurst, who told us your direction. We followed you as soon as could be."

"Let us be off. My thanks, Doctor Meredith."

"I shall continue to unearth details and write my findings to you." Doctor Meredith clapped his hands like a child and surveyed his books. "How exciting this all is."

The drive back to Terralton Abbey was a mere twenty-five minutes, but it took far longer than Bayard could withstand. Alethea would not wander afield alone, but what if she were accosted while in the shrubbery or the park?

When they were home, Bayard flung himself from the carriage before it had stopped moving. "Saddle horses for us," he ordered the groom and bounded up the stairs to the front door.

His neck tightened when Raven opened the door before he could reach it. "Alethea is gone."

"What?" Bayard stumbled on the last step.

"As soon as Ord spoke to me, I searched for her. She was not in the house so I had the servants search the grounds, but they found nothing. However, her cloak is still here. She may have been taken against her will."

Bayard shook his head. He could not contemplate the possibilities. "She took a shawl or a pelisse to walk in the shrubbery . . ."

"I spoke to her maid, who confirmed they are all still in her wardrobe. Lucy is also missing."

"Who saw her last?" Bayard strode with quick steps to his study, where he kept maps of the estate.

"Forrow said that Mrs. Coon visited her for a short while. I sent a servant to the rectory, but Mrs. Coon had just left to visit a sick parishioner and the maid did not know to whom she went nor why she visited Lady Alethea."

Bayard found his thoughts clarifying, his mind focusing. His breathing became hard and even. He needed all his faculties to find her, to find Kinnier. Alethea, Lucy, Mr. Golding, Kinnier. One of them would lead him to all.

On any other day, he wouldn't have noticed his study door standing partly open.

"What is it?" Raven asked.

"I did not leave the door open." He entered the study warily, but it was empty. Bayard's eyes swept the room as he strode to the desk . . . and froze.

A map already lay spread out. It was a well-used map, with markings from over the years, but there was a fresh ink mark over a corner of the woods. And in the centre of the map, as though carelessly tossed, was a reed pipe.

He knew it was Alethea's. His pipe was upstairs on his shaving stand.

"Get Forrow," Bayard barked. "Did anyone see Alethea in my study?"

Ian slipped out of the room.

"Ord, where did you see Kinnier?"

His servant studied the map and pointed to a spot perhaps three quarters of a mile from the inked X. "He was heading in that direction, all right," Ord said, nodding to the X.

"That's the old gamekeeper's hut," Raven said. "Your father whipped us for playing there because it was too dangerous."

"Those men'll be prepared," Ord said.

"I shall speak to my gamekeeper," Bayard said. "If anyone asks, we shall be gentlemen in the woods, doing a little shooting."

※

The hut was completely still, no light and no sound. Bayard approached slowly, watching for movement, careful not to step on twigs or rustle the undergrowth. Shadowed by the trees, the air was damp and stinging with cold, but the weather had made the leaves wet and silent. In the dimness he could see footsteps around the front door.

Then a sound whispered on the wind, a feminine . . . grunt. "Blast it!"

"Lucy!" Mr. Collum rushed forward.

"Wait!" Bayard said. They did not know if she was alone.

But it was too late. Collum had pushed open the wooden door and entered the hut. Bayard followed.

Collum knelt on the dirt floor, his arms around a small figure. The hands clasping his back were unnaturally white, the fingers curled and shivering violently. When Collum released her to take off his coat, Bayard saw that it was Lucy.

Her hair tumbled around her face, and dirt streaked her forehead. There was also a bruise at her lower jaw that made Bayard's jaw harden. She had no cloak, only her dark dress. Collum swept his greatcoat around her and she clasped it to her.

Bayard knelt before her. "Are you hurt?"

She shook her head, and her teeth chattered. "You must find Alethea."

"Where is she? Where is Kinnier?"

"Why did they take you?" Collum said.

"To ensure Alethea would come willingly," she stuttered. "Mr. Golding stole her from the house and brought her here, but when she saw me, she threw her arms around me. They had tied my hands behind my back." She showed her wrists, which had the deep red and purple marks of a rope. "They pulled her away from me, but not before Alethea slipped a penknife into my hand."

Bayard took the knife from Lucy. It was his, the one he had lent to Alethea that day at the stream.

"Mr. Kinnier arrived soon after, and they left me alone."

"Which direction did they go?"

She nodded to her right. "They left in that direction. They were already several yards away, and I think they believed I couldn't hear them. One complained of the cold and wanted to go back to the inn, but Mr. Kinnier said he needed both men as sentries. He said, 'Two sides are clear fields, but there is forested area to the north and west, and I need you both to be in place to ensure Dommick comes alone.'"

"That's the cemetery, milord." His gamekeeper shouldered his hunting rifle. "Poachers like that forested area since it's thickest."

Bayard rose. "Collum, take her to the house." He hesitated, then said, "And would you speak to my butler? Have him gather the footmen and watch over my family."

Collum nodded. "I shall ensure they are kept safe."

"Thank you."

The rest of them hurried out, heading to the cemetery. It was possible that Kinnier was not expecting them so soon and that they could ambush them.

Bayard prayed they were not too late.

❧

Alethea sat upon the wooden bench and shivered so violently that she made the uneven legs rock against the ground. The rickety seat was marginally warmer than the stone bench where Kinnier sat.

He regarded her with cold, impassive eyes. "I suppose a gentleman would offer his greatcoat," he said.

"Then it is fortunate you are no gentleman," she snapped. She had refused to ask him for covering against the cold, and even should he offer it, she would fling it in his face. She did not want the scent of his skin, perfumed with an under-thread of rotting wood, upon her body, surrounding her.

He sighed as if bored and looked away, fingering the pistol in his lap. He had one shot in that gun. She had no wish to die, but she had no wish for that shot to kill Bayard. If the gun discharged, someone nearby may hear and discover them, ruining Kinnier's plans to entrap Bayard. Kinnier was far enough away from her that even if he fired upon her, she may be able to dodge the bullet. She simply had to make him fire.

"The servants will know I am missing," she said. "You should release me and escape while you have time."

Mr. Kinnier gave a short laugh. "My dear woman, no one will notice you are gone. No one cares."

The words burrowed easily into her, for the cold had made her weak and her fear had cut holes in her armor. She had been lonely for so long, the feeling of isolation came to her like a familiar friend, whispering words that made her colder than the winter wind could chill her body. Bayard did not love her. She did not know if he could ever love her. She curled in on herself, not for warmth, but to assuage the pain in her heart.

And then a small voice spoke words that were not words. She heard the bubbling of the stream, smelled the ferns and the damp earth, felt peace settle about her like a blanket.

Yea, I have loved thee with an everlasting love.

The remembered Bible verse was like fire to the ice around her heart.

The Lord thy God in the midst of thee is mighty.

She was not alone.

God *loved* her.

God would take care of her.

She straightened in her seat. "If truly no one cares for me, then Lord Dommick is hardly likely to respond to your ransom note and bring my violin to exchange."

"Oh, he will. I have insulted his honour, and he will want to challenge me to regain it. Just as he has insulted my honour."

What honour? "What has he done to you?"

"What has he not done? Because of the accolades heaped upon his mediocre talent, the gods have cursed me with this creative desert."

Only now did she realize Kinnier had the melancholy, tempestuous attitude of Poseidon, god of the sea—quick-tempered, passionate, but volatile. It had probably stood him in good stead when he was happy and producing music, but now, in the depths of his frustration, he had lost his muse and was desperate to tempt her to return. "Do you believe the violin will restore all this to you? It will not."

"What do you know of it?" he flung at her. "There is power in that instrument you could never comprehend, much less harness."

"How would you know?"

"I know all about that violin, a gift from the countess to her beloved husband. He played it when he missed her, after her death. That violin has been imbued with all his emotional power."

Or all his sorrow. "You are placing too much significance to an inanimate object."

"Be silent!" His sudden outburst made her start, but he immediately reverted back to his calm, impassive self.

She had poked a stick at the beast and had not enjoyed its reaction. And yet she must poke him more, induce him to do something unplanned. "How did you know I had the violin?"

"Your Lady Arkright made my life a living hell," he said. "I could not discern her married name no matter how I tried to trace her when she left Italy. It was by pure chance I came across the inquiry made by your cousin, Lord Trittonstone, when he inherited. He wanted to know what Lady Arkright had bequeathed to you, and the violin was described and deemed not very valuable."

"She could hardly know you were trying to steal it," Alethea said.

"It belongs to my family. If Sondrono had not sold the land where the wood was grown and the new owner cut down all the trees . . . if his idiot heir had not sold the violin to a peddler after Sondrono died . . ."

So that was why Stradivari had never produced another violin with the same wood.

"You should have simply sold it to Mr. Golding." Mr. Kinnier nodded toward the tree line, behind which the solicitor sat huddled in the cold, keeping watch for Bayard to respond to the ransom note being delivered by the cadaverous man at this moment.

"He was not persuasive," Alethea said. "He simply made me curious to know why the violin was so coveted."

"If Dommick had not made those inquiries about the violin, and if people had not begun talking about it, none of this would have been necessary," Kinnier said.

"Or if your men had not botched the kidnapping at the concert. You really must hire better minions."

His face grew hard at her dig, but he did not explode at her again.

"You are too heavy-handed," she continued in a conversational tone. "You cause people to be desperate, and so they resort to desperate measures."

"Such as your marriage to Dommick?"

"I am surprised you did not sign a betrothal agreement with Wilfred sooner than you did."

He gave her a nasty smile. "I had wanted to explore other avenues before resorting to such a *desperate* measure."

She supposed she deserved that.

"In the end, it doesn't matter. If I had married you, you would be equally as dead." His face was frighteningly calm.

"Bayard will not bring the violin, and in the end, you will have killed us both for nothing," she said. She fought the panic rising in her. Too much time had passed. She needed to induce him to do something before Bayard received that note and arrived with the violin.

And died.

No, she had to trust God to take care of them both.

And at that moment, she saw him.

"No," she moaned.

Bayard approached the cemetery wall from the road. He opened the gate and entered, walking slowly. He carried her violin case.

"I received your note. However, Mr. Collum took exception to the blow your grey man delivered to Miss Purcell, so they have detained the man at the abbey."

"She was putting up too much of a fuss," Mr. Kinnier said in a conversational tone. "I am impressed you found her before she froze to death."

"I have brought your violin." Bayard held the case aloft.

In a flash, Kinnier was at Alethea's side and had yanked her to her feet. The cold had numbed her limbs so that she could not feel her toes, and she wobbled.

Kinnier pressed the gun to Alethea's side. "I require all your compatriots to reveal themselves."

Bayard had stiffened, and his eyes were fierce upon the pistol. His gaze darted to the forest beyond them.

Lord Ian and Lord Ravenhurst slowly walked from the trees.

They held their shooting rifles, but kept them pointed to the ground. Their eyes were equally wary as they moved to stand beside Bayard.

"Your servant as well," Kinnier said. "Did you think I would forget him?"

The bushes rustled, and Ord appeared. He also held a gun, but it was aimed at Mr. Golding, whose V-shaped mouth was a flat line. Ord prodded him with the tip of the rifle, and Mr. Golding stumbled forward.

"Let Alethea go," Bayard said.

Kinnier gave a bark of laughter. "Are you really that stupid? Put the case on the ground and open it, facing me."

Bayard was only a few yards away, so Alethea saw the violin when the case lid was removed. It looked like hers and not the fake.

"Play it," Kinnier said.

Bayard hesitated.

"Play it or I shoot her." He shoved the pistol hard into her ribs.

She hissed, not from the pain but from the nervousness of his casual handling of the gun. She hoped it did not have a hair trigger.

Bayard removed the violin and lifted it to his shoulder. He looked directly at her with serious eyes, as though trying to tell her something, but she did not know what. And then he began to play.

It was her violin. The tone echoed through the cemetery with low, deep notes that seemed to make the tree roots rumble in the depths of the ground. The song captured all the chill of winter, the dead of the leaves, the bite of the frost. It was melancholy reverence for the harshness of nature and the end of life.

She felt rather than heard Kinnier's sigh as Bayard finished playing. "You defile it by playing it," he hissed to Bayard.

"Let her go."

"Put the violin in the case and close it. Leave it on the ground, then back away."

Bayard complied.

"*All* of you back away." Kinnier punctuated with another jab in Alethea's ribs with the pistol.

They moved slowly, every line of their bodies rigid except for Mr. Golding, prodded by Ord, who shuffled along with resentment burning from his eyes.

Kinnier did not seem to care that Mr. Golding was held at gunpoint. "Pick it up," he told her.

She clasped the violin case to her, but nearly lost her grip when he grabbed her upper arm and thrust her forward. "Walk. Dommick, we will leave you now. If you so much as sneeze, I shall shoot her."

He kept the pistol pressed to her, his other arm around her. They moved away from Bayard, whose entire body was rigid.

Because Kinnier had her so close to himself, she clearly felt when his hand reached for a second pistol in his coat pocket. As he drew it out, he twisted to take Bayard in his sights.

"No!" Alethea swung the edge of the violin case at him.

The deafening reports of the two pistols fired almost simultaneously, punctuated by splintering wood and a blinding pain in her side. She gasped and fell, her head ringing. She saw Bayard clutching his arm. Blood was smeared across his fingers.

Then a third shot rang out from the trees and Kinnier jerked. Lying on the ground, Alethea felt the thud as both his pistols fell to earth.

With a roar, Bayard launched himself at Kinnier.

The two men flew away from her in a tangle of greatcoats. They both rolled, grass and mud clinging to them, and blood smeared from their wounds. Kinnier was on his feet first and he aimed a kick at Bayard's head, but Bayard jerked aside and sent a sharp jab at the man's torso. Kinnier grunted and went down on one knee.

Bayard followed with a second blow to the jaw, and Kinnier arced back to land on the ground.

The rage in Bayard's face was primal. He got to his feet to attack Kinnier again, but Lord Ian locked Bayard's arms in his own.

"Let me go!" Bayard roared.

Lord Ravenhurst had landed on Kinnier and flipped him over onto his stomach. He tore his cravat from his throat and began binding Kinnier's hands. The man was still dazed from the blow Bayard had delivered.

From behind the trees, a man with a smoking hunting rifle emerged, and Alethea recognized Bayard's gamekeeper.

And then Bayard was beside her, holding her close. She could feel the slamming of his heart.

"I am well," she said.

"You are not." He looked at her side.

She could see that the bullet had gouged a furrow in her skin, but it was not deep. "A flesh wound," she said.

He crushed her against him again. "I thought I had lost you." His voice was ragged against her throat.

"I thought he would kill you," she whispered.

And then his mouth was on hers and he was kissing her fiercely, frantically, over and over again. He kissed her cheeks and eyes and jaw and neck and then her mouth again, each kiss hard with relief.

And then he pulled back only long enough to say, "I love you."

The pain in her side was washed away by the elation that flooded her. "I love you," she said as he kissed her again.

They were interrupted at last by Lord Ian. "You two are highly improper, and bloody messes to boot. Shall we adjourn to the abbey? I am in dire need of a hot toddy."

Bayard wrapped his greatcoat around her, and she breathed deep of oak, lime, and warm musk. He kept her close to his side as they turned their steps toward the abbey.

Toward home.

EPILOGUE

I do not understand why I desired to do this again." Alethea paced the antechamber that led off of Lady Whittlesby's ballroom in her London townhouse. The music being played in the ballroom filled the antechamber, but Alethea could not enjoy it. Rather, the cats fighting in her stomach would not allow her to enjoy it. "My violin does not sound the same after the neck was replaced. And the tuning peg was loose this morning . . ."

"I checked it an hour ago, and it is in perfect condition," Bayard said from his position by the open door. "You are missing Clare's performance. There are several young men looking at her rapturously . . ."

"I can hear her, Raven, and Ian quite clearly. They are flawless." Alethea made a swift turn and paced in the other direction. "I, on the other hand, am certain I shall play the wrong note the moment I draw my bow."

Bayard watched her with sardonic amusement. "You are quite adorable when you are nervous."

She shot him a glare but did not stop pacing. "You are exceedingly complimentary this evening, Lord Dommick."

"You were perfect last week at Lady Jersey's dinner party."

"That was a performance in an informal setting in the drawing room after dinner. This is in front of . . ." She gulped. ". . . *hundreds* more people."

"Pretend it is simply the two of us in the music room at Terralton."

The memory made her stop her pacing to choke back a laugh, which had a slight note of hysteria. "The result of which scandalized Margaret, who still believes kissing is disgusting."

Bayard gave a wicked grin. "Yes, she nearly regretted your aunt's decision to make their home with us. Are you quite remembering to breathe, my dear?"

She had to concentrate to do so. "You should be very glad that this time, I am not in danger of fainting."

He suddenly pulled her close to him, and she gave a squeak of surprise at his strong arms around her waist, pressing her to him.

"Well," he said with a smile, "this seemed to work the last time."

And then he kissed her.

DISCUSSION QUESTIONS

1. Alethea suddenly finds herself and her aunt responsible for Margaret, a twelve-year-old girl. Have you ever had a responsibility suddenly thrust upon you? How did it make you feel? What did you do about it?
2. Bayard is dealing with a painful episode in his past, and it has turned into a bitter inner wound. Can you relate to his pain? What should his friends and family have done for him? What should he have done for himself?
3. Alethea, her sister, Lucy, and Bayard's sister, Clare, are threatened by a dangerous man who wants Alethea's violin for reasons they don't know. Can you understand why she did what she did? What could she have done better?
4. Because of his bitterness, Bayard feels emotionally cut off from his family and friends. Can you relate to how he feels? If he were your friend, what would you say to him?
5. Mrs. Coon, the rector's wife, is a strong Christian who is comfortable speaking about her faith. Can you relate to her, or do you know someone like her? What is your own way of sharing your faith?
6. Bayard keeps doing all he can to try to protect Clare, but he feels helpless and guilty for the trouble he brings to the people he loves. Have you been in a situation where things

were completely out of your control, and it seemed to be going from bad to worse? How did you feel? What did you do?

7. Alethea is upset at God because she can't understand why God would allow her family to betray her and hurt her so deeply. Have you been in a situation where you questioned why God allowed some evil to happen to you? How did you respond? How should we respond?

8. As things get worse, Bayard just tries harder to protect Alethea and Clare on his own and gain some sense of control over the situation. Have you ever felt this way? How did you respond? What would you have done differently from Bayard?

9. Bayard has been trying to protect Alethea and Clare on his own strength, but he has to learn how to completely trust God instead. What does he learn about himself and his Heavenly Father? How does that impact the choices he makes at the end?

10. When Alethea shares with Bayard about how her family betrayed her and how she was able to heal from the traumatic experience, he responds with a strong emotional reaction (and a sizzling kiss!). Why did her words mean so much to him? How did her words change his thoughts or attitudes?

11. The spiritual message of the book is: You are not alone, God loves you, and God will take care of you. The verses Alethea reads reiterate that: Romans 5:8, Romans 8:38–39, Jeremiah 31:3, Zephaniah 3:17. What does the spiritual message of the book and/or the verses mean to you?

12. What were the most appealing parts of the book for you?

ABOUT THE AUTHOR

CAMILLE ELLIOT fell in love with Regency romances when she was in ninth grade and has been reading them ever since. In her free time, she knits Victorian lace shawls, works with the youth group at her church, and leads worship for Sunday service. She also tries to discipline her disobedient dog, but usually ends up giving it a treat, which annoys her engineer husband. They live in San Jose, California.